Olivia Hayfield is the pen name of British author Sue Copsey. Sue is usually to be found in her office editing other people's books, while Olivia is likely to be in her writing hut at the bottom of the garden, wondering what well-known historical characters would be like if they were alive today.

Sue worked for several years as a press officer at London Zoo, and then became an editor at Dorling Kindersley UK. She and her husband later moved to New Zealand, where Sue continues to work in publishing. She is also the author of several children's books, including *The Ghosts of Tarawera*, which received a Notable Book Award from the Storylines Children's Literature Trust of New Zealand. *Wife After Wife* was her first adult novel.

Sue lives in Auckland with her husband and two children.

Also by Olivia Hayfield

Wife After Wife

Sister to Sister

Olivia Hayfield

PIATKUS

PIATKUS

First published in New Zealand and Australia in 2021 by Hachette New Zealand
(an imprint of Hachette New Zealand Pty Limited)
This paperback edition published in Great Britain 2021 by Piatkus

1 3 5 7 9 10 8 6 4 2

A CIP catalogue record for this book
is available from the British Library.

ISBN 978-0-349-4233-3

Typeset in Garamond by M Rules
Printed and bound in Great Britain by Clays Ltd, Elcograf S.p.A.

Papers used by Piatkus are from well-managed forests
and other responsible sources.

Piatkus
An imprint of
Little, Brown Book Group
Carmelite House
50 Victoria Embankment
London EC4Y 0DZ

An Hachette UK Company
www.hachette.co.uk

www.littlebrown.co.uk

For Helena
Not quite as red, but just as feisty

Cast of Characters

The Rose family

HARRY ROSE

King Henry VIII

Billionaire head of media giant Rose Corp (retired – in
theory). Still a devilishly handsome charmer.

CLARE ROSE

Catherine Parr

Fifth wife of Harry Rose. Kind and wise. Harry's rock.

ELIZA ROSE

Queen Elizabeth I, the Virgin Queen

Daughter of Harry Rose and his second wife, Ana. English student
at Oxford. Smart and vivacious with a jealous streak. Weakness
for glamorous men, but won't let them physically close.

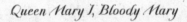

MARIA ROSE

Queen Mary I, Bloody Mary

Daughter of Harry Rose and his first wife, Katie. Acting CEO
at Rose Corp. Strict Catholic; lacks people skills. Troubled.

EDDIE ROSE

King Edward VI

Son of Harry Rose and his third wife, Janette. Schoolboy
at Eton. A fine, wholesome young man.

Eliza's Oxford friends

WILL BARDINGTON

William Shakespeare

Gifted English literature student. Active in Drama
and Poetry Societies. A drama queen.

KIT MARLEY

Christopher Marlowe

Studying English with Will and Eliza. Androgynous,
wildly creative, enigmatic. In touch with his dark side.

FRANKIE MALLARD

Sir Francis Drake;
explorer, first ship's captain to circumnavigate the globe

Geography student. A keen sailor.

LEIGH WALTERS

Sir Walter Raleigh;
explored the New World, bringer of tobacco and potatoes

Economics student. Heavy smoker.

Rose staff and board members

JOHN STUDLEY

John Dudley, Duke of Northumberland

Crony of Harry Rose; trustee of Eddie Rose. Ex-
Army, has grand ambitions for sons Gil and Rob.

ROB STUDLEY

Robert Dudley, Earl of Leicester

Editorial assistant at Rose Corp; childhood playmate of Eliza.
Good-looking metrosexual; an exuberant, twinkly-eyed charmer.

TERRI ROBBINS-MORE

Sir Thomas More

Fearsome editor of *The Rack*; long-time friend and colleague of
Harry Rose. Takes a special interest in Eliza. Nickname: Cruella.

CECIL WALSHAM

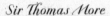

William Cecil/Francis Walsingham;
chief advisor/principal secretary to Elizabeth I

Consultant and later Chief Operating Officer at Rose Corp.
Reliable, all-knowing, wise, patient. Harry's spy.

FRANCESCA 'CHESS' LISLE

Lady Jane Grey

Eliza's cousin – daughter of Harry's sister Megan; board member.
Progressive, well-educated, feminist. Dating Gil Studley.

SEYMOUR MORRISSEY

Sir Thomas Seymour, Baron Seymour of Sudely

Brother of Harry's third wife, Janette; Eliza's step-uncle.
Trustee of Eddie Rose. Charismatic, with a dark side.

RICH MORRISSEY

Edward Seymour, Duke of Somerset

Janette's other brother; also a trustee of Eddie's.

ANGELO 'RIZZ' RIZZIO

David Rizzio

Adorable young production assistant at
Rose Corp. Sings while he works.

Rose relatives

MACKENZIE 'MAC' JAMES

Mary, Queen of Scots

Daughter of Harry's older sister, Margot James. Strikingly
attractive, strong-willed, ambitious. Questionable taste in men.

MARGOT JAMES

*Margaret Tudor;
married King James IV of Scotland*

Humourless older sister of Harry Rose. Holds one-third of
Rose shares. Lives in a Scottish castle; shoots things.

MEGAN LISLE

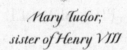

Mary Tudor;
sister of Henry VIII

Harry Rose's younger sister, married to his best friend Charles.

CHARLES LISLE

Charles Brandon, Duke of Suffolk

Harry's best friend and brother-in-law. A retired banker.

HELENA LISLE

Eleanor Brandon

Eliza's cousin; second daughter of Megan Lisle; an artist.

HENRY 'STU' BLUNT

Henry Fitzroy/Henry Stuart (Lord Darnley)

Son of Harry Rose and his mistress Bennie Blunt.
Grew up in Australia. A loose cannon — wild,
drinks a lot and avoids work. A bitter man.

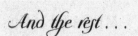

And the rest . . .

PHIL SEVILLE

King Philip of Spain

Billionaire head of US Christian media company
Hapsburg Inc. Right-wing fundamentalist. A snake.

AMY HART

Amy Dudley, née Robsart

Rob Studley's sweet, shy partner. A nurse. Often sad.

HAMISH EARLE

James Hepburn, Earl of Bothwell

A Scottish financier. Old friend of Mackenzie
James. Corrupt, with shadowy contacts.

CASSANDRA LISLE

no Tudor equivalent

First wife of Charles Lisle; a recovered alcoholic.
Runs a wellness retreat in Wales.

ANDRE SOKOLOV

no Tudor equivalent

Russian billionaire and owner of Premier League
football team. An evil man with no moral compass.

I would rather be a beggar and single than a queen and married.

ELIZABETH I (1533–1603)

Chapter 1

Eliza

'Bloody Maria,' said Terri. She took a savage bite of her apple and frowned at a bunch of high-spirited students gliding past in a punt.

Eliza was about to ask what her sister had done now, when the punter, a tall, rangy young man with a mop of chocolate-coloured curls, spotted them picnicking under a willow tree and yelled, 'Hey! Eliza Rose! *Shall I compare thee to a summer's day? Thou art more lovely and—*' He waved to attract her attention, lost his grip on the pole and fell over the side with a splash.

As the squealing girls hauled him back in, Eliza doubled over with laughter. 'Oh my god,' she spluttered. 'That was *so* on purpose. He's such a drama queen.'

'*. . . rough winds do shake the darling buds of May!*' the young man finished. He shook his head like a dog, fished out his pole, stood back up and gave an elaborate bow.

'Who the fuck was that?' asked Terri as the punt drifted away down the Cherwell.

'Will Bardington. He's in my English tutorial group. I love him. Sorry, what were you saying about Bloody Maria?'

Terri regarded Eliza for a moment. 'Part of me wants to just leave you in peace to enjoy your clichéd Oxford experience, even though it's a load of balls and punts, but the other part thinks I should keep you up to speed with what your psycho sister's up to. After all, you're going to have to come and restore sanity at some point.'

'What's she done now?'

'More on the tedious theme of cleaning up Rose publications, especially the women's mags. *Hooray!*'s Hot Bod of the Month is no more. Shame. It was an institution. And this week she took issue with a Celebrity Cellulite Secrets piece. Labelled it "body shaming", but it's just an excuse to ban exposed flesh.'

'But that stuff's totally par for the course,' said Eliza.

'That's precisely why she's pissed off. She's on a mission to change British magazine culture. It seems Rose will be spearheading the charge out of the cesspit of paparazzi crap. The *Telegraph*'s calling her the Clean-up Queen.'

'Maybe she should have stuck with Human Resources,' said Eliza. Before their father Harry Rose's forced early retirement, Maria had headed up Rose Corp's @People. Now she was Acting CEO.

'Yup. Should never have been allowed near editorial policy. Gotta say, I miss your dad. He wasn't a fan of sleaze, but he let the teams draw their own lines. Was very much hands-off. Apart from with your mum, of course. More hands-on with her.'

Eliza looked sideways at Terri, but she was gazing steadily ahead, her eyes hidden behind enormous sunglasses. She and Eliza's mother, Ana, had been great friends, and Eliza knew Terri's continuing mentorship was mostly to do with honouring Ana's memory. Terri and Eliza also knew more than anyone else about the true facts surrounding Ana's death. More, that is, apart from Harry Rose, and the Russian billionaire Andre Sokolov.

Eliza leaned back, supporting herself on her elbows. The May sun shone through the willow fronds, throwing dancing spots of dappled light onto the tartan blanket. In front of them, mayflies dipped into the water, creating tiny ripples and rings. Swallows swooped low, snapping up insects, and dragonflies zipped about and hovered.

From some distant ice cream van, the tinkle of 'Greensleeves' blew across on the breeze.

'Dad still won't talk about Mum,' said Eliza, popping a grape into her mouth. 'He always changes the subject when I ask about her.'

'He'll get there,' said Terri. 'But back to Maria. A word in her ear might help, before she does too much damage. Remind her she's meant to be running the big picture stuff past you, as per the arrangement with Harry.'

'Not sure she'd take a blind bit of notice, to be honest.'

'Give it a try – otherwise I'll have to speak to the board about reining her in. Mia's considering resigning.'

'Oh no,' said Eliza. *Hooray*'s editor had been with Rose for decades.

'She still hasn't got over Harry's departure,' said Terri. 'Any more of this and she'll spit the dummy and leave. And you can be sure Maria would recruit a replacement who'd back her clean-up campaign. If we're not careful, we'll end up with a bunch of 1950s *Good Housekeeping* clones.'

As Eliza enjoyed the bucolic scene, she couldn't work up any enthusiasm for being back in London, even if only for a short while. Late spring in Oxford was so seductive. The ancient, venerable feel of it all – the mellow stone colleges, the dreaming spires, the water meadows; the spirits of all those great minds passing on the academic torch.

Terri was right – she *was* a cliché. But in a way, this made her appreciate her good fortune all the more. She was aware of how lucky she was to be living this life. Never before had she had friends who inspired her like her fellow students did. When she was with them, anything seemed possible; they could – and would – change the world. Friends like Will Bardington and Kit Marley from her tutorial group, bursting with creativity. Frankie Mallard (Geography) and Leigh Walters (Economics), her closest female friends.

Conversely, Eliza's relationship with her half-sister, ten years her senior, was tricky at best, often fraught. If Eliza's new friends were shining lights, Maria was a shadow.

'Maybe Dad could talk to her.' *So I don't have to.*

'I thought the idea was to keep Harry at arm's length.'

Eliza sighed. 'True.'

Harry's daughters, and his wife Clare, had 'persuaded' him to step down from Rose Corp after revelations in the press about his affairs over the years, and his treatment of two of his wives. They believed he was at least partly to blame for Ana's and Caitlyn's deaths, and that he'd never clear his troubled conscience unless he accepted responsibility.

Harry and Clare were currently sailing the South Pacific on Harry's super-yacht *Janette*. On his video calls home, Eliza sensed he was relieved to be out of the public eye after his downfall, but that his exile was hurting badly. Rose Corp was his life, his identity.

Tough. He still remained tight-lipped on the subject of Ana, particularly on her death, and Eliza couldn't let it go. It felt unresolved; it niggled away at her, and she couldn't help prodding it, like a person worrying a painful tooth. She loved her father dearly, but his refusal to open up on the subject of her mother was exasperating.

'OK,' she said. 'I'll call Maria tonight. And I'll be back at Rose in the summer vacation. Maybe on *The Rack* again?'

'Does it for me,' said Terri.

'Great! I love working for you.'

'Christ, that's a first,' said Terri. 'Must do something about my soft spot. Can't be seen to be mellowing in my old age.'

Eliza knew it was all bluster. Terri Robbins-More's management style was notoriously tyrannical, but to writers, editors and designers, a job on *The Rack*, Britain's most-awarded magazine, was the stuff of career dreams.

Eliza wondered how old Terri actually was. She guessed about the same age as Dad – mid-fifties. When her hair had started to turn grey, she'd dyed her swept-over fringe white, and the rest back to her natural black. 'Your mum called me Cruella,' she'd told Eliza, 'so think of it as a tribute to her.'

'Your cousin's starting at Rose this summer, too,' said Terri. 'Came in for an interview. Considering the silver spoon wedged in her entitled millennial mouth, she doesn't seem too annoying.'

'Chess?' Francesca Lisle was the daughter of Harry's younger sister, Megan. 'She's cool. Very smart. Maybe she could work with you?'

'Nepotism may be accepted practice at Rose, but I prefer to choose my team based on talent and experience, not on who their bloody uncle is and how many shares they have.'

'But you didn't mind having me around?'

'Any complicity in that arrangement was down to your dearly departed mother's memory. Although I'll grant you're acceptably talented. But my benevolence does not extend to cousins. So no. Cousin Chess can look elsewhere. And maybe you should park yourself with Maria, keep an eye on her extremist tendencies. Offer to be an extra PA, or something.'

'She wouldn't want that.'

Eliza and Maria's work relationship was built on eggshell-thin foundations. They'd rubbed along during Eliza's recent stint at Rose, thanks to a shared need to demonstrate to Harry and others on the board that they were capable heirs to the business. Eliza had been right behind Maria's equality and ethics goals, although, from what Terri was saying, those goals seemed to have shifted significantly, from worthy to reactionary.

But Eliza suspected the lean to the extreme had always been there, waiting to emerge like a bug from a pupa, the minute the counterweights of Harry and Eliza were removed. She didn't trust Maria's motivation. There was far too much emotional baggage and religious conviction involved. Not ideal drivers for business strategy.

On a personal level, Maria still seemed to regard Eliza as little more than a painful reminder of the event that had wrecked her childhood – Harry's desertion of Maria and her mother, Katie.

Eliza was the 'bastard child' (actual words) of Katie's usurper, Ana Lyebon, the conniving seductress who'd forced Harry to divorce his saintly, devoted wife of many years.

Until Maria could move past that, there was probably little Eliza could do to improve their relationship. Although it might help if their father displayed less admiration for his 'genius' daughter in front of his 'worrisome' one.

'Eliza, love,' said Terri, touching her arm. 'Your sister's living proof that deeply unpleasant people with zero empathy should not be allowed to step into an important job based entirely on the "who's yer daddy?" principle of business. If we can't put the brakes on her, there'll be nothing for it but to bring back Harry. Like I said, I miss the old bugger, but it's probably best if he stays in the back seat. This is a girl power moment – the men have had their turn, now it's yours. Girl power *singular*, preferably. Far be it from me to conspire to treason, but Rose's future should lie with you, Eliza. *Only* you.'

Chapter 2

Harry

Harry Rose picked up his laptop and moved into the shade. Even at this early hour, the Pacific sun beat down with the ferocity of an angry wife.

The ever-cheerful Timmo, an Aussie crewmember with an uncanny ability to appear at the exact moment Harry needed something, placed an espresso in front of him. 'Thought you might be in need, Harry.'

'Indeed I was. Thanks, Timmo.'

'No worries.'

Harry smiled inwardly. He loved the South Pacific vibe. The yacht's crew was largely composed of Australians and Kiwis – excellent sailors, and so laid-back it was surprising none of them had fallen overboard.

'Sorry about the cricket, Harry. Still, only a warm-up, eh?'

'England are on form, Timmo. The World Cup will be wending its way home come July, you mark my words.'

'Small wager, Harry?'

'A hundred of your Aussie bucks says England for the win.'

'Shake on it, mate.'

They shook.

'Seriously,' said Harry, 'if business was this easy, I'd be a billionaire by now. Oh, wait . . .'

Timmo grinned. 'Can I get you some breakfast to go with that coffee, Harry?'

For a moment Harry fantasised about a full English. But Clare would be up soon, and sausages and bacon were strictly off-limits. It was a bore, but her fruit and fibre breakfasts had helped return him to his former glory (number eight in *Hooray*'s recent Hottest Top Ten), following his mid-life dive into drug addiction and overeating. He owed it to his beloved fifth wife (sixth, if his brief online marriage to Anki counted) to stay on track.

'Fruit, thank you, Timmo. And perhaps one smallish croissant.'

'Coming right up.'

Harry looked at the clock on his laptop. He needed to FaceTime Eliza, but it was still the weekend in the northern hemisphere and she might be out. Maybe on a date. He hoped so – it was about time. As far as he was aware, she hadn't ever had a proper boyfriend. And to think people said she was just like her father!

In some ways, yes. He'd seen how men looked at her, and her response to that. She was quite the flirt. But while she enjoyed the attention, she never let men close. And he had a nagging suspicion that might have something to do with him.

Was Eliza's famous stance on virginity, reported in Terri's 2018 opinion piece on Harry, and quoted in almost every article about his daughter since, a response to his own relationships over the years? In particular with her mother? Had she sworn off romance because she'd witnessed the damage it could cause?

Harry's conscience pricked him. He still had some way to go to win back Eliza's trust, following the revelations about Ana's death. All these years on, he knew he had yet to properly face up to what had happened to his second wife. Eliza was forever turning the subject of conversation round to her mother – and he was always deflecting her questions. It was time to be honest, to fill in the gaps. She deserved nothing less.

And the bigger issue remained, always there, often haunting his dreams. How could he make reparation for letting Ana down? For not seeing what had been coming? Could he really expect redemption without putting things right? For Ana's sake, as well as Eliza's.

Andre Sokolov's face appeared in his mind's eye. One day, he'd make that man pay.

But for now, he'd focus on Eliza. Harry was enormously proud of her achievements – straight As so far this term – but he worried there was too much work and no play. And zero romance. In many ways, Eliza displayed a maturity beyond her years, but in others she was inexperienced, unworldly, perhaps naive. He wished she'd let her hair down a little, gain some life experience.

She was driven; focused on her studies to the exclusion of almost everything else, apart from her involvement with the Dramatic Society. And even that had a purpose; she'd told him she was learning all she could about drama production as this was an area she wanted Rose TV to expand into.

It wasn't a bad idea, and he knew she wouldn't take it forward without a feasibility study. Eliza was nothing if not thorough, and was naturally cautious. However, when she was determined, she let nothing stand in her way. It seemed she'd inherited the steel backbone that had enabled his father to grow Rose Corp from a small Lancashire publisher into a national media giant. If Eliza wanted to expand Rose's production arm, he knew it would happen.

'There you go, Harry.' Timmo put down a small, disappointing plate.

'No croissant?'

Timmo pulled a face. 'I ran into Clare.'

'Ah. How does she do that?'

'Fuck knows. I'll try the other stairs next time.'

'Good man.'

Grimacing at the slices of melon and papaya and other wholly unappealing fruits with a scattering of seeds, Harry returned his thoughts to Eliza.

At the age of twenty-one, her grasp of business was astonishing. This was, of course, an inherited trait, but at his insistence she'd backed up her first-rate genes with a sound grounding in corporate strategy and management.

Harry had wanted her to study Philosophy, Politics and Economics, as he had, but she'd dug her heels in. 'I'll be a businesswoman for the rest of my life, Dad,' she'd said. 'Let me have this time studying English, just for the love of it. And we're a media company – it's all about words, right?'

As with most things in life, he'd let her have her way – on the condition she gained a sound business education during her gap year. So her time working with Terri in *The Rack*'s offices had been interspersed with periods in the finance, legal, marketing and production departments, backed up with a top-notch online course in Business Administration.

Harry had every confidence in her abilities, but life at the top would be tough, and she'd need his help to survive, at least at first. It was time for some one-on-one coaching on how to be ruthless, when occasion demanded. Like … now. Thanks to Maria, this couldn't wait until next year, when she finished at Oxford.

Eliza was Harry's natural heir, and he fully intended to put her on the throne. Maria would have to go – quickly, before she did lasting damage – while Eddie was still years off being able to play an active role.

He pondered on his elder daughter for a moment. How had he and sweet, gentle Katie produced this humourless harridan intent on enforcing her archaic values throughout Rose? Terri's latest report had been deeply unsettling.

It was time to push back, and Eliza would be his weapon.

Eliza

Eliza phoned Maria that evening. Her half-sister didn't do Skype or FaceTime, or social media. In fact, she didn't really do social.

'Hi, Sis! How's things!' Eliza cringed at her own hearty tone.

'Why are you ringing on a Sunday?' came Maria's gruff voice.

'Oh, just to find out how things are going. I hear you've launched an attack on sleaze.'

'You saw the *Telegraph*?'

'Terri visited today. Hey, it's great that—'

'Terri?'

'We had a lovely picnic by the river.'

'Eliza, are you ringing about work?'

Well, it'd hardly be for a girly chat.

'Partly. It's just . . . I'm feeling rather out of the loop. I don't seem to be getting copies of your emails. I thought I'd better check—'

'I don't work on Sundays; I don't even think about work. You should know that by now. I'm leaving for evening mass shortly.'

'Oh, sorry.'

'I have to go. Goodbye.'

Eliza sighed as she pocketed her phone. Maria was impossible.

Her earliest memories of her half-sister were from her visits to Wales. She'd been sent to stay with Katie and Maria on two occasions. She had no recollection of the first, which had followed Ana's death, but her memories of the second were vivid. She'd been nine years old, and she and her baby brother Eddie had stayed for several weeks following the death of Harry's third wife, the sweet-natured Janette.

Katie had been a great comfort after the loss of her step-mother. But Maria, in her late teens, had treated Eliza like something with a bad smell that had been deposited on the stone steps of the rambling old house. When Katie's back was turned, she'd called Eliza creative names based on the theme of bastard, and the vocabulary she'd used to describe Ana had been savage. *Whore. Witch. Godless. Slut.*

Finding Eliza sobbing in the garden, Katie had attempted to explain her daughter's behaviour – how difficult it had been for Maria to see her beloved father with another woman, and another daughter, and the effect his abandonment had had on the two of them. She'd told Eliza about her own prolonged periods of depression, during which she'd been unable to properly care for her daughter. It wasn't surprising she was a complicated teenager, prone to resentment and anger.

Maria's behaviour was less ferocious now – snide, rather than overt – but there was still enough friction for regular sparks.

'Why is your sister even working in a media company?' asked Leigh, when Eliza returned to the common room. Eliza's despondent expression must have said it all. 'I mean, why doesn't she just become a nun or something?'

Eliza slumped down beside her friend. 'You can't change society if you're not part of it, I guess. Last year she was still finding her feet. Seems she's not only found them, she's really putting the boot in. Steel-toe-capped ones. Terri says Maria's determined to "lift the moral landscape of the media". She's dreaming – that ship sailed decades ago.'

Leigh had been idly scrolling through her phone. She put it down. 'In a company that size, one person can't have that much power. What about the board – checks and balances?'

'Yep, we might have to bring them in,' said Eliza. 'She's like Trump. Step one: "You're fired"; step two: replace with a yes man.'

'She sounds terrifying.'

'She's just pulled a piece on celebrity cellulite when she'd decreed the women's mags should avoid body shaming.'

'Well, actually . . . how's that a crime?'

'She's got to be more subtle, Leigh. She's going in like a flame-thrower. Women's magazines thrive on our insecurity. Ten pages of ads featuring stick-thin women photoshopped to look even thinner, followed by how to smooth your curly hair, curl your straight hair, cover your blemishes, iron out your wrinkles; an article on celebrity weight-loss secrets – oh, and their cancer scares – and finishing with five decadent chocolate recipes you won't be able to resist. Why should readers feel bad about themselves?'

'Jesus. How exploited are we? So . . . you gotta be in favour of what she's doing?'

'To some extent, yes. She's just going about it the wrong way.

She's got no connection with people, she doesn't try to understand them. She's making herself so unpopular. Sheesh.'

'What else has she done?'

'Banned editors from dealing with the paparazzi. Authorised press only from now on.'

'Also not such a bad thing?'

'And, apparently, no alcohol at work. No more Friday-night drinks.'

'What? Now that *is* unacceptable.'

'I know, right?'

'What does your dad think about all this?'

'Not sure he knows what's going on. Though ... somehow he always seems to. He won't be happy. But I want to try and rein Maria in myself. Show Dad I don't need to go running to him every time there's a problem.'

Leigh's grey-green eyes, so striking against her dark skin, misted over. 'But lovely to know he's there if you need him. Imagine, Harry Rose ... '

'Oh god, not this again.' But Eliza couldn't help smiling.

All through Eliza's life, women had turned to mush over her father. Even now, in his fifties, he still regularly made the top ten in those hottest-men lists Maria was probably busy banning from Rose publications. His questionable record as a husband, along with revelations about his philandering, didn't seem to have dented his appeal.

'Talking of hot dudes ... ' muttered Leigh.

Will Bardington was striding across the room towards them. Following him was Frankie Mallard, the third of Bard's Babes, as Will called the three of them.

'Dried out, Will?' Eliza called.

'Eliza That-Which-We-Call-A-Rose. I was dazzled by the sight of you reclining on the riverbank and my pole took on a life of its own. 'Twas ever thus. What were you two so deep in conversation about?'

'My sister,' said Eliza.

'Ah, the Clean-up Queen. I was reading about her in the paper. Sounds like fun times at Rose. How are you two related? You're like day and night.'

'We might have been talking about her dad too,' said Leigh. 'A far more appealing topic of conversation.'

'Oooh, Harry Rose.' Frankie always looked mildly surprised, thanks to her wide-set eyes and arched eyebrows. 'I love a man with a big boat. Where is he at the moment?' Frankie was a keen sailor, with ambitions to take part in the round-the-world Ocean Race.

'My punt didn't do it for you?' said Will, flopping onto a seat and crossing one leg over the other with a flourish. Could Will not do anything without behaving as if he were on stage?

'Somewhere in the South Pacific,' said Eliza. 'Last time Dad FaceTimed, he was wearing a Hawaiian shirt. It wasn't pretty.'

'But *that* is,' said Frankie, looking over Leigh's shoulder. 'My god, he's not fair on a girl.'

'Or a boy,' said Will.

Kit Marley was making his way over. Across the room, books were lowered and cups of tea paused en route to mouths.

Kit was spectacularly beautiful, in an androgynous, undernourished way. His unkempt blond hair fell over his eyes, which were the colour of autumn leaves, and on past his shoulders. And he had this *walk*, as if he knew everyone was looking but couldn't give a toss.

But Kit wasn't just an unfeasibly pretty face. Eliza had recognised his genius from their very first English tutorial. His rambling critiques were difficult to follow, but undoubtedly brilliant. He got Shakespeare like nobody else.

Eliza had immediately pegged him as a future Rose recruit. She was going to bag that brain, use it to drive her vision for the company.

She'd need to work out how, though. Kit shied away from doing anyone's bidding, preferring to go his own sweet way. Sometimes he disappeared for days at a time, no one knew where.

Although she and Kit had been friends for more than a year now, he was still an enigma to her. Eliza liked to understand what motivated people, what made them tick. But with Kit she had no clue. She didn't get him at all. She'd need to figure him out if she was going to make him hers. Correction: *Rose Corp's*.

But as she watched him approach, Eliza conceded that her growing compulsion to understand this boy was perhaps coming from a place that wasn't all about being his future boss.

She chided herself. Kit was *not* relationship material. The exact opposite, in fact. Frankie had described him as 'lacking boundaries', and after one of his and Will's regular creative spats, Will had called him a slut.

'You say that like it's a bad thing,' Kit had replied.

'Shift up,' he said to Eliza, parking himself beside her. 'Where were you tonight?'

Will, Kit and Frankie had been to a Dramatic Society meeting, the first since their recent production of a play co-written, with appropriate drama, by Will and Kit. Eliza and Frankie had been active behind the scenes.

'I had an important phone call to make. How was the meeting?'

'Wasn't really listening,' said Kit. 'Except for the part about the guy from Working Title wanting to meet with me and Will.'

'Cool!' said Leigh. 'I told you it was only a matter of time, after that review in the *Guardian*.'

It seemed Fate was forcing Eliza's hand. 'Er . . . nope,' she said. 'No Working Title for you. I want you two at Rose.'

'Nepotism. An admirable vice,' said Kit.

'Pray continue,' said Will.

'Remember those discussions we had last year? About creating great things, even changing the world?' said Eliza.

'First-year fools,' said Kit.

'Don't mock – I was serious. I like to plan ahead. When I'm back at Rose full time, I want to focus on the TV side of things. I'm going to skew it more towards the arts. There's far too much sport. I'm thinking we'll commission content. Really good stuff. We have channels already, but there's nothing original to speak of.'

'I can do original,' said Will.

'Roseflix?' said Leigh.

'At the moment it's dreams in my head. But I intend them to become reality, and I want you two boys on board.'

'*Of the very instant that I saw you,*' said Will, '*Did my heart fly at your service.*'

'You do realize we'll now haunt you until you do it?' said Kit.

'Haunt away,' said Eliza. 'Let's make it happen.' She smiled at him, and when he smiled back, holding her gaze, something inside her lurched. And she saw him notice.

'Can I play?' said Leigh. 'Be your money lady?' Leigh was treasurer of the Dramatic Society.

'We'll certainly need a feasibility study,' Eliza replied, dragging her eyes from Kit's. 'Could be a thesis angle for you?'

Leigh's business brain was formidable, especially when it came to finding new areas to exploit.

'What about me?' asked Frankie, with a pretend pout.

'Well, if I'm being accused of nepotism – I'll sponsor your round-the-world boat.' Eliza grinned. 'We can plaster Roseflix logos all over it.'

'Chuck us a ciggie, Leigh,' said Kit, standing up.

'Don't, Leigh,' said Eliza. 'Filthy habit. Why are you still a smoker?'

'*All they that love not tobacco and boys are fools,*' said Kit.

'I love boys,' said Leigh.

'Don't we all?' said Kit, as the pair headed outside.

Chapter 3

Eliza

'You weren't serious, though, about the whole virgin thing?' said Leigh, as she and Eliza headed to the Turf Tavern on Friday night. The evening was warm, and the streets teemed with students heading to Oxford's favourite watering holes and clubs.

Once again, Eliza wished Terri hadn't included the virgin quote in the *Sunday Times* piece she'd written just before Harry's retirement. Her friends and family teased her remorselessly about it. She'd meant it at the time – her younger self had been appalled at the way adults lost their heads over the opposite sex, and the most obvious way to avoid that was surely to keep men firmly at arm's length.

That said, Eliza loved men, cerebrally speaking. She sparkled under the spotlight of male attention, and recognized that flirting was in her DNA. She was her father's daughter, after all. But she wasn't about to let her life goals be swept aside by what was essentially the body's biological imperative yelling 'procreate!' There was deep friendship, and there was physical attraction, but until the two meshed in some as yet unencountered and probably non-existent Mr Right, she refused to set off down the path of romantic disappointment. With this in mind, she put her recent inappropriate thoughts about Kit Marley firmly to one side.

'I was serious when I said it,' she said, dodging a bike as they crossed the road by the Bodleian Library.

'And now?'

'Still in no hurry. I haven't met any suitable candidates.'

'Not Will?'

Eliza laughed. 'You're fishing. No, not Will. And anyway, he only pretends he fancies me. It's all show. Go ahead and flutter your unfairly long eyelashes at him. You know you want to.'

'I don't think I'm his type,' said Leigh. 'His last girlfriend looked like Anne Hathaway.'

'Seriously, I'm sure he likes you. All this "Methinks a Rose is best" nonsense is just to divert attention.'

'Could you at least try and be less beautiful, then?' Leigh skipped in front of Eliza and turned round, walking backwards. 'Look at you, with your dazzling looks and talent for casually throwing together the perfect outfit.'

'This old thing?' Eliza stroked the soft leather of her jacket, worn over a cotton dress with a short full skirt and black Doc Martens. Her long curly red hair hung over her shoulder in a low side pony-tail, and her only make-up was a touch of mascara and a sweep of red lipstick. It clashed with the hair, but it worked.

Clothes were Eliza's weakness – the buzz she got when heads turned. Her addiction to such moments was perhaps a little sad, but she was what she was. DNA doing its thing again. Her mother had been a style icon.

Eliza had also inherited Ana's deep-brown eyes, while everything else – the red hair, tallness and pale skin with a scattering of freckles across the nose – was her father's. She wished she had Harry's rosy cheeks, though. No matter how bitter the wind or fierce the sun, her face stayed resolutely pale, if not the colour of actual snow.

'Will would be a bad choice for either of us, I think,' said Leigh. 'Though it's tempting. I think he just loves the drama of the chase.'

'So get caught! Live in the moment. Just don't get – you know. *Involved.*'

They made their way down the cobbled alleyway to the pub, where Will, Frankie and Kit were sitting at an outside table.

'Leigh! Eliza! Looking babelicious this fair eve. What's your poison?' said Will, rising from his seat.

'Chrissakes, Will,' said Eliza. 'I thought you were a lover of language. I'll get them in. Who's for another?'

'Well, I'd say that'd be all of us, the night is but young,' said Will.

Leigh went to stand beside Will, until he got the hint and shuffled along the bench. She winked at Eliza as she sat down. 'I'll have one of those unnecessarily strong ciders, please.'

'Same, please,' said Frankie.

'We're on pints of Bald Badger,' said Will.

'I'll give you a hand,' said Kit.

The two of them went inside and joined the queue at the bar. It was busy, and as a woman squeezed past carrying drinks, Kit put an arm round Eliza's waist and pulled her out of the way. He kept it there, and she noticed him watching her in the mirrored wall behind the optics, a small smile on his face.

'What?' she said, turning to look at him.

'Just admiring your red lips. Very . . . kissable.'

Eliza felt herself blush. Or at least, if her cheeks had just once in her life hosted the colour pink, that moment would have been now.

'Stop it, Kit.'

Yes, he was beautiful. But no, she wouldn't be going there. Where so many had been before.

'Stop it why?' His smile was wicked.

'Because . . . well . . . ' Those hypnotic eyes seemed to be snuffing out her words before they had the chance to leave her mouth.

'In all the time I've known you, I've never seen you with a bloke. How's that possible? You're utterly lush.'

She pulled herself together. 'I have standards.'

'Drop them, just for tonight.' His arm pulled her closer, and a shiver ran down her spine.

'A one-night stand? And then awkward for ever more? I intend to be your boss one day. I think not.'

'Why would it be awkward? It'd be nice. Trust me, I'm good at it.' He bent down and kissed her cheek, then released her. 'Are you buying these drinks, or what?'

Sitting next to Kit, Eliza sipped her cider, but all awareness of taste, or of the conversation around her, was subsumed by the sensation of Kit's leg against hers. Echoes of the thrill that had zipped through her in the bar rippled along her limbs.

She made a conscious effort to wrench back use of her faculties and join in the discussion – recent movies, Brexit (as per), the Extinction Rebellion protests, their plans for the summer vacation. In an effort to relax, she downed her drink far too quickly, but the alcohol only exacerbated her confusion.

'Are you with us, Eliza?'

'Sorry, what?'

'I said, do you want another of those?' said Frankie, grinning, her eyes flicking between Eliza and Kit.

After the second drink, and then a third, she stopped worrying that everyone would notice her discomfort; that Leigh and Frankie would be wondering if she was finally about to cave in the face of this irresistible, wholly unsuitable boy.

The sky grew dark above them, but the night air was warm and soft.

When Kit and Will went to buy another round, the girls leaned in.

'Eliza! What the heck?' said Frankie. 'You and Kit?'

'Don't know what you mean,' said Eliza, invisible-blushing again.

'Come *on*,' said Leigh. 'I can feel the heat from here. Did he finally make a move?'

Eliza glanced through the open doorway, but the boys were still buried in the throngs at the bar.

'What do you mean, *finally*?'

'He's always watching you. Like a cat stalking a mouse.'

'He came on to me earlier. Can you believe it? As if!'

'Still holding out for Mr Right?' said Frankie. 'That's fearsome self-control right there. Kit's totally the definition of temptation.'

'Wasn't it you who said he lacks boundaries?' said Eliza. 'I've seen the havoc guys like him cause. Harry Rose, anyone?'

'I'm not saying you should go out with him,' said Frankie. 'But it could be time to, you know, get a bit of practice for when Mr Right finally shows up? I mean, with all that experience, he's gotta know what he's doing.'

'Good point,' said Leigh. 'And what were you saying earlier? About living in the moment? Letting yourself be caught but not getting involved? Perhaps you should take your own advice, girlfriend.'

'*He's the Devil in disguise,*' sang Frankie under her breath, as Will and Kit returned.

Eliza rallied her sensible side as Kit sat down beside her, but soon acknowledged it was losing. Badly. More cider demolished her final defences, and when he turned to her and said, 'Shall we go?' she found herself looking into his eyes and saying, 'Lead on.'

She stood, swaying a little. Lifting her leg over the bench was a challenge.

'Where are you going?' asked Frankie, her eyes widening.

'To the Devil,' said Kit with a grin. He held out his hand to Eliza.

She smiled at her friends, shrugged and took it. Will's jaw dropped, before Kit led her down the alleyway into the narrow lane beyond.

Eliza took his arm, leaning on him. 'I appear to be a little drunk. Where are we even going?'

'My place.'

For a while they walked in silence, past the old three-storey houses leaning out above them, softly illuminated in the glow of the wrought-iron streetlamps. The night air had cooled, and Eliza pulled her jacket tighter round her.

'You cold?' asked Kit.

'Tad chilly.'

He put an arm around her and rubbed her shoulder.

'This is weird, Kit. I shouldn't have had all that cider.'

'It's good. You need to lighten up. You're always stressing about work. There's more to life.' His tone was characteristically flippant, but there was something different this time. Something that invited her confidence.

'It's not that easy for me. My future's all laid out; people expect things of me. I don't want to let them down.'

'Daddy's girl. I get that. But you should take time out while you're here. You won't get the chance again.'

'Come with me, Kit? To Rose? I meant what I said the other night.'

'Maybe.'

He kept his arm round her shoulder, and it felt good. Kit was right, she should lighten up. For the first time in her life, she was feeling ... what *was* she feeling? She had butterflies; she was nervous. But excited. Her heart was in her mouth. She'd never been down this path before. Kit was most certainly Mr Wrong, but ... she recognized the contradiction. He was dangerous, but she felt safe. In spite of his reputation, she trusted him.

'I've never had a proper boyfriend,' she blurted out.

'Never? Why the fuck not?'

'Always studying, I suppose. Pressure to get into Oxford. Then I was working at Rose. And I've never really met anyone I liked enough. Just had the odd snog at school. Didn't even like that very much.' She gave a small laugh. 'Maybe I'm frigid. No one's ever—'

'Turned you on?'

'No. I must be a late-blooming Rose.'

'Eliza, I don't do boyfriend.'

'I don't want boyfriend.'

'So what *do* you want?'

'I think I want ... you.'

He stopped walking and turned her towards him. 'Only one way to find out.'

Kit had an indecently beautiful mouth – the sort of full, pouty lips a girl would kill for. Eliza found herself touching them, tracing their outline.

He moved her hand aside and kissed her.

It was sweet, delicious ... addictive. A wave of heat pulsed down her body as his hands moved inside her jacket and up her back, pulling her close.

Not frigid, then.

She looped her arms around his neck, melting into him.

So this was what all the fuss was about.

He stopped. 'My place?'

She hesitated. 'Another kiss first?'

He led her into the shadows of a nearby alleyway, and as the kiss became intense, slipped his hand up her skirt.

And all at once, the exquisite sensations fled.

'No ... stop!'

'Why?' he said, not stopping.

She pushed him away. 'I said stop!'

He looked at her for a moment, then touched her arm. 'Hey, what's up?'

She didn't know. She had no idea what just happened. One moment she'd been in heaven, the next she'd been hit by a blind panic that came out of nowhere.

Maybe she was overwrought – her nervousness, the cider.

'God, I'm sorry, Kit. I ... I felt sick. Must be the drink.'

He smiled. 'Look, maybe I should just take you home. Perhaps this wasn't such a good idea.'

'But I want to, Kit. I really do. That was lovely, and it's ridiculous, me not having ... at my age. Maybe not the whole way, this time. Perhaps we could ... go out sometime? I like you. Quite a lot.'

'I run a mile when that happens.'

'Why?'

His smile faded. 'Don't try and work me out, Eliza.'

'You'd rather just be mates?'

He looked at her steadily, then smiled again. 'Time for bed. You in yours, me in mine.'

Chapter 4

Eliza

Eliza woke to a thumping on her door. Or was it in her head? She groaned and pulled the pillow over her eyes.

'Eliza Rose, get your lazy arse up this minute!' came Frankie's voice with its gentle West Country burr. 'We have much to tell and much to find out. We're going for brunch. Full English – best hangover cure. You know it makes sense.'

'Can I see you there?'

'OK, but there will be time penalties. No later than eleven at St Giles'. Got it?'

'Whatever. Got it.'

She hauled herself out of bed and tentatively sniffed under her armpits. A shower was what she needed, to clear her head too, but it was shared with others and there'd probably be a queue on a Saturday morning.

She pulled off the T-shirt she'd slept in, rolled on some deodorant, and dressed. As she bent down to lace up her Docs, blood rushed to her head and she drew in a sharp breath as pain pounded her skull. The thought of eggs nearly made her gag. But then . . . coffee.

She pulled her hair into a high ponytail without brushing it first – that'd just turn it to frizz – then went over to the basin in the corner of her room and splashed cold water on her face. Finally she brushed her teeth to get rid of the old carpet taste.

As she picked up her jacket, the memory of Kit sliding his hands inside flashed into her mind.

Oh my god, what was I thinking? How strong was that cider?

She sat down on the bed, her jacket in her lap, and closed her eyes for a moment.

No. The cider had simply helped things along. Kissing Kit had been divine.

So what had happened? Why the panic?

There was a rush of embarrassment as she remembered pushing him away.

She stood up, shrugged on her jacket, then picked up her phone and saw the red '1'. The text was from Kit.

KIT: Movie later? Tolkein?

She smiled.

ELIZA: Sure. Txt me details.

'So?' said Leigh, as Eliza pulled up a chair. The two girls had already started on their breakfasts.

'So yourself,' said Eliza.

'You first.'

'Too drunk, in the end. Bit embarrassing. He took me home.'

'Kit? A gentleman? Who'd have thought?' said Frankie.

'He is. He's lovely.'

'So that's it? You staggered home and said goodnight?'

'Pretty much.'

'So that's *not* it,' said Leigh. 'And?'

'Well … We did kiss.'

'Short kiss? Long kiss? Good kiss?'

Eliza grinned. 'What do you reckon? You've seen that mouth.

But sensible me won out – friendzone only.' It was a version of the truth. 'Over to you, Leigh. Did you get caught?'

'Well, when Will didn't crumple at the sight of you leaving with Kit, I figured I may as well offer comfort for his non-existent trashed dreams. That's not making sense, but you get what I mean.'

'I think so. And?'

'Clichéd romantic walk by the river. Very nice. He was almost like a normal bloke.'

'No sonnets?' said Frankie.

'Not a single line. He said nice things about my eyes, though. And my lips.'

'So are you an item?' said Eliza.

'Maaaybe. I'm kind of hoping so.'

Eliza's food arrived, the plate piled high, and she pulled a face at it. 'The Will Bardington of breakfasts – totally over-the-top full English.'

'Whereas Kit would be a hash brown with scrambled eggs and the blackest of coffee,' said Frankie. 'Eliza, you're holding something back. You kissed him, you say he's lovely, but you friendzoned him. Why?'

'Like I said last night, I'm waiting for Mr Right. I'm not giving it up for someone with the morals of a . . . I don't know. I'm hungover. Whatever a person with no morals is called.'

'Have to say, when I first met him I assumed he was gay,' said Leigh.

'He looks like a girl,' said Frankie, 'but he's outrageously sexy. How is that possible?'

Eliza wished they'd stop. She was conflicted enough, without having to think about the whole embarrassing episode again. She was glad when her phone tinkled and a notification flashed up: a message from Harry.

'It's Dad,' she said. 'I'd better read this.'

DAD: Sweetheart – can we talk soonest? Trouble at mill. Might need to send you south.

She tapped out a reply.

ELIZA: Sure, Dad, FaceTime tonight? 7 p.m. OK? 9 a.m.
your time, right?

DAD: Yep. Goodnight from the South Pacific xx

Eliza clicked on the camera icon, and Harry appeared. He was sitting on *Janette*'s deck sipping coffee, wearing sunglasses and a Panama hat, looking tanned and relaxed. The straight line of the horizon behind him bisected the deep blue of the Pacific and the cobalt blue of the sky.

'Hello!'

'Dad, you need to stop positioning your laptop like that. It's not fair. Turn it round so there's, like, a wall or something behind you.'

'I thought you'd be interested to see where we are.'

'Blue on blue. Sunny. Hot. I get it. Welcome to my shoebox.'

She lifted her MacBook, panning around the room.

'My shoebox years were some of my happiest,' said Harry. 'Youth is wasted on the young. How's things?'

'Good! Got an A on that Shakespeare essay.'

'Another one. Excellent.'

'And you?'

'Auckland this week. Should be in time to see England thrash the All Blacks. Or vice versa, probably. Then we head to Sydney.'

'Not so bad then, Dad?'

'Coping. How's the social life? Not all work and no play, I hope?'

'Been playing a bit, with my friends.'

'Girlfriends or boyfriends?'

'Both.'

'Anyone special?'

'Nope. Mr Right doesn't exist, I've decided.' She paused. 'I had a kind of a date last night, but he's definitely Mr Wrong.'

'Sometimes a bit of wrong is just what you need, right?' Harry winked.

'Dad . . . ' Eliza shook her head.

'I've been speaking to Terri.'

'Gah!' Eliza raised her eyes heavenwards. 'She told me to sort out Maria without running to you! God, you two.' Harry and Terri had always been thick as thieves.

'Terri's my eyes – I need hers until you're back at Rose. Look, Maria's really putting the wind up the staff. I know you two want to take responsibility, but we're still in transition and I need to be sure there's a safe pair of hands. Maria's are distinctly dangerous. She needs to understand any changes in strategy or personnel have to be run past you. And she *must* copy you in on each and every managerial email. This is non-negotiable.'

Eliza sighed. 'I can try, but you know what she's like with me.'

'Go down for a weekend, talk it through, face to face. I know it'll be difficult, but give it your best shot. If she won't be told – well, we'll have to bring in the board, and that could get messy.'

'Urgh. I've got loads of coursework to get through. But yes, Rose must come first.'

'Good. And then . . . how about flying down to Sydney at the start of your summer break?'

Eliza perked up at once. 'Really? That'd be great!'

She'd been on *Janette* once before, on her maiden voyage around the Caribbean. The thought of spending time on the yacht again, in the sun with Harry and Clare, was most appealing.

'I want you in that CEO position, the minute you finish next year. But I need to teach you . . . let's say the *finer points* of corporate management.'

'Oh, you mean a work trip. Well, I do want to talk to you more about expanding Rose's production side too. Commissioning things.'

Kit's face appeared in her mind. *Go away, I'm trying to concentrate.*

'Thinking ahead. That's good.'

'Can you email me your dates?'

'Will do.'

Harry sat back, putting his hands behind his head. 'So, Lizzie. Saturday night. What are you up to?'

'Seeing a movie with Mr Wrong.'

'Excellent. What's he like?'

'Gorgeous. Probably bisexual. A stranger to fidelity. And totally the coolest person I know.'

'Good grief.'

'Gotta go, Dad. Love you.' She blew kisses at the screen and ended the call.

As she changed into a summery dress and denim jacket, she thought about Kit. This wasn't a *date* date, but even so . . . that kiss. It was going to be a challenge not to stare at those lips.

Chapter 5

Eliza

As they left the cinema, Kit let rip with his critique. Eliza smiled as she listened to his stream of words which, as usual, were almost impossible to follow as he referenced obscure works, writers and directors.

'Shall we get food?' she interrupted. 'I'm hungry.'

'Food?'

'It's the stuff you eat.'

'Must we?'

'I'll pay.'

They found a table at Browns and, while Kit was in critique mode, Eliza took the opportunity to pick his brains on their current assignment: To what extent was Shakespeare's *The Merchant of Venice* influenced by Marlowe's *The Jew of Malta*?

His insight was, as ever, remarkable.

'How do you know all this stuff?' she asked. 'Seeing as you never attend lectures and don't seem to do any actual work?'

He shrugged.

'You got a scholarship, right?' she said.

'I shouldn't be here. I was meant to go to Cambridge.'

'How do you mean?'

'My father ... it doesn't matter.'

It was as if his face had shut down. He sat back in his chair, looking around him at the other diners. 'This place is boring.'

'Where do you like to eat, then?'

'I don't, really.'

She laughed. 'So you don't eat, you were meant to go to Cambridge – what else? Tell me about your family. I don't even know where you're from.'

'It's complicated. And not very interesting.'

'It is to me. Anyway, it can't be as complicated as mine.'

'Tell me about yours, then. You can leave out the dad part, we all know about him.'

'You first.'

He went quiet, watching her over the rim of his beer glass. 'OK. The parents travelled a lot for my father's work, so I was sent away to school. No siblings. My mother died; I have a step-mother but ... I don't get on with my parents. We're estranged.'

'No! That's terrible. Why?'

'Said all I'm going to say.'

'You don't like your step-mother?'

'Tell me about your complicated family.'

His expression told her not to push it. Poor Kit.

'My mum died too. I was pretty young – four.'

'Really? That sucks.'

'I remember her, though. Images of her, some of the things we did together. How she always smelled lovely. Then Dad remarried, to Janette. She was his third wife, after Katie and Mum. She was sweet. She died just after having Eddie, my little brother – he's at Eton. Then, a couple of years later, Dad got married again, to Caitlyn. She was a lot younger than him, a reality TV star. Caitlyn Howe – do you remember her?'

'No.'

'Oh, OK. Well ... she died too.'

'Jesus.'

'Yeah. Most people know all this; I guess you're not one for the tabloids?'

'Nope.'

'Caitlyn was very beautiful, and a lot younger than him. I think Dad had a kind of mid-life crisis moment with her. But she was nice; I really liked her. Dad kicked her out when she cheated on him with a pop star. He decided she'd only married him for his money. She ... Well, like I said, she died too. It was very sad.'

'How?'

'Suicide.'

'Shit.' Kit picked up the salt cellar and started fiddling with it.

'She was more fragile than anyone realized. I think there were drugs and a dodgy ex-boyfriend. To be honest, I don't really know. Dad won't talk about it. He won't talk about my mum, either.'

'How did your mum die?'

Eliza twizzled the stem of her wine glass, not meeting his eye. 'Some sort of blood poisoning. Toxic shock.'

'Toxic shock?'

Eliza looked up. He'd stopped fiddling with the salt cellar.

'Yes. It was out of the blue. Then there was Clare, and she's so lovely, perfect for Dad. They're really happy together.'

'So ... five wives.'

'Yes. And as you know, I also have a half-sister, Maria, from Dad's first marriage.'

They were quiet for a while.

'I think,' Eliza said eventually, 'I have a problem with men because of my dad.'

Where had that come from?

The thought that had been blundering about her brain all day, like some amorphous blob, had finally crystallised into a question: was her reluctance to get romantically involved something to do with her father possibly being complicit in her mother's murder?

Possibly complicit. Who knew? She only had his word that it had been carried out without his knowledge. She trusted him, of course. And yet, by his own admission, there was a chance he 'could have stopped it'.

'I'm sorry I freaked last night. I don't think it *was* the cider, actually.'

'The hand of God, maybe,' said Kit. 'Telling you to keep the fuck away from me.' He sat back in his chair, watching her.

Those eyes. What did you call that colour? Hazel? Amber? Gold?

'I thought you were an atheist.'

'That was meant to be ironic.'

'Oh. Right. Sometimes you're quite difficult to follow.'

'You want another drink?'

'Better stick with water.' She took a sip. 'But like I said, sorry about the reluctant virgin moment. We're all good, as mates? Even though ...' she felt herself invisible-blushing, 'kissing you was nice.'

He held her gaze. 'Eliza – it's just sex, for me. It's more than that for you.'

'Haven't you ever fallen in love?'

'*That perfect bliss*? Romantic love is a ridiculous notion.'

Her eyes slid away from his, but with a will of their own travelled down to his lips. *Oh god.* Really, there was no part of that face that encouraged coherent thought.

'You have a point. It's kind of ... logic doesn't seem to be involved.'

'Love's just another name for desire,' he said. 'For connection, maybe. The need to not be on our own. It's the worst of human frailties; turns people into morons.'

She thought of Harry. 'It makes good people behave terribly.'

'But terrible behaviour is also part of being human.' He grinned. 'One of the best bits.'

Eliza laughed. 'You're incorrigible. So fidelity isn't ever a thing for you?'

'Why would you restrict yourself to one type of ... I don't know. Ice cream. When there's so many flavours out there.'

'My dad—'

'I know, you said. But the chances are you'll end up with a bloke like him. Don't women subconsciously look for someone just like their father? And you're always talking about him.'

'Then I'm doomed. Unless I'm a fifth wife. He got it right in the end.'

He leaned forward again. 'So – do we understand each other, Eliza?'

'No more kissing?'

He smiled. 'Maybe on special occasions. You're right, it *was* nice. Want to come to a party?'

Two hours later, Eliza was chatting in the kitchen with a group of English students. Will had his arm draped around Leigh's shoulder.

'You two are cute together,' said Eliza.

'Eliza, darling,' said Will. 'What *were* you thinking, last night, with Kit? Was it a rush of blood to your fiery-red head? I thought you were my most sensible of friends.'

'Cider makes fools of us all. Fear not, I have seen the error of my ways.'

'Thank heavens for that.'

'Where is he, anyway? I need to go home.'

'Wrapped around a first year, last time I saw him,' said Leigh.

'And her friend,' said Will.

Leigh pulled a face. 'He's such a tart.'

Eliza experienced a stab of something, and Leigh noticed.

'You OK, Eliza?'

'Yep, I'm fine. I guess you two will have to see me home, then.'

Keeping her promise to Harry, Eliza went to see Maria the following weekend, staying in the St Katharine Docks apartment her father had retained after they'd moved to Richmond. Maria's flat was upriver in Westminster, but on the phone she said she'd prefer to meet at the office.

There was no hug, no kiss, barely a smile as Maria sat down at her desk, wordlessly indicating the chair opposite. She'd changed little in the past few years – same severe haircut, same sombre-coloured clothes worn with opaque brown tights and sensible shoes. Same thick eyebrows, drawn together in a frown.

On the desk was a photo of Katie and Maria, and beside it a statuette of the Virgin Mary. The two objects filled Eliza with a strange sadness; a moment of sympathy for her solemn sister, who'd never seemed happy in all the years she'd known her.

But the empathy was fleeting. The discussion was every bit as difficult as anticipated.

'I agree there's too much sleaze,' she said, interrupting Maria's diatribe on the degeneracy of the British public, 'and, yes, we need to respect people's privacy, but—'

'My mission is to improve the moral landscape of the media. We need to reverse what's happening. People today are unprincipled, perverted, godless—'

'Can we just leave God out of it? You know the core value of our media is quality. Well, mostly. I admit there could be less fluff and gossip, but let's go about it carefully and slowly.'

Maria didn't respond, her expression stony.

Eliza carried on. 'We should commission market research – back up any changes as being in response to the evolving attitudes of readers. Let's tread the middle ground, do it subtly, *encourage* the editors to make changes, don't order them or threaten them. Dad thinks—'

'You really don't get it, do you?' Maria's glare was fierce. 'I don't *care* what Father thinks. He's the *last* person who should be offering an opinion on what matters to women. And he has no right to interfere; he agreed not to. What do you think you're doing, running to him? You and Terri, that . . . *unnatural* woman.'

'Unnatural? What do you mean?'

'I won't discuss this now. And I'm not going to shirk in my duty to the British public. And to God – He's guiding me in this. It's time to clean things up. All this focus on sex, and on . . . deviants.

It has to stop. I intend to make family values the heart of our mission statement. I'll send it to you when it's finalized.'

'Mission statement?' said Eliza. 'You can't change that without the agreement of the board. Including Dad.'

'We'll see. And like I said, Father is irrelevant. Off on his *pleasure* boat with his *fifth* wife.'

'Clare's lovely! How can you speak about her like that?'

'Father doesn't deserve her.' Maria's eyes, fierce beneath her dark brows, settled on the photo of her mother. 'And how can I respect him when he discusses things with *you*, away at university doing precisely *nothing* for the business, rather than *me*, slaving away, pushing back the tide of sleaze single-handedly. But it was always this way, wasn't it? *Difficult* Maria and *delightful* Eliza.' The last sentence was spat out.

'Look,' said Eliza, trying to keep her tone reasonable. 'It was you, me and Clare who told Dad to butt out of the business. You can hardly blame him for going travelling.'

'I don't want to talk about him. I thought you were here to discuss strategy.'

'You should give Dad a break. Doesn't your religion say you should forgive people?'

'You have to ask for forgiveness before God will grant it. And you have to be penitent – you have to mean it. Father is a nonbeliever and he lives a selfish life.'

Things didn't improve after that, and Maria snubbed her suggestion that they should find somewhere to eat and chat about life in general. Maria's walls were impenetrable. All Eliza managed to extract was a vague promise to copy her in on emails, but Eliza doubted it would happen.

Chapter 6

Eliza

Trinity term drew to a close, and the girls went round to Will and Kit's for an end-of-term celebration. It was a poignant finish to a memorable year; Eliza knew the next would be far tougher, with finals to face. And in the meantime it was back to work at Rose, and into battle with Maria. But at least she had Sydney to look forward to.

They ordered in a curry, then sat on the floor drinking wine.

Kit was idly leafing through the *Guardian*. 'Hey, look at this,' he said, grinning. 'Remind you of anyone?'

The photo showed Donald and Ivanka Trump.

Eliza scowled. 'That's not remotely funny. How dare you compare my father to that man. They're not in the slightest bit alike.'

'Wash your mouth out, Kit,' said Leigh.

'Daughter's hot, though.'

'Don't *ever* mention them in the same breath again,' said Eliza.

'Jesus. Lighten up, babe.'

'I'm not your babe.'

'Yes, you are.' He put an arm round her neck and kissed her head.

She pulled away. 'And thanks for abandoning me at that party, by the way.'

'I'll make it up to you.'

'No, you won't.'

'Stop bickering, you two,' said Will.

'God, I'm going to miss you guys so much,' said Frankie, laughing. 'I can't believe I won't see you until October.' She was off sailing around the Greek Islands.

'*Summer's lease hath all too short a date*,' said Will. He stretched out on the floor, putting his head in Leigh's lap. 'We'll be back here shivering before you know it.'

'Did you decide where you're spending summer, Kit?' said Frankie.

'Italy. Maybe with Will.'

'Let me know when you're back, Frankie,' said Leigh, twirling one of Will's curls around her finger. 'I'll come over.' Both girls were from Devon.

'If any of you are up my way, on pain of death do you pass on through,' said Will, whose parents lived in Warwickshire.

'And you, Eliza?' said Kit. 'Where will I find you, if I get lonely?'

'I thought you didn't do lonely. I'll be on Dad's boat in Sydney, then back at Rose.'

'Let's meet up.'

'OK.' She finally smiled. It was hard to stay mad at him. 'Come up to town; I'll give you the tour of the Rose building. You too, Will. If you're going to work there, you should come visit.'

'So you were serious?' said Will.

'Deadly.'

'Then yes, we will come visit your big pink rose.'

A Rose Air member of staff ushered Eliza to *Janette*'s helicopter, waiting on the tarmac.

'Welcome to Australia,' said the pilot. And then they were off, flying north to the Harbour Bridge and onwards until they were above a marina at which were moored a number of enormous yachts. Eliza recognized *Janette*, and was suddenly overwhelmed with excitement at the thought of seeing her father again – it had been months.

The helicopter dropped slowly onto the helipad. As the rotors wound down, Harry and Clare appeared, waving. She unbuckled herself and took off her headphones, impatient to be out.

A crew member opened the door and helped her climb down. 'G'day!' he said. 'I'm Timmo. It's a real pleasure to meet Harry's daughter.'

'Good to meet you, Timmo!' Eliza called over her shoulder as she flew across the deck and into Harry's open arms. He was looking fit and healthy, and there was no sign of his limp. It was amazing what the love of a good woman could do for a man.

'Look at you, Lizzie,' he said, squeezing her tight.

'Please don't say I'm blooming, Dad.'

His familiar warm broad chest and the scent-of-dad made her feel like a child again.

'Clare!' she said, finally disengaging herself and hugging her step-mother. Clare's fair hair was pinned up in one of her trade-mark clever buns, with little plaits twirled around it.

She held Eliza at arm's length, giving her the once-over. 'Looking fresh as a daisy after such a long flight! You'll have to give me some how-to tips for RoseHealth.'

They headed towards a door, Timmo following with Eliza's bags.

'The weather's quite cool,' said Clare. 'I hope you've brought some warm clothes. Though we had someone go shopping for you – there are a few things in your wardrobe, just in case.'

'We'll be heading north,' said Harry. 'How do you fancy a spot of diving on the Barrier Reef?'

They led her down a flight of stairs to a wood-panelled, carpeted corridor lit by recessed ceiling lights.

'You're in the same cabin as before,' said Clare.

The suite still made her gasp. The bedroom alone was probably four times the size of her Oxford shoebox. There were floor-to-ceiling windows, and the decor was black and white, with thick, cream-coloured carpets.

'We'll leave you to unpack,' said Clare. 'If you need anything, just ring through to the staff.'

Having a billionaire dad certainly had its advantages.

Later, after a reviving nap, Eliza freshened up. Under the bright bathroom lights, her skin was alabaster white. She pulled a face at her reflection. 'Pale and interesting' may have been the thing in Victorian times, but down here among the outdoorsy Aussies, she'd stand out like a corpse. Cursed red hair. Was even a faint tan too much to hope for?

❁

Eliza gave an enormous yawn as they finished dinner.

'How's the jet lag?' said Clare.

'Oh, not so bad. I like the Rose Air first-class bed things.'

'The Rosebeds,' said Harry.

'One of yours, Dad? Really, in future you should leave the words to me.'

'Well, I hope it did the job, because we've got a busy day ahead of us tomorrow. I'm expecting John Studley – he's in Sydney at the moment, so I thought I'd take the opportunity to brief him on Maria's table-flipping adventures.'

John was a favourite crony of Harry's – they'd known each other all their lives. He was on the board at Rose, as one of Eddie's trustees now that Harry had signed over the majority of his shares to his children. John had been something high up in the Army, and Eliza found him rather intimidating.

John had two sons, Gil and Rob, who were close to Eliza in age, and she had happy memories of playing with them when the two families got together. Thanks to Harry, the brothers had done internships at Rose.

'Have you been in touch with Chess recently?' Harry asked.

'Not really. Terri said she'd been into Rose for an interview. Why?'

'She's dating Gil, apparently. John's pretty happy about that.'

Harry

As Eliza and Clare headed off to bed, Harry poured himself a brandy and took it out on deck. Leaning on the railings, he gazed at the night sky, its indifferent beauty providing a welcome distraction from the situation facing him tomorrow.

He sipped his drink and closed his eyes for a moment, feeling the brandy's warmth spreading, soothing.

How do I handle this?

Opening his eyes he looked up once more, as if seeking an answer from the heavens. Yet again, it was time for Harry to face up to his past. And yet again, he needed to have a difficult conversation with Eliza.

Just when he'd been regaining her trust, bringing their relationship back on track, something else – some*one* else – had resurfaced to sabotage his hard-won progress.

He downed the rest of his brandy in one gulp.

'Can I get you anything, Harry?'

He started at the voice behind him, and turned to see Rebecca, a blonde, long-limbed crewmember, smiling in a way that suggested 'anything' meant exactly that.

'Another of those?' she said, glancing at his empty glass. 'I could join you, if you fancy some company?' Her eyes gazed directly into his.

'One's my limit,' he said, hoping she'd pick up on his true meaning. 'But thanks for the offer.'

She pouted, then smiled again. 'Any time, Harry.'

He turned away.

'You've still got it, Harry,' said another voice, a moment later.

He held out his arm, and Clare tucked herself beneath it.

'I have indeed. And all thanks to you. I thought you'd gone to bed.'

'Something's troubling you, I could tell. Do you want to talk about it?'

'I think I probably do. You'd better brace yourself . . .'

Chapter 7

Eliza

'Before John gets here,' said Harry, as he and Eliza breakfasted next morning, 'I want to take you through the board membership. I know it's your first day, but it's important you understand who's got the clout. We might need it, the way Maria's carrying on. Then we can give John lunch, and he can bugger off and we can set sail. By this afternoon we'll be cruising past the Sydney Opera House and out to sea. How does that grab you?'

'Sounds brilliant.'

On the way to his onboard office, Harry took Eliza up to the bridge and introduced her to the captain.

'Captain Yates is a Kiwi,' he said, as she shook his hand. 'Far better sailors than the Aussies, but never let Timmo know I said that.'

'Too right,' said the captain.

Harry and Eliza made their way downstairs and sat down at a table looking over the marina. Pads of paper and pens had been laid out, along with a pot of coffee and cups.

As Eliza poured, Harry pulled a pad towards him and began to write.

'OK, Lizzie. Rose shares. This is how they're divided up.'

'I'm listening.'

'When my father died,' – he wrote *Henry Rose* at the top of the page – 'the company was wholly family-owned and the shares were split three ways between me, Megan and Margot.'

He drew lines down from *Henry* to *Harry*, *Megan* and *Margot*, like on a family tree. Then he drew a smiley face next to Megan, a grumpy one next to Margot, and a small crown next to his own name.

'As you know, when I stepped down I signed three-quarters of my third over to you three.'

He drew three lines down from *Harry* and wrote *Maria*, *Eliza*, *Eddie*, then sketched a grumpy face next to Maria, a smiley one next to Eliza, and a boy in a cap next to Eddie.

'Cute. With you so far.'

'Megan's intending to sign her shares over to her daughters, as Chess will be starting at Rose.' He added their names. 'From what I hear, Helena has no interest in working for the company, so she'll have a proxy vote.'

'No surprises there. She's wanted to be an artist forever.'

'Now, as for Margot's third, she's always been happy for me to act on her behalf, as long as she gets her regular income.'

'OK.'

'Back in the nineties, when I needed to raise capital for the football channel, a proportion of the company was sold.'

Eliza sat up straighter. That would be a certain Russian investor. 'Him?'

'We bought him out and onsold. Charles sorted it.' He wrote down *outside investors* next to the family tree and, after a moment's hesitation, drew a mean-looking bear then scored a line through it. 'Satisfying.'

'Dad—'

'Those shares – twenty-four per cent of the company – are now mainly held by investment companies. They don't interfere, as long as dividends and share prices hold up.'

'Right. And that's where Maria could be a problem?'

'Exactly. They'll notice if the share price drops significantly. We have to make sure that doesn't happen.'

'Who are Eddie's trustees again?'

'Me, John Studley, and Eddie's uncles Rich and Seymour.'

Eliza shuddered inwardly. *Uncle Seymour.*

Everyone had that one uncle.

The Rose and Morrissey families had kept in touch after Janette's death, for Eddie's sake. She and Eddie had been to stay with Seymour and his wife on several occasions. Her step-uncle was loud, flamboyant, full of swagger. He'd had a habit of appearing by her bed in the mornings, coming in without knocking, to let her know breakfast was ready, or just for a 'chat' – while his eyes roved across the shape of her body beneath the covers. He'd pat her bottom as she walked past, would 'accidentally' brush her breasts. In the evenings he'd sit next to her on the sofa, pushing his leg against hers, touching her knee when his wife wasn't looking.

Before her final stay with the Morrisseys, when she was a teenager, she'd been physically sick at the prospect of seeing Seymour again, but Harry had been grieving for Janette and Eliza hadn't wanted to add to his worries. So she'd gritted her teeth and gone, for his sake.

Now she avoided family gatherings that included the Morrisseys.

'John's recommended bringing an associate of his onto the board,' continued Harry, 'and to mentor you when you're full time. Cecil Walsham, a management consultant. I know him a little – he's a Cambridge man, but we won't hold that against him. When I started at Rose, my uncle, Richard York, showed me the ropes. I think it's a good idea to get you that level of support too.'

'Why have I never met your uncle Richard?' asked Eliza.

'He disappeared,' said Harry. 'It was all very mysterious.'

'Oh. But this Cecil – he's not family?'

'I think that's a good thing. Too many family board members can lead to infighting. I've done my research, and he seems a safe pair of hands.'

John arrived, still looking like a military bigwig with his closely cropped hair and crisp clothes. After the niceties, the three of them discussed Maria's moves to *improve the moral landscape* of the British press. Eliza told them about her sister's intention to place family values at the heart of a new mission statement.

'The mission statement's a no-no,' said John. 'She'll know that. Could be the excuse we need to call in the board?'

'My thoughts exactly,' said Harry. 'I'll speak to her, but if she's set on this course of action, well—'

'We'll need to rally the troops,' finished John.

Harry

Clare joined them for lunch. The sun had come out and the atmosphere was light as Harry and John shared anecdotes from their childhood. Their fathers had been big pals back in the day, and the two families had remained close.

As always, John talked (read: boasted) about his boys, Gil and Rob. Poor chaps. While Harry appreciated the value of sons to one's legacy goals, John was rather OTT in his ambitions for his.

'Are they still interning at Rose?' asked Eliza.

'Just finished,' John replied. 'Gil's training with the Civil Service. I'd like him to go into politics, eventually.'

Culminating in prime minister, if John had anything to do with it.

John turned to Eliza. 'He's going out with your cousin Chess. Isn't that splendid?'

Harry wondered whether John had somehow engineered their meet-up. Megan's eldest daughter was super-bright, and her father, Charles – Harry's best friend and brother-in-law – knew everyone who mattered. Chess would be the perfect politician's wife.

'It is,' said Eliza.

'Rob was due to start at one of the big accounting firms,' John continued, 'but Terri Robbins-More offered him a position on *The Rack* last week.'

'Oh!' said Eliza. 'That's great! But quite surprising, given her views on nepotism.'

'It's only a junior editor position,' said John, 'but Rob's ambitious, could make a go of it at Rose, I think.'

Did John anticipate that his position on the board, and the fact that Rob was Harry's godson and Eliza's chum, would speed his son's rise through the Rose ranks?

In fact, Rob Studley was unlikely to need a helping hand. He was clever – whip sharp – and possessed an exuberant, impish charm that would undoubtedly see him win at life. As a boy he'd been a cheeky little sod, rarely intimidated by his overbearing father, or by Harry.

Rob should probably be in the sales department, not Editorial. He'd be a natural.

A move to Sales would also put him out of range of Eliza, who seemed determined to work on *The Rack* again this summer, although Harry would rather she parked herself on the top floor to keep an eye on Maria.

He thought back to when Rob and Eliza were children. When the Studleys visited, the two of them would run off into Richmond Park, returning hours later with grazed knees, their clothes streaked with grass stains. There had been a broken arm on one occasion, and he remembered a park keeper coming for a quiet word after the pair had been caught harassing deer.

He smiled to himself as he pictured them standing in front of him, heads bowed for their telling-off, their curly hair – hers wild and red, his dark and floppy – tangled and full of grass seeds. Harry had never put a stop to their adventures. Rob had often been just what Eliza needed, what with losing two step-mothers and her father's ongoing life-and-wife dramas.

And that was all very well in childhood. But now, at Rose – probably not. Harry didn't want Eliza distracted. And he couldn't see Rob treating Eliza with the respect she'd be due as his superior.

Perhaps he'd have a quiet word with Terri.

Chapter 8

Eliza

As they finished up with coffee, Timmo brought a phone across to Harry. 'Sorry to interrupt, but I think you'll want to take this. That call you were expecting? Perhaps in private?'

Timmo was obviously more than a carrier of bags and bringer of coffee.

Eliza saw the smile leave Harry's face.

'Ah, right. Excuse me, all, this shouldn't take long.'

Eliza also noticed Clare's frown. She wanted to ask if everything was OK, but probably shouldn't in front of John.

'Well,' said John, 'I should be marching on. Eliza – come and see us when you're back in London. Come for Sunday lunch.'

'I'd love to.'

Eliza smiled as she thought of her childhood playmate. Rob's internship had coincided briefly with her time at Rose, but she'd only seen him once or twice, as they'd worked on different floors.

Harry returned, and Eliza noticed his distraction.

'I should wend my way, Harry,' said John. 'A pleasure as always to see you and your delightful family. Don't worry about seeing me off, if your man could do that?'

Harry waved Timmo over. 'Good to see you too, John. When

I'm home, perhaps we should consider golf. Do you think we're old enough now?'

'Good Lord, Harry. I thought you'd sworn never to.'

'I'll need something to fill the hours, when my tiresomely capable daughter properly takes over the helm at Rose.'

'Daughter-*s*, Dad. Plural?'

'We'll see.'

'I think I'll have a swim,' said Eliza, as John left.

'Wait,' said Harry. 'I need to speak to you first.'

Eliza was again aware of her father's discomfort. What was going on? Her stomach was tying itself in knots. What was Dad about to land on her now?

'OK.'

Harry sighed and ran his fingers through his hair.

Clare touched his arm. 'Tell her, Harry.'

'Where to start? Eliza, you remember back when . . . everything came out in the papers?'

Oh god. Another skeleton? Another affair? Or was this something to do with her mother?

'There was one revelation that never came. That may be about to change.'

'What the heck, Dad?'

'You know that your aunt Merry wasn't my first . . . other woman. Before her there was Bennie.'

Eliza breathed out. Not Ana. 'Yes, you told us.'

'We were together when Katie and I were first married. It ran its course and ended amicably, and Bennie moved out of London. After that we were only in touch via my lawyers. I sent her money. Because . . . ' He gazed out at the harbour. 'She had a son. My son.' He turned back to Eliza. 'Henry. He's the same age as Maria.'

What the f—

'I haven't seen him since he was a baby. Clare knows, Lizzie, but it never seemed the right time to tell you. I should have done so before. I'm very sorry I didn't.'

Anger bubbled up as she felt the rug being pulled from under her feet – again. 'So why now?'

'Because when Henry was still a boy, Bennie left her husband and moved – to Sydney.'

Eliza gasped. 'You don't mean—'

'He wants to meet me. This afternoon. I couldn't refuse, could I?'

Now Eliza felt sick. It was sinking in. Her father had another son. All these years, he'd had another son, and he hadn't told her. She'd thought they were so close. Her father was a cheating, lying . . .

She stood up and threw her napkin on the table. Tears pricked at the back of her eyes. 'How could you keep this from me? *HOW*?'

He looked stricken. 'Lizzie, please let me explain.'

'No. I don't want to hear it. Jesus, Dad! Not only could you not stay faithful to your wives, not to mention the havoc you wreaked in their lives, but you've kept *this* from *me*?'

'He was the other side of the world. I thought it wouldn't come up. I heard through Cranwell that Bennie had remarried, and apparently Henry loved his new step-dad; wanted nothing to do with me. He wouldn't even use the name Henry, which I chose. He calls himself Stu – his step-father's surname is Stewart.'

Harry took a long drink of water. He looked relieved to have dropped his bombshell, was regaining his composure.

'Funny how he's suddenly interested when his billionaire father's in town on his yacht.'

'Calm down, Lizzie. You never know, we might like him.' He looked at his watch. 'He'll be here soon. Sweetheart, I could really use your support on this. It was a shock when he got in touch. And – well, I'm curious, and quite excited. Maybe you should be too – he's your half-brother.'

'Fuck off, Dad.' She walked away without a backward glance.

Now Clare would be telling him to give her time to get used to the idea. How could Clare trust a man like that? Had Dad been unfaithful to *all* his wives, or just the first two?

Tears streamed down her cheeks; she swiped them away.

Back in her room, there was a tap on the door, and Clare's head appeared round it. 'Eliza?' She came over, wrapped her in a hug.

'I'm so sorry, Eliza. That must have come as an awful shock. I could kill Harry for not telling you before. He just buried his silly head in the sand, hoping it would all go away.'

'Well, that sounds bloody familiar,' said Eliza, sniffing. 'Dad's always had a responsibility deficit. A total inability to face up to his stupid mistakes. To blame someone else, or—'

'Shhh. It's terrible timing, yes. But he would have told you. Being in Sydney has just forced the issue. Obviously the boy wants to meet his father – actually, not a boy, he must be in his thirties. If it's any consolation, I think this will be difficult for Harry.'

'No consolation at all.'

'I'm rather hoping I won't be summoned. Is that bad of me?'

'No. Why should you be dragged into Dad's sordid past?'

'It's not Stu's fault, though, is it? Wouldn't you want to meet your dad?'

As she left, Eliza felt calmer. Clare was ever the voice of wisdom. Perhaps Maria was right – that fraud Harry Rose didn't deserve her.

She lay down on the bed, suddenly exhausted, and picked up her phone. She opened the Messenger window. What time was it in Europe? She was too tired to work it out.

ELIZA: R u awake?

She stared at the screen, willing him to respond.

KIT: It's 6 a.m. in Rome, of course I'm not awake

ELIZA: Rome! Nice?

KIT: Bellisima

ELIZA: Miss you. Having a shit day

KIT: Why?

ELIZA: If I tell, not a word. Not even to Will – is he with you?

KIT: No. I'm with Sofia

ELIZA: Ah

KIT: Tell me. Lips sealed

Eliza pictured those lips for a moment. Lucky Sofia.

ELIZA: Dad has a son he never told me about until today. He lives in Sydney and he's coming aboard

KIT: And that's a surprise because?

ELIZA: Thought we had no secrets now

KIT: People are allowed secrets

ELIZA: A son though!

KIT: Just talk to him about it. Don't judge. We all fuck up. He just seems to do it more than most

ELIZA: True. Sorry if I woke u. Good to chat

KIT: Any time, gorgeous. Stay cool XX

ELIZA: You too XXXX

She put down the phone, closed her eyes and fell asleep.

She awoke an hour or so later, splashed cold water on her face, then headed back upstairs.

Making her way to the pool deck, she was horrified to see Harry coming towards her with a tall, unshaven, sandy-haired man. The resemblance between the two was striking. He wore shorts, flip-flops and a shapeless, faded T-shirt. The fashion fan in her couldn't help asking, wasn't this the first time he'd met his father? What was he doing looking like a hobo?

'Eliza,' Harry said as they drew level. 'I'd like you to meet Henry – Stu. Stu, this is my younger daughter, Eliza.'

'G'day, Sister!' he said, grinning. His piercing blue eyes were slightly bloodshot and his hair was matted. He looked as if he'd been swimming – or surfing, perhaps. 'Great to meet you. There's no escaping that red hair gene, eh? I wish I could stick around, but Harry says you're about to set sail.'

Eliza wondered what to say. 'Nice to meet you too, um, Stu. Perhaps some other time, if you're ever in England?'

'I intend to be! Want to get to know my fam. Can't believe it's taken me this long. My step-dad didn't want me meeting up with Harry, but I'm a big boy now, I can make my own choices. So yeah, I'll be seeing you in the homeland, you can count on it!'

The pair carried on past, Eliza refusing to meet Harry's eye.

She went over to the railings and watched as Stu walked down the gangplank with Harry, and they shook hands. Then Harry abruptly left. He didn't look back.

Stu watched him go, his hand half-raised for a final wave. As Harry disappeared inside he dropped it, and walked off towards the car park.

That was her half-brother. Harry's son. It hadn't properly sunk in. She'd taken an instant dislike to him – but why? Because he looked cocky and dissolute, or because of what he represented? Her father's lies, his cheating. Wasn't Stu just another victim, like Maria? Another screwed-up, damaged person, part of the detritus of Harry's womanising? He hadn't looked back at Stu. Son dismissed.

Harry appeared by her side. 'Lizzie, can we talk?' He looked troubled.

'How was Stu? Looks a lot like you – when you were in your drinking and drug-taking phase.'

'Ouch. But you're right. He seems to enjoy a drink.'

'Come back to bite you on the bum, hasn't it? What goes round comes round.'

'I've really stuffed this up, haven't I? What can I do?'

'Try being honest. That'd be a start.'

'I hope he doesn't show up in England.'

'You didn't like him, then?'

'Come and sit down.'

She remembered Kit's message:

Just talk to him.

'Let me try and explain. I'd always wanted a son. Katie and I had enormous problems – a stillbirth and miscarriages, another stillbirth after Maria was born. That was part of the reason I took up with Bennie. I was very young – about your age – and things at home were pretty difficult.' He paused, his eyes searching hers.

'Go on.'

'Bennie asked me to stay away from Henry, because his step-dad wanted to adopt him. It hurt, but I made the decision to do that, thinking it would be best for Henry. I never stopped wondering about him – what he was like.'

Eliza couldn't help thawing, Dad looked so sad.

'It seems he didn't have the happiest upbringing. Bennie's marriage broke up pretty quickly and she came here and remarried. I get the impression Stu's a drinker. Addiction's a horrible thing. He's thirty-four; it's probably too late for me to make a difference.'

In spite of Harry's distress, Eliza couldn't bring herself to care about Stu.

'And now I'm worried. He spoke about coming over, connecting with his family, maybe getting a job at Rose. That's not going to work out.'

'No.'

'But I do have a responsibility. Like you say – it's come back to bite me on the bum. What should I do, Lizzie?'

She was aware of a shift in their relationship. Harry was asking her for advice.

'Maybe just go with the flow, see what happens. Perhaps he won't come.'

He sat back in his chair. 'I'm sorry for how I handled that. I promise – no more nasty surprises.'

Eliza smiled. 'You're all right, Dad. But there is something you can do to make it up to me.'

'Your negotiating skills are shaping up beautifully.'

She grabbed her moment. 'I want to know more about you and Mum. I know hardly anything. You never talk about her. I don't mean ... you know, how she died. I want to know about your relationship. What made you fall in love with her? What was she like with you?'

'Ah. I see.' He shifted uncomfortably. 'Well, I suppose we could talk about that sometime, while you're here.'

'Now's good. You met at work, right?'

He frowned, then looked away, his eyes settling at some distant point on the horizon.

'Well ... OK. The first time properly was at a tennis match. She was firing volleys at me like you wouldn't believe. Then I managed to hit her on the head with the ball – a rather excellent backhand, in fact – and she ended up sprawled across the tennis court.'

'So you literally hit on her!'

He smiled. 'Wasn't a saying in my day. But I suppose I did. It was something of a significant tennis match – it was the first time Charles and Megan had seen each other in years, and they fell in love that night. Must've been something in the air.'

'You fell in love that night too?'

'Do you believe in love at first sight?'

'I'm probably not the best person to ask.'

'I didn't, until I set eyes on your mother. I first met her, briefly, when I sat in on her job interview. I was curious, as it was organized by ... well, her sister.'

'Oh my god, Dad.'

Harry's ex-mistress, Merry McCarey, was serving time, following her attempted murder of Harry a year and a half ago.

'I know. I was bad.'

'Too right.'

'Your mother captivated me from the instant I saw her. But she didn't like me at all, at first. Thought I was too full of myself. Which I undoubtedly was.'

There was a deep rumbling beneath their feet, and the deck vibrated.

Harry stood up. 'Ah, anchors aweigh. This will have to wait.'

It was a start, at least.

❀

As *Janette* sailed majestically up the coast, the weather grew warmer and the skies cleared.

Harry spent the mornings coaching Eliza, teaching her more about Rose, the different strands of the business: the magazines, newspapers, websites, Rose TV, Rose Air. He peppered his lessons with nuggets of information on key staff.

'How do you know so much?' Eliza asked. 'Do you have spies?'

'Knowledge is power, Lizzie. Clichéd, but true. Knowing what motivates your staff is as important as understanding the balance sheet. The key is to surround yourself with talent. And you need people you can rely on and trust, who'll do all the legwork for you, giving you space to focus on the big picture.'

Eliza thought about Kit, Will and Leigh.

'Can I ask, Dad – where do you stand on nepotism?'

'Wholly in favour, if the people fit the job.'

'I have three super-talented university friends I want to employ. Two are creatives; they're already being noticed by theatre reviewers and producers. The other's a brilliant economist. She wants to go into corporate management. All three would be perfect for Rose's production company.'

'If they fit your vision, then yes, get them on board. But my advice would be to wait. Let's get the Maria situation sorted first.'

After the intense mornings – Harry's easygoing persona masked a hard taskmaster – Eliza would relax by the pool, or they'd take a helicopter trip inland or to one of the Barrier Reef islands.

On her last night she stood alone at the railings, gazing at the Milky Way arcing over the vast expanse of the ocean. In the warm night air, it was all achingly romantic.

If only she had someone to share it with.

She took out her phone and attempted a photo of the moon lighting a silver path to the horizon.

ELIZA: look – pretty!

KIT: WTF is that

ELIZA: Never mind. Home soon. Maybe see you in London? Xx

Chapter 9

Eliza

Eliza was sitting in bed with her laptop, catching up on her emails and thinking about her return to Rose the next day. Excitement was bubbling. Walking through The Rose's revolving doors into its lofty atrium after time away always felt like going home.

The building had such an energy about it. Dotted throughout the atrium's rose garden and tall trees were colourful benches and hanging egg chairs. Quotes from British writers were inlaid into the marble floor, and there were more on plaques tucked between the flowers as little surprises. The scent of roses filled the air (helped along by the innovative air conditioning).

The atrium was Eliza's favourite part of the building, and it was the result of Harry's original brief, which had included an area where staff could sit with their laptops away from the ranked desks of their departments. It worked. On the rare occasions when Terri gave Eliza a wordcount and a deadline, removing herself from *The Rack*'s busy offices into a leafy corner kick-started the ideas part of her brain.

The cafe overlooking the Thames had also become a creative hub. More of those laptops, plus coffee. Really, actual offices were so last century!

The Rose had won many architectural awards; it was a London icon. And, despite recent media coverage of Maria's clean-up campaign and the negative connotations of that, working at Rose Corp was still many a young person's dream. Eliza intended to make sure the company continued to attract the crème de la crème.

She was looking forward to catching up with Chess, who definitely fell into that category. Her cousin was working in admin, following her failure to secure the junior editor position on *The Rack*.

Which Terri had evidently offered to Rob. This still confused Eliza, given Terri's views on nepotism.

She smiled to herself as she pictured Rob's cheeky smile and mop of dark hair. She remembered how, when he was a boy – and on into adolescence – women had always felt compelled to ruffle those curls.

She wondered what Rob made of Terri. Most newbies were petrified of her.

Her spirits sank a little as she finally turned her thoughts to her sister. As per Harry's instructions, she would do what she could to keep an eye on Maria. But the thought of working on the top floor with her prickly sibling, rather than with the team on *The Rack*, had been too depressing. What would she even have done up there?

She'd had a better idea. Stealth could be a more effective strategy than face-to-face combat. Harry had taught her that. Biding one's time; gathering information. So during a conference call that morning, she'd explained her plan to her father and Terri, and had won them round.

By Monday morning – dull and grey – Eliza's time in the Australian sun seemed weeks, if not months ago. She decided to walk to work, as it wasn't far, but when she reached London Bridge those grey clouds let rip and there was nowhere to hide. By the time she'd crossed to the other side, she was soaked.

Stupid British weather. Stupid Eliza, forgetting an umbrella.

She was within a hundred metres of The Rose when there was a shout behind her. 'Hey! Lizzie!'

She turned to see the tall, dark and astonishingly handsome form of Rob Studley walking towards her, holding an umbrella, a big grin on his face.

'I heard you were back,' he said. 'How the devil are you? Apart from exceptionally wet.' He took in her bedraggled appearance and laughed, then bent down and kissed her cheek. His own was cool and fresh, and she caught a whiff of something delicious.

Aftershave? Rob?

'Not funny. I'm pissed off. How did I forget umbrellas are a thing in London?'

He held his so it was over them both. 'Pissed off? Why would you be pissed off on a wet Monday, with only five working days to get through before a weekend that will be equally shite? British summers, eh?'

'Maybe because this time last week I was cruising the Barrier Reef?'

'So I heard. Dad said he'd seen you. Hey, let's grab a coffee. Loads to catch up on, Lizzie.'

She'd forgotten he called her that. He and Harry were the only ones who did.

'Can't. Got to report to Terri. Not a good idea to be late on your first day back working for *her.*'

'Wait.' He took out his phone. 'Terri? Rob. I've just run into a sodden Eliza Rose. OK if we get a coffee before reporting in? If you say yes I'll fetch you one too, maybe even one of those buns you like.' He looked at Eliza. His eyes still had that twinkle. 'Yep, we'll be with you by nine-thirty latest. Thanks, boss.'

Eliza's jaw had dropped. 'Seriously, Rob? How are you not scared of her? How did she not say fuck off and get your arse in here now?'

'Nah, she loves me. Probably 'cause I give as good as I get. Come on, let's get out of the rain and into the Vaj. Oops, sorry. Probably shouldn't call it that in front of you.'

After The Rose had opened, Londoners had quickly given it a special nickname.

'Dad hates that name.'

'How is dear old Harry?'

'Same as ever.'

They made their way through the atrium and up to the cafe, and Eliza didn't miss the many pairs of eyes clocking the boss's daughter – or sister now, to be technically correct – with a good-looking junior member of staff. Gossip was ever a thing at Rose.

They sat down at a table overlooking the gloom of London on a wet Monday. She sighed as she sipped her coffee and took in the view. Low cloud hung across the city, and the Thames looked like sludge.

'Oh dear,' said Rob. 'Missing the sun? You're looking good, anyway. Is that a tan? Must be a first for you, Snow White.'

'Rude. It's probably joined-up freckles. My skin doesn't do gold. You look different, Rob. What've you done?'

'Smartened myself up now I've got a proper job. Discovered hair product. You like?' He ran his fingers through his pretty black curls, mussing them up.

She smiled. 'You always were ugly.'

'You too. Hideous.'

She felt the gloom lifting. Rob had always been great company. Full of fun. Full of . . . well, himself. But she didn't mind that; he was such a charmer, and nice with it. And this new look was pretty easy on the eye.

She admonished herself. Wretched DNA. Far too much of her father's.

'How do you like working here?' she asked.

'Love it. These offices – it's like Google, but without the teeth-gnashingly annoying part. And being on *The Rack*'s brilliant. Terri even lets me write the odd word.'

'Didn't you do maths at uni?'

'Only because it was easy.'

'Hey, I hear Chess is going out with Gil. How did that happen?'

'Arranged marriage,' he said, taking a bite of his blueberry muffin.

'What?'

'Ha. They knew each other vaguely – we met the Lisles a few times, if you remember? You know Charles, Harry and Dad are big mates. I'm convinced they're plotting to create an empire. They'll be marrying you off to me, if you're not careful.'

He paused for a moment, looking out of the window.

'Gil and Chess are great together, actually.' He met her eye again. 'She's bloody clever, isn't she? First from Cambridge, no less. Not sure Gil's up to the job, to be honest, but Dad's whipping him along, keeps asking when he's going to propose.'

'Seriously?'

'He's a military man; he has a strategic plan for everything in life, and that most certainly includes his sons. Like I say, watch out, Eliza Rose.' He winked. 'Right, we'd better get to work before Cruella notices we're not there.'

'You call her that?'

'You've seen the hair.'

'My mum gave her that nickname.'

'Did she? Ana Rose.' He got up to leave, putting a hand on her shoulder. 'It was so sad that she died. Poor you.'

'Yep. Well, like you say, we'd better go.' She pushed her own chair back. 'Hey, Rob?'

'Mm?'

'It's great you're here. This weather was bringing me down, but you just cheered me right back up.'

He smiled. 'You were always my favourite girl, Lizzie.'

They made their way to the third floor, and Eliza carried on into Terri's office.

'Hi, Terri!'

The Rack's editor raised her head. She didn't look happy.

'I'm back! What can I do?'

'Ask Harry to arrange a hit on your bloody sister?'

Eliza's smile faded, and she looked over her shoulder.

'Sorry, pet. Bad-taste joke. I'm just ... Maria has to stop this. She's *Acting* CEO. We've moved on from body-shaming issues to abortion. Needless to say she's anti, under any circumstances.'

'Oh my god. Can I sit down?'

'Do. Where's my bloody coffee?'

'Rob's just coming, someone grabbed him.'

Terri sat back in her chair, scowling. 'I wish I'd known you two were mates. My nepotism detector seriously malfunctioned. Sent Harry's niece away only to get a bloody godson.'

Eliza laughed. 'I can't imagine you offering *anyone* a job unless you thought they were highly capable. In fact, I'd have thought a privileged background would have the opposite effect.'

Terri went still.

'Sorry, Terri. You didn't ask my opinion.'

'No, it's ... fuck it, Eliza. Sometimes you're so like your mum.'

'Am I?'

'Where's that coffee?'

'Please tell me, Terri? How am I like her?'

She sighed. 'I was "encouraged" by Harry to employ Ana. It was a favour to Ana's sister, who Harry was having an affair with at the time.'

'Aunt Merry.'

'Yes. Her. This was way before there was anything between him and your mum. We were recruiting for *The Rack*, and the art director and I spotted her talent immediately. Otherwise no way would we have agreed to it. As things turned out she was a brilliant designer, but I was forever niggling her about that foot in the door.'

'I can imagine,' said Eliza.

'Harry fell for her and promoted her way too quickly. She thought it was because of her talent, but I was suspicious right from the start. I can see her now, standing in my office saying, "I would hope any career success is down to my talent and hard work." I told her she was deluded. I guess we were both right, in the end.'

Terri looked away, and Eliza saw her remembering. Given this news about their working relationship, it was surprising they'd become so close.

'Honestly,' said Eliza, 'I can't believe Dad had relationships with both sisters, *and* while he was still married to Katie.'

'He was quite the lothario. Ah, Rob. About bloody time.'

'Sorry, boss,' he said, bouncing over and placing her coffee and something in a paper bag in front of her. 'Got waylaid by Ellie. She wasn't happy with my review of Ed Sheeran.'

'I liked it. What was her problem?'

'Didn't like my use of the word "lame".'

Eliza snorted.

Terri picked up her coffee, back in editor mode. 'Right, you two. Get the fuck to work, and I don't care if you've known each other since the sixteenth century, I don't want you sloping off to the cafe every five minutes to catch up on family gossip. Eliza, you can proofread everything I'm about to email you. Hot-desking as usual, find one as far from *him* as possible.' She jabbed her pen in Rob's direction.

ELIZA: Hiiii!

CHESS: Eliiiiiza!

ELIZA: free for lunch?

CHESS: no :(but drink after work?

ELIZA: even better! The George 6 p.m.?

CHESS: c u there xxx

Eliza's proofreading was coming along slowly. She was still jet-lagged, and found her eyes drifting away from the screen to the view out of the window, or across the office to where Rob was sitting round a table with a group of editors and designers. He seemed to be doing most of the talking, even though he was probably the most junior member of the team.

He'd do well at Rose. And life here would be a lot more fun with him in it. Perhaps, later on, she could bring him onto her production team.

She should probably go and see Maria – and start actioning the spy-recruitment plan she'd discussed with Harry and Terri.

Before she could talk herself out of it, she took the pink glass lift to the top floor.

'Hi, Pippa,' she said to Maria's PA.

'Eliza! How lovely to see you again!'

Pippa had been promoted to replace Harry's assistant, Aleesha, who'd left in a huff just after Eliza's return to Oxford last year. According to Terri, Aleesha had 'missed Harry terribly', stayed 'for Eliza's sake', then walked out after a dressing-down from Maria on the subject of her too-transparent blouses.

'How are you enjoying working up here?' said Eliza.

'It's very ... interesting, thanks.'

The moment's hesitancy was exactly what Eliza had been hoping for.

'I hope we gave you a good pay increase.' She smiled conspiratorially, raising her eyebrows in the direction of Maria's closed office door.

'Haha, yes. Quite a good one.'

'I expect you deserve every penny.' Eliza winked. 'I hope my sister isn't too ... demanding, Pippa. It's important to my father and me that key staff are happy in their positions. If ever you feel uncomfortable with anything ...'

Eliza let her words hang in the air. Pippa would be aware Eliza was due to return to Rose full time next year, and the reminder that Harry was there in the background wouldn't hurt.

She saw Pippa working it out.

'There *have* been one or two things I've been a little worried about. Bearing in mind my loyalty is to Rose, rather than to any one particular person.'

'I'd imagine things have been a little difficult, at times?'

'More than a little, truth be told.'

'Oh, that's disappointing. I'd be happy to discuss your concerns, off the record of course. Are you free for lunch sometime this week? Off base, perhaps? No need to inform Maria.'

'That would be great, Eliza.'

'Cool. Why don't you book us somewhere and email me.'

She looked over at Maria's office door again. 'Is it OK if I go through?'

'I'm afraid she's got someone with her—'

Just then the door opened and a dark-haired man in an expensive-looking suit emerged, Maria behind him.

'What are you doing up here, Eliza?' said Maria.

'Eliza Rose?' The man stopped and looked Eliza over. His accent was American, and he was attractive in that clean-living, all-American, square-jawed way.

'That's me,' said Eliza, 'Mister . . . ?'

'Seville. Call me Phil.' He held out his hand, and she shook it. His grip was firm and his nails beautifully manicured.

'Eliza's doing work experience,' said Maria, coming to stand next to him. Her cheeks were slightly flushed, and she seemed . . . fluttery.

'I came to say hi, as it's my first day back,' said Eliza.

'I'm busy. Now, if you'd move, so I can show Mr Seville out?'

'It's a real pleasure to meet you, ma'am,' said Phil to Eliza. 'I'm sure we'll be seeing more of each other.' He smiled, revealing perfectly straight, blue-white teeth. He probably had those 'walk with me' meetings and used Bluetooth things a lot.

'Will we?'

'Oh yes. Goodbye now.' His rather intense blue eyes lingered on her before he turned to Maria. 'A pleasure, Ms Rose.'

'Do call me Maria, please.'

'Maria. I look forward very much to seeing you again soon.'

Maria touched her hair and . . . *simpered*.

Phil left, and Eliza followed Maria into her office.

'Who's he?'

'He has media interests in America.' Maria sat down and started reading a document.

'Oh? Wait.' Eliza realized the name was familiar. 'Phil Seville? Isn't he the evangelist guy with all the God TV channels?'

'*God TV?*' Maria gave Eliza a withering look. 'You mean Christian broadcasting and media. He's head of Hapsburg Inc.' Her demeanour changed. 'A most interesting man.' Her eyes were definitely sparkling. 'We have similar views on many things.'

'But isn't he, like, a fundamentalist? Not your religious bag, I'd have thought.'

'The most important principles and beliefs tend to transcend religious boundaries. Pro-life, family values – we see eye to eye on many things.'

Eliza felt uneasy. 'OK. Well, I came to say hi, but I guess this is a good time to remind you about, you know, our conversation. About copying me in on things.'

'You're doing work experience, you're not management.' Maria looked down again, carried on reading.

'I'm on the board, and I'm technically on study leave before coming back full time. You've got to keep me in the loop. Dad talked to me about it while we were away.'

'Oh, I'm sure he did.' She didn't look up. 'How *was* your *holiday*?'

'It was lovely! Clare and Dad are having a great time. It's not so bad for him, being retired, I think.'

Maria said nothing.

'So, this Phil. Is he just a business contact?'

As Maria looked up, Eliza cocked her head to one side and smiled.

Maria blushed. 'He's an inspiring man, and I'm delighted to have made his acquaintance. He wanted advice regarding the media landscape in Britain, as he has an interest in increasing his involvement here.'

'Mutual interests as well as a cool few billions in the bank – can't be bad!'

'I need to get on.'

'I'm meeting Chess for a drink after work. Don't suppose you'd like to come?'

'I don't drink, and it wouldn't be appropriate. She's very junior. Eliza, please go. I'm busy.'

✦

The rain had stopped, so Eliza and Chess carried their drinks to an outside table. Eliza was looking forward to a serious catch-up with her cousin; they'd been close all their lives.

'So ... I've been hearing all about you and Gil.' She grinned. 'Rob thinks John's looking to create a dynasty.'

'Oh god, John's a pain,' said Chess. 'He keeps asking Gil when he's going to "make it official". Embarrassing, much?'

Her pale-red hair, a straight version of her mother Megan's, hung like a well-behaved curtain around her shoulders. Eliza had always been envious of it when they were girls, despairing of her own unruly curls.

'I call him the Major,' Chess continued. 'He's like one of those throwback British Empire dudes from India.'

Eliza laughed. 'I saw him in Australia. He's well pleased about you two.'

'Hm. I should imagine that has little to do with my personality.'

'Rob called it an arranged marriage.'

'Well, if we do tie the knot, he can forget about little heirs to his empire for many, many years to come. I'm loving Rose – the company, if not the job. I suppose you'll be my boss after uni? Hope that won't make things awkward.'

'I think all sorts of shit might be about to hit the fan. Probably shouldn't talk about it, but you're going to be a shareholder, right? On the board?'

'Already am. Mum's signed her shares over to Helena and me. She never could be bothered taking an interest.'

'Why did you choose admin?' said Eliza. Chess's degree was in modern languages, but she was good at just about everything.

'I didn't. Maria put me forward for it. She said as a graduate trainee I should get inter-departmental experience, and this was a starting point.'

'I see.'

'Bloody Rob, getting a job on *The Rack*. I interviewed for that, thought I did quite well. Obviously Terri Robbins-More wasn't impressed. Or maybe she was just beguiled by Rob's twinkly eyes.'

'No – she hates people getting jobs because of who they know,' said Eliza. 'If she hadn't been aware you were my cousin, you'd have walked it. Ha, she didn't realize I know Rob, she's really pissed off about it.'

'Not surprised. You and Rob together always meant trouble.'

Chapter 10

Eliza

'What's up, Busy Lizzie?' said Rob, perching on Eliza's desk. She was thumping her keyboard unnecessarily hard as she fired off emails chasing overdue copy.

Eliza didn't look up. 'I had an argument on FaceTime with Dad this morning.'

'What about?'

'Brexit, again. He *still* thinks it's totally the right thing for Britain! Dad and Boris are chums – they were at Eton and Oxford together. What a pair.' She stabbed at the delete key, erasing the word 'please'.

'You're a remainer, then?'

Finally, Eliza looked up.

And all at once, her mood improved.

Rob was wearing jeans and a white linen shirt, and there was designer stubble. He looked – there was no other word for it – hot.

'Well?'

Eliza realized she was staring. 'Sorry. I'm still coming to terms with Fashion-Forward Rob. Yes, of course I'm a remainer. It's all so frustrating!'

'Chill, Lizzie. I actually came to see if you fancied *A Midsummer*

Night's Dream at the Globe tonight – me, you, Chess and Gil. Amy's got to work, so I've got a spare ticket.'

'Amy? Who's Amy?'

'The missus. Did I not mention her?'

'You've got a missus? How did I not know that?'

'You did not ask that.'

'Who is she?'

'Rob, you stupid arse!' a voice hollered from across the office. 'I said where's my *coffee*, not copy!'

'Sorry, Terri – on my way! Bloody hell,' he muttered. 'What's up with the boss? Her cage is rattling fit to burst.'

'Maria's really ramping things up. That's why Dad FaceTimed me. He thinks we'll have to call a board meeting to bring her under control. Wait, why am I telling you this? Go and get Terri's coffee – and forget you heard that.'

'Right. Globe tonight. Yes?'

'You're on.'

❁

Before heading to the theatre, the four of them went for a drink at The George. They sat fanning themselves with beer mats on this hot, sultry, midsummer-ish night. England was in the grip of a record-breaking heatwave; today the temperature had topped thirty-seven degrees.

Eliza snapped a selfie with the ancient inn in the background, and sent it to Will and Kit: *Off to see Midsummer Night's Dream at the Globe. Jealous?*

Will replied: *What the Puck? Serious attack of the green-eyed monster. Stratford's dull as ditch water. Bring on Michaelmas.*

She smiled. He was home from Italy, then. Was Kit? She missed her friends.

'Get off your phone,' said Rob. 'Who're you messaging?'

'A Shakespeare nut, to make him jealous. He's called Will.'

'Of course.'

'He's from Stratford.'

'Puffling pants?'

'Definitely. Drama queen in every way. But cute.'

She put the phone away. 'So tell me about *Amy*,' she said, nudging him. 'Who is she, what is she, how long, how serious? Leave nothing out.'

'Who and what – a nurse. How long – quite long. How serious . . . ' He glanced at Gil.

'Amy's lovely,' said Chess. 'Really sweet.'

'Thought *I* was your favourite girl,' said Eliza, with a pout.

'You are.' He grinned. 'She's my favourite *woman*.'

Chess rolled her eyes.

'Where does she work?' asked Eliza.

'At Kingston Hospital. She used to be up near us, in Coventry.' The Studleys were a Midlands family, with a sprawling old manor at Kenilworth. 'We met when I broke my leg last year.'

He looked at his watch. 'Time we were off, team. Starts in fifteen.'

After the play, Rob walked Eliza home. As they crossed London Bridge, the night air was tropical-balmy. Monday's dull-grey cityscape had morphed into a romantic, prettily lit version that demanded you slow down.

'Not so bad, is it?' he said. 'Now the rain's stopped.' They paused to lean on the parapet, looking across to the floodlit Tower of London, peering down as a party boat chugged through the arch beneath them.

'You're quiet, Lizzie. Everything OK?'

'It's just . . . I can't help thinking about my step-mum. Caitlyn. She jumped.'

'Oh god, I remember,' said Rob. 'We were – what? Twelve or thirteen?'

'Yes. Poor thing. Who'd have guessed what was going on in that beautiful head? Dad certainly didn't.' Eliza turned her back on the inky water.

'Amy . . . she's kind of like that. Fragile.'

Eliza looked at him in surprise. 'What, you mean she gets depressed?'

'I didn't know, at first . . . ' He hesitated, looked away.

'That must be hard. Do you live together?'

'Yes.' He went quiet, his eyes settling on the Tower.

Clearly there was some problem. Eliza was aware of a twinge of satisfaction; a sense of . . . possessiveness.

'I should come clean,' he said, turning to her. 'You're my oldest friend, after all.'

'Come clean?'

'I'm married, Lizzie.'

What the f—?

'No. You're kidding!'

'It happened on holiday, in Bali. Impulse thing, on the beach.'

He held her gaze, waiting for her response.

'But . . . how did I not know? Dad would've told me – and your dad, in Sydney – he didn't say a word!'

'He refuses to accept it. Says it's meaningless, not legal. He hit the roof when he found out; he's still of the generation that thinks marriages should be *advantageous*.'

'So I hear.'

This was *most* dispiriting. Eliza acknowledged the daydreams that had been flitting around in her head, unbidden. Of nights on the town with Rob, Chess and Gil; a little summer flirtation.

'But, Rob, you're so young.'

'Yep. Far too young; hadn't even finished my internship. I do have this disappointing tendency towards impulsiveness.' He blew out a breath. 'Can I be honest with you?'

'Of course.'

'I'm kind of regretting it now. It was probably a mistake.'

Again he held her gaze, and she had a sudden inkling that the 'now' had something to do with her.

'But you do love her?'

'She's adorable. Sweet; angelic. Not a bad bone in her body.' He grinned. 'Beautiful body, actually.'

'Tsk, Rob.'

'She's kind of opposite to me. Quiet and ... not very self-confident.'

'Don't your parents like her?'

'Dad doesn't approve of her at all, because she's ... well. Of no strategic importance. I think part of me got married as an act of rebellion. You know what it's like, having an in-your-face dad who you sometimes just really want to piss off.'

'Yup. With you there. So it's a case of marry in haste, repent at leisure?'

'In a nutshell. And now she knows I'm having second thoughts, and she's had this depression ...' He rubbed the back of his neck. 'I don't actually know what to do, Lizzie.'

'I'm not the best person to talk to about relationships, to be honest.'

Eliza started walking again, and Rob fell into step.

'I remember you saying after Caitlyn died, that you'd never marry,' he said. 'That it only led to misery.'

'Can't say I've changed my mind. Looks like you should've listened to me.'

'You still single?' He looked sideways at her. 'No one up at Oxford?'

'Nope. Haven't we just watched a play that tells us how love turns people into fools?'

Kit's wicked grin came to mind: *Terrible behaviour is also part of being human. One of the best bits.*

'I did like someone, but he's ... that would *certainly* have been foolish. Maybe I'll meet Mr Right one day, but I'd really rather it wasn't now, with so much on my plate.'

'But you'll *always* have a lot on your plate.' He put an arm round her and gave her a quick squeeze. 'You should make the most of now.'

'Can I buy you lunch?' said Chess on the phone, a week or so later. 'I could do with some advice.'

'Sure. The cafe?'

'Actually, can we go somewhere with no ears or eyes?'

Eliza suggested the riverside bistro she'd been to with Pippa. Maria's PA was now Eliza's top-floor spy, and was quietly forwarding emails to Eliza's personal email account.

Chess was scrolling through her phone when Eliza arrived. 'Look at this,' she said. She held up an Instagram post, and Eliza recognized her cousin Helena's distinctive painting style. 'I think I've lost my sister to Paris. She's met a hot French guy and they're living in a garret room in Montmarte. How sickening is that?'

Eliza sat down. 'Following her dreams. As everyone should.'

Chess frowned. 'Why so wistful?'

'Oh, I guess we all have escape fantasies from time to time. People – cute men, actually – keep telling me to let my hair down. To live in the moment. Like that's easy for me to do.'

'What cute men? Rob?'

The waiter came to take their order, giving Eliza an excuse not to answer.

'So. Can you guess what I wanted to talk about?'

'Not work, I hope. Gil?'

'Indeed. He's popped the question.'

'Oh! But – how long have you been seeing each other?'

'Since March.'

'That's not long, Chess. Why the rush?' She thought of Rob's revelation. 'You could just move in together, see how it goes?'

'He's quite old-fashioned.'

'You mean his father is.'

'Well, yes. I do see the hand of the Major in this. He seems to be assessing me on my suitability as the wife of a future politician. I don't think he'll be happy until Gil makes prime minister.'

'So what are you going to do?'

Chess smiled. 'I'm a independent, feminist career woman.'

'You are.'

'But I'm going to say yes.'

'What? Really?'

'I'm also marshmallow inside when it comes to Gil. I can't imagine anything lovelier than being his wife.'

'Then, congratulations! He's perfect for you.'

'You think?'

'Remember when we played princesses, and made up our ideal princes? Before we discovered feminism, obviously. Gil is exactly that prince you made up. Handsome, intelligent, beautiful manners—'

'Looks good on a horse,' said Chess.

'Always a plus.'

Their food arrived.

'So you don't think I'm a throwback, or a disgrace to the sisterhood?' said Chess. 'For wanting to tie the knot with my true love at an unfashionably young age?'

'You know my views on marriage. But then your dad's only had the two wives.'

Chess laughed. 'Seven between them, good grief. Wifeaholics. So, Eliza. Will you be my chief bridesmaid? Remember how we promised each other?'

'I'd love to, as long as you don't expect me to reciprocate. I'm never getting married.'

'Of course you will!'

'Nope. Never. I'll write that in blood, if you want. And I'll need a say in the dress. No frills, no pastels.'

'Heh heh. Actually, thinking about it, Rob will no doubt be best man, so maybe making you chief bridesmaid isn't such a great idea.'

'Oh, I think our days of practical jokes are behind us,' Eliza replied.

'Hm. I didn't mean that. I'm more worried about being upstaged, what with your pizazz and Rob's new metrosexual look.'

Eliza smiled. 'He has changed, hasn't he? But I kind of miss the old scruffy version.'

'So cute now, though. Those Studley brothers, eh?'

Eliza thought back to the heart-to-heart on the bridge. 'Rob and I had a chat the other night. Chess – why didn't you tell me he's married?'

'Ah. I was surprised you didn't already know – you two were always pretty close. When I realized you didn't, I thought I'd let him tell you himself. It's a massive sore point with the Major, and his mum's not best chuffed, either. His parents kind of ignore it – like, because it happened on a beach in Bali with some local non-Christian ceremony, it doesn't count. But apparently it does. All legal.'

Eliza fiddled with her napkin. 'He told me he's regretting it.'

'Did he?' Chess looked concerned. 'Gil said Rob's always been one to act first, think later. Let's just hope things work out.'

Eliza had a hunch they wouldn't.

'OK, I'll be your bridesmaid,' she said, steering the conversation back into its comfort zone, 'if you promise a frill-free dress in a non-pastel shade.'

'Gil's talking about a December wedding.'

'Like Dad and Janette's Christmas wedding, remember? I demanded the bridesmaids should wear sparkly pink. What was Dad thinking, letting me get away with that?'

'Uncle Harry's always been wrapped around your finger. It must be hard for Maria, you're so obviously his favourite. Hey, she called me up to her office yesterday, supposedly to see how I was getting on, but she started quizzing me about shareholdings. What do you think that was about?'

Eliza frowned. 'I'd have thought she could easily access that information. But I don't know why she'd suddenly be interested.'

Had Maria got wind of Harry's intentions to round up the board?

'I asked her when I could move on from Admin,' Chess continued. 'She wants me to stay where I am for now. To be honest, I'm bored witless. All I do is input stuff into a computer. Gil keeps nagging me to do something about it – so does the Major – but I'm new, I don't want to make waves. What do you think I should do?'

'I can't do much about it yet, Chess.' She thought back to the diagram Harry had drawn, illustrating who owned what. 'I've got even fewer shares than you, come to think of it.' The realisation made her uncomfortable. 'But then . . . so has Maria.'

'Really?'

'But hang in there. When I'm back next year, no way will I leave you to moulder in Admin.'

'That's good to know.'

'So. When are you going to let Gil know it's a yes?'

'No time like the present – I'll tell him tonight. Exciting!'

Eliza was at the office early the next day and, after checking through her emails, texted Chess:

> ELIZA: Did you tell him yes?

> CHESS: I did! Only immediate family know so please don't tell. Or it's turquoise polyester for you.

Rob appeared, coffee in hand, and claimed the desk next to hers. A delicious scent – a combination of aftershave and espresso – wafted across.

'Morning, Snow White,' he said, swivelling his chair to face her. 'Heard the news?'

'I have! Chess is a happy lady.'

'Gil is too. Man, I mean. I just hope he didn't propose to score brownie points with Dad.'

'Don't ever let Chess hear you say that.'

'We're going to take a bottle of fizz or two over to St James's Park after work to celebrate. You'll come?'

'Oh! Well, yes. It would be churlish not to. Is Amy coming?'

'No, still working nights.' He winked.

'You need to speak to Human Resources,' said Gil, topping up their glasses with Moët. 'Or whatever ridiculous name they call it.'

'@People,' said Rob. 'Who came up with that piece of corporate shite?'

'Dad,' said Eliza. 'He thought it suited the Rose vibe. Idiot.'

It was a beautiful evening, and the grassy areas of the park were scattered with tourists and office workers. And lovers. Lovers were everywhere.

'Tell them you've learned all you can in Admin,' said Gil, 'and you're ready to make the move.'

'I will,' said Chess. 'Can we not talk about work? We're meant to be celebrating.'

Rob, lying on his stomach next to Eliza, threw a hunk of bread to a passing family of ducks.

'Don't feed the birds,' said Eliza.

'You're not the boss of me,' he replied. 'Actually, you are.'

'And don't you forget it, or there will be consequences.'

'Whip me?'

'Any time.'

Chess rolled her eyes. 'You two.'

Eliza was on her third glass of champagne after eating very little all day. People kept telling her to chill, so she'd decided to do exactly that. If she couldn't let her hair down with these three lifetime buddies, then when could she?

'Did you read *Fifty Shades of Grey*, Eliza?' said Chess.

'No.'

'Liar,' said Rob.

'Well, yes then. But only in my capash . . . capashitty as a monitor of current publishing trends.'

'It's such tosh,' said Chess.

'Methinks the lady in *grey* doth protest too much,' said Eliza. 'Hey, Gil – have you noticed how Chess often wears grey, in many shades. Perhaps she's trying to tell you something.'

Gil looked across at Chess. 'Can this be true, babe?'

'Can what be true? You haven't read it – have you?'

'One gets the gist.' He grinned an evil grin, straddled Chess and pushed her down onto the grass, grabbing her wrists and saying,

'*Clink, clink.*' Then he lowered himself on top of her and said, 'You're mine now. You said yes.'

'*Oh my!*' said Chess, in an American accent.

Gil kissed her, and Eliza felt herself invisible-blushing as it seemed they weren't about to stop anytime soon.

'Awkward,' said Rob. 'Walk?' He stood up and held out his hand.

Eliza grabbed it and stood up too quickly, stumbling forward into his arms. 'Oops. I seem to be a little tipsy. I blame you. All this talk of being foolish.'

His arms tightened around her for a moment, then he took a step back. 'Be as foolish as you like, Lizzie. I promise to see you safely home. Come on.' He grabbed an unopened bottle of champagne and their glasses.

The sun was setting, streaking the sky above Buckingham Palace with bands of gold and pink. They found a spot beside the lake, and Rob popped the cork, which flew off and landed in the water with a splash, scattering birds.

'You're determined to kill a duck.'

He shifted closer, until their shoulders were touching.

'Here's to foolery,' he said, lifting his glass.

She clinked hers against his, sighing in contentment. Being with Rob was so easy.

'Would you look at us, all grown up,' she said. 'Weird, isn't it? But nice. Did I mention I'm so pleased you're at Rose?'

When he didn't respond, she turned to look at him. And registered the expression in his eyes.

Her heart began to thump.

No. *Not* a good idea.

He touched her cheek. 'Is this a foolish notion, Snow White?'

'A married man? Perish the thought.'

He smiled, and pushed her curls back from her face. 'Crazy hair.'

Her hand took on a life of its own, and she found herself running her fingers through his silky dark curls. 'Too much product,' she said. 'I think I'm probably quite drunk. Don't even think about taking advantage.'

'But how can I be expected to behave when you look at me like that?'

'Like what?'

'God, Lizzie. When did you get to be so beautiful?'

He kissed her.

Thoughts tumbled through her head.

Chess and Gil might see.

Gosh, this was nice. So . . . assured.

But . . . Rob! Her childhood playmate. Her *married* childhood playmate.

This was wrong.

But it's divine.

He stopped. 'Sorry. Probably shouldn't. Blame the champagne.'

'Indeed. I guess in letting you do that, I was just proving a point.'

'What point?'

'That I can be foolish. I hope Chess and Gil didn't see.'

'I think they know, Lizzie.'

'Know what?'

'How I feel about things. About you.'

'Me?'

'That mistake I made suddenly feels a whole lot more serious.'

His eyes were pulling her under. She turned her gaze to the lake, the birds silhouetted on the water as dusk deepened. A chill had crept into the air.

She pulled her jacket tighter, aware of sobering up. 'It was just a drunken kiss, Rob. Forget about it. No way am I having a thing with a married man. We rewind to best mates, OK?'

'OK, boss.' He smiled. 'Might have to do some serious thinking.'

'You do that. And now we should get back to Chess and Gil.'

Chapter 11

Eliza

'My office – now,' said Terri.

Eliza's head was full of cotton wool – and pain. The hangover was every bit as bad as she deserved. The sum total of her achievements in the three hours since she'd arrived at work had been an email to Terri and a message to Chess.

Each time she tried to focus on work, her mind veered off to last night's moment. Last night's stupid, impulsive, moment.

Last night's unforgettable moment.

Rob was nowhere to be seen this morning, and she didn't know whether the delay in the awkward moment to come was a good thing or a bad one.

'Shut the door,' said Terri.

'Is there a problem?' The room seemed to tilt as Eliza sat down.

'I was expecting your update on outstanding copy.'

'I sent it.'

'No, you just messaged me a gif of Spongebob looking green.'

'Oh. Sorry, that was meant for Chess. My cousin – she's working in Admin. The one you—'

'I know who bloody Chess is. Eliza, you look like a bag lady this morning. Hungover is not a look I encourage in my department. What's going on?'

'Sorry, Terri. Chess just got engaged to Rob's brother. We were out celebrating.'

'Your lot are still arranging marriages, then? Fuck's sake.' Terri gave Eliza a long, hard stare. 'Look, Eliza, there's nothing wrong with letting your hair down occasionally—'

Something inside Eliza snapped. 'God! I wish people would stop telling me how to live my life.'

'Better get used to it,' said Terri. 'Has the penny not dropped? The future of Rose Corp lies on your shoulders. *Yours*. Harry wants you as CEO, and Harry always gets what he wants. You need to be ready.'

Her expression softened. 'Yes, you can let those charmingly unruly curls out of their ponytail occasionally, but only if you don't let that interfere with your professional life. You've been ... distracted all week. You need to keep focused.'

As Terri continued, Eliza felt the weight of it all settling back onto her shoulders.

'Maria's tightening the screws. She just sent me an article about the backlash against the new abortion law in Ireland. She wants me to interview some woman she called "inspirational". There's no way. Maria *must* be reined in.'

'You could do the interview but make it a stitch-up?'

'Nope. Any articles on "sensitive" issues must from hereon be run past the Acting CEO for copy approval. New edict.'

'My god.' Eliza remembered seeing an email in her inbox, subject heading *Copy approval*, but she hadn't got round to opening it.

Terri was right, she needed to up her game. And to stop being ... distracted.

'Look,' said Terri. 'You'll be getting a notice about a board meeting any time now. You have to be ready when Harry makes his move.'

'Right.'

'Do your homework. Now go and nurse your hangover, and

for fuck's sake don't have any more of them until we've got this sorted.'

◈

The board meeting was arranged for the week before Eliza's return to Oxford. She was making a huge effort to focus on her work, to let nothing – and no *one* – divert her.

Rob carried on as if the kiss hadn't happened, which was fine, as far as Eliza was concerned. Rob didn't do awkward; he kept up the banter, made the odd suggestive comment – it was business as usual. She attempted to wipe the kiss from her memory, telling herself it had been nothing but a moment of drunken foolery.

Part of her remained unconvinced.

◈

On the morning of the board meeting Eliza put on the clothes she'd carefully picked out the night before. She was going the full executive: grey suit, white silk blouse, black kitten heels; hair wrangled into a restraining up-do.

She'd spent the previous weekend in Richmond. Harry and Clare seemed happy to be back, but Eliza sensed her father itching to return to Rose. She wondered what they were going to do about that.

They discussed the Maria situation as they took a walk in Richmond Park, scuffing the first of the autumn leaves. Harry was still tanned, and his cheeks were rosy in the fresh air.

'It should be an easy win,' he said. 'If Maria refuses to change direction, the board will vote on her mission statement proposal. She won't have the numbers to carry it through. She'll either have to resign, or agree to follow the direction the board wants her to take. Assuming she stays, we'll give her time to bring things back on track, and if that doesn't happen – and I'd imagine it won't – well, that's when we vote her out and you in, Lizzie.'

He made it sound so simple.

❁

'Hi, everyone,' said Eliza, sitting down beside Harry at the board-room table.

John Studley, Chess, Harry and Pippa were already there.

Agendas were laid out, along with pads of paper and plastic bottles of water. Eliza made a mental note to speak to Pippa about replacing those with glass jugs. Sheesh, what was happening to Rose's green ethics?

She looked at the agenda. The two main items were 'Mission statement' and 'CEO appointment'.

The door opened, and Eliza shivered. *Him.*

Seymour and Rich Morrissey walked in, all swagger, expensive suits and wide grins, greeting everyone effusively. Eliza avoided the eye of her step-uncle Seymour, as Harry reached across to shake hands. He had no idea, of course, that Seymour was a perv.

Maria came in, grim-faced. She took the seat at the head of the table, and dropped a folder of papers loudly in front of her. 'If we're all ready?'

They murmured that they were.

'We're here at my father's request. He's briefed me on the reasons.' She paused, and looked at each of them in turn before continuing. *Death stare.*

'Apologies have been received from Helena Lisle and Margot James.'

'Noted,' said Pippa.

'As you'll be aware,' Maria continued, 'my recent focus has been on consolidating Rose's core values. The trouble, as I see it, is that there's no single underlying goal or purpose to our activities. It's a loose collection of offerings, with no cohesion, no *mission*. Take the Green Rose brand, for instance. It's way off topic, too far from Rose's roots.'

'Nice pun,' said Harry.

Maria ignored him. 'Or *The Rack*. It's become little more than a mirror for the liberal left, reflecting back its own values, full of questionable themes and featuring people on the fringes of society at the expense of the moral majority.'

'You mean like the LBGTQplus community?' said Eliza.

'I do not deal in trendy acronyms, Eliza,' said Maria. 'And please don't interrupt.'

Harry sat back in his chair and rubbed the side of his face.

John was looking unconcerned, and Chess was staring fixedly at the table. Eliza didn't look at Eddie's uncles.

'I have drafted a new mission statement to reflect Rose's core values, but this needs a majority vote from the board before we can draw up a strategic plan.'

'Maria, you're not going to get it,' interrupted Harry. 'You're Acting CEO, and one of a team. You're the only person interested in going down this road, so pull your head in, do what's required of you until Eliza comes back full time, and then – *only* then – should you start making any strategic changes.'

Maria looked at him steadily. 'In fact, Father, I'm not the only one who considers Rose should spearhead Britain's return to more family-orientated values.'

'So let's just vote on it,' said Harry, exasperated. 'All those *against* a new mission statement along Maria's lines, raise your hands.'

Maria looked as if she was about to insist on conducting the vote herself, then pursed her lips and said nothing.

John, Chess, Harry, Eliza, Rich and Seymour raised their hands.

'And I have Helena's proxy vote here,' said Chess, indicating a document in front of her, 'which is against redrafting.'

'Now all those in favour of redrafting the mission statement,' said Harry.

'Wait,' said Maria. She slid a bunch of papers out from her folder. 'I have here Margot James's proxy vote. This counts for around twenty-five per cent of the company shares. Together with mine, that makes nearly thirty-two per cent—'

'As compared to nearly fifty per cent held by myself, Eliza, Eddie, and Megan's girls,' said Harry. 'Maria, did you not pay attention in maths?'

A laugh escaped Eliza, but everyone else looked horribly embarrassed.

'If you'd excuse me one moment, Father?' Maria left the room. No one said a word.

'What the hell is she up to?' muttered Harry to Eliza.

'No idea. But I have a bad feeling.'

And all at once, Eliza worked it out. 'Oh my god. Phil Seville.'

As she said his name, the door opened again and Maria ushered the American billionaire into the room.

'Everyone, I'd like you to meet Philip Seville, head of Hapsburg Inc. Hapsburg has bought the majority of the publicly owned Rose shares, equating to twenty per cent of the company, and therefore is entitled to a say in the direction we take. Philip and I will lay out this direction in a new mission statement.'

Phil bestowed a dazzling smile on each of the stunned faces around the table.

'I'm delighted to make your acquaintance, folks,' he said, taking the seat next to Seymour. 'Especially yours, Harry – we've met before, but not properly. I've already had the pleasure of meeting your lovely daughter.' His eyes lit on Eliza, and stayed there a while before turning to Maria. 'And Maria and I have been working towards a sea-change mission statement that I know Britain needs very much right now. As does the world, but one step at a time, eh, Father?' He looked up at the ceiling.

Maria giggled. *Giggled*.

Eliza could feel the heat coming off Harry. It was like sitting next to a time bomb counting down its final seconds. He was furious; he was going to go off like he'd never gone off before. A US evangelist with a right-wing agenda had stolen a chunk of the company from under his nose. Phil, Maria, and horrible, humourless Aunt Margot had joined to form Harry's trio from hell.

Eliza had let her father down. She'd been asked to keep an eye on Maria. Both Harry and Terri had wanted her to work up here, on Maria's floor. But no, she'd selfishly wanted to work on *The Rack*. All she'd done was to recruit a spy who, it turned out, hadn't been aware of what Maria and Phil were up to. And, she finally admitted to herself, she'd let herself be distracted by that boy across the office; the memory of his kiss, the look in his eyes.

And now Maria was going to pull apart the forward-looking company Harry had built up over his lifetime – his legacy – and replace it with a means to a political, religious end.

'Gentlemen ... and ladies,' said Phil, making it clear that was the natural order of things. 'I'll be based in London while I work with Maria moving forward, and we'll be consulting you throughout, of course. I don't intend launching Christian channels here in the UK, at least not immediately. What works in the US wouldn't necessarily be effective here. Instead we'll work with what we already have, bringing it in line with a more morally focused mission statement. That statement will be with you all by the end of next week.

'Perhaps, Pippa,' he continued, 'we should wrap this up? Accepting, of course, in light of the recent vote, that Maria will now be CEO.'

Eliza was still waiting for Harry to explode, or to come in with one of his cutting comments that would let everyone know he was still in charge.

But he didn't.

Now Eliza felt sick. They'd forced Harry to retire because of mistakes he'd made in his personal life – mistakes Eliza was beginning to understand, as she grew up and made her own. If they hadn't done so, then Maria would still be in HR, and Eliza would be at Oxford, unconcerned as to what was happening at Rose. Harry would still be at the helm of one of Britain's best-loved companies, sailing it into innovative new waters.

What had they done?

Chapter 12

Eliza

Eliza was head down, focused on her work. She loved being part of *The Rack*'s team, but since the board meeting had been feeling detached; that she should instead be working towards putting things right.

But how?

Her desk phone buzzed. 'There's a package for you in reception, Eliza,' said Terri's PA. 'Needs signing for.'

'Fuck's sake.'

She seemed to be picking up Terri's bad habits. Or maybe she was passive-aggressively resisting Maria's family values, soon to be enshrined in a new mission statement.

'Do you want the courier to bring it up?'

'Good plan,' said Eliza. 'Sorry for the swear – I'm rushing to meet a deadline.'

'Off-brand language,' called Rob from the next desk. 'Mind I don't report you to our Dear Leader.'

'Chairman Maoria?' said Eliza.

'Big Sister is watching you.'

And Little Sister was watching Rob, far too often, in spite of herself.

Eliza turned back to her computer. Too many distractions. When she wasn't brooding on the Maria situation, she was trying hard – and usually failing – to ignore the ever-evolving Mr Studley. Today he wore some sort of shoelace necklace thing over his snowy white T-shirt, and her gaze kept drifting to his arms, which were quite tanned after all this sunshine.

He was the very definition of a hot desk.

Stop it, Eliza.

Hot-desking was such a stupid thing. Whoever came up with such an idea? Eliza wished she had her own space, one she could configure so as to avoid those twinkly brown eyes; one where the neighbouring desks were occupied by people she could happily ignore.

'Eliza Rose. *Where thou art, there is the world itself.*'

Eliza gasped and swung round in her chair. 'Will!'

And Kit.

'Sign here, please,' said Will, plonking a large brown envelope on her desk.

Eliza leaped up and threw her arms round him. 'Why didn't you call! Oh my gosh, it's so good to see you!'

Her eyes met Kit's.

He smiled his lazy smile. His hair was sun-bleached almost white, and his amber eyes seemed to take up twice as much of his face as before.

'Hello, gorgeous,' he said.

As he hugged her, she felt the angst of the past week draining away, as if it had all suddenly ceased to matter. She buried her head in his shoulder and closed her eyes, breathing him in. His hair tickled her nose; he smelled smoky.

'Miss me?' he said.

'So much!'

She squeezed him tighter; she could feel his bones.

'You're even thinner,' she said. 'Have you not been eating again?'

'You can feed me up.'

She pulled back a little and smiled at him.

'Ahem,' said Will. 'Eliza, darling, if you could put Kit down for one moment? We bring you the result of our summer labours. This one's for you, not the Dramatic Society. Do with it what you will.'

Eliza let go of Kit and picked up the envelope. As she did, she noticed Rob watching them, his eyes flicking between her and Kit.

'A script?' She slid a sheaf of A4 out of the envelope.

Most Human of Saints, read the title page.

'Thomas More?' she said, turning over the first few sheets.

'Save it for later,' said Kit.

'I will. Gosh, I can't *wait* to read it!'

'I like your big pink rose,' said Will. He looked out of the window. 'And you're practically next door to the Globe.'

'Oh, you're going to *love* it here,' said Eliza. 'Hey, let me give you the tour, and we can grab something in the cafe. Food, Kit.'

As she closed her computer window, Rob caught her eye, raising his eyebrows.

'This is Rob,' she said, as they passed his desk. 'One of our editors, and ... an old friend. Rob, meet Will and Kit, from uni. They're writers. Exceptionally good ones.'

Rob shook their hands. 'What sort of thing do you write?'

'He writes dark,' said Will, looking at Kit. 'Very dark. I attempt to lighten him up. I usually fail.'

'Is this new one dark?' said Eliza.

'It explores a troubled soul,' said Kit.

'Your own, one might surmise,' said Will.

'Fuck off,' said Kit.

'No swearing, Kit. Sister's house rules,' said Eliza.

'Welcome to the house of fun,' said Rob.

'Why thank you,' said Kit, and he gave Rob an outrageously sexy smile.

Rob's eyes widened.

'Thomas More's troubled soul?' said Eliza. Really, Kit was a disgrace.

'And Henry the Eighth's,' he said. 'Thomas More's soul wasn't for sale. Couldn't say the same for Henry's.'

'I'm loving this already,' said Eliza.

She glanced over to Terri's office as they headed for the lift, but it was empty.

'Rob's cute,' said Kit.

'He's spoken for, sorry,' said Eliza. 'And straight.'

'Is he yours?' said Will.

'No! But we've been friends since childhood. Have you seen Leigh, Will?'

'She came up to Stratford for a few days. I took her to see *King Lear*, but she doesn't really get Shakespeare. And she really pissed off my parents with her smoking.'

'Oh dear.'

After a bite to eat in the cafe, Eliza showed the pair Rose's TV studios, where a small number of programmes were produced. 'It's mainly news, sport, and breakfast TV. It's bland central at the moment. Even blander now Maria's in charge. When I'm full time, if things go to plan, we'll keep the news, take a good look at the daytime stuff; the football's—'

'Pointless,' said Kit. 'Like all sport.'

'Far too much football, for sure,' said Eliza. 'We'll need to keep some, though. It's a major earner for Rose. But I want a big, shiny new production department. Honestly, guys, I can't wait. Think of the possibilities. A new golden age of British drama. The time is so right for this.'

'As are you, Eliza Rose,' said Will.

Chapter 13

Eliza

It was late October, and Michaelmas term was in full swing. The wind carried the scent of frosts to come, and college scarves were once again wrapped around student necks.

The three girls were renting a house close to the centre of town. Early in the mornings Eliza would walk by the river as mist rose and swirled along the banks, thinking about the day ahead, the situation at Rose.

She remembered Harry telling her how he'd always felt drawn to the Thames, how he liked to sit and watch it when he needed to think. How there was some deep connection that worked its magic. She was finding the same. DNA again, perhaps. She liked to think about how this river, called the Isis here, was on its way to London to flow past Richmond then onwards to Terri, Chess and Rob, and all the others at work in The Rose.

Harry, John, and their new consultant, Cecil Walsham, were developing a plan to ensure Maria and Phil couldn't wreak too much havoc at Rose. Harry had told Eliza to focus on her finals, to enjoy her last months at Oxford, not to worry. She *was* focused, and enjoying, but having trouble with that last part. Her biggest worry was that Harry thought she wasn't up to the job, that she'd let him down.

'No, Dad,' she'd said, during a video call on her first weekend back. 'I want to be involved. I've been mulling it over, thinking about how we can tip the balance back in our favour. Could Aunt Margot be brought back on side?'

'Scary Big Sis?'

'Come on, Dad. I thought there was no such thing as a woman immune to your charms. Doesn't everyone love a cute little brother? Surely you can win her over. After all, she owes you. Last time you did as she asked, you got shot.'

'Excellent point. I'm liking the way you think. And we have Cecil. The man has networks like you wouldn't believe. He's been doing a spot of forensic accounting. He's traced Mr Seville's corporate raid back to the holding company he's been hiding behind – Armada, it's called. Cecil's been careful to stay in the shadows, but let's just say, Seville's share of Rose is already not what it was.'

'Won't he notice?'

'Cecil's been extremely subtle in his manoeuvrings. The man's a strategic genius.'

'Wow, go Cecil. So if you can swing Scary Big Sister . . .'

'Things will start to fall into place.'

'I have to say, I'm quite partial to the season of mists and mellow fruitfulness,' said Will, sipping his pint as they sat outside the Head of the River. In front of them, the green waters of the Isis flowed quietly by.

'Can't be doing with that poem,' said Eliza. 'Too overblown.'

'So fruity,' said Kit. 'All that swelling and ripeness, and the close-bosom friend part.'

'Clammy cells,' said Eliza.

'Last oozings,' said Kit.

Eliza snorted.

Kit slipped an arm round her shoulder. '*Unless a tree has borne blossoms in the spring you will vainly look for fruit on it in autumn.* Remember that, Eliza.'

'Remember that why?'

'You have yet to blossom, yet you are forbidden fruit.' He kissed her cheek.

'You two are so weird,' said Leigh. 'You're always touching, and talking in riddles. It's like you're having a thing. The thing that wasn't a thing. *Are* you having a thing?'

'Theirs is an affair of the mind,' said Will. 'Never try and understand.'

Leigh and Frankie left for afternoon lectures, and Will took himself off to Blackwells, leaving Kit and Eliza sitting in the autumn sun.

'I finished your script,' said Eliza.

'Took your time,' said Kit. 'And?'

'I read it through twice. It's brilliant, Kit. Congratulations. You really got inside Thomas More's head.'

'Henry's was more interesting. Thomas allowed his conscience to dictate his actions. And look what happened to him. Henry negotiated with his. Clever man.'

'You think? I love how you've flipped the good versus bad. And how you explore Henry's mind – and, oh my god, the part where you have him selling his soul for a son. Like a different take on Dr Faustus. Honestly, Kit, I can't wait to get started on this. It's going to be huge – even bigger than *Wolf Hall*! Marley and Bardington. What a combo.'

'Yup, my name first.'

Eliza tutted. 'Why do you two have to be so competitive? You spark off each other – you're both brilliant.'

'Better sup up,' he said. 'I said I'd meet Bard in Blackwells.'

They walked along the riverside path, carpeted with golden leaves.

'How's the love life?' said Kit. 'Found your daddy substitute yet?'

'Too much going on to worry about men. And you? Still playing every field and water meadow in Oxford and way beyond?'

'Meh. What about that bloke at the office? He's into you.'

'Rob?' Eliza tried to keep her face impassive. 'We've been friends for ever. I love him to bits . . . as a mate.'

'Come on.'

There was no point in denying it. Kit could read her mind. 'OK, I might have a crush, but he's . . . spoken for, and I don't want the distraction. I can't afford it. I need to focus on work.'

'Wait.' He touched her arm and stopped walking.

Eliza's red woollen scarf was hanging loose. He took one end and slowly looped it behind her head, once, twice, pulling her closer.

His eyes were catching the low rays of the autumn sun, gold on gold.

'*Feuillemort*,' she said softly, caught in their hypnotic gaze. 'Dying leaves.'

She felt their strange connection, like he had a hotline to her soul.

For a fleeting moment it was as if a shadow passed over his face.

'Metaphorical bullseye,' he said. His eyes moved past her to the river beyond. 'Sometimes you have to go with the flow. Let things play out.'

'Things? What things?'

'Things . . . ' He met her gaze. 'It's down to Fate.'

'You're confusing me again. And surely you don't believe in Fate?'

'I get a sense . . . like . . . it won't be easy. You and him.'

'Now you're freaking me out.'

'Never mind, forget I said that.'

He set off walking again.

🌑

'What do you think?' asked Eliza, swivelling her laptop to show Frankie and Leigh the bridesmaid's dress on the screen. It was a strapless gown in a beautiful shade of green that she knew would suit her colouring – and Helena's. Chess, Helena and Eliza. Two strawberry blondes and one full-on redhead. There was no escaping that Rose gene.

'It's stunning,' said Leigh. 'What's your cousin thinking, putting you in that? She must have great faith in her husband-to-be.'

'You generally do, when you're getting married,' said Frankie. 'Hey, what's the best man like? 'Cause, you know, traditionally . . . '

'It's the groom's brother, Rob. I've known him all my life. He used to pull my hair a lot, pushed me into the lake at Richmond Park one time.'

'But is he hot?' said Leigh.

'Give it a rest, you two. But since you ask, yes. Very. And he always used to save me his last Smartie, even if we didn't see each other for months on end.'

'Aw!' said Leigh. 'So . . . a spot of best-man-on-bridesmaid action might be welcome? You'd only be keeping up a fine tradition.'

'He's married.'

'Shame,' said Frankie. 'If you wear that, his wife had better watch out.'

◈

December arrived. Chess and Gil were getting married in an ancient church close to the Lisle's rambling Suffolk farmhouse.

On the eve of the wedding, Gil, Chess, Eliza, Rob and Helena went for a rehearsal at the church, then on to the village pub.

'Just an orange juice for me,' said Chess. 'Don't want to be fluffing my lines tomorrow.'

'Only two words matter,' said Gil, as they found a table by the fire. '*I* and *do*.'

Chess kissed his cheek.

'Cute,' said Rob. 'How's it going, Helena? Hear you've got yourself a Frenchman. Letting the side down rather, aren't you?'

'Englishmen are so threatened by Frenchmen,' said Eliza.

'Our mother speaks highly of them,' said Chess.

'She does,' said her younger sister, who looked like a boho

version of Chess. 'Uncle Harry said she had a ball when she was a chalet girl in the French Alps.'

'With my mum,' said Eliza. 'Funny to think of them having those lives. Kind of the same as us, but different.'

'Do you think history repeats?' said Helena. 'Sometimes I feel like I'm living out some predestined path, like I've done it all before.'

Chess tutted. 'Artists. You always were the family flake.'

'I think you're on the right lines,' said Rob. 'Except it's not destiny pushing me and Gil, it's our bloody dad.'

'Yup,' said Chess. 'Good job I love you, Gil, otherwise I'd be feeling very much the sacrificial lamb tomorrow. The guest list's like a *Who's Who* of people to invite to your son's wedding if you want him to be PM.'

'I assume Maria's not coming,' said Eliza, 'now she's bailed on Dad in favour of Phil the Pill?'

'Sent her feeble apologies,' said Chess. 'Probably too embarrassed to show her face. The face that never smiles.'

'Been smiling quite a lot, actually,' said Rob.

'What?' said Eliza.

'Word on the office grapevine is she and Phil are putting in long hours on their missionary position – sorry, mission statement.'

'I heard those rumours too,' said Chess.

'Seriously?' Eliza thought back to Maria's flutteriness around Phil.

'She's had highlights,' said Chess. 'And her shoes are far less sensible.'

'Oh my god.'

What would it mean for Rose if Maria and Phil were to become a couple? Or worse? She wondered if Dad knew about this. *Of course* he'd know.

'When's Amy getting here?' said Chess, turning to Rob.

'Early in the morning.' He glanced at Eliza.

So tomorrow she'd meet Amy. Eliza had to admit, she was intrigued.

❀

'Oh my gosh, I'm gonna cry,' said Eliza as Chess turned to face Eliza, Helena and Aunt Megan, fluffing out the silk skirt of her dress.

'I already am,' said Megan, fishing in her clutch for a tissue. 'Darling, you look absolutely stunning.'

'And so do you all,' said Chess, wiping away a tear of her own as she looked at her mother. 'Green was definitely the right choice. Mum, stop blubbing or my make-up will be beyond repair. What we need is a glass of something fizzy to steady our nerves. Anyone? There must be some?'

'I'll go,' said Eliza. She'd finished getting ready, and excitement was bubbling at the thought of the day ahead. It had been so long since she'd had an excuse to dress up – not since the college ball. The dress fitted like a glove, giving her the full hourglass. The hair and make-up girl had been a magician, working with her hair ('quite difficult') to create an artistic French twist, with a few shining curls pulled free to frame her face. She'd performed make-up wizardry on Eliza's dark eyes and pale skin ('so luminescent'), and had agreed red lips were called for to finish the look, which had a distinct touch of the Rosetti.

She was still barefoot – the high heels were lofty enough that she needed to minimise shoe time.

As she entered the kitchen, Rob came in the back door carrying a box of flowers. He was in full morning dress and looked . . . *Oh my lord. That's just not fair.*

He stopped dead when he saw her.

'Jesus, Lizzie.'

She smiled. 'You like?'

His dark eyes said it all.

'Could've worn shoes.'

'I came down for champagne.'

'Steady. We know what that can lead to.'

He put the box down on the table, went over to the fridge and took out a bottle. 'May as well get a head start.'

'I have to take it upstairs, the bride's waiting.'

Rob looked at his watch. 'They can wait a minute. Let's have a cheeky one ourselves first.' He took glasses from a cupboard and popped the cork.

Eliza perched on the kitchen table. 'I guess we're finally grown up. Chess looks amazing. I got a bit tearful, thinking back to the old days.'

He passed her a glass of champagne. '*You* look amazing. Very grown-up.' He touched one of the stray curls around her face, then twirled it round his finger. 'Well-behaved hair.'

Their eyes locked, and the kitchen door opened.

Rob stepped back as Helena came in. 'Eliza, what happened to the ... oh.'

'Champagne?' said Rob. 'Just sorting it. I believe the provision of calming alcohol is one of the best man's duties. After you, Lizzie.'

Chapter 14

Eliza

The organist struck up the Wedding March (could Chess not have come up with something more original? Or was this the hand of the Major at play again?) and the bride and groom headed back down the aisle.

Chess and Gil's happiness was infectious, and Eliza's smile was wide as she followed them down the aisle towards the church doors, the congregation snapping photos and mouthing *Congratulations*.

She hooked her arm through Rob's, and he looked down at her and said, 'Hello there, lovely cousin-in-law.'

Eliza laughed, and leaned her head on his shoulder for a moment.

John Studley, on the end of a pew, caught Eliza's eye and smiled.

'Parent alert,' she whispered in Rob's ear. 'Risk of strategic alliance: moderate to high.'

Rob whispered back, 'Risk of complying with irritating yet suddenly appealing parental ambition: high to extreme. Contributing factor – I can see down your cleavage.'

She was spluttering with laughter as they drew alongside Harry, a few pews further on.

'I see nothing much has changed with you two,' he said. 'Still up to mischief.'

Over his shoulder she noticed a pretty girl with honey-coloured hair staring at them. Her troubled expression suggested this was Amy.

Outside, as the photographer called 'Bride and bridesmaids, please', Eliza's eyes followed Rob as he went over to – yes, definitely Amy – and kissed her cheek, then her lips.

Eliza felt something stab her.

Well hello, green-eyed monster. Fancy meeting you here.

The reception was in a stately home surrounded by gardens that looked glorious, even at this time of year. In the entrance hall the bridal party greeted guests in front of a huge Christmas tree decked out in hundreds of twinkly lights.

In the reception room the walls were hung with wreaths decorated with the intertwined letters F and G. Bundles of mistletoe hung from the crystal chandeliers.

Promising.

Amy was nicely tucked away across the other side of the room as Eliza sat down at the top table. Place cards had positioned Eliza and Rob like bookends around the bride and groom and their parents, but Rob quickly switched his own with his father's, so he was next to Eliza.

'Stealth manoeuvre. Nicely done, Son,' said John, sending an appreciative glance Eliza's way.

'Alert level: DEFCON1,' Rob said as he sat down. 'Parent approves of place-name swap.'

'As do I,' she said, smiling at him.

As the meal progressed, she was careful not to drink her wine too quickly. She was too hyped, too aware of Rob next to her. She was chief bridesmaid – she needed to stay in control.

Dessert arrived, and as Rob chatted with Aunt Megan on his other side, turning on the charm, making her laugh, Eliza realized who the new Rob – this version who'd replaced the scruffy imp – reminded her of. Dad. He had the same way with words, the same magnetism, the same naughty glint in his eye.

Dad. Rob. Two of a kind.

Kit's words popped into her brain: *Found your daddy substitute yet?*

Oh my god.

She looked across at Harry, sitting at a nearby table, and he gave her a half-smile as he listened to whatever a random relative was telling him, her face flushed, looking like she'd won the seating-plan lottery.

Eliza smiled back. Her father was looking ridiculously handsome today, for a man of his age. Eliza had clocked the number of people making sure their 'bride and groom' photos had him in the background. Hashtag Harry Rose.

'Dessert wine, Snow White?'

'I'll pass. I'm taking it slowly today. I made myself a promise, to be sensible and sober.'

'What? Why ever would you do that, today of all days? Remember, lovely Lizzie, the road to Hell is paved with good intentions, but, more importantly, the road to Heaven is paved with bad ones.'

'OK, pour.'

'I hope our champagne moment in the park wasn't responsible for the vow of sobriety?'

'Not really. It was more Terri giving me a bollocking. The day after, she said I looked like a bag lady.'

Rob snorted. 'Cruella.'

There was a tinkle as Uncle Charles tapped his glass. The talking died down.

'Fuck,' muttered Rob. 'I forgot about my speech. See what you do to me?'

Uncle Charles's words were warm and funny, then Gil spoke and toasted the bridesmaids. Finally, Rob stood up.

'Hi, I'm little bro.' He flashed his cheeky smile, and everyone smiled back.

Eliza shook her head a little. *Eating out of his hand already.*

'I wasn't sure how to start this speech, so I googled brother quotes. I found this. *A brother's love exceeds all the world's loves in its unworldliness.'*

There were murmured *aah*s.

'No idea what that means,' he said, 'so I tried again.'

There were chuckles.

'*We know each other as we always were. We know each other's hearts. We live outside the touch of time.'*

Rob's mother wiped away a tear.

'Gil, I know your heart, and now it belongs to the lovely Chess. Welcome to the family, gorgeous. You're far too good for him.' He winked. 'Totally the wrong brother.'

Chess blew him a kiss.

He told the requisite embarrassing story, then said, 'And before we raise our glasses to the happy couple, I'd like to endorse Chess's choice of bridesmaids. Well done, littlies,' he said, waving to the flower girls who were playing on the dance floor. 'And Helena and Eliza . . .'

But he was looking only at Eliza.

'Breathtaking.'

The words dried up as he held her gaze.

She couldn't look away.

Gil coughed, and Rob came out of his trance. 'Sorry, Gil. Please raise your glasses, everyone . . .'

'How did I do?' he said, as he sat down. 'Did I embarrass myself?'

'Slightly, perhaps. But you got the job.'

'What job?'

'My sidekick at Rose. One day.'

By the time the dancing started, Eliza was approaching the reckless stage of champagne consumption. Sobriety be damned.

Rob had gone to sit with Amy, and Gil hauled Eliza to a table of his civil service workmates. 'Everyone, meet Eliza. She likes to dance. Chaps, form an orderly queue.'

She *did* love to dance, and the music was good. She kicked off her shoes and her inhibitions, and wasn't short of partners.

A slow number came on, and the guy she'd been dancing with – rather sweaty, his fringe plastered to his forehead several inches below hers – pulled her into his arms. She couldn't help grimacing as he rested his head on her shoulder.

Then she noticed Rob and Amy, a short distance away. Amy was leaning on Rob's chest, her eyes half closed. Rob's were on Eliza, and were full of mirth.

She pulled a face.

The dance ended and Rob came over, his arm round Amy's shoulder.

'Lizzie, come and meet Amy. Let's go grab a drink.'

She followed the pair into the bar, and Rob went to order.

'You two know each other well,' Amy said, with a hesitant smile. She was quietly spoken, and her face was delicately beautiful, in a . . . forgettable sort of way. Regular features, small nose, wide, light-blue eyes.

'We do. Our dads are big pals.'

'Harry Rose. Gosh. Fancy having a dad that famous.'

'He's retired now. You're a nurse, I hear.'

'That's right. I love your dress, Eliza. And Chess looks so pretty, doesn't she?'

'She does.'

'So you're still at university?'

'Yep.'

'Are you enjoying it?'

'I love it. Great course, great people.'

Eliza looked past Amy towards the bar, and saw that Gil and Chess had joined Rob. Catching her eye, Rob beckoned her over.

'Eliza, we're leaving soon,' said Chess. 'Can you come and help me with the dress?'

They made their way upstairs, and Chess was quiet.

As Eliza undid the tiny buttons down the back of the wedding gown, Chess said, 'How do you like Amy?'

'Truth? She's not what I expected. With Rob being so lively, I mean.'

'I guess anyone would find it difficult.'

'Difficult?'

'Eliza. You and Rob – not the subtlest.'

'He's just flirting.'

'And so are you.'

'Well, who wouldn't? Anyway, best man and bridesmaid, it's expected.'

'If I was Amy I'd probably stab you,' said Chess, stepping out of the dress.

'If I was Amy I'd definitely stab me.'

Chess laughed.

Eliza set about hanging up the dress.

'Maybe you should stop, though,' said Chess. 'I think Amy's pretty upset.'

'What was Rob thinking?' Eliza said, before she could stop herself. 'She's so not his type. He should be with someone sparky. Amy's so, I don't know. Colourless.'

'Been at the champagne again, Eliza?'

'It's a wedding, Chess.'

'Look. Gil and me. We saw you that time, in the park.'

'Oh. Well, it was just a kiss.'

'That was not just a kiss.'

She's right.

'And he's married, no matter what the Major says.'

'Are you ready? You don't want to be wasting wedding-night time nagging your cousin.'

As the happy couple headed for the waiting car, Chess grinned at Eliza and threw the bouquet at her.

'Dad paid her to do that,' said Rob's voice behind her. 'Come and dance with me?'

'Where's Amy?'

'I introduced her to Harry. She'll be happy with him for a while.'

Finally, was Eliza's only thought as she melted into him on the dance floor. His arms tightened around her; he was warm and smelled musky. She pressed her nose to his chest and breathed in deeply.

Any remaining space between them quickly disappeared, and the sensible thoughts – about Amy, about having to work with Rob in years to come – were swept aside by the sensations flowing through her.

I want Rob. I want to kiss him again. I want to feel his hands on me.

'Lizzie,' he said, drawing back. 'Can we talk?'

She nodded, heart in her mouth.

He led her through the entrance hall, to the shadowy gardens beyond.

It was cold outside, and Rob put an arm around her shoulders, rubbing her bare skin. They walked a short distance, then he stopped.

'Rob—'

He kissed her. It was briefly tentative, and then they were making up for lost time. The weeks in the office, resisting the pull.

Eliza felt herself falling.

She stopped. It was too much. 'Rob – what are you doing?'

'Maybe . . . falling in love?'

'This is crazy,' she said. 'You and me, we're best mates. How can this be happening?'

'I know. Who'd have thought? Madness.'

'And Amy?'

'Seriously, Lizzie. I've tried, but I can't stop these feelings. I can't stop thinking about you.'

She took a step back. 'Same. But I can't do this. You're married. And we'd better get back; we'll be missed.' She set off walking, her mind in a whirl.

He caught her up.

As they neared the entrance, they saw Harry standing in the porch, watching them.

Oh god.

'Eliza – a word. Rob, go find Amy.'

'Right, Harry. I'll ...'

'Go, Rob.'

'Dad—'

'Come with me, Eliza.'

She followed Harry to a corner of a small lounge, where a few guests were enjoying quiet respite from the celebrations.

'Eliza. John told me today, about Rob's so-called marriage.' His expression was grim.

'Yes, I know. He's—'

Harry interrupted. 'John's opinion on the validity of that aside, what on earth are you doing? Is it the wine and the wedding, or is there something more going on here? Because that girl – his wife – is pretty upset.'

'It was just a best man–bridesmaid kiss. You know how fond we are of each other.'

'Don't lie. You're better than this.'

The disappointment in his voice filled her with dismay. Until anger swept it aside. *Hypocrite!*

'Am I, Dad? Or is it in my genes?'

Harry looked taken aback. 'OK. Granted, I haven't been the greatest role model.' His expression softened. 'Funnily enough, my affair with Merry began at a wedding, in full view of Katie. History repeats, as they say. What a fool. But I don't want you making the same mistakes I did.'

She had no intention of doing so. Any future relationship with Rob would be on *her* terms. And those didn't include sharing.

'Rob says he made a mistake. But don't worry, no way will I be going there while he's still married.'

'Be careful. You know I like Rob, always have. But he's a wide boy.'

'Dad!'

'He is. That lad could talk his way into anything.' He looked thoughtful for a moment. 'We could do with him in Sales. But that's beside the point. If there are problems with Amy, he needs to sort that out before he even thinks of moving on to you.'

'She's so not right for him, though. I mean, what was he thinking, Dad?'

'Not necessarily. I had quite a chat to her, and she's lovely. Shy, but I got her to open up.'

'Boring, though.'

Harry shook his head, smiling. 'No doubt at all whose daughter you are, Lizzie.'

'Yours.'

'Ana's.'

'How do you mean?'

'The way you're talking about Amy – it could be your mother talking about Janette. All she saw was her ordinariness. She called her a moron.'

'Janette was sweet.'

'Katie was too. They didn't have your mum's glamour or charisma, but they were kind, and they had inner strength. Same with Clare. Look, don't play with people's feelings, Lizzie. You're half Ana, half me. That's quite a combo, if I say so myself. Men will fall at your feet. Don't smash their relationships just because you can. Fragile people break. Look what happened to your aunt Merry, to Caitlyn. I'm afraid Amy reminds me a little of Caitlyn.'

'Rob said something like that.'

'So take a step back. I expect you've both had a fair bit to drink, you got carried away with the moment. You'll be back at Oxford soon, he'll be in London. Leave him be. Focus on your studies. You don't need the distraction.'

Harry

'Eliza's having a good time,' said Clare, watching her dancing with one of Gil's friends.

'Hm. I just caught her kissing Rob. And we're not talking peck on the cheek.'

'Really?' Clare grinned. 'Lucky Eliza!'

'What?'

'Well, he's gorgeous! And there's obviously quite a spark there. You can't miss it. It's about time she had some romance in her life. Is he going out with the other girl, or is she just his wedding date?'

'Amy. They're married, in fact.'

'*Married?* Gosh, the family kept that quiet.'

'A Bali beach wedding, probably not worth the paper it's written on. John's furious; you know what he's like with his sons. But whatever the legal technicalities, I don't want Rob messing Eliza about.'

'Perhaps John's the reason why Rob and Amy ran away to the beach.'

'My thoughts entirely. But rebelling against your father isn't a reason to get married, which Rob's obviously realized. Idiot.'

'Poor thing.'

Harry looked over at Eliza, and his heart constricted.

'Rob's all right,' he said, 'but I don't want Eliza falling for him. She has zero experience of men, and he's way more ... worldly than she is.'

'Sounds like you at that age. Married, with a roving eye.'

'A tad unfair.'

'Harry, you have to let her find her own way, make her own mistakes. Do you honestly think she's capable of running a business empire, but can't look after herself when it comes to men? Take a step back, let her get on with it.'

'I don't want her to get hurt, that's all. If Rob's serious, he needs to sort things out with Amy. And if he's not serious, he'll have me to answer to. Plus Eliza's got finals coming up. She shouldn't be thinking about anything else right now.'

Clare shook her head. 'So when you were blazing a trail at Rose back in your twenties, women weren't a thing for you, Harry?'

He couldn't help smiling. 'All right, Barr. Point taken. I should leave her be. But if young Studley puts so much as a toenail wrong ...'

Clare squeezed his hand. 'Being a dad's hard. But Eliza has her head screwed on. Be there for her, but don't interfere.'

He lifted her hand and kissed it. 'God, it's annoying, how women always know best.'

Eliza

Next day, there was a brunch for relatives at a local cafe. Rob and Amy would be there.

Eliza drove back to Oxford instead. She took the country route, enjoying the wide East Anglian skies and the bare winter fields lit by low sunbeams. The driving time gave her the opportunity to think about yesterday.

She tried a little self-analysis. Why did she find Rob irresistible? There were plenty of obvious reasons: the looks, the charm, the infectious smile. Always fun.

But perhaps it was more about the shared history. With him she felt . . . at home.

By the time she reached Oxford, she'd decided on a way forward. She'd focus on her work, keep Rob at arm's length, at least until he'd made up his mind about Amy. Zero flirting. Or maybe just a tiny bit. They'd go back to how they'd been before – partners in crime. Mates.

For now.

Chapter 15

Eliza

Eliza spent the Christmas break at Richmond, enjoying family time, catching up with Eddie.

Maria stayed away. She'd phoned Harry to make her excuses and, according to Clare, it hadn't gone well.

'I'm afraid your father had something of a meltdown,' she said to Eliza as they prepared the vegetables for Christmas dinner. 'I couldn't help overhearing; he was shouting. I understand why he's angry – he explained all that business to me, about the vote, and Maria being full CEO now. But if he wants her to listen to *him*, and not this American, he's going about it the wrong way.'

'True. Maybe I should talk to him about it?'

'He might listen to you. I've never warmed to Maria, but the way Harry treats her compared to you … well, it's no wonder things between them are fraught.'

But on Boxing Day, before Eliza had the opportunity for that discussion, Maria's name flashed up on her phone.

'Maria!' she said. 'Happy slightly belated Christmas.' She thought it wise to lay on the Christmas spirit – Dad would need her to keep the lines of communication open.

'And to you, Eliza. God's blessings on you and the family.'

'Right. Did you have a good Christmas? Where were you?'

'Can we meet? I'm back in town.'

What was she up to now?

'Why don't you come to Richmond?'

'Terrible idea. I need to see you, Eliza. Not Father.'

They arranged to meet the following day for lunch, in Covent Garden. Eliza went early to browse the sales, treating herself to a new dress from Agnès B.

As she walked along Floral Street she glanced upwards, then stopped for a moment. Mum's office. This was where Ana had died. Where she'd been killed.

She saw the sign on the door: *IQ Design*. It was still going, then. The name had apparently been Terri's idea, the initials standing for Ana's nickname: Ice Queen.

The mother she remembered hadn't been cold at all.

Eliza had walked past here many times before, but today the moment seemed more poignant. After her recent chats with Dad and Terri, her mother had been in her thoughts. She remembered shiny long hair, dark eyes; she'd been beautiful, had always smelled lovely. But most of all she remembered someone full of hugs and smiles and love.

At least, until Dad's car crash.

Then she'd lost the baby she'd been expecting, and the atmosphere in the house had changed. Eliza had a vague memory of Ana being horrible to Harry. Snappy, impatient.

And then Dad had gone.

She looked up at the windows of IQ Design and felt a deep sadness. If only she'd had more time with Ana. And she wished the matter of the loose ends around her death had been resolved.

Reaching the cafe, she saw Maria sitting by the window. Heck! Chess had been right – there were highlights. She'd had her eyebrows done too. It had lifted her face; she looked younger. Happier.

'Maria! You're looking so nice. I love the hair.' She kissed her sister. 'Bit of cheeky shopping,' she said, holding up the carrier bag.

'I like their stuff,' said Maria, reading the name on it.

What? Talking clothes with Maria?

After discussing Christmas and the weather, Maria said, 'Eliza, I need you to smooth the path with Father for me.'

She thought carefully about how to respond. 'I can see that would help. I appreciate you're doing what you believe is right at Rose, but maybe you could have gone about it differently?'

'No, it's more personal than that. Phil and I are getting married.'

Shit!

'Oh! Wow, um ... congratulations.'

'Thank you. There'll be an announcement this week. Phil's people are handling it. It won't be a big wedding, but ... I'd like the family to be there. Do you think Father will come?'

'Of course he'll come. I know things have been tricky, but you're his daughter. And look – what you did, it's business, and you did it for what you thought were the right reasons. Dad's got to respect that; I'm sure he's pulled similar tricks himself. You don't get where he did without a spot of ruthlessness.'

'Thank you. I didn't want to have to do it that way, but I knew you and he would never agree to my policies. Father was retired, you were away at university – I didn't want to wait. And ... I also didn't expect to, well, develop feelings for Phil.'

'You seem happy.'

'I am.' She smiled. 'For the first time in so many years, I'm actually happy.'

The lunch was the closest they'd ever come to being friends. Eliza promised to speak to Harry, and Maria promised to keep Eliza up to date with what she and Phil were planning for Rose. Although Eliza suspected any opposition to those plans would continue to be ignored.

Back in Richmond, she sat Harry down. 'I caught up with Maria in town.'

'I thought you were hitting the sales?'

'That too. But Maria wanted to see me. And, well, there's no easy way to say this. She's engaged – to Phil.'

Harry didn't often swear in front of his children, but this time he let rip.

She waited for him to stop, saying nothing.

' . . . and of course he's only after her because of her position at Rose. Why can't she see that? What a . . .' And off he went again.

'Dad—'

'How could she be so *stupid*. Is she doing it to spite me?'

'DAD!'

'Sorry.'

'Believe it or not, she's in love. She's like a different person. She's happy.'

'Well, that won't last, once she realizes why he's marrying her.'

'Give them a chance, Dad. Maybe he does love her. They seem to think the same way.'

'Don't be ridiculous. He's a businessman; he's worth billions. And he's powerful. Strong links to the Republican Party and the religious right. Love has nothing to do with it. He's just after establishing a transatlantic dynasty.'

'She's promised to keep me in the loop, says she'll let me know what they're doing at Rose.'

'Do you believe her?'

'Maybe. I think she's changed. Perhaps happy Maria will work better for us than angry Maria. And, Dad, you should go see her. Take advantage of the thaw. Try and overlook what she's done, work with it, be a tempering influence. If you show her you care, she'll listen. I'm sure of it.'

'So you think it's my fault, the anger?'

'What's important is what you two think.'

Finally, Harry smiled. 'Eliza the Wise. Never mind Rose, you should've gone into politics. The diplomatic service, perhaps.'

The following day, Eddie asked Eliza if they could take a walk in Richmond Park, just the two of them.

Her brother was fourteen now, and had grown up into a highly likeable young man. Everyone loved Eddie. He even got on well with Maria. He was clever, showing an aptitude for science, and had a quiet air of confidence and calm.

It was a cold, crisp day and they were well wrapped up, Eddie's face half-buried in a scarf wound several times round his neck and halfway up his face. His hair was the exact same colour as Harry's before he'd started going grey, but his eyes were Janette's.

'Eliza,' he said. 'Can I ask you something – between us?' His voice, which was breaking, squeaked a little.

'Sure, ask away.'

'How old were you when you knew you wanted to work at Rose? With Dad?'

The question took her by surprise. 'Oh. I guess I've always known. Never questioned it. It was just a thing.'

'Right.'

'Why?'

'Promise not to tell?'

'Cross my heart.'

'I don't want to be a businessman. I want to be a doctor, maybe a surgeon. Medicine, anyway.'

Eliza was quiet for a moment. Dad wasn't going to welcome this news. He doted on Eddie, assumed that in a few years' time he'd be following in Eliza's footsteps.

Perhaps Eddie would change his mind as he progressed through his final years at school and then university. He was still very young. But as he looked across at her, waiting for her response, she saw her brother was clear in his mind.

'Eddie, you must follow your dream,' she said. 'You'll make a brilliant doctor. Dad might be upset for a while, but there's Maria and me to carry on his work. I'll back you up all the way. Don't say anything to Dad yet, but please, don't worry about it.'

'Thanks, Eliza. You're awesome. The best sister in the world.'

Chapter 16

Eliza

It was Hilary term at Oxford again, and revision was piling up as they approached final exams.

After months of on-again, off-again, Leigh and Will had broken up, but were still friends.

'I just can't take the drama,' Leigh said, as she talked it over with Frankie and Eliza. 'A low mark on an essay, the faintest criticism of one of his poems – anything can set him off. "No one understands my work!" I spend so much time mopping his brow it's ridiculous. I'm done.'

'If I didn't know about you and him, I'd assume he was gay,' said Frankie. 'And he's *very* close to Kit.'

'They have a love–hate thing,' said Leigh. 'They're so competitive. Kit even accused Will of stealing his ideas. *Major* drama. Still, not my problem any more. On da market again, girrrrls. Let me know if you spot any likely talent. Curl-free would be good.'

'How about you, Eliza?' said Frankie. 'Still off men?'

'Absolutely. Had a shaky moment at my cousin's wedding, but staying strong now.'

Leigh and Frankie were busy applying for jobs, Leigh in corporate management, while Frankie's priority seemed to be 'not boring'. Eliza was investigating an internship at Rose for Leigh, and had asked Harry if Frankie joining *Janette*'s crew might be a possibility.

She'd assured Will and Kit she wanted them at Rose, but had been honest about the Maria situation. Rose TV had optioned *Most Human of Saints*, to prevent them from taking it elsewhere. It was the best she could do, for now.

An invitation to Maria and Phil's wedding arrived. Eliza had been hoping for one of the fancy Catholic churches – Westminster Cathedral, perhaps. But the venue was an evangelical church in North London. When she googled it, the church was described as a place where 'the Lord Jesus is exalted as the only sufficient sacrifice for the sins of the fallen human race.'

Looked like this wedding was going to be full of joy. Probably alcohol-free, too.

'I don't get it,' she said, as the five of them sat outside the Turf on a Saturday lunchtime. 'Katie and Maria were full-on Catholics. I assume Maria still is. Shouldn't Phil respect that?'

'Are you kidding?' said Will. 'As far as Phil's lot go, women exist only to serve men.' They didn't have to wait long for the supporting quote. '*For man did not come from woman, but woman from man. Neither was man created for woman, but woman for man.*'

'I'd join that church,' said Kit.

'It's surely a means to an end,' said Eliza. 'A controlling thing. Phil's not stupid, he can't really believe all that stuff.'

'*Religion hides many mischiefs from suspicion,*' said Kit.

'Yep, his mischiefs being bigotry and sexism. You see what I'm up against?'

'All religion is ridiculous,' said Kit. 'As far as I'm concerned, Heaven's right here on Earth for the taking. And Hell, which is equally appealing.'

'True,' said Will. 'I fully intend my last months in Oxford to be an homage to hedonism.'

'Same,' said Kit. He turned to Eliza, sitting next to him. 'Make me immortal with a kiss?'

'No.'

He put an arm around her shoulder and kissed her cheek. *'Come live with me and be my love, and we will all the pleasures prove.'*

'Still a no.'

'You're boring. How about you, Will?'

'Are you on something, Kit?' said Leigh.

'Maybe. *Resist temptation, and your soul grows sick with longing for the things it has forbidden to itself.'*

'Holy shit,' said Frankie. 'Ain't that the truth. Who said it?'

'Oscar Wilde,' said Kit. 'For what temptations do you grow sick with longing, Frankie?'

'Don't answer that,' said Eliza, anticipating her reply.

'Truth?' said Frankie. She looked Kit in the eye. 'You.'

Kit turned to Eliza, eyebrows raised.

She shrugged.

'Come, my little duck,' he said to Frankie, holding out a hand.

'Well, fuck me,' said Leigh, shaking her head.

'Both of you?' said Kit.

'Stop it!' said Eliza. 'Just get out of here, you two, if you're going.'

Later, Will was quiet as he and Eliza took a walk through the botanical gardens.

She glanced over at him. 'What happened back there. I think you minded. Am I right?'

'I did, my sweet. You know my heart.'

'Oh, Will. Of all the people you could have fallen in love with.'

He smiled ruefully. *'His unkindness may defeat my life, But never taint my love.'*

'I don't get him, Will. But I'm not going to stop trying. Maybe he'll sort himself out, let someone close?'

'You and I probably know him as well as anyone does. Which isn't saying much.'

'Just keep working with him, writing amazing stuff. Maybe that's the best way to connect with him, for now.'

He searched her eyes. 'So you aren't hankering after him yourself?'

'No. He's delicious, of course.' She looked away as the memory of Kit's kiss sidled in. 'But you were right, about it being an affair of the mind. And, besides, I like someone else.' For once, she allowed herself to picture Rob's face. 'I *really* like someone else.'

❁

Eliza returned to Rose during the Easter vacation, and Maria suggested she join her on the top floor. Eliza was pleased the thaw in relations was continuing. She'd be able to get a handle on what Maria was up to, plus she'd be out of Rob-temptation range.

Unless it was a case of Maria keeping her enemy close, of course.

On her first day back, her sister suggested lunch, and did most of the talking. Almost every sentence began with 'Phil'. She was radiant, full of plans for their Easter wedding, the honeymoon, and working at Rose with her husband-to-be.

'We'll be such a team,' she said. 'But between you and me, what I want more than anything is a child.'

'Surely there's no rush,' said Eliza. 'Don't you want some together-time first?'

'It's not our decision. God bestows children if and when *He* wills it. I'm hoping that's very soon. It's the most important thing in the world to me, Eliza. Imagine what it must be like to have a child.'

'I'm good, thanks.'

'I'm hoping God will bless us immediately.'

Eliza supposed Maria wouldn't be using contraception.

She remembered what Harry had told her about his and Katie's fertility problems – the miscarriages and stillbirths. She hoped Maria's God would be kinder to her.

ELIZA: I'm back! Sneaky coffee?

CHESS: Now? Am bored out of skull

They caught up properly on news, having exchanged only the odd message since the wedding.

'How's Rob?' Eliza asked, spooning the froth from the bottom of her coffee cup, not meeting Chess's eye.

'Fine. He's really enjoying Sales.'

'Sales?'

'Didn't you know? He's moved over to TV.'

'How did I not know that? I'm supposed to be in the loop.'

'It was Maria's doing, apparently. Harry suggested it. Rob was so pleased – and *very* relieved. He thought he was persona non grata after ... I heard Harry caught you two kissing at the wedding. What were you thinking, Eliza?'

'I *wasn't* thinking. Dad gave me a talking to. But hey, it's great news that Dad and Maria are communicating, better still that she's taking notice of him.'

Later, Eliza went to see Terri. Maria may have extended the olive branch towards the family, but Terri was struggling.

'She won't be happy until I resign,' she said, pushing her glasses up onto her black and white hair. 'And if I don't, she'll find a reason to fire me. I'm on Death Row.'

Rose without Terri was unthinkable. 'Can you ride it out? Until I'm back in summer? And I know Dad won't let that happen in the meantime.'

'She loathes me; so does Phil. Call it a personality clash. All I can do is make the magazine politically neutral, avoid anything controversial, and hope you manage to swing things back further down the line. It didn't help when Maria found out about Layla.'

'Who's Layla?'

'My girlfriend.'

'Ah.'

'Are you surprised?'

'Not really. I always kind of assumed.' She remembered Maria calling Terri *that unnatural woman*. How could anyone think that way in this day and age? 'I'd better get back upstairs. Please, Terri, don't ever think about leaving.'

❀

At lunchtime the next day, Eliza was sitting in the atrium, messaging her Oxford friends in their group chat. Light was flowing down through the glass roof hundreds of feet above her head, reflecting off the polished marble floor and illuminating the tall trees in their tubs.

Groups of people sat around chatting, their voices echoing across the bright, airy space, and younger members of staff occasionally slid down the glass slide that spiralled down through the centre. In spite of Maria's morality check, the Rose building still had a good vibe.

'Hello, stranger,' said a voice, and she looked up to see Rob smiling down at her. 'Room for me on there?'

She shuffled along the wooden seat, even as her heart began to thump.

'Rob. Loving the salesman look.' He was in a dark-blue suit, with a pale-blue shirt and thin spotted tie. His hair was shorter, and there was a tidy beard.

It was all rather gorgeous, but his eyes weren't as twinkly as usual.

'Are you enjoying your new job?' she asked as he sat down. 'I only just found out.'

'It's full-on. I'm missing Terri, oddly. But yeah, it's good. Harry's suggestion, apparently.'

'Probably a good one. He told me you could talk your way into anything.'

'Hm.' He put his elbows on his knees and looked up at her sideways. 'Not quite anything.'

She resisted the urge to touch his hair. 'I got a bollocking off Dad, after he saw us. Sorry I haven't been in touch, I thought it best we had some space.'

'Likewise. I needed to sort my head out.'

'How's things with Amy?'

'Complicated, but I'm on it. So, Lizzie – have we had that space now? Shall we get a coffee?'

'I don't know. Too many eyes.'

'Doesn't matter – people know we're mates.'

'Rob—' She looked away.

He said nothing for a moment, then stood up. 'It's OK. I get the message.'

Before she could respond, he was walking away.

Back in the office, she texted him: *Sorry. Still friends?*

There was no response.

Maria had asked for her thoughts on a number of budget forecasts, but Eliza couldn't concentrate. She sighed, resting her chin in her hand, staring out of the window. There was nowhere for this thing between them to go, not while he was married. She missed the flirtation, the banter, the lingering looks. But she would *not* be that sad other woman, waiting around while he dithered and procrastinated.

Complicated, but I'm on it.

Was he? In what way was he *on it*?

She sat up straighter. She needed to know the score.

She texted him again: *Don't blank me. Can we meet after work?*

Still no response.

Half an hour later her phone finally pinged: *George 6.30?*

In the loos, she put on lipstick and let her hair loose. This felt like an actual date. No Chess and Gil, no family, no workmates; just the two of them. And she had butterflies.

It's not a date, it's a chat.

Eliza was ten minutes late, but she was still there first. How aggravating. She ordered a glass of wine, then sat at the bar scrolling through Instagram, not registering any of it.

Rob appeared by her side, and she didn't miss the barmaid's appreciative glance.

'Sorry I'm late,' he said. 'We lurched from one crisis to another today. You all right for a drink?' He waved the barmaid over (unnecessary – she was already making a beeline), then kissed Eliza's cheek. 'I wasn't blanking you, it was just all going off at work.'

'Sure.'

They took their drinks over to a booth and she sat down opposite him.

'Lizzie?'

'Rob.'

He hesitated, then said, 'Can I come and sit next to you?'

She looked at him properly, and understood. He was nervous too. It made her want to touch him.

'Why?'

'Might make it easier. What I want to say.'

Do I want to hear this?

'Sounds serious. When did you ever do serious?'

'Truth? Since I was eight. About the time I pushed you in the lake.'

She laughed. 'OK, come on round.'

She moved along, and he sat down and immediately took her hand.

'You're not going to propose, are you?'

'It's a thought.'

She laughed again. 'Just for the record, you know I'm never getting married.'

'Never say never.'

'I'm saying it. Never. So – what's on your mind, Roberto?'

'You are. All the time.'

Her heart leaped.

'Not seeing you these last few weeks ... well, I missed you. Loads. I like being with you.'

'I missed you too. But like I said, it was best we had some space.'

'Lizzie . . . ' He took a breath. 'I love you. I think I always have. I'm going to end it with Amy. Ask her for a divorce.'

He loves me!

She looked down at her hand clasped in his. *Eliza and Rob.* It felt right. It felt wonderful.

'I think I love you too, Rob. But . . . I don't know if I'm ready for this. I've got finals coming up. Can you give me some time?'

He stroked her palm; she was melting again.

'How much time, Lizzie?'

The pull was too strong, the temptation too great.

'I'd say, about five minutes.'

The night was cold. Rob undid his wool overcoat and wrapped her in it, as she put her arms around his waist.

'Finally, no spies,' he said. 'No parental or sibling eyes.' He kissed her, and the feelings rushed in.

'Can I stay tonight?' he said.

She considered his words. She was ready; she trusted him. She wanted Rob to be her first.

But she wanted all of him.

'Better not, I think. Until you've sorted things properly with Amy. Moved out.'

He groaned. 'Are you sure?'

'Cool it, Rob. It's taken us all our lives to get here. We can wait a bit longer.'

Chapter 17

Eliza

Eliza woke to sunlight pouring through the sheer curtains of the balcony windows.

Welcome, clichéd sunny morning for person newly in love.

Oh my gosh – I am. I'm in love!

'*Yoooou, you make loving fun*,' she sang in the shower. It was an old song off one of Clare's favourite albums. *Rumours*, if she remembered correctly. No doubt there would soon be plenty of those flying around at Rose.

After smoothing her hair into long waves, she put on the dress she'd bought in Covent Garden back in January. It was the colour of sunshine, and short. Yellow dress, red hair – loose, today – red lipstick. Why not? Ankle boots to finish. She twirled in front of the mirror.

Oh yes.

She set off for the office, and smiled to herself as heads turned on London Bridge. She felt like a woman in a shampoo advert.

Striding into the atrium, she waved to the receptionists and took the lift up to the top floor.

'You look lovely today,' said Pippa.

'I feel lovely.'

'Why's that then?' said Pippa with a knowing smile.

'Kind of a hot date last night. But shhh.'

Pippa grinned. 'What with you and your sister, it's Romance Central round here.'

Eliza knocked on Maria's office door, which was closed. If she'd looked through the pink-tinted glass she'd have noticed the person in there wasn't Maria, before opening it.

'Er, Eliza, she's not—' called Pippa.

'Oh. Sorry, Phil! Maria not in yet?' It was the first time she'd seen Maria's fiancé since the board meeting.

'Come on in, Eliza. How lovely to see you again, looking so bright and pretty.'

Phil was sitting at Maria's desk, jacket off, his white shirt as dazzling as his teeth. It would be rude to back out again. She stood awkwardly, just inside the door.

'Please, come on in, sit down. We haven't had a chance to get to know each other, and we'll be family soon. Family is the most important thing in the world. After God, of course.'

'Right. I'm looking forward to the wedding.' She sat down opposite him.

'As am I. Maria is going to make a wonderful wife. In this day and age it's not easy to find a woman of substance who agrees with my views on marriage.'

Hardly surprising.

'Yes, well . . . it's lovely to see her so happy.'

He came round to her side of the desk, leaning a hand on it.

He was uncomfortably close. She could smell his aftershave. Boss, if she wasn't mistaken. *Ironic.*

'I know you and Maria don't see eye to eye on Rose Corp's future direction, my dear, but I trust that won't affect our relationship. I hope, as family, we can all get along just fine. Especially you and me.' He looked into her eyes, then at her dress, then her legs, almost all of which were on show.

Then his eyes met hers again, and he smiled, slowly. 'That's a very lovely dress, Eliza,' he said, his voice husky. He stood up and took a step towards her.

Oh my god.

There was a voice from the doorway. 'Eliza?'

'Maria!'

Eliza pushed her chair back so quickly it almost tipped over.

Her sister's eyes were on Phil, who was leaning nonchalantly on the desk again. The leer had given way to a brotherly smile.

Maria's eyes narrowed as they moved to Eliza, and to her legs. Had she seen Phil's ... what *was* that? Had he been about to touch her?

'I just wanted to catch up, Maria.' Eliza tried to keep her voice steady. 'I'll come back later.' She headed for the door.

'And when you do,' said Maria, as she moved past her, 'perhaps we could discuss whether your – ' her eyes moved to Eliza's legs – '*attire* is appropriate. It shouldn't be necessary to spell out dress codes to executive staff.' She lowered her voice, so that only Eliza could hear. 'But then, I suppose it's difficult to escape one's background. History repeats, as they say. I believe your mother seduced her boss.'

The loathing in Maria's eyes took Eliza straight back to those times in Wales, and she flinched.

But no. She wasn't a child any more. There would be no more cowering.

'I'll wear what I bloody want. If your fiancé sees a pair of legs as a temptation from God, that's his problem.' She didn't look at Phil. 'And probably yours. But it's not mine. There is no dress code at Rose. This place is all about creativity. Expressing yourself. Great things get done by enabling, not by dictating. Today I woke up happy, hence the dress. I feel good in it. When was the last time *you* felt this good, Maria?'

She swept out, and immediately took the lift down to *The Rack*'s floor.

Her assertive words had been a response to Maria's, but in fact Phil's behaviour had left her shaken. Why, though? It had been basically little more than a leer. Had he really intended to touch her? Phil wasn't stupid; he wouldn't do that in Maria's office, would he?

She was glad to find Terri alone.

'Was never one for yellow myself,' she said, as Eliza sat down heavily. 'But it works for you.'

'Terri—'

'Something up?'

'Phil. I just ran into him in Maria's office.'

'Think of it this way. Your day can only get better.'

'He . . . harassed me. It was . . . it frightened me, Terri.'

'Harassed you how?'

'It was the way he looked at me.'

Terri snorted. 'Fuck's sake, Eliza. Most blokes look at you like that. Have you not noticed before?'

'I think he was about to touch me. If Maria hadn't come in . . .'

'*What?* Are you OK?'

'I think so. But Maria—'

'She'll probably blame you. Now you'll have husband-seducer to add to Daddy's favourite.'

'She implied that's what I am. My mother's daughter.'

'Tosh. Ana was the seduc*ee*. Although . . . Christ, that dress she wore to the Christmas party.'

Eliza let out a shaky laugh.

'Are you sure you're all right, love?'

'Yep. I'm just . . . I'm a bit hyper today.'

'Any other reason?' said Terri, with a small smile. 'Might it be connected to this . . . exuberant colour palette? Wait. Eliza Rose, is that pink I see on your cheeks?'

'Impossible.'

'I'd always thought so. Therefore something's clearly changed. Tell.'

'Is this how you interview your victims for *The Rack*? Dad calls you The Terrier.'

'Better believe it.'

'Just between us?'

'Naturally.'

Eliza prepared herself. What Terri – perhaps Mum's closest friend – thought, really mattered.

'What do you think of Rob?'

'Ah. History repeats. Again and again.'

'God, not you as well. Maria just said that. What do you mean?'

'Your wretched father, of course. Rob was my protégé, as was your mother. Harry gave them both to me, then stole them away again.'

'Oh. So you think Rob's all right, then?'

'So you're together, then?'

'You guessed?'

'Eliza, love. The temperature in this office when you two were in it was off the charts. If you hadn't been returning to Oxford, I'd have got rid of one of you before something combusted.'

Eliza giggled. 'He is hot, isn't he? We're kind of together, but it's not official. He's . . . well, he's married.'

'Yup.'

'You knew?'

Terri gave her a look.

'Ah, right. But he's getting a divorce, and then I guess we'll be a thing. An item. Do you think that'll be a problem, with us both working here?'

'It won't be ideal, you being his boss. It all fell apart when Harry and Ana tried to work together. There's no point worrying about it now, though. He's in Sales, you're up on the top floor and there's uni in the meantime. But I'd say keep it to yourselves, for the time being.'

ROB: How's your day?

ELIZA: Shaky start, OK now

ROB: Why shaky?

ELIZA: Tell you later?

ROB: cafe at 1?

ELIZA: 'A thousand eyes see all I do'

ROB: Who said that?

ELIZA: No idea. But can we make it off base? How about Caffe Uno near the Golden Hinde? Nobody from here ever goes there

ROB: With good reason

ELIZA: To love is to suffer

ROB: Fair enough. Laters x

Rob arrived first, and Eliza enjoyed his reaction as she walked over – this look was working a treat.

'Cool dress,' he said.

'Aiming to please.'

'You look like one of those rocket lollies we liked when we were kids. Mostly yellow with orange and red on the top.'

'Was thinking more Amal Clooney at Harry and Meghan's wedding.'

'Top girl – she knocked it out the park. Did you go to that?'

'No, but Dad and Clare did. Apparently Dad tried to out-Clooney George, with the whole dapper older-man look.'

'The coffee here's not great,' said Rob. 'I suggest you get a smoothie instead.'

'I've already got one of those,' she said, ruffling his curls. 'Be right back.'

'So what was the shaky start?' asked Rob, as she sat down.

'I bumped into Phil. He was in Maria's office. Alone. He was

all like, "Let's get to know each other, we're going to be family."
I've got a horrible feeling he meant "know" in the biblical
sense. And then he got *this* close.' She held her hand in front of
her face.

'He's a creepy arse.'

'He so is. And he's getting married! He's meant to be in love
with my sister.'

'Yeah, well. What you said before – what Harry thinks about
it. He's probably right, about being after her for her position.
A guy with Phil's power and money could have his pick of
dumb-ass beautiful women willing to be his "helpmate". With
Maria he gets to spread his nonsense throughout Britain without the bother of setting up a separate entity. If I were you, I'd
avoid him.'

'Good plan.' She sipped her hot chocolate.

'So, Lizzie. I'm moving out at the weekend.'

Oh my gosh, it's actually happening!

Her face broke into a smile, but then she registered his
expression.

'I guess that's going to be hard for you.'

'Very. I've just got to hope it doesn't push her back into depression. Might have to ask Chess to be on stand-by.'

'Where will you go?'

'Mum and Dad's London pad. I've told them I'm moving out,
and I *may* have mentioned you had something to do with it.'

'And?'

'Wanted to punch Dad's smug face, to be honest.'

She took his hand and laced her fingers between his. 'It feels
good, Rob. It feels right.'

He took a breath. 'Lizzie . . . what will Harry think?'

'Leave Dad to me. He likes you, Rob. He told me.' She didn't
mention the 'wide boy' comment, and tried to forget the 'you don't
need the distraction' part.

❀

Eliza opened her messenger window.

Bard's Babes

ELIZA: Remember how I said I was staying strong, menwise?

FRANKIE: Is this to do with your 'shaky moment'?

LEIGH: best man?!! Hot guy who pushed you in lake?

ELIZA: the very same

FRANKIE: saw him in FB wedding pics – guy with dark curly hair?

ELIZA: name of Rob

LEIGH: we warned you about that dress

FRANKIE: invite him to Oxford IMMEDIATELY!

ELIZA: calm down!

FRANKIE: That's lovely. Seriously I'm so pleased for you

ELIZA: Thx. GTG, miss you xxx

Eliza went to Richmond for the weekend. As she and Harry took their usual stroll in Richmond Park, the biting March wind turned Harry's cheeks pink. But Eliza was in her personal warm bubble as she took his arm.

'You're looking well, Lizzie,' he said, patting her hand. 'It's good to know both my daughters are happy at last.'

'I *am* happy, Dad. Um, I wanted to tell you why.'

'Think I may have guessed. Young Studley?'

'What! Honestly, Dad. How the f—? How did you know? I swore Terri to secrecy. Ah, wait . . . John?'

'Yes. But I saw how you were with him at the wedding. It was clear this had moved on from that flirting thing you two have always done. I had my doubts, as you know. But Clare told me to let you get on with it.'

'What flirting thing?'

'Since you were . . . I'd say thirteen, fourteen? Confession time – John and I have had a bet on for years, about when you two would get together.'

'I *knew* it!'

'I just won five hundred quid. Ha! But he heartily approves. Not so sure I do. What's he doing about Amy?'

'He's moving out, as we speak. Asking her for a divorce.'

'I see.'

Eliza registered his frown. 'Dad, don't dismiss Rob as some sort of pretty-boy charmer. There's a lot more to him. He's smart, ambitious, and we're into the same things. And . . . he knows me so well. He sees the real me, not the rich girl with the famous dad. I just love being with him.'

'That all sounds reasonable,' said Harry. 'As long as he accepts your heart belongs to Daddy.' He winked.

'Ew, Dad.'

Chapter 18

Eliza

> ELIZA: Hi, was maintaining radio silence at weekend as thought it best. How did it go?

> ROB: Horrible. Have moved into the flat. Come over tonight?

Was there a sleepover implication in that text?

> ELIZA: Sure

> ROB: Shall I come up to your office 6ish? Can go home together

> ELIZA: OK xx

Home together. Those two words.

By six o'clock, Maria, Pippa and the receptionists had left, and Eliza was sitting alone at her desk beside the tall windows that looked out across the Thames. The evening sun was reflecting off the glass towers of the City, and down below, the tourist hordes milled around on Bankside, getting in the way of office workers heading for the trains, tubes and buses.

Rob strode in, loosening his tie, looking right at home. There was something of a swagger going on, but when you looked like that, you could afford to swagger.

'Welcome to the top floor, Mr Studley,' she said, coming out from behind her desk.

He grinned. 'Are you all alone at the top of your pink tower, Ms Rose?'

'It would appear so.'

'Then it's OK if I do this?'

He picked her up by the waist, sitting her on her desk. His eyes locked on hers as he put a hand on each of her legs and pushed them apart, moving between them. Then he kissed her, his arms round her waist, pulling her towards him.

Heavens, this was gut-meltingly gorgeous.

He pushed himself against her and muttered, 'So, Ms Rose, have you ever done it on a desk?'

She managed to stop herself from shoving him off. Just.

She wanted to be honest with him, but in the face of his obvious know-how, was hesitant about sharing the sad depths of her own inexperience.

She put a hand on his chest. 'No, Rob. I haven't. Not loving that chat-up line, actually.'

'Sorry. I got carried away.' He pulled a contrite face. 'Shall we go, then? Back to mine?'

Eliza slid off the desk, pulling her skirt down. 'Rob – how many girlfriends have you had?'

'Had? Or *had*?'

Oh god, this was going downhill at a rate of knots.

'Well, I don't know. Both?'

'You're meant to have these conversations afterwards, Lizzie. In bed.'

'I just want to know. It's a simple enough question.' Suddenly, she really needed to know.

'OK.' He ran his fingers through his hair. 'Before Amy, three – no, four – proper ones. Several flings, one-night stands, whatever. Some probably ill-advised. I was a bit of a tart at uni, to be honest. Wild oats sown near and far. But I got it out of my system.'

She said nothing.

'Look, let's go home. Start this evening over? I messed that up big time, didn't I? What can I do to make it better?'

Eliza thought for a moment. This was probably as good an opportunity as any for the truth. 'OK. Time for some honesty from me, too. Your youth may have been misspent, but mine was a model of propriety. I studied hard, didn't go out much. I don't do casual, I don't do flings. I hardly ever do dates.'

He grinned. 'Hard to please. Makes me feel special.'

'No, what I'm trying to say is … I'm inexperienced.' She was horrified to hear a tremor in her voice.

He registered it too, and the grin faded. 'God, I really blew it, didn't I? Look, none of the others meant anything. Not compared to this. To you.'

'Really?'

He took her face in his hands and kissed her, gently this time. 'I love you, Lizzie. I'll do whatever it takes to make you happy. You're the boss of me.'

'It's true, I am.'

◈

The Studleys' London pad was a loft apartment near Leicester Square. The walls were white, the furniture was white, the floors were pale bamboo.

'Wow,' said Eliza, taking off her boots.

'Wine? Beer?'

'Wine, please.'

He took a bottle of red from a wine rack that doubled as a work of art, and poured them two glasses. 'You're quiet,' he said, kissing her nose. 'Don't you like the flat?'

'No, I do. It's just … not cosy, I guess.'

But her silence had nothing to do with the decor.

How do I tell him? How will this go? Will I panic again? Surely not. It's Rob.

They took their drinks over to a huge white leather sofa.

She took a sip, then shifted closer to him and leaned her head on his shoulder, tucking her feet up beside her. 'Rob, I have something to share, and it's not easy for me.'

He put his arm round her. 'What's on your mind?'

There was no point in skirting around the truth, using euphemisms, whatever. 'OK, here goes. I'm a virgin.'

He looked at her in surprise. 'Holy fuck.'

'Hm. I thought you might say something like that.'

'So when you said *inexperienced* . . . I have to admit, that comes as something of a surprise. You've never exactly shunned male attention.'

'I almost had a thing, with someone at Oxford. But I . . . he wasn't really boyfriend material.'

'Kit?'

'What? Well – yes. But I was quite drunk when we . . . and he didn't really want to, either. Because we're such good mates. And we'll be working together. It would've been awkward.'

'But you and me are mates. And we'll be working together.'

'Good point. But you're not a promiscuous pansexual who thinks fidelity is ridiculous.'

He laughed. 'My god.'

'He's . . . well. You've met him.'

'Louche?'

'Utterly. Looks to die for. Brilliantly clever. God knows what goes on in his head, though.'

'But back to us?'

'Yes. Look, Rob. I'm feeling insecure about my lack of experience, and I need you to understand that. Will you help me?'

'You mean will I teach you sex? Lizzie Rose, that is possibly the most stupid question anyone has ever asked me.'

She laughed, and the moment lightened.

'Shall we start now?' he said.

He pushed her back gently, until she was lying down, and moved so he was beside her.

They took it slow, and while one half of her appreciated his undeniable skill, the other half mourned that it had all been learned with someone else – lots of someone elses.

He knew exactly what he was doing: how to remove clothes without anything getting tangled or caught, which bodily buttons to press, what to whisper in her ear, what to do with his fingers, his lips, his tongue, for how long. It was heavenly, it was glorious; she sighed, she moaned. His consummate skill swept her along, daring her to falter.

Eventually he said, 'Do you want to give it a try?'

'Yes.'

'I won't hurt you.'

But as he manoeuvred she froze, and then, out of nowhere, panic hit. A fear so intense that for a moment, she forgot where she was, who she was with.

'Stop!'

She sat up quickly, taking deep, gulping breaths.

What just happened?

Just like with Kit, it had all been perfect, and then it wasn't. Something had been triggered.

Was there something wrong with her?

'I'm sorry,' she said, breathing quickly. 'I don't know what happened.'

'Don't worry, Lizzie.' Rob sat up and wrapped her in a hug. 'First-time nerves, I expect. Another lesson or two and you'll be scaling the heights like you won't believe.'

She had a feeling she wouldn't.

The fear was real. She knew that now. It was nothing to do with Rob, or Kit. It was something inside her head.

Later she caught a cab home and lay awake, mulling things over, reliving the moment. Perhaps Rob was right. Perhaps, after a few more goes, the panic would disappear and she'd be like a normal person, stopping over at his place, spending hot, lazy weekends in bed.

But deep down, she doubted that would happen.

Was it as she'd first suspected – a trust issue? Was her reluctance to get intimate something to do with her father's treatment of women? And one woman in particular – her mother?

Chapter 19

Eliza

Maria and Phil's wedding was a small, happy-clappy affair. The Studleys and Lisles were in attendance, and as Eliza and Rob shuffled into the pew behind their parents, John turned round, clocked Eliza and Rob holding hands, and remarked, 'Splendid!'

Harry caught Eliza's eye and winked, and she couldn't help laughing. 'You owe Dad five hundred quid, apparently, John.'

'Worth every penny, my dear!'

'Chrissake,' muttered Rob.

The contrast with Chess and Gil's wedding was marked. Given the wealth between them, Eliza supposed Phil believed low-key was what God expected of an evangelical Christian, though to her it felt off, half-cocked.

The pastor called Phil 'one of the world's chief defenders of Christian values'. 'And chief attacker of women's rights,' hissed Chess.

'*Those who appear the most sanctified are the worst,*' whispered Eliza.

'Who said that?' whispered Rob.

'Elizabeth the First.'

Maria wore a cream-coloured suit with a small hat; there were no bridesmaids, no best man. But she was flushed with happiness, and Eliza wiped away a tear as she remembered the solemn, damaged girl who'd resented her all these years. She hoped things would go well for her now. Perhaps she'd have that child she so desperately wanted. Perhaps a child would finally make everything right.

Harry looked bored throughout the ceremony, while Rob, Gil, Chess and Eliza reverted to their giggly teenage selves as an earnest guitar trio took to the stage to sing a heartfelt song specially composed for the occasion.

Afterwards, at the low-key wedding reception (no dancing, no alcohol), Harry took Eliza aside. 'Lizzie, let's escape. I want to talk work. This reception's so dull, we might as well.'

They found a sofa in the hotel lobby, and Harry fetched them large drinks from the bar.

'So here's the plan,' he said.

'What have you been up to?'

'Maria and Phil will be safely ensconced in the Bermuda house for the next two weeks. Hopefully Phil will be suitably distracted from work matters.'

'If Maria has her way, they'll be busy making babies.'

Harry pulled a face. 'So while the cats are away, I intend bringing Cecil Walsham in to meet you. Cecil will be your white knight, believe me. And as you suggested, I've been to see your aunt Margot. Turns out Maria didn't give her *quite* the full picture. Margot thought Maria's reforms were all about losing the sleaze, she didn't know about the right-wing Christian agenda.'

'Sneaky Maria. So you charmed Scary Big Sis?'

'Impossible. But I did talk her round. We should bide our time, choose our moment carefully. Oh, and Margot's also intending to gift some of her shares to her daughter, Mackenzie. She's been working in Brussels, but because of Brexit, she's decided her future lies in Scottish politics. Therefore I don't see her wanting an active role at Rose, but I thought you should know.'

Eliza had still never met her Scottish cousin.

'OK, Dad. I'll see the heads of department, to let them know we're on top of things. Do you want to come with me?'

Harry smiled. 'You're the boss. Use me as you think fit.'

✺

Harry came to the office early, to brief Eliza on Cecil. They headed to the cafe first, and staff acted as if Harry were a cross between their long-lost father and a member of the royal family (one of the popular, good-looking ones). He happily posed for selfies as they made their way over to the window.

Eliza smiled as she watched him. The media revelations that had so shocked Rose staff back in 2018 had clearly been forgotten. Or they'd all forgiven him, which was understandable in the face of his overwhelming charm.

Like skittles in the path of a bowling ball.

As they carried on, Eliza noticed him limping a little. 'How's the leg, Dad?'

'Been playing up a bit. I blame this wretched weather. I'm looking forward to being back on *Janette*; we're going to sail down the California coast to Mexico. Mark – you remember Captain Yates? – is keen to have your friend Frankie on board, by the way. Apparently they've been video calling.'

'That's great! Thank you.'

'Look at that view,' said Harry, as they sat down. 'I may moan about the weather, but this is still the greatest city in the world. Nowhere to touch it. Right. Down to business. Let me tell you about Cecil . . .'

Harry painted a picture of the steadiest of hands, unflappable, all-seeing, all-knowing. A rock. 'One of the keys to success is having a loyal, clever sidekick who does all the legwork for you. I had Tom Wolston. I more or less left the running of the company to him, while I did the strategic thinking. Cecil will be your Wolston.'

'I remember Tom. Why did he leave?'

Harry looked uncomfortable. 'Your mother may have had something to do with that.'

'Mum?'

'Wolston played by the rules when it came to the law. Ana was pushing me on my divorce; Katie wouldn't budge. I replaced Wolston with Cranwell, who was, let's say, less of a rules man.'

'Mum made you get rid of Tom?'

'I would have done anything for her. If you ever fall for someone like I fell for Ana, try and remain objective. Or at least, sane.'

Eliza laughed. 'Was it that bad?'

'I was a man possessed.'

'Cranwell was the guy who went to the press about Mum's death, right?'

'He was out for revenge. I'd sacked him for sexual harassment. He . . .' Harry paused. His eyes slid away from Eliza's and settled on the view again.

They moved down to the Thames.

'Behaviour sometimes follows a pattern, I have come to realize.'

'Cranwell's?'

'Mine.'

'How do you mean?'

Harry seemed to be having trouble finding the words. His eyes met hers again, and she flinched at the look in them.

'Dad?'

'Cranwell assaulted Caitlyn. I'd summoned her to the office when her ex-boyfriend tried to blackmail me. The extortion attempt was nothing to do with her. I knew that, deep down, but I couldn't forgive Caitlyn's infidelity. I turned my back on her, left her in the hands of Cranwell and her low-life ex. That evening, she threw herself into the Thames.'

Eliza pictured her step-mother. She'd been tiny, beautiful, full of life; had always loved playing with Eliza and Eddie. They'd adored her.

'But, Dad, if anyone should have understood infidelity . . .'

'I know. But it hurt. And I did something similar with your mother – buried my head in the sand, wanting to forget about it all, while Sokolov closed in. And all in the name of money.'

'You're a good person, Dad, and you're facing up to your mistakes. It's just taken you a while.'

'Lizzie, promise me you'll never let yourself be manipulated by a man.'

'I won't.'

'You think Rob's OK with you being his boss?'

'I'm pretty sure he enjoys it. Thinks it's fun.'

'Right. Well, it's probably not ideal, but it's early days. As long as you're happy.'

'I am. Very.'

'Good.' He looked at his watch. 'We'd better wend our way, Cecil will be here any minute.'

Pippa showed Cecil in to Eliza's office. Harry made the introductions, and Cecil looked Eliza in the eye and firmly shook her hand. His own was cool. She guessed he was in his mid-forties; medium height, brown hair in a sensible style. Earnest, intelligent eyes assessed her; there were faint frown lines between them. Something about him said 'dependable'.

'I'm delighted to meet you, Eliza. Harry speaks highly of your capabilities. He's filled me in on the situation here at Rose, and I hope I'll be able to assist in a consultant capacity—'

'Consultant only until Eliza's full time,' interrupted Harry. 'Then, pending her approval, you will be too. Whatever it takes, Cecil, consider yourself lured.'

'I see.'

The three sat around the table, talking strategies and future directions, and it felt right. Eliza knew – this was her place, her destiny. If only they didn't have the whole Maria and Phil business to sort out first.

Then, all at once, it was Trinity term – she'd be leaving Oxford in a matter of weeks. The daffodils had fluttered, danced, and left; the cherry trees were frothing with blossom, and there was a waxy blue haze of new leaves on the willows along the Cherwell.

On May Day eve, Eliza, Leigh and Frankie went over to Will and Kit's place.

'Food – I remember this!' said Will, snapping the lids off the Chinese meal the girls had picked up.

The goal was to stay up all night. Tomorrow they'd be making their way down to Magdalen Bridge to watch the sunrise.

'I guess I can catch up on sleep in my nine o'clock lecture,' said Frankie.

'Good plan,' said Kit, spearing a prawn wonton with a chopstick. 'Might make it into double figures – I'm one lecture ahead of you, Will.'

'No, we're both on eight, remember?'

'Eight lectures? In how long?' said Leigh.

'Since ever,' said Will.

Eliza shook her head. What would it be like to be so good at English that you could skip lectures and tutorials, do next to no revision, spend your final term in the pursuit of pleasure, and somehow still get a first? Because she knew that would happen.

After their meal they sat on cushions on the floor, drinking bottle after bottle of wine, the conversation rambling through politics, future plans, favourite childhood TV programmes, the meaning of life ... at which point Frankie fell asleep with her head on Leigh's shoulder.

Kit fetched his guitar and sang to them, his head tipped forward, his long hair hiding his eyes. His beautiful, soulful voice spoke straight to Eliza's heart. She recognized the old seventies number 'Woodstock', and sang softly along: *'And I feel just like a cog, in something turning ...'*

Then she couldn't sing any more.

'Eliza, are you crying?' said Will.

'How could anyone not?'

Kit looked up.

'Come here, sweetness,' Will said.

She shuffled over and curled up in his arms.

'Why so sad?'

'Because all this will end soon. What lies ahead, after Oxford . . . sometimes it feels like too much. The responsibility, Dad's expectations; the fight with Maria.'

'You'll have us,' said Will. 'All for one, and all that.'

As Kit finished the melancholy song, she fell asleep.

❦

At five o'clock, Eliza was gently shaken awake by Leigh. 'Time to go – drink this,' she said.

Eliza sipped the hot coffee, trying to work out whether she was drunk or hungover. Somewhere between.

The five set off through the dark streets, rubbing their arms against the chilly air, joining the crowds heading to Magdalen Bridge.

As dawn broke on May morning, and the gothic spires were silhouetted against a pale-blue sky, the sound of the young choristers singing 'Hymnus Eucharisticus' rang out from the top of the Great Tower and the crowd fell silent.

Standing behind her, Kit slipped his arms around Eliza's waist and she leaned back against him. Once again, she felt the presence of all those who'd come here before her, listening to the sweet voices of the choir celebrating spring.

Our endless numbered days.

People were recording the singing, their phones glowing bright in the half-light. But Eliza wouldn't need help remembering this.

Then the bells pealed and they set off back along the High, where morris dancing and other strange forms of revelry were already in full swing.

'Pagan worship does it for me,' said Kit, as a green-horned goat loped past, followed by a walking tree.

As they ate enormous breakfasts at the Turf, Will said, 'So, Eliza. Your Rob's up next weekend. Will we love him or hate him?'

'I'm *so* excited to meet him!' said Frankie.

'You'll love him, everyone does,' said Eliza. 'He's not into theatre or poetry, Will, but he loves a good movie.'

'I'll reserve my judgement,' said Will. 'Our standards on your behalf are beyond stratospheric.'

'You three need to get on. Trust me.'

'Why?' said Kit.

'Because I have plans for him. You could be working together soon.'

'Does it for me,' said Kit.

Eliza gave him a look. 'No. Mine.'

'Him, or me?'

She grinned. 'Both.' Taking him by surprise, she kissed him on the lips.

'Oh my god, you two,' said Leigh.

Later, Will, Kit and Eliza went to a lecture on Elizabethan and Jacobean popular theatre, where they slept on the back row until it was time for their tutorial.

❀

'Eliza, there's a fuck-off car outside,' said Frankie. 'I'm guessing it's Rob's.'

It was Friday evening a week later, and the girls had already finished their first bottle of end-of-the-week wine.

Eliza joined her friends at the window and saw Rob getting out of his silver Porsche, sunglasses on, swinging his Paul Smith jacket over his shoulder. He grabbed a bunch of flowers and a bag from the passenger seat, pressed his key remote, and headed up the path.

'Oh my *god*,' breathed Leigh. 'That's indecently hot.'

'Holy shit,' said Frankie. 'Fan me, someone.'

'Shut up, you two,' said Eliza, smiling. 'It's just a boy.'

But as she watched Rob approach, she acknowledged their expletives were justified.

She opened the front door. 'Welcome to my humble abode. Mangy old carpet, very little white, and I'm afraid no espresso machine – only a plunger.'

She was aware of her friends' heads poking round the living room doorway.

'But I do have a Frankie and a Leigh. Come and meet them.'

He stepped inside and held out the bouquet. 'Cliché bunch of flowers, but at least they're not roses.' Their scent competed with cool evening air and citrusy aftershave.

She took them from him and kissed his cheek. 'They're gorgeous, thank you.'

He kissed her on the lips, pulling her to him. He didn't stop, and her pulse began to race.

'Maaaan,' said Leigh, behind her.

He stopped and peered over Eliza's shoulder. 'Leigh?'

'Hello, Rob. Are there any more like you at home?'

'And I'm Frankie.' She came to stand by Leigh's side. 'Welcome, Rob. We have wine, but there's beer if you prefer. And crisps. We know how to live, here at number twenty.'

Rob was grinning like the Cheshire Cat. 'A wine would be nice. But first I should get out of my London and put on my Oxford. Although I don't have a scarf, and I'm unsure as to sweatshirt or jumper. What do you think?'

'A tightish T-shirt should do it,' said Leigh.

'My friends are shameless, I do apologize,' said Eliza. 'Come upstairs, I'll show you to your room.'

'My god,' said Rob, as he took off his work shirt and rifled through his holdall. 'They're dangerous.'

'Incorrigible,' said Eliza.

'I love them already.'

'Clearly reciprocated.'

'So . . . this is your bedroom.' He looked around at the art posters, the framed photos of Harry, Clare and Eddie, the one of Ana; piles of books on the floor, clothes slung over a chair.

'Sorry, slightly messy. But I hoovered.'

He kissed her. 'Do you want to stay up here for a bit, or would that be antisocial?'

'We've got all weekend. If those two let me near you.'

Downstairs, the girls had opened a second bottle of wine. Eliza watched Rob turning on the charm. He was shameless too. But

Rob was Rob, and she enjoyed the banter as he sat between her two friends on the sofa.

She went to the kitchen, returning with a bag of Kettle Chips.

'Crisps!' she said, throwing them at Leigh, who caught them, saying, 'Dinner! Where would we be without the humble potato?'

They'd arranged to meet Will and Kit at the pub. The boys were already there, standing close, sharing what looked like an intimate joke.

Rob raised his eyebrows at Eliza. 'Are they a thing?' he muttered.

'Who knows?' she said.

The evening was a raucous one. Will and Kit were living up to their vow of hedonism, having already spent the afternoon drinking together. Frankie, Leigh and Eliza did their best to catch up, whipping Rob along with them. Will and Kit laid into Rob about his designer stubble, pretty hair and expensive clothes, but he gave as good as he got.

'Eliza,' said Will, 'we love Rob. But what does he have that I have not? What is he that I am not?'

'He's not a tosser,' said Eliza. 'Of curls.'

They went on to a party, got gloriously drunk, and by the time they were home Eliza didn't have to worry about *sleeping* with Rob. She passed out on his chest, fully clothed.

Nobody got up before noon. Eliza and Rob lay in each other's arms, talking, kissing, a little more, but not a lot, because every time Eliza shut her eyes, the world lurched.

'Do you party like that all the time?' said Rob.

'You mean excessively?'

'Like there's no tomorrow.'

'Will and Kit have made a commitment to hedonism. We're just supporting them in that.'

'Kit's . . . I found it hard to get a handle on him.'

'Nobody can. He's a complete enigma.'

'What you said before – he's bi?'

'He's everything. He'll probably hit on you at some stage. Just warning you in advance.'

'Even though he knows I'm with you?'

'The concept of fidelity is beyond his understanding.'

Rob propped himself up on an elbow, looking down at her. He licked a finger and wiped beneath her eye.

'Probably should've washed my face before bed.'

'You look . . . dissolute. It's sexy.'

He kissed her, and as she closed her eyes the bed seemed to drop away. She opened them again.

He carried on. What must she taste like? Pretty gross, surely? She sensed he was digging in for the long haul, as things heated up. She so didn't need this right now.

'Sorry, I think I'm going to be sick.'

She walked quickly to the bathroom and slammed the door, wincing at the noise it made. Then she sat on the toilet, her head in her hands.

Eliza didn't feel sick, just gross. And not at all sexy. She didn't need to put herself through the whole lovely build-up/major panic business again, certainly not right now.

She gave it five minutes, flushed the toilet and made her way back to the bedroom.

To her surprise, Rob was up, a towel round his waist. 'Is the shower free?'

'Oh, yes. No one else is up yet.'

He left the room.

Eliza went over to her mirror and took in the panda eyes, the tangled hair. Those she could deal with. The mess in her head wasn't so easy to sort out.

After taking a shower she set about restoring life to her face with a little make-up. Now she looked a whole lot better than she felt.

Rob was alone in the living room, sipping coffee. 'I made you one,' he said, indicating a steaming mug. 'We could go and find brunch?'

The thought of food almost made her gag.

'Not up to it,' he said, noticing.

'How come you're looking so fresh?'

'I didn't mix my drinks, paced myself. I like to stay in control.'

She picked up her coffee and sat on his lap. 'I'm sorry. You must think I'm a disgrace.'

'You seem different here, that's for sure. But hey, you were a wild child too.'

'Only when I was with you. You led me astray. Shall we go punting? We could take wine – hair of the dog.'

'Yes to the punting, but let's lay off the booze? Because ... I'd like us both to stay in control today. I'm going home tomorrow, so tonight – Lesson Two?'

Eliza's stomach clenched. It could have been for one of three reasons: hangover, nerves or anticipation.

✹

Rob was in the living room with Frankie and Leigh, the sound of their laughter floating up the stairs. Eliza was changing for the evening. She mulled over her underwear selection.

She felt her spirits sagging, and wished she could just go to sleep, curled up in Rob's arms. But that wouldn't do. Rob was on a mission, convinced he could make her want him enough. Would he be as understanding this time, if it all turned to custard?

Eliza was fairly sure it would.

They ate at a candlelit bistro a few streets away, and as always the conversation was easy, fun, relaxed.

'Hey, a quick work thing while I've got you,' she said, as they started on their main course. 'What do you think about Rose TV commissioning original content – drama, movies, maybe. Good-quality stuff.'

'Sounds great. I could speak to a few people? But that's probably not my job. I might be stepping on toes.'

'Hm, you know what Dad says? If you can't promote someone over their manager, create something new for them.'

He laughed. 'How would that look, making a fancy new position for your boyfriend?'

'I'm talking theoretical – at the moment. I'd love you to read some of Will and Kit's stuff, there's nothing out there like it.'

'I can believe it.' His voice was deadpan.

'I'm totally seeing you as a wheeler-dealer producer, sweet-talking money out of film and TV executives. Maybe even Hollywood ones, eventually. You'd be a natural. What do you think?'

She saw him visualising that 'fancy new position'.

'I think whatever you set your mind to, me and you can make it happen.'

'What a team we're going to be, Rob.'

The relaxed conversation, the candlelit dinner, just one glass of wine. It all set Eliza up nicely for what was to come.

In her black lacy underwear, she lay down on the bed, fanning her hair across the pillow.

Lesson Two was every bit as lovely as Lesson One, and Eliza wondered if this time . . .

Rob was utterly confident it would happen, she could tell. His lack of hesitation, his assurance, gave her own confidence a boost, and once again they reached the point where he asked: 'Do you want me now, Lizzie?'

She did.

And then she didn't. It all crashed again. Her eyes flew open, full of fear.

He lay down on his back and pulled her on top of him. 'Try it this way. You're in control.'

But the moment had passed; she couldn't do this.

She buried her face in his chest and burst into tears. 'Rob, I think there's something wrong with me. I think I have . . . issues.'

He stroked her hair. 'How do you mean, issues?'

'I think . . . deep down, maybe I don't trust men. Can't get intimate with them. Because of Dad.'

'But you and he get on so well – you're very close.'

'Yes, we are. But . . . his history, the way he treated Mum, and his first wife, and Caitlyn. Cheating on them, turning his back on them.'

'Perhaps you should see someone? Like, a therapist?'

She pictured it – an earnest psychiatrist asking about her relationship with her father; encouraging her to explore her body.

'I can't do that, I just can't!'

'Why not?'

'Too embarrassing,' she said, sniffing.

'I think I've done all I can.'

'And it was lovely. Right up until the last part.'

And then it came to her. 'I'll talk to Clare. She'll know what to do.'

'Good plan. Look, Lizzie, I'm not going to lie. I don't know how long I can go on like this. I haven't had sex in months.'

Eliza's eyes widened. 'Rob! Is it really that important to you?'

'Yup. I want you very, very much.'

'Oh. I understand. I think. Well, obviously not as well as you do. Let me talk to Clare. But I've got finals coming up. It might take me a while.'

He looked at her for a moment, then smiled. 'In which case I might have to give you a different sort of lesson. I'm only human.'

'How do you mean?'

'Let's try a little experiment . . .'

Chapter 20

Eliza

As finals approached, Eliza went to ground, revising hard, venturing out only for tutorials. It was a grind, and she was feeling the pressure, so FaceTiming Rob in the evenings was welcome relief.

His banter always made her laugh and – well, he was one of the few people she knew who looked good on an iPhone screen.

When Maria returned from her honeymoon, however, the 'How's work?' part of their conversations became noticeably less upbeat. 'Don't worry about it,' Rob said, when Eliza remarked on the fact. 'Just concentrate on your exams.'

But eventually she prised it out of him. The sales team was battling an attempt by Maria to bring TV offerings in line with the new family values mission statement. This involved a new rating system, bleeping out expletives from each and every programme, and cutting scenes that Maria considered too graphic. Content that was less explicit but which still crossed her line would be scheduled for viewing after ten p.m., which was a nightmare watershed for the sales team to work with. It would all be expensive to do and complicated to organize.

'It's what the bloody parental lock's for,' said Rob. 'And we already have the whole "sexual content may offend" thing.

But what's really freaking everyone out is that she's requesting schedules way ahead, and scrubbing anything that doesn't fit her *family values*. It's censorship, based on two people's personal prejudices.'

'Yep,' Eliza replied, 'and it's so off brand. Rose is all about pushing boundaries, not turning back the clock. I appreciate you telling me, Rob. Try and ride it out. I'll be there in a few weeks, and Dad's keeping close watch. Don't push back – I don't want her marking your card. And keep me informed – be my spy?'

'I will. But don't fret. Just keep your head down and ace those finals, Lizzie.'

❀

Eights Week provided welcome relief from the pressure of exams and sister-related worries, thanks in no small part to Pimm's.

It was early evening, and the five of them were sitting on the grass opposite the boathouses at Christ Church Meadows, watching the last of the races.

'Rowing – pfft,' said Frankie, as a boat swung into the centre of the Thames to avoid being bumped by the one behind. 'Where's the skill in that?'

'It's absurd,' said Kit.

He was looking gloriously pretty today, in a disreputable way, with his ripped jeans, bare feet, and a tight black T-shirt. Had he cut his hair all year? It fell over his eyes, and Eliza couldn't resist shuffling over and pushing it back.

'Better,' she said. 'You have the most beautiful eyes, Kit. Why do you hide them?'

'Steady, Eliza,' said Leigh, sipping her Pimm's. 'This stuff's a lot stronger than it tastes.'

'Don't listen to her,' said Kit with his lazy smile. 'Let Bacchus be your guide.'

'The wine chap?' said Eliza. She took a long drink then turned her straw towards Kit, slipping it between his lips.

Holding her gaze, he sucked.

'Also general intoxication,' he said, 'fertility and . . . ' He leaned forward and kissed her quickly, but not that quickly. 'Ecstasy.'

She tasted mint. 'Mmm. Kit, you're too delicious.'

'He who sups with the Devil has need of a long spoon,' he said, running a finger down her bare arm. *'I have brought you a ladle.'*

She shivered.

'Kit, get off Eliza's shoulder,' said Will. 'Come sit on mine instead.'

'Food, we need food,' said Frankie, 'or we'll never make it to sunset.' She handed round sandwiches and crisps from a carrier bag.

'Remember how last year we had a hamper with actual plates?' said Leigh.

'And fancy nibbles from Marks & Sparks,' said Eliza.

'Now look at us,' said Frankie, glancing over at Kit, who was lying down with his eyes closed, looking like a beautiful homeless person.

As the races finished and the crowds left, die-hard students partied on into the night. One team set fire to an old rowing eight, and people danced, silhouetted in the flames. Girls and boys were kissing in the darkness, and the wine flowed on. Others, including Will, jumped into the river.

Eliza embraced Bacchus that night. In a matter of weeks, Oxford would be a memory, she'd be battling it out with Maria, and there was the whole virgin situation to be faced. So for now, she'd live in this moment, sobriety and the future be damned. She flung caution to the winds, threw off her clothes, and joined Will in the river.

❋

Trinity term drew to a close, and Leigh was the last to finish her exams. Traffic on the High Street ground to a halt as students spilled out of the exam hall, red carnations pinned to their gowns, blinking in the sunshine, unable to believe it was all over.

As tradition demanded, Eliza and the others met her outside

and sprayed her in confetti and champagne, then they left arm in arm for the pub. At sunset, they collected blankets, food and wine, and took it all down to the river.

Later, as a distant bell chimed the midnight hour, calling time on their Oxford years, their last night progressed into something which, looking back, Eliza would never quite understand.

She was prone on the grass, gazing up at the moon and stars above. After drinking for so many hours, coherent thought was no longer possible; there was only sensation and emotion.

Linkin Park's 'Minutes to Midnight' was playing out of a Bluetooth speaker, the singer's fragile voice and the acoustic guitars flinging Eliza's soul up to the heavens. She was feeling bereft. She didn't want this to end, didn't want to go back to London. She wanted to stop time.

Kit appeared beside her, a silhouette in the moonlight, his hair silvery. 'Come with me.'

'Not sure I can stand up.'

He hauled her to her feet, and she leaned on his chest and put her arms round his waist. They danced together, barefoot on the cool grass, and he said, 'You wanted to stop time.'

'You can read my mind. How is this possible?'

'I always know what's in your head,' he said softly. 'And in here.' He placed his hand on her heart, and she felt its heat.

'Marley, your powers are not of this world.'

'We've been here before, Eliza. Don't you feel it? Time isn't the same for everyone.'

'Kit, please don't do the existential thing. I'm not strong enough tonight.'

He took her hand, pulling her away from the river.

'Where are we going?'

He led her to an ancient oak, and into its shadows. He sat down, resting against the gnarly old tree trunk. Eliza slumped between his legs, her back against his chest, her head on his shoulder. They sat quietly, looking out across the water meadow, bathed in moonlight.

The silver air crackled with magic.

Kit held up his phone and snapped a selfie, then showed it to her. Their faces were beautiful in monochrome; Eliza's skin was glowing, Kit's hair pale as he leaned his head on hers.

A soft breeze rustled the leaves above them.

'Send that to me? I'll keep it for ever. Me and you. Here, now.'

'For ever, now. It's all the same. Time isn't linear. It runs in circles, in loops.'

'So now you're a physicist? How do you know these things?'

'I just do. Like . . . ' He paused. 'Like I know I'll die young.' He tightened his arms around her.

It sounded like a throwaway comment, but even in her befuddled state, she knew it wasn't.

It was all too much – the beauty of this moment; Kit's ramblings. She burst into tears.

'Shh . . . Forget it. Just dark thoughts.'

'Kit – I don't want this to end.'

He wiped away her tears, and she took comfort in his warm body, feeling their connection, the magic in the air.

They sat in silence for a while, then she sat up and looked at him. 'I don't think I'll ever understand you, or what goes on in your beautiful head. But whatever happens, me and you – we're for ever.'

He smiled. 'Yep. We'd better go; the others will think we've run away.' He took out his phone and messaged the photo.

'Maybe we *should* run away,' she said.

As Eliza stood up, her phone buzzed. She pressed the home button and the time flashed up: 12.00 a.m.

'That's odd.'

'What's odd?'

'The time. It says midnight.'

He smiled again, taking her hand as they headed back.

'Ah, Titania and Oberon,' said Will. 'Where have you two been? Fairyland?'

'Something like that,' said Eliza. She looked at Kit, who winked.

Leigh and Frankie were asleep beneath a blanket, and Eliza

sat between Will and Kit as dawn approached and the darkness melted to grey.

'*Moon, take thy flight, now die, die, die, die,*' said Kit, his voice soft.

The horizon turned palest pink, and then the golden sun rose over the spires and the water meadows. Nature was silent, watching, as night and its magic slipped away.

Chapter 21

Eliza

As Eliza settled back into her London life, that night at Oxford began to feel like a dream. Another time, another place, another Eliza.

Kit and Will had gone off to France, looking for any work that would enable them to live and write together until they felt the need to come home. Frankie was sailing in Spain, and at the end of summer would be flying to LA to meet *Janette*. Leigh's internship in Rose's finance department had been approved, and she was now in London. Eliza was happy to have her friend here, though of course they wouldn't be able to hang out as they'd done at Oxford.

Everything was different now.

And then there was Rob. He'd come over Sunday night, just two days after she'd finished at Oxford. Her head had been all over the place; she'd been unable to shake off the echoes of that night. They followed her round – the feelings, the magic, the moonlight; sitting beneath that ancient oak. Kit's strange ramblings. She couldn't recollect his words; only her reaction to them. She felt his absence as an ache.

When Rob arrived she was dressed in jeans and T-shirt, barefoot, her hair in a ponytail fastened with an elastic band. No make-up. Probably still looked tired – it had been one hell of a hangover, after all. (She was off alcohol now. Dry July seemed like a sensible plan.)

Rob had swept her up, kissing her enthusiastically. Her body had responded, but at first her mind refused to join in. It was too soon. It was still full of the intensity of those last days. The studying, the exams, the partying, the farewells, the tears; the knowledge that the door was closing on this golden time and that from hereon, it was real life all the way.

'Lizzie Rose, what *do* you look like?' he'd said when he put her down. 'Time to ditch the student, girl. You have half an hour to get your glam on if I'm to be seen with you at Ristorante Frescobaldi.'

'Seriously? I've wanted to go there for ages. Right. Give me ten.'

'Make it thirty – I have standards.'

Changing into a designer dress and doing her hair and make-up had helped shake off some of those echoes, and by the end of the evening Rob had wrenched her mind back to London. He'd been on great form, charming and funny and attentive and, best of all, he'd said after kissing her on the doorstep, 'I won't come in. We've got work tomorrow and I can see you're tired. And you'll need to get your head back into London. I understand – I saw what your life was like there.'

'It wasn't always like that weekend.'

'No, but it'll still take a while to adjust. Say the word when you're ready to move things on, with me. Until then I'm happy to chill, take in a movie, whatever you want.'

I love this man.

'Rob, you're the best.'

He'd kissed her again. 'Goodnight, Lizzie. Sweet dreams – of me?'

'Yes, Rob. Dreams of you.'

Back on the top floor, Eliza was relieved to see only Maria and Pippa were in – there was no sign of Phil.

'It's great that you're full time now,' said Pippa, as Eliza perched on her desk for a chat. She lowered her voice. 'Between you and me, we could do with a little lightening up round here.'

'Grumpy?' said Eliza, looking over at Maria's closed door.

'Workwise, yes. She's still smiley when Phil's around. Though he's not here much. Um, Eliza … Maria hasn't actually let me know, will I be working for you both now?'

'I need to talk to her. I don't even know what my job title is. Does she have time this morning?'

Pippa checked her computer. 'No meetings scheduled.'

'OK, can you block off an hour? I'll go have a chat.'

She tapped on her sister's door and went in. 'Hello, stranger! How's married life?'

Maria looked up and frowned. 'Eliza. Are you back already?'

'I am. For good. Can we have a chat? Or maybe I should call it a meeting. Now that I'm official. What do you think we should call me? Deputy CEO? Is there such a thing? What do you think?'

'If I could get a word in?'

Maria stood up and walked over to the door. 'Pippa, a coffee for Eliza and green tea for me, please.' She shut it behind her. 'I have important news.'

Oh god. What was she going to lay on her now? 'Fire away.'

And then the frown disappeared. Instead of returning to her seat behind the desk, Maria pulled over a spare chair and sat down beside Eliza.

Odd.

'I'm going to have a baby, Eliza. I'm pregnant.'

'Holy shit!'

Maria was so happy with her news she didn't even admonish Eliza for using either of those two words.

'Two months, I think. Due December or January.'

'Gosh, Maria. That's the most amazing news! Have you told Dad and Clare?'

'Not yet. I wanted to tell you first, for a number of reasons. The first being … well, Eliza, I know we've never been particularly close …'

Understatement!

' . . . but I'm hoping that will change now. Family, I have come to realize, is the most important thing in the world.'

Funny, that's what Phil said.

'I'd like you to be involved in your niece or nephew's life. Also, you should know, Phil and I firmly believe a mother's place is at home. So I'll be leaving Rose in the autumn. Phil will continue to play an active role, and I'll still attend board meetings, but the day-to-day running of the company – that will be over to you.'

Eliza was stunned. 'But, Maria, your policies – you know I don't agree with them. I can't carry those on for you.'

They went quiet as Pippa brought in their drinks.

Maria's frown was back. 'Phil will be ensuring our strategic plans are carried through, you can count on that.'

'And you can count on me to oppose them.'

Maria pursed her lips.

Eliza remembered Harry talking about Phil's share of the company – *it's not what it was* – and how he'd been to see Aunt Margot. Another vote might sink Maria and Phil, once and for all.

'Huge congratulations, anyway.' She stood up and hugged her sister. It wasn't exactly returned, but there was a pat on the arm. 'I know how much you wanted this, I'm very happy for you.' It was true.

It seemed the ideal solution, the perfect way forward. Maria would settle into a life of motherhood and servitude (*good luck with that*), and the board would wrest control from Phil's happy-clappy hands. Eliza would take over, mentored by Cecil, guided by Harry. She'd progress Rose's new production arm, bring Kit and Will on board, and let the editors and heads of department get on with their jobs.

The future was looking bright. Rose-y.

❖

A week or so later, Eliza invited Rob round for dinner. It was the first time she'd cooked for him, and she'd foraged at Borough

Market for the sorts of things she knew he loved – local, organic, artisan. That sweet-scoffing kid was quite the foodie these days.

But he was subdued as he picked at his hand-dived scallops.

'You're not your usual self,' said Eliza. 'What's up?'

He looked down at his plate. 'Nothing, I'm fine. This is tasty.'

'No, you're not fine.'

'OK.' He met her eye. 'It's Amy. Chess went to see her; she's not doing so well.' He put his fork down and sat back, raking his fingers through his hair. 'I feel bad. I know we haven't really talked about it, but ... she was devastated, Lizzie. And Chess has been picking up the pieces.'

Eliza hadn't given Rob's ex a minute's thought over the past months, but now she allowed herself a moment's sympathy.

'Chess hasn't said anything to me.'

'No, I asked her not to, with you doing your finals. Amy hasn't really made any friends down here; she's lonely.'

'I'm sure she'll soon find someone else.'

'She's ... Lizzie, she's being difficult, about the divorce, and I don't want to push too hard while she's not well. So it could take a while.'

Eliza remembered Harry telling her about his and Katie's long-drawn-out divorce. 'My mum had to wait forever for Dad. I think it more or less scuppered their relationship.'

'Things are different now, though. Probably a year, tops.'

'Hm.'

This was annoying. The Rose family was ever a subject of interest to the British public, and Harry was as well known (OK, *notorious*) for his love life as he was for his achievements as head of Rose Corp. If the press picked up on the fact that Eliza was dating someone who was still married, and that she was the reason for that marriage break-up, it wouldn't be a great start to her career.

She had a distinct image in her mind of how she wanted to be portrayed. The new face of Rose – a strong, independent young woman blazing a path. Firmly in control, steering Rose into new waters, launching a golden age of British TV drama. It would be all about her work, *not* her private life.

Perhaps she should rethink things. Maybe they shouldn't be seen in public yet. Keep their relationship below the radar until his divorce came through.

Rob was still picking at his food. Clearly whatever was going on with Amy was playing on his mind.

Maybe she'd save that conversation for later.

She smiled, trying to lighten things up. 'Kit says women subconsciously look for someone just like their father. I hope you don't turn into a serial monogamist.'

Rob frowned. In fact, he bristled. God, he was hard work tonight.

'Kit? What would *he* know? Not exactly the expert on relationships.'

'I was just joking. But don't dismiss Kit. He's wiser than you think. He said things between you and me would be rocky. In fact . . . ' She thought back. 'He knew we'd get together even before I did. How did he know that?'

'What do you mean, rocky?'

'No idea. Kit just knows things.'

'Ignore the crazy boy. Things between us will be sublime. And I'll be stopping at two wives, so you can forget your history repeats nonsense.'

'*Wives?*'

She was amused to see him blush.

'I'm married to the job, Rob. Better get used to that.'

After dinner they lay on the sofa watching a movie. Thankfully Rob seemed to have unwound, and Eliza's attention was soon diverted from the TV as he produced a box of hand-made chocolates.

'Fetch,' he said, holding one between his teeth.

It started out as the sort of play-fight they'd had as children, laughing and wrestling, pinning arms down, ending up on the floor. By the time they were on the third chocolate, Eliza was lost in the delicious sensation of dark-chocolate-flavoured kisses.

By the fourth she was aching for him, but the dilemma was real. Take things further and risk it all going belly up again, or stop now? And she really didn't want to stop.

'I'm full up,' she said.

'But are you satisfied?'

'I think not.'

'I can probably help with that.'

And so it went, over the following weeks. They found ways, and Eliza fell more deeply in love with Rob. She explained her rationale for being discreet, and they avoided being seen together in public. At the office they'd steal the occasional moment, though the glass walls were unhelpful.

Terri wasn't fooled, and gave Eliza a talking to, calling her unprofessional.

'Your mum and Harry would never have carried on like this,' she said, after walking in on them in Eliza's office.

Which had Eliza asking, 'What were they like together, at work?'

'Nobody had a clue what was going on. But that all changed at the Christmas party. Nineteen ninety-three, it would have been. Harry was still married to Katie, though it was common knowledge that was all very shaky. Harry didn't let on to anyone about Ana.'

'What happened at the party?'

'Your mum looked incredible. A gold Versace number, slit to the thigh. Harry used to do this whole welcoming thing where he'd talk to people as they arrived. When she came in he snogged her, right there in front of everyone. Have to say, it was quite hot.'

'Really! I'm so going to tease him about that.'

'Yeah, do. It'll take him back. They left the party together. He once told me it was the best night of his life and nothing would ever come close.'

So that must have been when they'd first slept together.

It was time to talk to Clare. Rob deserved all of her. She wanted them to have that best night of their lives.

Chapter 22

Eliza

'Ah, John. Good to see you. Where's my five hundred quid?' asked Harry.

It was Clare's birthday, and the Lisles and Studleys had been invited for an al fresco lunch at Richmond – always a gamble in England, but happily the sun was blazing down out of a clear blue sky. Eliza and Rob were sitting with Harry, Clare, Charles, Megan, Chess and Gil on the wide stone terrace that looked out across the gardens to the park beyond.

'Harry, old boy,' said John, as he and his wife joined them. 'Never been so happy to part with my cash.' He clapped Rob on the shoulder. 'Good work, Son.'

Harry winked at Eliza. 'I'll put it towards the dowry.'

'No, spend it,' she replied. 'I'm never getting married. I've seen where that can lead.'

Clare laughed heartily. 'I love this generation.'

'They're killing it,' said Charles. 'Wish we'd had Tinder in my day.'

'Dad!' said Chess.

'I seem to remember you did perfectly well without it,' said

Harry. 'Before he married you, of course, dear sister.' He raised his glass in Megan's direction.

'Touch of the pot and the kettle, dear brother?' said Megan.

'Honestly,' said Eliza to Chess. 'What were our dads like?'

Over to their right, Eddie and a schoolfriend were knocking a ball about on the tennis court, and down on the lawn, Maria and Phil were strolling back from a walk round the grounds. It was Phil's first time to Richmond, and Eliza expected Maria would be making her announcement today.

The caterers served lunch at a long table set out under the pergola. Dappled sunlight filtered through the roses rambling overhead, and a gentle breeze flapped the tablecloths and kept them cool. Harry was on fine form, sitting opposite Eliza and next to Rob, and Eliza smiled as the pair of them bantered. *Those two.* And when they moved on to their mutual love of fast cars and Harry said, 'You can take the Aston for a spin while we're away,' Eliza knew Rob had made the grade.

Phil was sitting opposite Eliza, a couple of seats down, and she noticed his eyes on her. A lot.

As the caterers served dessert, Harry tapped a teaspoon against his glass. 'Friends, offspring, hangers-on. May I take this opportunity to toast my beautiful and wise Clare, who several years ago brought me back from the brink of all sorts of horribleness. If Fate hadn't thrown us together, I'm fairly sure I'd be six feet under. She is my rock, and I love her to distraction. Please raise your glasses to Clare, everyone.'

'To Clare,' they said, and Eliza mouthed *Beautiful* as Harry caught her eye.

'Despite what Eliza might have to say on the matter, I would highly recommend the married state,' he added, before sitting down again.

'May I say something too, Harry?' said Phil, taking everyone by surprise.

'By all means,' said Harry, though his eyes switched from sentimental-warm to killer-cold within milliseconds.

'Maria and I have an announcement.' All eyes went to Maria, who was looking radiant. Pregnancy seemed to be agreeing with her. Eliza had been surreptitiously looking for a bump, and thought she detected a small one.

'God in his graciousness has blessed us,' he said. 'We're expecting a child. Harry, sir, your first grandchild.'

Harry looked stunned.

'My goodness!' said Clare. 'What marvellous news! Congratulations, you two!'

'Thank you,' said Maria, blushing. 'I'm so thrilled.'

'Well, yes,' said Harry, pulling himself together. 'Well done, Maria. Grandpa Harry. Good god.'

'As you know, folks,' said Phil, making it all about him again, 'family is at the true heart of Christian life, and therefore Maria will be leaving Rose to stay home and raise our children.'

Eliza didn't meet Harry's eye – he'd probably be looking somewhere between overjoyed and relieved.

'I, of course, have my responsibilities at Hapsburg, and will be dividing my time between the US and the UK. So we have decided Maria should prepare for the birth in a place where she'll be cared for by someone with similar views on childbirth to our own.'

'Phil,' said Eliza. 'Perhaps Maria could tell us herself? I think we'd all like that.'

Phil's dazzling smile faded. 'My wife likes me to speak on her behalf.'

'Maria?' said Eliza.

'I'm happy for Phil to tell you.'

Chess caught Eliza's eye and shook her head a little.

'If I might continue?' said Phil. 'As you know, Maria grew up with her mother at a retreat in Wales.'

'Can we move along to something we don't know?' said Harry, looking stroppy.

'Maria will stay at the retreat as a guest of Cassandra Lisle. She'll be in a nurturing environment where natural childbirth is practised, in line with Maria's belief that there should be no medical intervention in this beautiful process. She will be in Cassandra's hands, and God's.'

'Make ready the beanbags,' said Charles.

'Shh, Dad,' said Chess, trying not to laugh.

Eliza remembered Cassandra well from her visits to the retreat. A recovered alcoholic, she had, according to Harry, changed radically from the time she'd been Charles's fun-loving wife. She remembered floaty dresses, home-grown veggies, a propensity for talking in inspirational quotes.

'I object,' said Harry.

'Why, Father?' said Maria.

'The child will be Welsh.'

'Unacceptable,' said Charles.

Eliza spurted out some of the wine she'd been sipping. 'Stop it, you two,' she said, attempting to swallow her laughter. 'This is important. Maria, is that wise? What about monitoring the pregnancy? And what if there are any problems during the birth? It's miles from the nearest hospital.'

'Giving birth is the greatest joy given to a woman by God,' said Phil. 'Maria would rather put herself in His hands than the hands of your National Health Service.'

'Probably a lot safer,' said Harry.

Eliza noticed the hurt in Maria's eyes. Not only had Phil hijacked her news, Harry was treating the whole thing as a joke. He was incorrigible.

She leaned across Charles to Maria and grabbed her hand. 'Maria, I'll come and see you. I'm so looking forward to being an auntie.'

'Thank you,' she said, smiling gratefully.

Poor Maria. Eliza's words had been spur of the moment, based on a sudden protective instinct. She didn't trust Phil, and Cassandra, while well-intentioned, was virulently anti-science. Putting Maria under her care, with no input from medical professionals, was surely a risk.

❀

'Hey Clare,' said Eliza later. 'Can we take a little walk?'

'Love to!'

They set off down the steps to the lawn, and Clare hooked her arm through Eliza's.

Eliza took a breath. She'd been rehearsing what to say.

But Clare spoke first. 'It's lovely to see you and Rob so happy together. He's a real charmer, but genuine with it. I like him very much. And I have to say, he reminds me of Harry.'

That's not helping.

'Clare . . . can I tell you something majorly embarrassing that's worrying me quite a lot?'

'My goodness! Of course you can. Anything at all.'

She swallowed. 'It's . . . well, me and Rob. We haven't . . . slept together. What I mean is, I haven't ever gone all the way. With him or anyone.'

'Oh, I see.'

Eliza glanced at her step-mother. She was looking surprised.

'Well, you once said you wouldn't give it up for anybody! You'll know when the time is right.'

'No – it *is* right. I want to. We tried, but . . .' Eliza stopped walking, her eyes fixed on the ground in front of her.

Clare put an arm round her. 'What happened, sweetheart?'

'I freaked. I couldn't go through with it. I don't understand why.'

'Gosh, Eliza. You poor thing.'

She kept her eyes on the ground. 'Without going into embarrassing detail, we've found ways. Rob's . . . he's quite experienced and he's taught me things, does things . . . So we've done all the other things, but we haven't been all the way.'

She finally looked at Clare. 'I – I don't know what to do.'

'So it's just . . . intercourse that's the problem?'

'Yes.'

'You probably need time, to take things slow.'

'But what if there's something wrong with me? What if bits of me don't work? Or maybe my mind's messed-up?' She heard the note of panic in her voice. 'I thought maybe it was to do with Dad and what happened with Mum – a trusting men thing.'

'Does Harry know?'

'No! God, no.'

They started walking again.

'Talk to Rob, tell him it's a big deal for you. If you love each other, I'm sure it'll work out. Unless . . . ' She frowned.

'Unless what?'

'Well, obviously, if there's been sexual abuse—'

'No. Not that.' She wondered whether to mention Seymour. Did being touched by a pervy uncle count as abuse? It probably did, but she found it hard to believe her problem could stem from that.

'I think . . . maybe I need professional help?'

'I see. Well, I have plenty of contacts through RoseHealth, people in the field of psychiatry and so on. There are probably some sex therapists in there. Do you want me to see if I can find someone?'

'I think I do. I'm scared, Clare. I know I seem really up front, but I find it difficult to talk about. It'll have to be someone I feel comfortable with. Someone like you.'

'Leave it with me, Eliza. I'll be in touch.'

The night before her first session, Eliza couldn't sleep. The thought of talking to a complete stranger about her sex life was terrifying.

But talking to kind, calm Dr Thompson turned out to be easy. It was all so matter of fact, like discussing the weather.

'Now we've talked about the physical side of things,' she said, at the end of the first session, 'I feel we're ready to move on to the psychological side. Next week I'd like to talk about your relationship with your father.'

'Oh god. I knew it.'

'Let's see how we get on. And, Eliza, I think this will work for you. It'll take time, but I can tell you're a very determined young lady.'

Maria's baby bump grew in direct proportion to her waning interest in work. She was transformed – and distracted – by her pregnancy, and by September was only going through the motions. Finally she announced she would leave at the end of October, and began delegating her remaining work to Eliza.

Phil had been picking up Maria's slack, keeping the family values mission on track. But Eliza had been meeting with the heads of department: *Go along with it for now. Can't say too much, but things will change.*

Maria's last day arrived, and staff scraped together enough money for a few baby clothes. Most wrote *Good luck!* and little else in the leaving card. There was no party.

Eliza took over Maria's office, which was the largest on the top floor, though still nothing like the size Harry's had been. That had been turned into a soundproofed crèche. Eliza always enjoyed the surprise on people's faces when they came in for meetings and found themselves walking past a colourful room full of kids.

Harry had been biding his time, and came in the week after Maria's departure, along with Cecil. Phil was in the States. The American would be expecting them to make a move, Harry said, so they needed to tread carefully, time it right. Not yet. Not while Phil was on the alert. They pencilled in a board meeting for the end of the year.

Later, Eliza, Cecil and Harry made their way to The Shard, for a dim sum lunch.

'There's one more coming,' said Eliza as they took their seats. Leigh was several months into her internship, and her managers were keen to keep her on. But Eliza had other plans for her.

She'd given Leigh the venue and time, but hadn't told her who else would be joining them. So her friend's face when she saw Harry was a picture. Eliza grinned as she remembered Leigh sighing over him, back in Oxford: *'Imagine, Harry Rose . . .'*

As Eliza made the introductions, she didn't miss the appreciative look Harry gave her friend. Leigh scrubbed up well in her work clothes, all long dark limbs and glossy black hair, her almond-shaped eyes currently obliterated by stars.

'Delighted to meet you, Leigh,' said Harry. 'I look forward to hearing first-hand what Eliza got up to at Oxford.'

'We're here to talk work, Dad.'

'But it would be impolite to do so straight off. Leigh, come sit beside me, tell me everything.'

Leigh was blushing, giggling.

Chrissake!

'Well, Mr Rose—'

'Call me Harry.'

'She worked very, very hard. She put the rest of us to shame.'

'Well, that's all quite boring. What about the interesting part?'

'OK. She loved a good party. Partial to cider and Pimm's. Would you like to hear how she swam naked in the Isis on the last night of Eights Week?'

'Leigh!' said Eliza. 'Oh god, what have I done?'

Cecil was laughing heartily. Eliza had got to know him better over the past months, and was in awe of his abilities. He'd proved an enormous help, guiding her, teaching her the finer points of corporate management. Most importantly, he'd made it clear that in future, she'd be able to leave most of that to him, enabling her to focus on strategies and ideas. Talking of which . . .

'So can we discuss work now?' she said, interrupting Leigh's description of that time when Eliza and Will had sown cress seeds in their tutor's computer keyboard.

'Perhaps we should,' said Cecil.

'To be continued,' Harry said to Leigh. She was just lifting her glass to her lips when he followed through with a smile and a wink. Leigh mistimed the sip, and wine dribbled down her chin. Embarrassed, she dabbed at it with her napkin.

Really, if Leigh was to come on board at a more senior level, she'd have to get a grip.

'*If* we're all ready?' said Eliza.

'Are we?' said Harry to Leigh.

'I think so,' breathed Leigh.

'As you know, I like to plan ahead,' said Eliza.

'She does,' said Harry to Leigh.

'So once we ... well, once we're able to make decisions unencumbered, I'd like to move my ideas on Rose TV forward.'

'Summarise where you're at,' said Harry.

Eliza felt the rush. She'd been bursting to share more of her thoughts with him. Harry loved a good movie, a well-told story, a great play.

'You know I'm planning a big expansion in the production side of things. Films, TV series, like Netflix. Original content. Here, in the UK, but expanding into the US, selling to the networks over there as well as broadcasting on our own TV channels here. I want to get two writers I know from university on board – Will Bardington and Kit Marley.'

'They're in a league of their own,' said Leigh to Harry.

'Their latest script has been optioned by Rose TV,' Eliza continued. 'And I'd like to involve Leigh on the development side – she's already done a feasibility study on this for her thesis – and Rob on the sales side. We should start small, contracting in the best industry professionals while we're still learning the ropes. We'll need to properly research the market, assess the competition and so on.'

Eliza paused, waiting for Harry's reaction.

He was sitting back in his chair, listening carefully. He looked over at Cecil, raising his eyebrows.

Cecil nodded.

Harry smiled. 'Make it happen, Lizzie.'

Chapter 23

Eliza

Eliza sent a message into the group chat: *Will + Kit – where are you?*

It remained unopened. The boys seemed to have dropped off the face of the planet. It could have been for any number of reasons, but Eliza was hoping it was a creative one.

'If you really want to employ those two, you'll have to take them in hand,' said Rob. He was sitting on Eliza's sofa, flicking through the TV channels while she loaded the dishwasher. 'I mean, you can't have them flouncing around Italy or wherever, just emailing you unfinished bits of things with a vague promise to turn up at some point.'

'Any email would be good. Even a postcard,' said Eliza, sighing. It was frustrating, not being able to get the ball rolling properly on Rose TV, plus she missed the boys. A lot. Especially Kit.

'I wanted to talk about something else,' said Rob. 'You done with the dishes?'

'Sure. Coffee?'

'I'll make it,' he said, getting up. He'd bought her an espresso machine like his own, but she hadn't been able to get the hang of it.

'What did you want to talk about?' she asked, hoping it wasn't her therapy. She'd been keeping him up to date, and he was being wonderfully supportive.

'Well ... us,' he said. He came over, putting his arms around her from behind. 'Amy's coming to terms with things. The divorce will be in the pipeline soon.'

'Thank god for that.'

'So, I was thinking. Now things are progressing, maybe we could move in together? How about it, Lizzie?'

She turned to face him, putting her arms around his neck. 'It's a lovely thought.' She kissed him. 'But like I said before, can we hold off until it's all finalised? I'd rather wait until you're properly free. You know I have to think about my public image.'

'Lizzie, it's the twenty-first century. Nobody gives a stuff if I'm technically still married. I'm separated, I'm getting a divorce. I just want us to be together. I want to come home with you after work, wake up with your crazy hair across my pillow, bring you coffee, go food shopping with you. I want us to be—'

'I'm sorry, Rob. I'm ... it's too soon.'

He kissed her nose. 'Come on. I've been waiting for you since I was eight.'

She smiled. 'Rob, can I be honest? It's not only about my image. I don't think I'm ready for that level of commitment. I love you, so much. But I want to be ... independent. For a bit longer. I like living by myself. I love having you over, going to yours, but keeping my own space. And with so much going on at work at the moment—'

'At the moment? You think that'll change?'

'Well ... probably not, I suppose.'

He looked so disappointed; she felt bad. She wasn't entirely sure why she'd said no, in spite of the reasons she'd given him. It had been a gut reaction.

He sighed, running his fingers through his hair.

'You know I love you, Rob.'

'Do you? You won't sleep with me, you won't live with me. Lizzie, I need more.'

She kissed him again, this time with feeling, and felt him respond. He picked her up and sat her on the countertop. 'Lizzie, I want you so much . . .' He kissed her neck, and she gasped as the sensation zipped down her body.

Things progressed, steamily, but this time took a different turn.

'Can we try?' he said. 'It's been so long.'

She froze. 'You know I'm still having therapy. You said you'd be patient.'

'No one could have been more patient.'

She wondered – should she try again, while her therapy was still ongoing? Showing willing might help smooth things, now she'd turned down his invitation to move in.

'Well . . . I suppose we could give it a go.'

He carried her to the bedroom. This time there was no taking it slow, no waiting for his cue. It was like being ravaged. She could have said stop, but she didn't want to. It was wildly exciting.

Maybe this was the key. Maybe she just had to give in to it, let him do his thing. Lord, but he was on fire, kissing her deeply, losing himself in her, driving her on.

'Yes, Rob. Do it,' she gasped.

But then, out of nowhere, the panic hit and she was fighting him off. She squeezed out from underneath him and flew to the bathroom, slamming the door behind her.

Eliza sat on the edge of the bath, her head in her hands. She was trembling – this time the fear had been more intense than ever.

What's wrong with me?

There was a tap on the door. 'Lizzie? Are you OK?'

She opened it with shaking hands, and he took her in his arms. 'I'm so, so sorry,' he said. 'I should've waited.'

She said nothing.

'Lizzie?' He looked down at her. 'God, you're white as a sheet.'

She pushed him away and grabbed her robe from the bathroom door, quickly putting it on and tightening the belt round her waist.

'Lizzie, for chrissakes. Talk to me.'

But she couldn't. How could she explain, when she didn't

understand herself? All she knew was that right now, she wanted to be alone.

'I'm sorry, Rob, I need some time by myself. To think. I'll call you.'

His expression was bewildered. 'Don't shut me out. I love you, Lizzie. *Please* talk to me.'

'I can't. I need to work things out, and I really, really need to be alone.'

He continued staring at her, and his eyes filled with tears. 'Lizzie—'

'Please! Just go!'

Finally he swung round and returned to the bedroom.

She waited in the hallway until he reappeared.

'I'm so sorry, Rob,' she said, touching his arm. 'I'm messed-up and I need to find out why. I'll call you,' she said again, as he opened the front door.

He looked down at her, went to speak but stopped. He shook his head and closed the door behind him.

Eliza sat on the sofa, staring into space. Her phone, in front of her on the table, vibrated.

KIT: Still in France. You need me?

ELIZA: yes

KIT: Time to come home?

ELIZA: please can you?

For the rest of the week, Eliza avoided Rob.

ROB: How you doing? Please forgive?

ELIZA: Need to see therapist. Give me space? Will be in touch soon x

ROB: OK. Take care. Miss you x

Maybe she was being unreasonable, but she wanted to talk to Dr Thomson before she saw Rob again. Echoes of the fear that had gripped her were ambushing her dreams and distracting her at work. She wondered why, this time, her reaction had been so extreme.

A voice in her head whispered: *He tried to force it.*

She was dismayed when she couldn't get an appointment until Tuesday, the day after a scheduled meeting with Rob, Leigh and Nikki Jones, the Head of Rose TV.

Eliza had moved Leigh across to The Greenhouse, Rose's research department, to further develop the feasibility study for the new production company, working title: RoseGold. And Rob had been seconded from Sales to Production, where he was being mentored by Nikki. This seemed to include much lunching with industry players, of whom, according to Nikki, Rob was already one. 'He's a natural,' she'd said to Eliza. 'And he doesn't half remind me of your dad.'

The meeting was in the Rosebud – the room used for brainstorming sessions. There were beanbags, cubes and cushions, and whiteboards were built into the walls.

When Eliza arrived, Leigh and Rob were already reclined on beanbags, Leigh pointing out something on her laptop to Rob.

'Hi,' Eliza said briskly. 'Sorry I'm late. Leigh, shall we start with your figures?'

'Whoa,' said Leigh. 'Nikki's been delayed, so how about a catch-up with coffee first?'

Suddenly, Eliza had no idea how to do this.

Rob noticed her discomfort. 'Lizzie, how is there not a coffee machine in here? I'll go fetch – maybe you should update Leigh while I'm gone?'

Thank you, you lovely man.

'Sure, thanks, Rob.' Her eyes followed him as he left the room.

'That had the feel of a strategic move,' said Leigh, watching her watching him. 'Are you two having trouble navigating the whole *you're the boss* scenario?'

'It's complicated. I can't really explain, sorry.'

'OK, I won't pry. But I hope things are all right. You two are so good together. The way you spark off each other – I was counting on that as a key driver of our success.'

'We'll get it back. We just need to work some things through.'

Rob returned, and as he passed her a coffee their eyes locked. He smiled, and her heart lifted, the misery of the past week lightening a little.

Nikki arrived, and for the next hour or two Leigh talked them through figures and projections, and Nikki and Rob ran through the production and sales side of things. The marketing department would need to come on board early, Nikki said, as the plan was to start with an announcement – a PR blitz. Rose was going to be a big player in film and TV production.

'Once we have the green light from the board, I'll need Rob on this full time,' she said.

'You OK with that, Rob?' said Eliza.

'More than OK.'

'Good. I *think* Kit and Will are on their way back, though who knows with those two. When they finally show up, we might have to put electronic tags on them.'

Nikki left to pick up her children from the crèche.

'I guess we're just about done, then?' said Rob.

'Quick drink on the way home?' said Eliza.

'Sounds good to me,' said Leigh.

'Sorry, can't,' said Rob. 'In fact ...' He looked at his phone. 'Shit. Late already.'

'Anyone we know?' Eliza said, jokingly.

He paused. 'I'm seeing Amy. I need to talk through some things with her.'

❀

Eliza sat on the sofa, a box of Belgian truffles in her lap. The green-eyed monster was back, and the need for chocolate was overwhelming.

Right now, Rob was with Amy. Where were they? The house that they'd chosen together? A cosy pub?

Sweet, adoring Amy, who'd been more than happy to defer to Rob. No *who's the boss?* issues there. And no bedroom issues, either.

Chapter 24

Eliza

Eliza was back in Dr Thomson's comfy armchair. She picked up her tea and noticed her hand was shaking.

So did Dr Thomson. 'Are you worried about discussing your father, Eliza?'

'Maybe. But, as you know, we have a great relationship. We're close.'

'Nevertheless, it's no secret that he's had quite a ... colourful love life. How do you feel that's affected your own relationships with men?'

'I've only had one. You know about the problem with that.'

Kit's face came to mind. 'OK, maybe two. But the other one ... well, I fell at the first hurdle. Probably just as well,' she added.

'Does what your father thinks of your partners matter to you?'

'Yes.'

'Has he ever discussed his love life with you?'

Eliza shifted uncomfortably. 'Kind of. As you know, I wondered if I had trust issues because of his habit of flipping off one woman and moving on to the next. But we've talked more about all that recently. Things weren't always what they seemed.'

'I see.'

For the next hour, Dr Thomson gently coaxed out Eliza's thoughts about Harry's relationships with women, in particular, his treatment of Ana.

'Maybe, deep down, I hold him responsible for her death,' said Eliza. 'Because he cheated on her, then turned his back on her when she was in danger. And Caitlyn – I loved her. He basically drove her to suicide. If the man I love and respect above all others can behave in that way, how can I bring myself to trust *any* man? How can I let Rob ... well, inside, I guess.' She gave an embarrassed laugh. 'And people keep telling me he's a lot like my dad, which isn't helping.'

'The mind,' said Dr Thomson, 'the way we physically respond to things – everyone's different, things are rarely black and white.' She paused, looking down at her notes. 'Eliza, during our first session you referred to a – let me see – a "creepy uncle".'

'Oh god, Seymour. Yes.'

'You said he touched you inappropriately. When was this?'

Eliza shuddered inwardly. 'A few times, when Dad was married to Seymour's sister, Janette, and then a couple more after she died.'

'So a man into whose care you'd been entrusted abused that trust.'

'Too right he did.'

'And to recap – your trust in your father was perhaps severely compromised when you discovered he ... let's say, he failed to protect your mother and step-mother.'

Was this it? Was this the reason for her problem?

'Dr Thomson ... Rob and me, we tried again. I know I shouldn't have, while I'm still in therapy, but I ... well, I felt I owed it to him.'

'Why did you feel that, Eliza?'

'He asked me to move in with him, and I refused. I felt bad about it; I wanted to show him how much I love him.'

'Why did you say no to moving in?'

'I wanted to keep my independence for a while longer. And he's still married.'

Dr Thomson paused. 'I'd surmise that your reluctance to commit and your response to sex are connected. What happened when you tried?'

'I completely freaked. I couldn't stop shaking.' Eliza finally burst into tears.

Dr Thomson handed her a box of tissues, waiting for her to compose herself.

She took a shaky breath. 'Dr Thomson?'

'Yes, Eliza?'

'If you think it *is* a trust issue – will I ever be able to lose the fear?' Her heart was in her mouth.

'We can devise strategies and see what works for you.'

'How long will it take?'

'Hard to say. We'll probably need another half a dozen sessions, then perhaps you can resume relations with Rob, see how it's working out.'

ELIZA: Hi. I'm getting there. Let's catch up next week?

ROB: Whenever you're ready. Missing you so much xxx

ELIZA: Cool. Will text again soon. Miss you too xxx

'Two visitors in reception for you,' said Pippa that afternoon. 'Will and Kit?'

The PA's mouth dropped open as Eliza flew past her, heading for the lifts.

In the atrium, milling with fashionably dressed Rose employees, the pair stood out a mile in their tatty jeans and misshapen jumpers, their backpacks beside them on the floor.

After the despondency of recent days, Eliza felt an enormous surge of happiness. 'Oh my god, have I missed you two!'

'Likewise, my lovely carrot top,' said Will, squeezing her tight.

She turned to Kit. 'You came. What perfect timing.'

'Come here.'

He wrapped her in a hug, and she felt her angst dissolve, as if he were absorbing it all. She closed her eyes and rested her head on his shoulder.

'Your people are ogling, Eliza,' said Will.

She pulled back. 'Where have you been?' she asked, touching Kit's face. 'What have you been doing?'

'As little as possible. Ran out of money, though.'

'Have you been writing?'

'I started something. What's going on with you?'

'Let's go somewhere more private.'

She called Pippa. 'Hey, I'm taking the afternoon off. Can you reschedule everything?'

'Where are we going?' said Will.

'My place. It's not far to walk. Shall I call Leigh?'

'She's here?' said Will.

'Yes.'

'Then let the party begin.'

So many reasons to let her hair down. So many reasons not to stop at just the two drinks, or three, or four . . .

'Call it a belated celebration,' said Leigh, topping up their glasses. 'Firsts for all five of us. Wish Frankie could be here. Didn't we do gooood?' She looked at Will and Kit, sprawled together on the sofa. 'Though how you two managed it, I'll never understand. Do you have a pact with the Devil or something?'

Eliza put on a playlist from their time at Oxford. 'So – are you in London for good? Where are you staying?'

'We're homeless. But we might not have been as idle as you're supposing,' said Will.

'How so?'

'We're here for job interviews.'

'But—'

'Just in case. You're not the boss lady yet, correct? Do you think your Rob could lend us some suitable clothes? Can't really turn up like this, and we're completely skint.'

'I'm sure he will.' Eliza sighed. 'But I should probably tell you – things between us are a bit tricky at the moment. We're on a sort of break. Just temporary.'

'Why?' said Kit.

'It's complicated.'

'You can tell us,' said Will.

'No, I can't. Anyway, you can stay with me. And I'll take you clothes shopping and get you decent haircuts. Think of it as an advance.'

❀

It was past two in the morning. Leigh had gone home, and Will was asleep on the sofa. Eliza fetched a duvet, and he muttered softly as she arranged it over him. She smiled and kissed his forehead, hit by a wave of wine-induced sentimentality.

Kit was standing by the window. She slid her arms round his waist, resting her head on his back. 'I'm so glad you're here. When you're not around, I feel kind of . . . lost.'

'Let's go for a walk.'

'But it's gone two!'

'Perfect time for a stroll.'

'I always knew you were a creature of the night.'

They walked along the embankment to the looming hulk of the Tower, its boxy symmetry illuminated by floodlights. Out on the river, barges and other Thames workhorses chugged along purposefully and a little mysteriously, their dark, lumbering shapes a contrast to the daytime ferries that scuttled to and fro.

The city's glow radiated upwards, masking the night sky.

London – never quiet, never still. Its long, long history; its hint of magic.

Eliza was reminded of their last night at Oxford.

'Same river,' said Kit.

'Reading my mind again, Marley.'

'It's not that hard, Rose.'

She peered down at the Traitors' Gate below them. 'I walk past this every day, but it still gives me the creeps.'

Kit looked across to the walls of the Tower. 'This whole place screams.'

'I know what you mean.' Eliza shivered.

'That wasn't a cold shiver, but let me warm you up anyway,' said Kit, putting an arm round her.

'I am a tad chilly.'

'You said that once before.'

'Did I?'

'So . . . you and Rob. What happened?'

'He wanted me to move in with him. He tried . . . to rush things, I guess. It was all moving too fast for me – he's still married. I have to think about my public profile. Harry Rose's daughter with a married man. What do you suppose the press would do with that?'

'History repeats.'

'Yep. Marriage-wrecker, just like my mum. And my dad. The part about Rob being separated would be roundly ignored for the sake of a good story. I've been mulling it over.'

Telling Kit about the problem was helping her resolve it in her mind. 'I think we should cool things right down until his divorce comes through.' She snuggled in to Kit. 'And . . . I love him, but I'm just not ready for that level of commitment. Plus there's . . .' She stopped herself. She didn't need to share *everything*.

'The virgin thing?'

She looked at him in surprise. 'Oh, that's embarrassing. How did you know?'

His smile was secretive. 'Intuition.'

'You freak me out sometimes. But . . . yes. I'm getting help. Therapy.'

His smile turned mischievous. 'I could help.' He pulled her closer, and she felt a burst of something as wicked as his smile.

'Stop it, Kit. Do *not* sully our beautiful friendship with your . . . your . . .'

Jesus, his eyes. Those lips.

He was laughing at her. He was too beautiful. He was ...

'Just ... stop it!' She pulled away from him. 'So? Am I doing the right thing, making him wait?'

'When it comes to relationships, I'm probably not the best person to ask.'

'But you know my mind and my heart. Who else would I ask?'

'You already know the answer. Yes, make him wait. Keep control.'

He leaned on the parapet, looking out at the river. 'What's she like, his wife?'

'Quiet. Sweet. A nurse. Bit boring, really.'

'Nurse Nobody or Queen Eliza. A no-brainer for someone like him. No wonder he bailed; his eyes are on the prize.'

'No, he's not like that.' She moved close again. 'He's known me forever. He loves the real me.'

'You sure about that? Rob's a player.'

'Maybe. But I actually think he has a problem with me being the boss.'

'He's an alpha male. Needs to be top dog.'

'But you do like him, right?'

He turned to her. 'Babe, nobody's good enough for you. Apart from yours truly, but I'm a fuck-up. This you know.'

He was smiling, but there was something in his eyes.

'You are, Kit.' She put her arms round his waist. 'Maybe you should have therapy too?'

He snorted. 'Nobody could sort out my shit, believe me.'

'Why don't you tell me about it?'

He pushed her away gently, and set off walking. 'Come on, Rose,' he called over his shoulder. 'Time for bed.'

She hurried to catch up. 'Right. You in yours, me in mine.'

Chapter 25

Eliza

> ELIZA: Lunch tomorrow?

> ROB: We can do better. Dinner? I'll book

> ELIZA: OK. Make it somewhere VERY discreet!

He was already there, sitting by the pub window with a pint. He hadn't noticed her come in, and she stopped for a moment, watching him, her heart in her mouth. Adorable Rob. *Why* couldn't she give herself to him completely?

He spotted her and grinned. 'Lizzie. Figured you might need a large one.' He indicated a gin and tonic.

His eyes were twinkling. He was assuming it was all back on.

She went to sit down opposite, then changed her mind and sat beside him. He kissed her cheek, then, after a moment's hesitancy, her lips.

'I'm sorry,' they both said at once.

'No, I am. Really,' said Eliza. 'I shouldn't have shut you out. Thanks so much for understanding.'

'I shouldn't have pushed it,' he said. 'Hey, I have good news.

Amy's finally playing ball. I've got myself a lawyer – he says the Bali wedding was legal, so we have to do everything properly.'

'Right. How long will it take?'

'Six months to a year. So, Lizzie – we've had some space. We're all good now, right?'

She took a breath, reminded herself what was at stake. 'Well ... yes. But I've been thinking things through, and I've talked some more with Dr Thomson too. I won't go into that now, but we're working on a strategy.'

'That's good.'

'Rob,' she said, meeting his eye. 'I'm sorry, but I want to wait until you're properly free. Divorced.'

He frowned.

'If all goes to plan at the board meeting, I could be CEO soon. The spotlight will be on me, there's no escaping that, and I'd rather be single while that's happening.'

'*Single?* Lizzie—'

'Let me finish. I want the media focusing on my work, my career, my plans for RoseGold. I don't want them diverted by my love life, especially when they're bound to drag up Dad's past again. That's so going to happen if they profile me.'

'I see.' He paused, and shook his head. 'Shit, Lizzie – that's a long time to wait.'

'I know. I'm sorry. It won't be easy.' She smiled. 'But I'm worth the wait, aren't I? And it doesn't mean we can't see each other, as friends and a bit more. A stolen kiss here and there. Could be kind of exciting, right?' She took his hand, holding his gaze, willing him to see things from her point of view.

He was quiet for a moment, considering. 'OK, Lizzie. It sucks, but if that's what it takes. We'll do this on your terms. I'll do what I can to hurry things along with the divorce.'

Her relief was profound. She put her arms round him and kissed his cheek. 'We can have regular catch-ups at Caffé Uno.'

He laughed. 'I guess the best things in life are worth terrible coffee.'

'Rob ... you're my best thing. Always.'

Harry

Phil and Maria were virtual attendees at the board meeting, Phil from New York and Maria from Wales. Their images appeared on the drop-down screen at the end of the boardroom.

The number of board members physically present was down today. Just Harry, John, Cecil, Chess and Eliza. Helena and Margot were voting by proxy again, as were the Morrissey brothers, who had sent their apologies.

'Good morning,' said Phil, with a flash of his ridiculously white teeth. 'And hello, my dear.' He peered at his screen and gave a little wave, which Maria returned with a simper. Really, the pair of them were so off-brand. How on earth had they ended up in charge? They were like a couple of aphids, sucking the life out of Rose, leaving it drooping. Harry couldn't wait to pick them off and squash them.

He gave a small smile. It was about to happen. Everything was in place. Nobody would be pulling anything heinous out of a hat today.

'Shall we begin?' said Eliza, sitting at the head of the table.

Harry allowed himself a moment of pride as he switched his gaze to his other daughter, the antithesis of Maria. Over the months since Maria had left, Eliza had surpassed his expectations, which had already been high. She'd taken on board everything he'd taught her, adding her own touch and inspiring a fierce loyalty in Rose staff even beyond what he'd experienced himself. She listened, she facilitated, she genuinely cared. She brought out the best in people, giving them the opportunity to shine, to be part of the company narrative.

Cecil was hugely impressed by her business acumen and her ability to think strategically, to see beyond the 'what' and the 'how' to the 'why'.

'We have apologies and proxy votes from Helena, Margot, Rich and ... Seymour,' Eliza said. 'I suggest we move immediately to my proposal that the current mission statement be replaced with an update, which will be based on the original drafted by my father and his team.'

'Nothing's changed in terms of numbers since the last board meeting,' barked Maria. 'Why are we doing this, Eliza? You're wasting everyone's time.'

Harry glanced at Phil, but he was looking down, as if examining his fingernails. He probably was. They were as well tended as his teeth.

'I formally propose,' Eliza continued, 'that the current mission statement, as written by Phil and Maria, be superseded by a new one, to be drafted and circulated for approval. Those in favour, please.'

Harry, John, Chess, Cecil and Eliza raised their hands.

'Helena's a yes,' said Chess. Pippa nodded.

'As is Margot,' said Harry. 'She is more easily persuaded of the value of a middle way than you are, Maria. No one likes an extremist. Not even a grumpy aunt.'

Maria's eyes widened, then she pursed her lips. 'That's most disappointing. And rather underhand of you, Father.'

'Needs must. How are those votes stacking up, Cecil?'

'With Armada's reduced shareholding, we have a clear majority.'

Everyone looked at Phil, who snapped back to attention.

'What in the hell do you mean, *reduced shareholding*?'

'I'm afraid we've bought you out, give or take,' said Harry. 'Sorry, old chap. Your Armada's been blown out of the water. You really shouldn't have aimed your cannons at the Brits. It was never going to work. We simply don't enjoy your brand of god bothering.'

Maria sucked in a breath.

'Sorry, Maria. I did try to warn you. Perhaps you should listen next time.'

'Dad—' said Eliza.

'Shall we wrap this up, Lizzie?' Harry looked at his watch.

Maria's image suddenly disappeared from the screen as she cut the connection.

'I'll be in touch,' Phil said abruptly. He still owned around ten per cent of the company shares and therefore would have a degree of influence, but his team of three was now a team of one.

His image disappeared too.

'Oh,' said Eliza. 'I suppose that means . . .'

Maria and Phil's family values mission statement had been metaphorically screwed up, thrown in the bin and set on fire.

'I'd like to propose a second motion,' said Harry. His face broke into a grin. 'That Eliza Rose be voted in as CEO.'

An enormous smile spread across her face. 'Oh!'

'Congratulations, Eliza,' said Cecil, holding out his hand. 'Great things start right here.'

'Hear hear!' said Chess, coming round the table to give her cousin a hug. 'This is wonderful!'

'No more admin for you!' said Eliza.

'Bravo!' said John. 'Splendid!'

'I'll formally request the votes of the absent members,' said Cecil. 'You'll be acting CEO until we get their nods, but I'm sure it'll be a formality.'

As Harry watched Eliza – incredibly, her face was pink – he was overcome with emotion. His little girl, the apple of his eye, his true heir.

'Write your name across the sky, my darling girl,' he said, hugging her tight.

❀

'Watch Seville ditch Maria now,' said Harry, as he and Eliza headed off to lunch.

'I don't think so, Dad. She's his dream subservient woman, and soon she'll be the mother of his child. And didn't I tell you to stop being mean about her?'

'So magnanimous in victory. Let's just say, certain things came to light during our tit-for-tat raid on his shares. He's not a person I want involved in my grandchild's life.'

'What things?'

'Need-to-know basis. Useful if we have to go to war again at some point.'

'Gosh, Dad. You're always one step ahead. I still have lots to learn.'

'You're doing way better than fine. Where are you taking us?'

'The pub. There are two people I want you to meet.'

'Is Rob joining us?'

Eliza looked at him, and he saw her elation fade for a moment. What was going on there? Studley had better not be messing her about.

'No, Leigh and Rob won't be coming today. I wanted you to meet the creatives.'

'Your university pals?'

'Yes. Hence the pub. I thought informal would be best.'

Entering The George, Eliza led the way over to two tall, skinny lads with a lot of hair between them, drinking pints at the bar. She introduced the one facing Harry as Will Bardington.

Harry shook his hand. 'Delighted, Will.'

'Likewise, Harry.' He had lively brown eyes, and a high forehead from which brown curls cascaded. 'A pleasure to meet the father of our lovely Eliza. We couldn't adore your daughter more.'

The blond one was . . . good lord. When he turned round, Harry found himself face to face with a disconcertingly beautiful boy with the most unusual gold-coloured eyes.

'This is Kit Marley,' said Eliza.

Harry didn't miss the way she briefly touched his arm, and got a smile in return that spoke of a close intimacy.

What was going on here? Was this why there was a problem with Rob?

'Good to meet you, Harry.' There was a knowingness about the boy, as if he'd figured Harry out even before he'd said a word.

'And you, Kit,' he said, shaking hands.

'Dad – Will and Kit are utter geniuses, ready to take the world by storm with our productions. And yes, that build-up is entirely justified.'

They found a table, and Will and Kit took Harry through some of their ideas for drama and film. Will spoke with actorish aplomb, his eyes alight. Occasionally he'd pause, and Kit would lob in a sentence or two that beautifully enhanced Will's words. The boys' eloquence, their vocabulary, was extraordinary.

'Well, chaps,' Harry said, as Will finished with a flourish. 'I very much like the sound of this, and RoseGold has my full support. Anything you need.' He held out his hand, and the boys shook it, grinning. 'Having said that, Eliza's in charge now, of course.'

'Officially!' she said. 'I'm acting CEO, as of today. Maria and Phil have been voted out.'

'Hallelujah!' said Will. 'All hail Eliza.'

Kit gave her a small smile. 'And so it begins.'

She held his gaze, and as Harry saw the look in them, he wondered again about Rob.

He narrowed his eyes. There was something most unsettling about this boy. A sexual magnetism and . . . a hint of something dark. He had an air of detachment, yet the connection between him and Eliza positively sizzled.

Kit was *not* what a father would want for his daughter.

'While I'll help in whatever way I can,' he said, 'one has a yacht to catch.'

'Already, Dad?'

'After Christmas. Off to LA, then sailing down the coast.'

'With Frankie on board! How brilliant.'

'Indeed. My spies tell me she's getting on *exceptionally* well with Captain Yates.' Harry winked.

'Honestly. How is your spy network more efficient than me messaging Frankie?'

'This is true. And don't you forget it.'

Eliza

Harry and Eliza headed back, leaving Will and Kit in the pub.

'Let's walk by the river,' said Harry, as they reached Bankside.

'OK. So – how do you like Will and Kit?'

'You did well, getting them on board. I don't think I've met anyone quite like them in all my time in this business.'

'There's something about them.'

'Will's use of language is remarkable. His way of describing things. Does that come across in his work?'

'Oh yes.'

'Kit – I think the darker of the two? More complex? You and he seem ... close?' He gave her a searching look.

'We are. He understands me – he's my soulmate.'

'I see. He's not responsible for ... are there problems with Rob?'

'No. Well, sort of. I've told Rob I want to cool things between us, until his divorce comes through. I thought that would be sensible, given my new role. There's bound to be media interest.'

'Wise move. Well done.'

'And it's nothing to do with Kit. He doesn't do relationships. His behaviour would make even *your* toes curl.'

'Ah. I got some sense of that.' Harry looked relieved.

'He and Will are staying with me at the moment. I love hanging out with them.'

'And your thing with Kit; it's definitely platonic?' That penetrating gaze.

'Like I said, yes. Why? Don't you like him?'

'He's ... hard to pin down.'

Eliza grinned. 'Give up now.'

'And he's ... well, quite something to look at.'

She chuckled, and nudged him. 'Do you fancy him, Dad?'

'Don't be ridiculous,' he spluttered. 'But I wonder ... is his creativity perhaps enhanced by something? I have some experience with addiction.'

Her smile faded. 'I think Kit does whatever it takes to produce his best work. But he doesn't need chemicals to kick his brain into the zone. It's phenomenal. The things he sees, knows. The way he can read my mind. It's like he's my ... I don't know. My shadow. Always there, even when he's not.'

They stopped and leaned on the parapet, looking down at the sludgy water slapping the wall below them.

Eliza thought back. 'Something strange happened with me and him on our last night at Oxford. I should probably mention we'd had a few wines, but even so it was ... I can't explain it. Kit said some of us exist outside of time. And then ... time seemed to actually stop. I swear – my phone proved the fact. Does that sound mad?'

She was expecting one of Harry's cutting comments, but instead he said, 'No, it doesn't.' He seemed to be weighing up whether to tell her something. 'There have been times when I've felt something similar. When Ana and Janette died, and when I was in a drug-induced half sleep. And ... I've never told anyone this before. When I was shot, I had what I believe is called a near-death experience.'

Eliza looked at him in surprise. While Harry was a deep thinker, and loved to talk philosophy, he rarely discussed religion or spirituality. His views on Maria's faith were scathing, and she'd always assumed he had zero belief in an afterlife, or any realms other than the one in which he existed, here and now.

'Seriously?'

'Clearly the brain at these times does things far beyond our comprehension. I've read about it. Quite a lot.'

'What happened?'

'My mind – maybe my soul, whatever it was. It was outside my body. I could see myself, below. There were others in the room, as well as the surgeons and nurses. Not people – shadows. Presences. They were discussing whether I should live or die. Whether I'd made amends for ... a past life, I think. Or maybe this one.'

'My god.' Eliza was shaken. Every time she thought she understood her father, some new insight would blindside her.

'I've come to the conclusion it was my brain shutting down,' he said, staring out at the river. 'All that stuff on my conscience taking on some form of imagined reality. Who knows? But it's stayed with me. The mind, Lizzie. It's an unknown realm, wouldn't you say?'

She took Harry's arm and leaned her head on his shoulder. 'They let you live. You must have come right in this life.'

'*There are more things in Heaven and Earth . . .*'

'Oh my god. Don't *you* start.'

Harry laughed. 'Young Will does like his Shakespeare.'

'Thanks for sharing that. Have you ever told Clare?'

'No. Only you. And it's between us. One doesn't want to sound like a fruitcake.'

'Hardly. Your mind's the sharpest I know.'

He patted her hand. 'Well, I have to say, that was all quite existential for a Tuesday lunchtime.'

'I do love you, Dad.'

'And you're my best girl, Lizzie. But we'd better go. You have an empire to run.'

Chapter 26

Eliza

ROB: Happy Christmas Snow White! xxxx Love the
Ray-Bans and the leather jacket but most of all the
box of hair products. Haha. Did you like my presents?

ELIZA: The necklace is beautiful Rob. Thanks SO
much! Also the Chanel handbag full of Smarties.
Perfect! Love you and really wishing we were
together today xxxx

ELIZA: Happy Christmas Mr Marley. Kind of speechless
when I opened your present. Was going to ask how
you knew. Then I remembered, you just do. ILY xxxx

On Boxing Day evening, the family was sitting by the fire in the
drawing room. Clare was reading her novel, while Harry, Eliza
and Eddie were deep into a game of Scrabble.

Eliza and Harry were well-matched and hugely competitive,
while Eddie wasn't really concentrating, busy on his phone.

After many an hour pitched against Will and Kit, Eliza's
vocabulary was pleasingly vast. (Will, however, was a terrible

cheat, always making up new words.) Harry was irritatingly good at slipping high-scoring letters into gaps, and also had a knack of using triple-word scores that seemed unreachable.

Earlier, Harry had taken a call from Cassandra. 'I could hear her quite clearly,' he said, 'considering she's in Wales.'

Eddie rolled his eyes.

'Was she phoning about Maria?' said Clare, looking up from her book. 'How is she?'

'I'm afraid Cass has some concerns, though you know what I think about her *wellness* philosophies.' He slid an E, an X and an E onto Eliza's *CUTE*. The X was on a triple-letter score. 'Thirty-two, I think you'll find, Lizzie.'

'What concerns?' said Eliza, pursing her lips.

'She was quite vague. I think perhaps one of you should speak to Cass – Clare? You're the nurse.'

'She must be due any time?' said Eliza.

'That's the thing. Apparently Maria's being quite obtuse about it. And Cassandra's focus on everything natural isn't helping. There's been no monitoring or scans, any of that. Cass said that was Maria's choice, because if any problems *had* been detected, she's anti-intervention anyway. Couple of nutters, the pair of them.'

'She told me she was pregnant back in June,' said Eliza. 'I think she said she was due end of December or January.'

'What exactly are Cassandra's concerns, Harry?' said Clare.

'She thinks Maria's small for her dates. And apparently Maria's upset because Phil's hardly been in touch. What did I tell you, Lizzie?'

'Perhaps I should go to Wales and make sure she's all right?' said Clare.

'You won't have time. I don't want to put off flying to LA.'

'I'll go,' said Eliza. 'I can take a couple of days off work. Cecil's got everything under control.'

'It's so nice to see you two getting on,' said Clare, 'after all these years.'

'That *might* be putting it a bit strongly, especially after the last board meeting. But I want to make sure she's OK. She was so happy about this baby. It would be terrible if anything went wrong because nobody's checking up on her.'

She placed QUEENLY on a double-word score and wrote down *38*.

❋

Celtic Mists Wellness Retreat was exactly as Eliza remembered. Her last visit had been for Katie's fiftieth birthday celebration, thirteen, maybe fourteen years go. Katie had died a few years later, and Cassandra now ran the retreat by herself.

The front door of the rambling Welsh stone house flew open and Cassandra greeted her with a hug. She wore leggings and a brightly coloured hand-knitted sweater, her feet in sheepskin slippers. She hadn't changed a great deal, but her long frizzy hair, held back with a scarf, had gone grey.

'Eliza, darling! Good heavens, look at you! You're the very image of your parents. You have your mum's eyes, but otherwise you're all Harry.'

Eliza hadn't realized Cassandra had known her parents as a couple. This trip was suddenly looking more interesting.

As they went inside, the smell of the place – a blend of old carpet and pot pourri – took Eliza straight back.

'I'll show you to your room, then we'll have a cup of tea. Maria's having a nap. I'm so pleased you're here; she needs a friend.'

It was the same room she'd stayed in as a child. As she unpacked her bag, she looked out of the old sash window with its deep stone windowsill, to the rolling hills beyond, remembering. Her eyes fell on the vegetable garden below, and for a moment she saw Katie, trowel in hand, looking up at the window and waving.

Eliza felt a pang of loss. She'd usurped Katie's own daughter in Harry's affections, but Katie had never shown resentment, had never said a word against Harry. No wonder he still called her Saintie Katie.

Back downstairs, as Cassandra brewed tea, she repeated her concerns about Maria. 'She seems distracted, worried. Phil's only visited her once. I didn't like him at all – he more or less dismissed my way of life because it doesn't include God; only nature and the human spirit.'

'Phil the Fraud,' said Eliza, sitting down at the familiar scrubbed pine table. 'Making billions out of evangelizing. It can't be right. His TV ratings are huge, and so are his advertising rates. All of which means he can generously donate to the political party that will advance his sexist, bigoted aims. I don't trust him, not one bit.'

'Heavens, Eliza. You've marked his card.'

'Dad thinks he only took up with Maria to get a foot in the door of a British media company. He could be right, but Maria's mad about Phil. Anyway, Dad kicked him into touch at the last board meeting, so he's got next to no influence at Rose now.'

'Good old Harry. I was always a massive fan.' She placed a mug of tea the colour of urine in front of Eliza.

'He liked – likes – you too.'

'No, you were right the first time. We got on like a house on fire when I was still with Charles. Everything changed when ... well, when Katie lost another child. I blamed myself when she went into early labour, after a row between Megan and me. Poor Katie. Your mum was there when it happened. It was what pushed me into rehab.'

Eliza sat up straighter. 'Did you know Mum well?'

'No, I only met her twice. That first time was before Ana and your dad were together, obviously. But I do remember Harry watching her that night – it was *The Rack*'s launch party. She looked stunning. Poor Katie was seven months pregnant; she felt like a lump next to your mum. Ana was with her fiancé.'

'Percy?'

'That was it. Wavy fair hair. Smiley.' Cassandra pushed a plate of muesli slices across the table. They looked like squares of gravel. 'Poor man never stood a chance once Ana caught Harry's eye.'

'Well, I'm kind of glad she did.'

'Haha, yes. Worked for you! But, Eliza, I've been thinking about Katie, what with my worries about Maria. She had a terrible time of it with her fertility problems. Stillbirths, miscarriages; she really went through the mill. It made me think – even though Maria's set on natural childbirth, and I'm all in favour of that – maybe we should get her checked out. I don't want something going wrong and then having Phil sue me for lack of care or whatever. I suggested a check-up, but she refused. I'm worried she's got her dates wrong – she's not as big as she should be.'

Eliza sipped the tea, trying not to grimace. She couldn't identify the flavour, but in an attempt to rescue her tastebuds took a bite of the muesli slice. Matters didn't improve.

'The dates sounded right to me,' she said, after ungluing her teeth. 'Could the baby just be small?'

'I don't know. Something's not right. See what you make of it, when she comes down.'

◈

A little later, as Eliza lay on her bed reading the latest draft of Will and Kit's script (this was going to be *huge*), she heard movements in Maria's room next door. She slid off the bed and made her way onto the landing.

'Maria, it's Eliza,' she said, tapping on the door. 'Can I come in?'

Her sister was dressed in a maternity top and leggings. Eliza tried to keep her eyes on Maria's face.

'Cassandra told you I was coming?'

'Yes. I suppose it's nice of you to visit.'

'So your due date's the middle of January?'

'I feel it will be soon.' Maria stroked her rounded stomach, and Eliza finally looked down. Cassandra was right – from Eliza's admittedly sketchy knowledge of these things, that didn't look like a full-term bump.

Rather than stare, she looked around the room. There was a beautiful bassinet draped in white lace, and neatly arranged on shelves were folded piles of baby clothes and nappies, and a baby monitor still in its box.

'Shall we take a walk outside?' said Maria. 'I could do with some fresh air.'

'So you've been feeling well?' Eliza said, as they opened the gate to the field beyond the garden. The sun had already dipped behind the hills, casting the valley into shade. Frozen puddles cracked beneath Eliza's boots.

'Very well, yes. And you? How are things?'

'Oh, you know. Work's fine, but my love life's slightly shambolic.'

'No, I didn't know.' Maria looked over at Eliza, considering. 'We've never really had those conversations, have we?'

'How's Phil?'

'Very busy. He gets in touch when he can. He's looking forward to our baby's arrival, obviously. He likes Elijah for a boy, Sarah for a girl.'

'Lovely! Eli or Sarah. Aunt Eliza heartily approves.'

'I'm afraid Phil doesn't approve of *you* at all. He thinks you're ...'

'In league with the devil?'

Maria smiled. 'Something like that. But I'm glad you're in charge at Rose now.'

'You are? Why? I thought you'd be angry.'

'When you fall in love and have a family, then you'll realize what's really important in life. But in the meantime ... I like seeing you doing well.'

Eliza looked at her sister in astonishment. Could love really change a person so profoundly? Maria's fire had been well and truly doused.

'OK, I have to ask – who are you, and what have you done with the real Maria?'

'Pregnancy truly is an amazing gift.'

Eliza told Cassandra she agreed – the bump looked too small. Maria should be checked out.

'If she won't be examined by a doctor, maybe a midwife? One who's into natural childbirth?'

'Worth a try,' said Cassandra.

By the end of the following morning they'd found one they thought might meet with Maria's approval. Bronwyn Morgan offered to come over.

They told Maria over lunch – bowls of Cassandra's homemade watercress consommé. Eliza tried not to gag as the soup, which tasted like washing-up liquid, slipped down her throat. It was all coming back to her now – Cassandra's cooking. She remembered how the food, and Maria's cruel words, had made her desperate to go home to London.

'So the midwife's views are entirely in line with yours, Maria,' said Cassandra. 'No drugs, no intervention. I'd like her to attend the birth, and thought it would be useful for you to meet her first, so the two of you can discuss your birth plan.'

'I don't make that plan, God does,' said Maria.

'Yes, well. But you're happy to meet with her?'

Maria looked mutinous. 'I'm not doing any tests. And I don't want to be prodded.'

'No prodding,' said Eliza. 'We promise.'

◉

Bronwyn was small and brisk, middle-aged, with short grey hair. Cassandra reiterated Maria's wish for everything about the birth to be natural.

'I've brought many a little life into this world,' Bronwyn said, in a strong Welsh accent, 'without the need for anything more than a big push from Mum and a helping hand from me.'

Cassandra took Bronwyn upstairs then joined Eliza back in the kitchen.

They were still washing up the lunch things when Bronwyn reappeared. 'Eliza? Maria would like to see you, dear. Cassandra, could I have a word?'

Eliza's heart sank as she noticed Bronwyn's troubled expression. She made her way upstairs, finding herself slowing down as she neared Maria's room.

What had Bronwyn discovered about the baby? About Eliza's little niece or nephew – Dad's first grandchild. Was there something terribly wrong with it? She went cold at the thought.

She tapped on the door and opened it.

Maria was curled up on the bed, her eyes wide and staring.

Eliza hurried over. 'Maria! What's wrong? Is the baby all right?' She sat down beside her and stroked her back.

Maria turned her head and met Eliza's gaze. The despair in her eyes was heart-wrenching.

'Maria?'

'I don't understand, Eliza. I don't understand.'

'What don't you understand?'

'It can't be true. Tell me it's not true.' Her voice rose. 'Who is that woman? Did God send her?'

'Bronwyn's an experienced midwife. What did she say, Maria?'

Cassandra and Bronwyn came in, and Maria started to cry. Great, heaving sobs.

'Eliza?' said Bronwyn in a low voice, beckoning. She took her onto the landing. 'Did she tell you?'

'No. Is the baby . . . is there something wrong with it?'

Bronwyn put a hand on her arm. 'There is no baby, Eliza. I'm afraid it's a phantom pregnancy.'

'*What?*'

'I examined Maria, and persuaded her to do a urine test, which confirmed my suspicions. It's all in her mind.'

Eliza's hand flew to her mouth. 'But . . . the bump. Surely that's not possible?'

'Phantom pregnancies are rare, Eliza. There's usually a psychological reason. Sometimes when a woman's desperate for a child – *really* desperate – the mind tricks the body into thinking it's pregnant. All the symptoms are there. It can be so powerful that hormones are produced – the stomach enlarges, the breasts swell; there might even be milk.'

'Oh my god. Poor Maria.'

Eliza was reminded of her conversation with Harry, about the power of the mind. 'Poor, poor Maria. How will she ever get over this?'

Chapter 27

Eliza

'How do we tell her husband?' asked Cassandra as they drank tea in the kitchen. Eliza made it this time – camomile, to calm the nerves.

The midwife had advised them to let Maria rest, to give her time to come to terms with this heartbreaking situation. Once she accepted the truth, her bump would disappear – although Bronwyn recommended a thorough check to rule out anything else that might have caused the symptoms. Cysts were mentioned, but the other word beginning with C hung in the air.

'Surely she should tell Phil herself,' said Eliza. '*I* don't want to tell him. When was he next due to come?'

'Not until the birth.'

'What a supportive partner. He probably thinks it's all women's work, just wants to be presented with a pretty, pink, sweet-smelling baby when it's all over.' She sighed. 'I suppose I'll have to tell Dad. I actually think he was quite excited about being a grandpa.'

Cassandra smiled. 'He'd make a good one. I remember him with Maria when she was small. He was lovely with her.'

'I wonder when that changed? He's quite mean to her now.'

'Well, you know Maria's history. She went from two happy

adoring parents to a chronically depressed mother and a father who was never there. There was a time when only the housekeeper paid her any attention.'

Eliza put down her mug on the table with a bang, making Cassandra jump. 'I'm going for a walk – and I'll ring Dad.'

She strode across the fields, keeping up a brisk pace against the cold – and as an outlet for her frustration. Eventually, feeling calmer, she climbed onto a wooden gate and sat looking out across the valley. Little clouds formed in front of her face as she breathed deeply, letting the natural beauty wash over her.

No wonder Katie and Cassandra had settled here. She was beginning to understand what they'd been running away from.

There was only one feeble bar on her phone, but she gave it a go.

'Lizzie! How's Welshness?' said Harry.

She didn't bother with the preliminaries. 'Dad. It's not good news. For reasons that are quite difficult to understand, Maria's not pregnant after all. She just imagined she was.'

'What? You mean . . . a phantom pregnancy?'

'Yes. All the symptoms, but no baby. She's devastated.'

'My god.'

For a moment, neither said anything. Eliza remembered her sister's words, spoken only yesterday, about the power of love, about what really mattered.

'Dad, I think you need to come to Wales.'

'Can't. We're flying out in a couple of days.'

He really didn't get it.

'No, Dad. You *need* to come to Wales.'

'She's got you there, she doesn't need me.'

The anger made a swift return. 'For god's sake, Dad! What if it was me? Would you come if it was me?'

'Well . . . yes. But you and I are close.'

She gripped the phone harder. 'And why do you think that is?'

'Because we get on. Because you're my—'

'Favourite?'

'What's your point, Lizzie?'

'That list of women you've treated badly in your past. You might want to add your daughter to it.'

He went quiet. 'Where's all this coming from? Ah, wait. Have you been discussing me with Cassandra?'

'Yes, but this is coming from me. She mentioned how lovely you were with Maria when she was little. Then it seems you pretty much ignored her. No wonder she's such a screw-up. Have you never thought perhaps *you* might have something to do with that?'

'Is that what you believe?' She heard it in his voice. Her answer mattered to him.

'You know what? All my life, people have told me how I'm the apple of your eye. Your favourite. And all this time I basked in it. What must that have been like for Maria? If you don't want another messed-up woman on your conscience, you should come to Wales. And don't say you can't. We have an airline. Reckon you can rebook that ticket.'

Harry arrived the next day. Cassandra and Eliza had spent the morning with Maria, reassuring her that she and Phil would still be able to have a family once she got over this upset.

Eliza spotted the Aston Martin coming up the driveway, and they went out to meet him.

'Look at him, Eliza,' said Cassandra, nudging her. Harry appeared out of the beautiful car, dressed in jeans and a chunky cream sweater.

'That's just so unfair on other men.'

Eliza snorted. 'Please stop. I have issues with women finding my father sexually attractive.'

'Hello!' said Harry, slamming the car door and coming over. 'Cass, darling. So good to see you – it's been a while.'

'Harry. It's wonderful that you've come. I think you and Maria will both benefit from some healing time together.'

'Hm. We'll see. Just doing as I'm told, as per. The Rose women are very much in charge now. Frightening times.'

'Come and see Maria,' said Eliza.

'Already?'

'Yes, already.'

Harry

Eliza put a hand on Harry's arm and said, 'Don't blow this, Dad. Be kind. Think back to that little girl Cassandra was telling me about, the one you adored. Not the difficult one.'

He tapped on the living room door and opened it. Maria was sitting by the fire, staring into the flames. She looked up as he shut the door behind him, and the grief in her eyes took him straight back.

Katie.

He swallowed. That expression – it was Katie's, after the loss of Summer, their first stillborn child.

He hurried over. 'My poor girl,' he said, wrapping her in a hug.

Her tears came, and for a long while neither said a word.

'Are there tissues?' he said, gently letting her go.

'Yes,' she said, sniffing. 'But they're so organic they disintegrate with one nose blow.'

Harry laughed, glad she'd offered a way back to the light. 'Cassandra hasn't changed, then.'

He pulled up a chair next to hers. 'She and Eliza have filled me in on what's happened. I couldn't be more sorry. About ... well, all of it. What's happened to you here; our disagreements at work. Not being around enough when you were little. I fear I may be responsible for—'

'My unhappiness? Partly, Father. But you weren't responsible for Mother's death. I'm still trying to get over that. She was all I had, until I met Phil.'

'You had me, and Clare and Eliza.'

'No, I didn't. You've always excluded me.'

He was quiet for a moment. 'Perhaps. I'm sorry. Will Phil come to take care of you?' He acknowledged the passive-aggressive element in that question. Maybe the best he could do for Maria in the short term was to prepare her for what was surely to come.

'He doesn't know what's happened. I can't face telling him. I don't know how to.' The tears started again. 'How could God be so cruel? I can't understand why He'd do this to us.'

Her words gave him another jolt. They were Katie's, after one of her miscarriages.

'You know I'm not a believer, Maria. But that tired old cliché *Everything happens for a reason* – perhaps there's something in it. We've all noticed how you've changed since you met Phil. You've become a warmer person, and people have responded to that. It'll take you a while to get over this, but try and hold on to happy Maria; let go of angry Maria. Be part of the family. Eliza's always tried to be your friend. Don't push her away any more. Or me.'

'Thank you, Father. For coming today. I do feel a bit better now.'

'Would you like to join us on *Janette*? A spot of California sun could be just the ticket.'

'It's kind of you to offer, but I want to be with Phil.'

Harry bit his tongue. She'd learn the truth, soon enough. And when she did, she was going to need her family. Thanks heavens Eliza had made him come.

'Very well. But if you change your mind, there's a berth with your name on it, less than a day away. It would mean a lot to me if you came. Remember that, sweetheart.'

Harry joined Eliza and Cassandra in the kitchen.

'Maria's gone for a lie down. Any chance of a cup of tea? None of your herbal nonsense, Cass. Just a good strong brew of English breakfast.'

'Well, Dad?'

'There were hugs, Lizzie.'

'Seriously. How did it go?'

He sat down. 'You were right, as usual. I don't have the greatest report card where number one child's concerned. I've promised to try and make amends, if it's not too late.'

'That's great. I'm so pleased.'

'She doesn't want to come back to work yet. I think it's time we contacted Phil, put him in the picture.'

Maria joined them for dinner, and sat quietly as Harry and Cassandra shared memories. She was calmer, her eyes less haunted.

Afterwards, Harry went into Cassandra's office to call Phil.

He was teeing off in Hawaii.

Hawaii. The man who claimed family was 'at the true heart of Christian life' was playing golf on a tiny dot in the Pacific, on or around the due date of his first child. Even Seville's private jet with a helpful tailwind from God couldn't make Wales in less than twenty-four hours.

Nevertheless, the poor blighter was in for a shock and Harry thought it kindest to tell him quickly, before he had the chance to assume Harry was ringing with good news.

'Harry?'

'I'm most dreadfully sorry, Phil. I'm afraid it's bad news.'

'Bad news?'

'Maria's ... unwell. Mentally, rather than physically.' He explained about the phantom pregnancy.

Phil was silent.

'So I'm afraid she's going to need some time to get over this,' Harry finished. 'Shall I go get her, so you two can talk?'

'No.' There were voices in the background, then Phil called, 'Play on, I'm nearly through here.'

Harry bristled at his casual tone.

'You might call it an illness, Harry,' said Phil. 'I would call it the hand of God.'

'What?'

'It's clearly a sign, a judgement on our marriage. I will need to pray to Him for a way forward.'

'Your way forward needs to be off that golf course and onto

a plane. Eliza and I are supporting Maria, but it's you she wants to see.'

'I'll be in touch, Harry. Thanks for calling.'

It had taken less than five minutes.

Harry's blood was boiling as he returned to the kitchen.

He filled Eliza and Cassandra in. 'He's waiting for guidance on a way forward,' he said. 'A way out, he means. And good bloody riddance.'

❀

As Harry hugged Eliza goodbye, she said quietly, 'Another big tick on that conscience score card, Dad. You're getting there.'

Maria would stay on for a while under Cassandra's care. She'd have counselling at the retreat, and Cassandra would arrange a doctor's appointment to make sure she was physically fit. Maria would let Harry and Eliza know her plans once she'd talked to Phil.

Harry had a bad feeling about that.

Chapter 28

Eliza

Another grim January to get through. So many months before the return of the warm weather. So many long dark nights to come, the face-numbing walks to work, the trees devoid of leaves, no flowers, the bitter wind whipping across London Bridge. And tights. Every day.

Eliza and Cecil were finalising the structure and logistics of RoseGold. Rob was now working full time with Leigh in the Greenhouse, while Kit and Will were on contracts, working from home while RoseGold was still in development. They'd been burning the midnight oil while Eliza was away, refining *Most Human of Saints*.

As she lay on the sofa, listening to them running through their latest revisions, it was like being back in their English tutorials. This was her happy place. Will was reading More's lines, and Kit Henry VIII's. The king was battling his conscience, deciding the fate of the saintly humanist, perhaps the greatest mind of his time. And, as Will pointed out, an Oxford man.

Kit was cross-legged on the floor, while Will was striding about delivering his lines with feeling. At one point Eliza interrupted. 'Henry wouldn't say that. He needs to be more conflicted.'

'Yep, flag that line, Will,' said Kit. 'He's got Anne Boleyn on one shoulder and his conscience on the other. How does he feel about that choice? Anger and self-loathing. He knows a sentence of treason is morally wrong, but there's no way he can turn back now.'

'Poor man,' said Eliza.

'Tyrant,' said Will.

'Both,' said Kit.

Later, as they tucked into bowls of noodles, Will said, 'Eliza, sweetness. As the Bard said, unbidden guests are often welcomest when they're gone. Should we be looking for our own place?'

'Stay as long as you want. No, scrub that. Never leave? But I might have to teach you to cook.'

A few days later, the weather turned bitterly cold, and snow was threatening. Eliza was still at her desk at eight o'clock, reading over the draft press release announcing the expansion of Rose TV into RoseGold. She should go home, but the walk wasn't appealing.

ELIZA: You guys home?

WILL: In the Dickens. Great pies. Also quiz night – Kit and me are killing it. Coming?

ELIZA: See you there

As she put down her phone, there was a tap on her door. She looked up.

Shit.

It was the first time she'd seen Phil in anything other than a suit. The black on black of his trousers and turtleneck sweater emphasized the alarming brilliance of his teeth and eyes – and the way those eyes ran over her made her stomach turn.

She was alone on the top floor, apart from a cleaner she could hear vacuuming in the reception area.

'Phil, what a surprise!'

'I'm glad I caught you, Eliza.' He shut the door behind him. *How did he know I'd still be here?*

'I'm going to see Maria tomorrow. I thought it would be good to talk to you first.'

So far, so normal brother-in-law.

'That's great news. She's been longing to see you. Have a seat – would you like something to drink? Tea? Beer?'

'Beer, sure. Make it a large one.'

That didn't sound very evangelical.

She went over to her mini-fridge and poured him a glass. As she returned to her seat, he stared at her legs. Blatantly. *Nothing subtle about that at all.*

Her spine prickled as she remembered the last time she'd been alone with him. It would be prudent to let someone know she was up here with Phil.

'Sorry, I just need to send a text. I'm meeting our creatives. I'll let them know I might be late.'

ELIZA: R u still here? Phil's turned up in my office. Feeling nervous

ROB: Yep. Shall I come check on you in 5?

ELIZA: Thank you x

'I'm so sorry about the baby, Phil. Such an awful thing to happen to you and Maria.'

Phil crossed one leg over the other and sipped his beer, watching her carefully. 'God works in mysterious ways, Eliza.'

'So does the human mind. She wanted a child so badly she had all the symptoms. I'm afraid she was in a terrible state when she found out there was no baby. But I think she'll come right, with your love and understanding.'

'Eliza. Nothing makes sense if you don't look at it in the context of God's will. Why did God afflict Maria with a phantom pregnancy? Was it to punish me for being tempted by her position here at Rose, rather than by her suitability as a helpmate, which is what God intends a wife to be?'

'Or perhaps it wasn't all about you? For goodness' sake, don't say such a thing to Maria. She's still very fragile. We need to give her all the support we can to get over this.'

'Maria will be guided by her husband and by God. Not by her sister. I have to decide how to move forward.'

'You do still love her, right?'

'Maria was everything I was looking for in a wife.'

'Was?'

'I'm seeking God's guidance.'

Eliza couldn't contain her anger any longer. 'For heaven's sake, Phil. Look, I'm no psychiatrist, but Maria had a troubled childhood. I expect her longing for a family has something to do with that. Her mum had similar issues – depression, fertility problems. She's getting counselling, but she needs *you*. Go and support her, talk to her. Love her. Don't *blame* her, or God.'

Phil's demeanour changed. The faux-troubled expression disappeared. He smiled, and stood up. In his black clothes, with his black hair, he was like a tall shadow.

Eliza's heart began to thump.

'I'll talk to Maria,' he said, 'but, frankly, I'm not sure she and I have a future together.'

Looks like Dad was right all along.

'But surely – you wouldn't leave her? How would that fit in with your "till death us do part" vow? Aren't your lot anti-divorce? I know Maria's are.'

'Corinthians tells us a Christian is not obliged to stay with a spouse who does not share his religious viewpoints, and that this justifies seeking a divorce.'

'But she *does* share your viewpoints!'

'We disagree on many points of doctrine.'

'You guys can always find a Bible quote to back up your

self-serving views. I bet there are plenty of other parts that say divorce is wrong.'

'So you know your Bible, do you, Eliza? Are you able to give an example of such a quote?'

'Enough, Phil. You need to leave. And you should know that I loathe everything you stand for. You're sexist, you have no compassion, and you don't deserve my sister.' Eliza stood up, heading for the door, but Phil blocked her path. He looked down at her, breathing heavily.

'While you,' he said, 'are shameless, with your short skirts and your red lips.' His eyes fixed on her mouth. 'A disgrace to womanhood. God sent you to tempt me.'

She stood firm. 'You know what? You *should* divorce my sister. Go ahead and do it. She deserves better. You're nothing but a hypocrite who twists God's will to serve his own ends.'

He grabbed her arm, pulling her towards him. 'So angry, Eliza,' he said softly. 'Someone needs to teach you a lesson.'

The door opened and Rob came in. His eyes went to Phil's hand on Eliza's arm. 'Everything OK here?'

Eliza shrugged off Phil. 'I'll encourage Maria to agree to a divorce, on the condition you sell your remaining shares back to Rose and have nothing to do with this company ever again. Agreed?'

Phil's eyes flicked between Eliza and Rob.

'I think what Eliza means,' said Rob, coming over, 'is that it's probably time for you to fuck right off.'

'Let me know your plans,' Eliza said. 'Email me. Copy in Harry.'

Phil opened his mouth to speak, then shut it again. He left.

'Holy shit,' said Eliza, sinking onto the edge of her desk. 'Oh my god, poor Maria.'

Rob perched next to her. 'You OK? That looked pretty heavy. Was he ... do you think he was going to touch you?'

'I need punishing, apparently. Something to do with my short skirts.'

'Jesus.'

'Yep, Jesus told him to.'

Rob smiled. 'But you were right back at him – so bad-ass.'

'I don't know whether I want to punch someone or curl up and cry.'

'Need a hug?'

'Please.'

He held her tight. 'You want to go get a drink or something? Shall we get you out of here?'

'I'm meant to be joining Will and Kit – it's quiz night at The Dickens.'

'God, the very thought. Is there prize money? That'll sort their rent for the foreseeable.'

'Killing it, apparently.'

He let her go and took her hands, kissing them one at a time. 'Can I come?'

'Of course.'

They left the building and set off for St Katharine Docks. The wind was bitter, and they hunkered down in their coats and scarves.

'So Will and Kit are still at your place?' said Rob. 'How's that going?'

'It's great. I'll be sad when they move out.'

'How's your liver bearing up?'

She laughed. 'They're different at home. We've been working on *Most Human*. It's one reason I don't want them to go. I won't be able to be so hands-on.'

'God, the girls at work all want to be hands-on with Kit.'

'Only the girls?'

Rob laughed. 'Good point.'

'I'm sure he'll oblige,' she said.

He looked sideways at her. 'Does that bother you?'

A fierce gust of wind buffeted them as they reached London Bridge, whipping away her, 'No – why would it?'

She took his arm, snuggling in. 'Sheesh, this weather. Have you read the latest version of *Most Human*?'

'Yep. Your boys are certainly on fire. We'll be ready to green light it soon, once the budgets are approved by the higher-ups. Leigh thinks the US is key. She says we should go over there to meet with producers and distributors. Harry says he can hook us up with the right people.'

'He's been advising you?'

'We were in touch while you were in Wales.'

She looked up at him. 'I told him what happened, with us. Not the details, obviously. Just that we're waiting on your divorce before we're a proper thing again. He thinks it's a wise move – that I should focus on work at the moment.'

Rob pursed his lips. 'Hm. Have you ever thought maybe we should stand up to our dads a bit more? You always do what Harry wants. Especially when that means avoiding me.'

He had a point. 'Maybe. And as for yours . . .'

'Yup. I hate thinking how pleased he'll be when we're together again, his empire-building all back on track.'

He grinned down at her. His curls were blowing about in the wind, and his eyes were sparkling in the dark.

Her heart skipped a beat. She stopped walking. 'Rob . . .' She bit her lip. The wind played with a lock of hair that had escaped her scarf, blowing it across her face.

'Hair chaos,' he said, tucking it back in. He stroked her cheek. 'I'm waiting for my cue. You're in control.'

'Now's good.'

They kissed, and the strength of feeling that surged through her was overwhelming.

'God, Lizzie,' he said, when they finally pulled apart. 'This waiting's doing my head in. How am I meant to function? It's torture.'

'True. I guess we could try a spot of pie therapy in The Dickens? I'm bloody freezing.'

He laughed. 'Right you are. Lead on, Macduff.' He put an arm round her shoulder and they headed off again.

'That's a misquote, actually,' she said.

'You're such a nerd.'

Chapter 29

Eliza

Eliza stood at her office window, pondering the Maria situation. London this morning was grey on grey, the sky leaden. Across the apathetic Thames the windows of the City's towers were matt, as if there were no light for them to reflect. People on the riverside below were hurrying along, heads down, intent on reaching somewhere warm.

What would Maria do now? Once she was recovered she could return to work but, truth be told, she wasn't cut out for corporate life. She hadn't fundamentally changed – at least, her values hadn't – to the extent that Eliza was going to welcome her back with open arms.

Her phone pinged.

FRANKIE: Harry and Clare say hi :) :)

There was a photo of Frankie standing between Harry and Captain Yates. Smiles and shorts, the sky and water behind them blue.

ELIZA: Not fair. Soooo cold here! Hey – word has it you and the captain???

FRANKIE: That would be most unprofessional. He's my boss!

ELIZA: So that's a yes?

FRANKIE: I love your dad now.

ELIZA: FFS. When u setting sail?

FRANKIE: Harry and Clare want to spend some time here in LA first so not sure. Can't wait to sail this baby down the coast!

Later, Eliza came out of a meeting with Cecil to find a note on her desk: *Pls call Cassandra. Urgent.* Her heart sank.

'Cassandra? It's Eliza.'

'Thanks for calling back. I'm afraid Maria's had a setback.'

I thought you might say that.

'Phil was supposed to be coming today. She's been counting down the hours. He rang to say he's been unavoidably called back to the States. What sort of a husband is he, Eliza?'

Poor Maria. But it was better that this relationship was put out of its misery now, rather than later.

'An ex-husband. Soon. He paid me a visit last night; we had words. Looks like Dad was right all along – he was mostly after her for her position at Rose. I think he's going to divorce her. I actually hope he does.'

'Maria didn't say anything about a divorce.'

'She probably doesn't know yet. I'll need to warn her, or she could have a nasty surprise in the post. I'll call her later, when I've worked out what to say.'

⬤

Something in Maria's voice told Eliza she knew the truth.

'I don't think he'll come back, Maria. I saw him here, in London. I'm so sorry, but to be honest, I think you'd be better off without him. The way he twists God's words to serve his own ends, it's not . . . well, it's not Christian.'

'You saw him?'

'He wanted to find out how you were. I said you needed love and understanding. His take on things was a little different.'

'He thinks God doesn't see a future for us. Eliza, why would God not want us to be together?' Her voice was bleak.

'Maybe because God realizes Phil's a fraud. Not a good man. Maybe God has something better planned for you. Something where you can make a difference – by yourself, not as someone's *helpmate*.'

Maria sighed. 'I don't fit in this world, Eliza. I feel like I'm in the wrong century. I won't come back to Rose for a while. Perhaps I won't come back at all.'

'Whatever you decide, I'll be right with you.'

Eliza ended the call and looked out across London. Dusk was already snatching the feeble amount of light that remained on this raw midwinter day.

Her heart bled for her sister, but she reflected that this whole distressing episode had brought the family closer together – and, unwittingly, Phil had solved the whole sister-versus-sister problem.

'Thank you and goodnight, *helpmate*,' she said.

✹

Later, Eliza FaceTimed Harry to fill him in on the situation. He was sitting on *Janette*'s pool deck; Clare leaned in to give Eliza a wave.

'You both look . . . warm,' said Eliza. 'How's La La Land?'

'Everyone here's appropriately insane,' said Harry, 'but it's always fun in short bursts. So what did you want to discuss?'

'Maria.' She updated him, leaving out the part about Phil wanting to punish Eliza for her tempting ways. 'So he's cleared off – and don't say *I told you so*, I hate it when you do that. I'm worried he'll make some sort of claim on her share of the business. Do you think he would?'

'No need to fret. I have dirt on Mr Seville. There's tax evasion, political donations from so-called charity funds, all highly suspect.

His duplicity is masterful – but obviously he wasn't counting on a Cecil.'

'Or a Harry.'

Once again she was reminded why, even in 'retirement', Harry was one of Britain's most powerful men – and why it was never a good idea to piss him off.

'What's next on the agenda?' he said.

'Ready to press Go with RoseGold. We're putting out a media release. And a social media blast – Twitter, and so on.'

'Good. You should formalise your team members' roles. And Cecil will need to come on board full time too. Make him Chief Operating Officer.'

'Right.'

'Rob tells me you're looking into co-funding your first production with a US distributor?'

She took a moment to enjoy the image of Dad and Rob talking business. He was properly part of the family firm now.

'Yes indeed.'

'I have a proposition for you. One I think you might like.'

'You going to give us some production money, Dad?'

'Better. I thought the five of you could come over, while we're in LA. You can invite potential co-producers on board *Janette.*'

'That would be brilliant!'

The last of her despondency flew. On Dad's yacht with her team, bringing her vision to life.

'I'm sure you can charm your way into funding for your first series,' he said. 'And, of course, US producers will be queuing up to pitch ideas to you for future film and TV. Tell Rob and Leigh to liaise with me. I'll leave Will and Kit to you.'

The press release announcing RoseGold was sent out to UK and US media, and the response was huge.

ROSE CORP SET TO BE MAJOR PLAYER IN TV AND FILM read the headline in *Variety.*

LONG LIVE THE NEW ROSE QUEEN! said the *Telegraph* (subhead *Clean-up Queen Steps Down*).

HARRY ROSE'S TRUE HEIR, said *Hello!* and there was a photo of Harry and Eliza eating strawberries at last year's Wimbledon.

Rose Corp's PR department was inundated with requests for interviews with Eliza. Such interest was inevitable, but she didn't want it all to be focused on her. All her life, the media had been obsessed with Harry, and she'd watched and learned how he used that to his advantage. And, like Harry, Eliza was determined to keep her own private life just that. There would be a public face and a private one.

She deflected some of the attention by pointing reporters towards Will and Kit, who were poised to be the new darlings of the arts world. They were already regulars at the Groucho Club, and Will was only too happy to offer frank opinions to the media on current drama and literature, while Kit enjoyed winding up journalists with his provocative and usually unfathomable pronouncements on the arts, sexuality, politics and religion.

Trying to keep some modicum of control over their image, Eliza asked Terri to do a piece on the pair for *The Rack*. Her resistance was predictably fierce. Putting Eliza's university pals on her front cover would be a 'blatant piece of nepotistic puffery'. It was out of the question.

'Dad loves them,' said Eliza.

'That's not helping your case.'

But then Eliza took the three of them to lunch.

'Holy fuck,' said Terri, afterwards. 'Humble pie for pudding. I want those two writing for *The Rack*.'

'Nope, they're all mine,' said Eliza. 'Sorry.'

'Nice one, team,' she said to Will and Kit that evening. 'Ms Robbins-More's praise is hard won.'

'She's magnificent,' said Will. 'And she got our take on Thomas More immediately. Really related to the character.'

'Hardly surprising,' said Kit.

'Well, they do share a surname – half of one, anyway,' said Eliza.

'A little more than that,' said Kit.

When Eliza saw the cover design – *New Era for Rose* – featuring the three of them, she almost wept.

'So much hair,' said Rob.

In the photo, Eliza was sitting on a golden chair, deliberately chosen to suggest 'throne', and Kit and Will were standing either side, hands on her shoulders. The stylist had played up her long red curls and pale skin and had dressed her in a beautiful long gown of rose pink and gold.

Will and Kit were in gold-coloured suits, their tousled locks tumbling artistically over their collars, looking like a louche pair of *enfants terribles*.

When the issue came out, the cover was shared everywhere. *Brits set to take TV and film by storm* tweeted *Entertainment Weekly*.

They were ready to go.

Meetings were set up with producers, flights were booked, and Eliza and Leigh took themselves Hollywood-power-clothes shopping.

Rob, Kit and Will perfected their pitch for *Most Human of Saints*. Normally the meeting would be on the producers' own turf, but Harry's personal invitations to join him on *Janette* had worked like a dream. They had their captive audience.

'Ready to slay,' Leigh said, as they finally left the office at close to midnight, the night before they were due to fly out.

A limo was waiting at LAX, and they had an *Is this for real?* moment as it whisked them off to Del Rey Landing.

Harry and Clare welcomed them aboard *Janette*.

'Hello, Rob,' said Clare, as he kissed her cheek. 'Isn't this all terribly exciting?'

Eliza introduced Leigh, Kit and Will to her step-mother. They were looking around them in astonishment.

'*If money goes before, all ways do lie open*,' said Will.

'That's the general idea,' said Harry.

'Timmo!' said Eliza.

'G'day, Eliza!'

'Frankie!' said Leigh, as their friend appeared in crew uniform.

'It's like the start of a Famous Five book,' said Harry. 'All together again for the hols. Down, Timmo!'

Eliza laughed. 'Five Go to Hollywood. So good to be back on board, Dad. Thanks for this.'

She was in the same suite as before. She showered, and changed into a stripey sundress. *No tights!*

On the pool deck, Harry was chatting with Rob.

'Something to drink?' he said.

'Wizard. Ginger beer?' Eliza sat down next to him.

'Good one,' said Rob. 'Where's Dick and Julian?'

'Probably off on one of their adventures.'

'I'll leave you to it,' said Harry, finishing his beer. 'See you at dinner, children.'

'He says I owe him five hundred quid,' said Rob, once Harry was out of earshot. 'Apparently Dad's claiming it back – we weren't officially together for long enough.'

'Tosh. There was no small print. Dad earned it fair and square.'

They looked out over the marina, where the sky was turning pink. It was peaceful; the only sounds were the cry of seagulls, the *clink clink* of ropes on masts, and the puttering of small boats coming back to their moorings.

'Isn't it lovely?' said Eliza.

'It is. As is your dress. You look like a Brighton deckchair.'

'I could do with a stroll after sitting on that plane for hours. Shall we?'

They walked down the gangplank, passing Frankie doing something with a rope. She caught Eliza's eye, raised her eyebrows at Rob and winked.

Indeed, Rob-in-shorts was a pleasant surprise. Eliza was so used to seeing him in a suit these days. His bare legs took her back to summers past, running wild in Richmond Park, hiding in the long grass pretending to stalk the deer.

'I used to love how you always saved me your last Smartie,' she said, as they set off along the boardwalk.

'No, I gave you the blue ones. 'Cause I didn't trust them.'

'No, you definitely saved me your last ones.'

'I wouldn't have done such a thing for a girl.'

'You so did.'

'Remember how we used to turn the tubes into blow-guns and fire them at the deer?' he said.

'And sherbet fountains. You always gave me the liquorice.'

'Obviously, 'cause I hate liquorice.'

'Rob, stop trashing my childhood memories of you being sweet to me.'

They walked around the basin past the yachts, then headed onto an esplanade. The sun burned gold, dripping onto the horizon, and they stopped, leaning on the railings as it hit the sea. The clouds lit up in shades of pink, purple and gold.

'That's just unfair on a couple trying to be discreet,' said Eliza. 'Stupid sunset.'

Rob put an arm around her waist. 'True. But we're practically in Hollywood, therefore an appropriate response is expected. I now turn to you, tuck your hair behind your ear, and suggest that while we're hidden away on a big boat, no one will notice if we let our guard down.'

'You think?'

He turned to her and tucked a curl behind her ear. 'Not quite sure what happens next.'

'I run my fingers through your hair and remind you we're here to work.'

She ran her fingers through his hair.

'I reply, There's more to life than bloody work, Lizzie.'

'And I say, It's all about priorities. I need to be in the right head space for all this. And so do you.'

Rob shook his head. 'I then ignore you, and do this.'

He kissed her, and resistance was impossible. There was an over-whelming sense of coming home.

'That was lovely,' she said, after a while. 'But seriously. No more until the job's done.'

Chapter 30

Eliza

The next two days were a blur of meetings, pitches, pressing the flesh, tweaking their presentations, listening to Hollywood executives pitching their own ideas. Evenings were spent debriefing.

Before the first meeting, Eliza thought she might throw up from nerves. Could she really be doing this? Presenting to hard-nosed Hollywood executives?

Harry helped things along. He began with introductions, building them up, laying on the English charm. Then Eliza outlined RoseGold's mission, emphasising their goals of originality and excellence, before handing over to Rob for the big sell. His exuberant enthusiasm transitioned beautifully into Will and Kit's pitch, Will adding drama, Kit's words transfixing some and confusing others. Finally, Leigh concluded with the business side of things. The team soon had it down to a fine art.

On the final day, Harry said he'd bet a cool million they'd have their pick of partners and projects. They were drinking champagne on deck; celebration was in the air.

Another beautiful sunset beckoned, and Eliza looked over at Rob. They'd spent no time alone since that first day. After two glasses of champagne, feeling the stress lifting, the time was right to slip away.

But before she could say anything, Kit appeared at her side. 'Hey, come for a walk?'

'Now?'

Her eyes flicked over to Rob, who gave a small shrug.

'OK.'

Kit bought them beers from a bottle store, and they sat on the harbour wall, looking out to sea. Now that the pitches were done, he'd changed into a faded blue T-shirt, shorts and flip-flops. With his tousled blond hair, he fitted right in here in California.

'To you,' he said, clinking his bottle against hers. 'You pulled all this together.'

'I'm exhausted.' She edged closer and leaned on him. 'Kit – you and Will. You're on the brink of something amazing. Just ... stay true?'

'You mean don't go the full Hollywood.'

'Never do that. Some of those guys we met. It's like they'd sell their souls for success.'

'*Hell is empty, and all the devils are here.*'

He lit a cigarette.

Eliza grimaced. 'I wish you'd give up. Cigarettes aren't a substitute for food. Do you have a death wish?'

'Very possibly.' He draped an arm around her shoulder. 'How're things with Rob?'

'Good. He reckons he'll be divorced by summer. How about you? Kit – are you and Will ...?'

'He's in a huff, didn't you notice?'

'No – why?'

'Caught me with Timmo.' He laughed, and dragged on his cigarette.

Eliza bristled. 'For god's sake, Kit. That's just cruel.'

He said nothing.

She looked at him. 'Do you really not believe in love?'

'Meh.' His face was impassive; he gazed out to sea.

'Why are you like this? I'm so open with you. You know it all. Well, most of it. Why can't you be the same with me?'

He glanced at her briefly.

'Kit?'

'Sorry. I guess . . . I had it. Once. It was stolen from me and I'm not going there again.'

'Who?'

'Nope. That's all.'

It was way more than she'd ever got before.

'But, Kit, everyone gets their heart broken at least once. It doesn't mean you can't try again. And it definitely doesn't mean you go around breaking other people's. Make it up with Will; treat him right.'

He hopped down off the wall and stood facing her. 'Let's go.'

'Catch me.' She jumped, and he caught her round the waist.

'And, Kit?'

'What?'

'You've had it more than once. Love, I mean. You've got it now.'

They set off back, and he kept an arm round her. It felt nice. Really, a soulmate who happened to look like the most beautiful of Greek gods was a wonderful thing. Even if he was . . .

'*Timmo*, Kit?'

He grinned. 'Gotta love those blokey Aussies.' He threw his cigarette butt on the ground.

Eliza stopped. 'Pick it up. You may be trashing your own life, but can you at least keep the planet beautiful?'

'Jeez, you're such a control freak.' He picked it up and flicked it in the water.

'Kit!' What was wrong with him today? 'Why are you being obnoxious?'

'I am?'

She stood facing him. 'You should really sort your shit out.'

'Not a hope,' he said. He met her gaze, and for a moment she glimpsed something.

She touched his cheek. 'I wish you'd talk to me.'

'I do. You just don't always listen.'

'I promise to listen, Kit. Any time you want.'

He looked at her for a moment. 'Thanks, babe.'

Taking her face in his hands, he kissed her, gently. She tasted cigarettes.

He leaned his forehead against hers. 'Help me stay true.'

'I will.' She put her arms around him, hugging him tight.

They set off walking again, and as she glanced up at *Janette*, she saw Rob standing at the rails, watching them.

'Oh god, I think Rob saw that.'

'Good. Keep him on his twinkly fuckin' toes.'

Eliza eyed the clothes in her wardrobe, wondering what to wear for their last night. She was looking forward to winding down. Their days here had been relentless, intense, with so much at stake. Her chance to realize her dream distilled into short, sharp, back-to-back meetings.

Jeans and T-shirt were calling – she'd done quite enough power dressing. But she wanted to look good for Rob. He'd been brilliant; she owed him so much. Tonight she'd show her appreciation, and would prove she was indeed aware that there was more to life than work.

She wondered what he was feeling about what he'd seen. He had a problem with Kit, this she knew. They were chalk and cheese. Alpha male and . . . whatever Kit was. A lone wolf, perhaps. Rob always seemed wary of him, didn't get him, or their friendship.

She chose a short black dress, slipped on strappy heels, tamed her hair into glossy waves and finished with a spritz of musky perfume.

Timmo whistled as she emerged onto the deck.

Really, Timmo?

'Cheeky,' she said, and blew him a kiss.

She spotted Rob talking to a crew member. Rebecca, of the unfeasibly long tanned limbs, waist-length blonde hair and big blue eyes that were currently locked on Rob's.

Eliza went over to the railings, hoping he'd shake off Rebecca and come join her.

Frankie got there first. 'Harry's given me the night off! Did I say I love your dad? We're on the top deck. We have beanbags and champagne.'

The thought of lying on a beanbag with Rob was most appealing. 'Be right there.'

She went over and touched his arm. 'Sorry, excuse me,' she said to Rebecca. Gosh, she was disappointingly flawless, close up. 'Rob, I'm going up to the top deck. See you there?'

His eyes searched hers for a moment. 'Sure. I'll be up soon.'

As Eliza climbed the stairs, she looked out across the marina to the open sea. A huge full moon had risen; it hung in the sky like a spotlight, its reflection fragmenting into flashes of silver that danced on the water.

The gentle tinkle of ropes on masts blew across on the soft, warm breeze.

It was time for some serious letting off of steam. The five relaxed beneath the night sky, the stress of the week behind them.

Some time later, there was still no sign of Rob. *Where is he?*

Was this something to do with her harbourside walk with Kit? Rob hadn't often seen her and Kit together outside of work; he probably didn't realize that was just how they were.

Tired of waiting, Eliza rolled off her beanbag and moved over to Kit.

'Is there room for another on your beanbag, Mr Marley?'

He held out an arm and she lay down next to him, resting her head on his shoulder, kicking off her shoes, stretching out her legs.

'Oh, this is nice. Wow, look at that moon.'

She closed her eyes, and the mix of champagne, relief at a good job done, and Kit's warm, familiar body, filled her with a deep peace.

'Eliza!' hissed Leigh.

She opened her eyes and Leigh raised her eyebrows, nodding in the direction of the stairs. Eliza saw Rob, watching them.

'Rob!' she called.

He came over, not taking his eyes from hers. There was no twinkle in them.

Perhaps sharing Kit's beanbag hadn't been the most sensible idea.

'Draw up a beanbag,' she said.

The others had stopped talking. Tension had chased away the magic.

She forced a smile. 'Pour yourself a glass of bubbles. We should raise a toast to our success. You did brilliantly. Dad reckons we'll get what we want, and more.'

'Does he.' His tone was flat.

The air was heavy with silence.

'Well, we all know how important *Harry's* opinion is. But to get what you want, you have to know what that is. It's a shame you don't.'

She attempted to sit up. 'But—'

'I'll leave you to your –' his eyes locked with Kit's – '*friends*.'

He turned abruptly, and headed back towards the stairs.

There was a pause, then Will said, '*To be wise and love, exceeds man's might*.'

'Do you want to go after him?' said Kit.

Did she? She acknowledged the hurt. But there was anger, too, that he could speak to her like that.

'No. He's being a douche. He can just . . . ' She couldn't say any more. Tears pricked the back of her eyes.

'Hey,' said Kit. 'Don't stress. He'll work it out. Forget about him for tonight – get pissed. Party. Live in the moment.'

'Music,' announced Will. 'Frankie, can we sort a speaker?' He fiddled with his phone.

Frankie made a call and a crew member appeared with a couple of speakers, followed by another with more food and champagne.

A favourite song from their Oxford days came on and Will danced, bottle in hand.

Frankie flicked a few switches on a bulkhead and the deck lights went off. Everything turned silver.

'Will met by moonlight,' said Kit.

Eliza chuckled. Kit absently stroked her arm, and she felt herself relaxing again. He was right, she *should* live in the moment. When would she next get the chance to party on a super-yacht with her best pals? Rob, with his wrong conclusions, could wait.

Hours later, when they finally ran out of steam, Will fell dramatically backwards onto a beanbag, arms akimbo, and Leigh and Frankie joined him on either side, snuggling close under a blanket. '*To sleep,*' he said, closing his eyes. '*Perchance to dream . . .*'

Radiohead's 'Street Spirit' was playing, and Eliza was wrapped in Kit's arms, lost in a swirl of music. *Fade out . . . Immerse your soul in love.*

The California moon finally slipped below the horizon, its work done, leaving a dome of black sprinkled with stars that faded out where the sky met LA's orange glow.

When the music stopped, Eliza and Kit curled up on their beanbag together and fell fast asleep.

Chapter 31

Eliza

Timmo woke her a couple of hours later, with coffee. 'Harry sent me to find you. Says he's having breakfast if you want to join him.'

Eliza sat up, pushing her hair out of her eyes. 'Thanks, Timmo.'

His eyes lingered on Kit.

'He's not worth your time,' she said.

'What?'

'Never mind.'

Timmo left, and she looked down at Kit, still sleeping peacefully, then across at Leigh, Frankie and Will, curled up together, eyes closed. She smiled. If those powerful Hollywood executives could see them now, like a bunch of exhausted puppies in their baskets.

She took her coffee over to the railings and watched the watery sun climb higher in the pale morning sky. A lone seagull cried mournfully from the top of the mast behind her; joggers were running along the boardwalk far below, gaping at *Janette* as they passed.

As her brain began functioning properly, she allowed in memories of the night before. A fierce pain hit as she wondered what Rob had been up to. Had he hooked up with Rebecca?

She looked across at Kit, still fast asleep, his face half-hidden behind his mess of hair. The pain eased a little. *What would I do without you?*

She remembered the look Rob had given him, before he'd flounced off. She was going to have to sort this out. Her relationship with Rob aside, those two would be working closely together, and she couldn't afford the clash of egos. She needed Rob to understand; she'd have to explain their friendship – again.

She returned to her cabin to shower and change, then went to find Harry. He was by the pool, talking to Timmo, who stood up when he saw Eliza approaching.

'G'day again, Timmo,' she said.

'Not really. You're all leaving us today.'

'I'll miss you, Timmo.' She touched his arm.

'Can I get you some breakfast?'

'Just another coffee?'

'Coming right up.' He left.

'You're leaving quite a trail of unrequited love,' said Harry.

'It's not me he's crushing on.'

'It isn't?'

'I make that four people Kit's managed to hurt this week.'

'Ah. Two of them being you and Rob?'

She sighed. Harry missed nothing.

'What's going on?' he said. 'Why didn't Rob join in your party?'

'He saw me with Kit and got the wrong end of the stick. Like it's any of his business.'

'Ah.'

'I need him to understand there's nothing going on.'

'Nothing at all?'

'I *told* you. Why do men have such a problem understanding male–female friendship?'

'A little disingenuous of you, when the friend is Kit.'

'Whatever.'

'Sort it out, Lizzie. Apart from anything else, you need Rob on side for what's to come – he's dynamite. It's him you'll have to thank when the offers start rolling in.'

Harry was right. Hurt feelings aside, it was important Rob knew his efforts were appreciated.

'OK, I'll talk to him. But can I just drink my coffee now? I've had, like, one or two hours' sleep. On a beanbag. My back hurts.'

Harry smiled. 'I'm glad you had some time out; you've got so much hard work ahead of you. Be nice to Rob today. He's your best ally, he'd do anything for you. Between him and Cecil, I'll know my girl's in good hands.'

●

Back in her room, Eliza started packing her things.

> ELIZA: Hi, can we take a walk?

> ROB: Why?

> ELIZA: only 2 hours sleep don't ask difficult questions

He didn't reply for a while.

> ROB: c u in 10?

> ELIZA: thanks

She had an idea, and rang through to Timmo, who arranged for a car to be waiting. 'And can you let Harry know? We'll probably be back around lunchtime.' Their flight wasn't until early evening.

'Have you had breakfast?' she asked, as they walked down the gangplank.

'Not hungry,' said Rob. 'Surprised *you* can face food.' He shoved his hands in his shorts pockets. She couldn't see the expression in his eyes, behind his Ray-Bans.

'In fact my alcohol consumption was only moderately excessive last night. I thought we could go to Venice? Get breakfast and walk along the beach?'

'You're the boss.'

It wasn't far to Venice Beach. Already the boardwalk was buzzing with street performers, skateboarders, tourists, artists. Finally Rob began to unwind as he enjoyed the vibe.

She took his arm. 'Rob . . . you didn't . . . with Rebecca?' She looked sideways at him, trying to catch his expression before he responded.

He frowned. 'What? Of *course* not.'

'But . . . she was coming on to you, I didn't imagine that.'

He shook his head. 'She wants to get into acting, and obviously thought the casting couch was still a thing. I told her she was letting the side down, that we've moved on. I had an early night. By myself. I was knackered.'

Eliza's relief was profound. She nudged him. 'She probably wasn't only after you for your big parts.'

At last he cracked a smile.

They stopped to watch a busker, then bought waffles from a stall and sat on a bench overlooking the beach.

Eliza took a breath. 'Rob . . . last night. I wanted to be alone with you; to be with you – properly. But—

He leaped in. 'So why were you kissing Kit? I saw you.'

'I didn't kiss him. He kissed me. Because . . . we'd had a heart-to-heart. He was saying thanks; it's just how he is.'

He shook his head, frowning. 'Tell him to back off.'

'Rob – I need you to understand. I'm not going to stop hanging out with Kit. We're very close. But seriously, there's nothing physical.'

He pushed his sunglasses up onto his head, and she was relieved to have access to his eyes again. They were full of uncertainty.

'Are you telling me the truth, Lizzie?'

She was touched by the rare glimpse of vulnerability. 'I am, yes. I promise.'

He looked away from her. 'He's so . . . '

'I know he is. But it's you I love, Rob. Very much.'

He kissed her, and the need for more words flew.

'Sorry,' he said, when they finally pulled apart. 'About last night's hissy fit.'

'Me too. I should have come after you.'

'So . . . we're OK?'

'Please god let it be so. And now we have a whole morning, just the two of us. No eyes – no work people, no stupid British press, no annoying parents . . .'

'And no Kit.'

Chapter 32

Eliza

Over the following weeks, deals were sealed and RoseGold took over an entire floor of The Rose. The funding the team had secured, plus a generous budget approved by the board, meant they could employ well-established industry executives – the best in the business.

Eliza wanted to make Will Head of Drama and Kit Head of Creative, mostly because the titles amused her. But Harry had a quiet word.

'Nepotism is all well and good, Lizzie, but you really don't want to be pissing off the underlings. Keep your boys as freelancers. When they've proved themselves, then you can bring them onto the staff.'

She dug her heels in over Rob, however, making him RoseGold's Head of Production. It was the job she'd have chosen for herself, had she not been CEO. She could hardly call him 'Personal Sidekick'.

And she plucked Chess from the abyss of Admin, giving her a production manager role.

'Fuck's sake,' said Terri, when the new positions were announced.

Casting and location scouting began, and the filming schedule was drawn up.

Eliza, often alone in her office, wished she could be back in the thick of it, rather than presiding from the top floor.

'It's a shame, RoseGold's your baby, but we hardly see you,' said Chess at their regular lunch.

'I sometimes hate being stuck up there with only Pippa and Cecil for company. I miss just hanging in *The Rack*, doing dogsbody jobs but having fun. Being CEO sucks sometimes.'

'So it's true about it being lonely at the top.'

'It is. Everyone treats me differently now, like they think twice about what they say.'

'That's only natural. Maybe you should be making more of the upside – all that lovely dosh. And the fact that you're the new darling of the British media. Honestly, I can't open a newspaper without seeing your ugly mug staring out at me. Hey, why don't you buy yourself a fancy new place? You've been living in Harry's London apartment for a while now.'

It was a thought. Somewhere spectacular. Will and Kit had recently moved out. They'd bought a beautifully renovated terraced house in Dalston, and when they weren't working, were usually carousing in local clubs and bars or hanging out at the Groucho. She missed them.

Perhaps Rob could help her look for somewhere. It would be lovely, once the divorce came through, to kick-start their relationship in a place they'd chosen together.

'Are you going to Aunt Margot's funeral next week?' she said, changing the subject.

Harry's elder sister had recently died, 'after a short illness', the papers had said. 'Probably from boredom,' Harry had commented when he asked Eliza to attend the funeral on the family's behalf.

'I am, yes,' said Eliza. 'Dad doesn't want to fly home for it. Pretty remiss of him, but they never got on. He's given me strict instructions to suss out our Scottish cousin's intentions with regards to her inheritance – as in practically a third of Rose shares.'

'Yikes,' said Chess. 'Let's hope she's like her mum and mine. Sit back, do nothing and watch the money roll in.'

'Fingers crossed,' said Eliza. 'So ... we'll finally get to meet the mysterious Mackenzie James. Dad says she works in politics. Probably hates the English. Should be an interesting meeting, anyway.'

❀

The weekend before the funeral, Maria came up to London. She'd phoned saying she'd made some decisions and wanted to let Eliza know what those were.

They walked along the embankment as a fierce wind churned the Thames.

'Phil's divorcing me.' Maria's face was pinched from the cold; she looked ten years older than when she'd been 'pregnant'.

'I'm so sorry, Maria.'

'Don't be. God has revealed to me Phil's true self. He's not the man I thought I married.'

'I know.' Eliza linked her arm through her sister's. 'You deserve better. You'll find someone else.'

'That's not what I want. From now on I will love only God.'

Eliza felt uneasy. Was Maria intending to return to Rose, to resume her crusade?

'I'm going to give you control of my shares.'

Oh!

'Phil's selling me his, and I'll add those to them. I'll need the income, but I don't want a role in the company, not any more. This will make your stake more secure, and it will free me to do what I feel God has planned for me. I'm going to do missionary work overseas. I'd like it to be with children.'

A lump formed in Eliza's throat. 'That's a wonderful plan!'

'I'm aware that I do tend to frighten children, rather, but I'm hoping God will teach me how to overcome that.'

'She will, I'm sure,' said Eliza with a grin.

Maria laughed. 'I can't believe I'm saying this, but I'll really miss you.'

It was only the second time Eliza had visited Aunt Margot and Uncle Robbie's gloomy Scottish castle. As for the first . . . she tried to avoid thinking about that terrible time, when Harry had been shot by Mad Merry, as he insisted on calling his former mistress.

'Christ Almighty, Henry Rose's dominant gene didn't take any prisoners,' said Uncle Charles, his eyes on Eliza's Scottish cousin as they gathered in the great hall.

Eliza laughed. It was true. Aunt Megan, Chess and Eliza were all variations on a red-haired theme: pale red and curly, pale red and straight, flaming red and curly . . . and now here was another version. Cousin Mackenzie. Light auburn and wavy, with gold-brown eyes to match. And those other Rose traits, there they were – tall, pale skin, high forehead. She was strikingly attractive, and moved with a grace that drew the eye.

Realising she was the focus of their attention, Mackenzie came over. 'Eliza, Francesca, Aunt Megan – we meet at last!' Her Scottish accent was soft and melodic.

'This is my husband, Charles,' said Megan. 'We're so sorry about your mother, Mackenzie.'

'Och, don't be. We didn't see eye to eye. We hardly saw each other, once I left home. She didn't seem to care much for her English family, either. All these years and I've never met you before. It's a shame.' She turned those unusual eyes on Eliza. 'You and I have a wee bit of catching up to do. And I want to meet Harry. I've been a fan for many years.'

'You must come down to London when he's back. He'd love to meet you too, Mackenzie.'

'Call me Mac, everyone does.'

'I hear you work in politics?' said Megan.

'For now. Getting fed up with it, to be honest. Too many big egos. Maybe, now I've inherited Mum's share of Rose . . . can I talk to you about that sometime?' She looked Eliza squarely in the eye.

The remark sounded off the cuff, like the thought had just

occurred to her. But Eliza could tell – she'd planned this. Cousin Mac wanted in. It was too soon to know whether this was to be welcomed, or treated with caution. On the one hand, with all the recent expansion, there could be a role for her, and she certainly had charisma – in bucketloads. But on the other ... Mac's share of the business was larger than Eliza's, and she had a political background. Eliza felt a niggle of unease.

'Of course,' she said. 'Next time you're down, let's have a proper chat.'

It had taken a lifetime for them to meet. Surely a trip to London would take some time to eventuate.

Chapter 33

Eliza

Eliza flicked through the *Guardian* as she took a break at her desk. She registered the date, 1st May, and smiled a melancholy smile, remembering May Morning back at Oxford, listening to the choristers singing from the Great Tower. Only a year had passed, but it seemed a lifetime ago.

Rob's divorce seemed to be taking for ever. It was almost a year now, and here they were, still skulking about, snatching the odd coffee, the occasional kiss.

She shut the newspaper and threw it to one side. Gah! It was *so* frustrating! Here she was, a high-flying, powerful woman at the head of a company doing amazing things. She'd been nominated as Business Roundtable Woman of the Year and *Vogue* had just called her 'spectacular'. And yet she was a twenty-four-year-old virgin who, thanks to the British public's voracious appetite for celebrity gossip, was unable to be with the man she loved.

She'd invite him over tonight. She needed to know – how much longer?

'Beer?' she asked, going through to the kitchen.

'Sounds good.' He plonked a box of handmade chocolates on the worktop. 'For later.' He looked her in the eye and her stomach clenched.

'I phoned for pizza, hope that's OK,' she said, pouring their drinks.

'Something nice and cheesy? Like all the lines I was thinking up on my way over.'

'Such as?'

'How much I love you. How this waiting's so hard; how I just want everyone to know we're together.'

'About that—'

'How amazing you are. Everyone at work thinks you're incredible.'

'Really?'

'Yeah, of course.' He grinned. 'Kit calls you Eliza the Kaiser, but other than that . . . '

'Bloody cheek!'

He slung his leather jacket over a chair, chuckling, then hopped up onto a barstool.

She passed him his beer and came to stand in front of him.

'Here's to moving on,' she said, clinking her glass against his.

He opened his legs and pulled her between them.

'Rob, how much longer will the divorce take?'

'We're just hammering out some final stuff. Two months max, I reckon.'

'That's good news.'

He twirled a lock of hair around his finger. 'So, I'll finally get to see your crazy curls spread across my pillow. Yes?'

'My therapy is almost complete. Whether or not it's worked remains to be seen.'

'Define "almost".'

'For the sake of argument, let's say two months max.'

'But in the meantime . . . '

'Did I see chocolates?'

As Eliza walked to work the next morning, she had an *everything's perfect* moment. It was a glorious spring day and the Thames was twinkling in the sun, the boats chugging along like cheerful characters in a children's book.

Rob's divorce was on the horizon, and RoseGold was bowling along beautifully. *Most Human of Saints* was on schedule and on budget. Everyone involved felt it in their bones – this was going to be a classic. BAFTAs would surely follow, and the US distributors were salivating.

The team had shortlisted a dozen possible future productions, aiming to whittle that down to two. Their brainstorming sessions were the highlight of Eliza's working week.

Cecil, now officially ensconced as COO, was a godsend, the steadiest of hands on Rose Corp's helm. She knew for sure he was Harry's spy, but in a good way.

And she was now confident that her therapy would yield a good result. During her last session, Dr Thomson had suggested she tell Harry about her problem. Unbottling her resentment, explaining the part he'd played in creating her mistrust, would apparently be an important step along the road to resolving the issue.

Eliza had baulked at the suggestion, but Dr T had gently talked her through it, certain that this would help.

'Morning, Pippa!' she called as she swung past her PA's desk.

'Hi, Eliza. Um, can I have a word, when you're ready?'

'Sure, you want to bring us both a coffee?'

Five minutes later, Pippa sat down opposite Eliza.

'What's up?' Eliza gave her a big smile.

Pippa returned it. 'All's going well with Rob, then?'

'How very dare you. But yes. And I know I can rely on your discretion.'

'Of course. Two things that might bring you down, I'm afraid.'

'Really? What things?'

'First up, I'm sorry to say Kit Marley's in trouble. Got himself into a fight last night in Soho. He spent the night in the cells.'

'What!'

'Will rang. He wants to talk to you.'

'OK, I'll call him. Bloody hell. What's the other thing?'

'This one's ... Eliza, I don't quite know what to say. I had a call from someone who gave his name as Stu Blunt. He said he was ... your *brother*. He sounded Australian. Says he's in London and wants to meet up.'

Shit. Shit shit shit.

'Oh. Right. Thank goodness Dad's home this week. I'll have to speak to him. Not a word, Pippa.'

'So ... who is he?'

'My half-brother. The result of one of Dad's flings. If the press find out, we'll be in for another media bomb. We so don't want that.'

'Right. Shall I put him off?'

'Yes. I'll talk to Dad, find out what to do.'

'OK. And talking of Harry, he asked me to make sure the corporate hospitality marquee was sorted for Wimbledon.'

'Dad and his tennis.'

'I told him it's all in hand.'

'Excellent. Looking forward to it.'

When Pippa left, Eliza phoned Will. 'What the heck, Will? Kit in a brawl?'

'He's quite the hothead these days, my sweet. Can you come see him?' Then his voice lost its drama. 'Actually, Eliza, I'm worried about him. His fuse seems to have shortened.'

This didn't make sense. Kit was the most laid-back person she'd ever known.

'I'll come over tonight.'

❀

Will let her in. 'He's not looking so pretty. The police let him off with a warning. He socked an *Independent* theatre reviewer and got one back, twice as hard. I'll go fetch a takeaway, leave you two to talk.'

Kit was lying on the sofa in the book-lined living room, reading a literary journal. 'Eliza. What are you doing here?'

She saw the bruising around his eye, and was more upset than she'd expected. 'Kit!' She hurried over and squatted on the floor next to him. 'What's this all about?' She gently touched his face.

He caught her hand, and didn't let it go.

'Just a spat. Theatre reviewer didn't know what the fuck he was talking about. Guess I got a bit wound up.'

'Kit, you don't get wound up. Had you been drinking?'

'Nope.'

'Anything else?'

' . . . Maybe.'

Eliza's heart sank. 'Don't, Kit.' She lifted his hand and kissed it. 'Look, I've never shared this with anyone, but I promised to help you stay true. Dad had an addiction problem, for years. It nearly sent him over the edge. He kicked it, with Clare's help. I don't want anyone I love to go through what he did. Will you stop?'

He stared up at the ceiling. '*That which nourishes me destroys me.* You can't imagine what it's like, here in my mind. I need to leave it, every now and again.'

Her heart missed a beat.

'Don't – please? And brawling; that's not you. You're gentle.'

He turned his gaze on her. 'You and Rob—'

'Don't change the subject.'

'No, it's good. I want you to be happy. Just . . . make the most of this time with him.'

A shiver ran down her spine. There was something about the way he'd said it.

What was going on?

'His divorce is nearly done, then we'll be properly together.'

'*Properly.* It's all such a jumble. A muddle. I can't see it.'

Eliza breathed a sigh of relief when Will appeared with the food.

Kit's ramblings, on the rare occasions she understood them, were sometimes too disturbing.

Harry

The weekend after Harry and Clare's return, Eliza went to Richmond. She was looking happy in her skin (so pale, in contrast to Harry's own tan), and he sensed she was now comfortable in her new role. Of course, his eyes at Rose had been keeping him up to speed with developments. Everything he was hearing was good — better than good — and Cecil was quietly nudging things back on track on the rare occasions when her inexperience led to mistakes.

'Three things, Dad,' she said, as they walked through Richmond Park.

'Good things or bad things? Secrets, one assumes, seeing as you plotted to get me by myself again.'

'One good, one possibly unwelcome. The third . . . ' She swallowed. 'There's something I want to talk to you about. It's hard for me, but I need to do it.'

Was this something to do with Ana? What had Eliza learned? He'd rather hoped the barrage of questions about her mother had ceased.

'Right you are,' he said. 'Where shall we start? With the unwelcome one?'

'OK. Stu's in London. He's been trying to see me. I've put him off so far.'

This didn't come as a surprise. Number One Son was proving tenacious in his attempts to connect with his English 'rellies'.

'Ah. He's been in touch with me too. I said we'd catch up when I was home.'

'Dad, what do we do when the press find out?'

'I'll have something ready. Happy to welcome long-lost son into the bosom of the family, etc. I'll just have to make sure he's on the same page. We don't want him selling his story.'

'Right. So are you going to meet up with him? What if he wants a job?'

'Let's hope he doesn't. I was thinking of organising a family gathering – a birthday do, maybe. My fifty-eighth, ye gods. Close friends and family, like we did for Clare's. What do you think?'

'That would work. Keep it in the family. Have you told Eddie?'

'On the to-do list.'

'Don't put it off, Dad.'

'And the good news?'

She smiled, and did a little skip. 'Rob's divorce is imminent – just a couple more months, probably.'

This also wasn't a surprise. Harry's spies were thorough.

'That's good.'

'Yes,' she said, 'the end is finally nigh.'

'And the difficult thing?'

A cloud crossed her face. She kept her gaze ahead, not meeting his eye. Harry had a horrible feeling his Russian nemesis was about to barge his way back into his conscience.

'I've been having therapy.'

This *was* a surprise. Lizzie was surely the most resilient of Roses. A hardy perennial. Was this something to do with her childhood?

His old companion, guilt, joined Andre in the wings.

'Therapy?'

She stopped and squeezed her eyes shut for a moment. She was biting her lip.

He went to touch her arm, but she took a step back.

'Eliza?'

He saw her swallow.

'It's ... I ... oh god. Right. Dad, I won't look at you while I say this, because it's hard.'

He frowned.

'That family joke,' she said, gazing across the park. 'About me being a virgin. Well ... I still am.'

'Nothing wrong with that, Lizzie,' he said, after a pause. 'I'm sure you have your reasons.'

'I do. But it's not a choice, Dad. It's a problem. A psychological one. Hence the therapy.'

Harry didn't respond, sensing her difficulty.

'In a way I'm like you,' she said. 'I love the opposite sex. And I like kissing and ... so on with Rob. And I almost had a thing with Kit, at uni. Remember when I called him Mr Wrong? That showed me I wasn't ... frigid. But I had a panic attack when he tried to take things further. That put the brakes on our relationship, which was probably just as well, because I believe in fidelity and he doesn't. Which kind of brings me to you, Dad.'

'I have a feeling you're going to tell me my terrible example has put you off ... things.'

She gave a small laugh, but didn't smile.

'Sorry, Lizzie. I can't believe I'm being so prudish. Me of all people.'

She looked at him briefly, then turned away again. 'No, it's hard to talk about with you, obviously. But I've been discussing you with my therapist, Dr Thomson. Clare found her for me – she's brilliant.'

'Clare knows about your problem?'

'I swore her to secrecy. And it seems my problem – why I can't ...'

'Give up your virginity?'

'Yes. It's a trust thing. To do with how you behaved towards women. And someone else's behaviour too, but mainly you.'

She was quiet. 'OK, I'd like to look at you now.' Her voice was unsteady.

She met his eye, and suddenly there were tears and her face twisted with emotion.

'You cheated on your wives, Dad. On Mum. You let her down; you turned your back on her. She died because of *you*. You drove Caitlyn to suicide.'

Her voice rose, and the tears spilled over. 'You had a secret love child who's probably a messed-up alcoholic. You sent Aunt Merry mad – she tried to kill you.' She swiped at her cheeks. 'Do you have *any* idea what all that has done to me? I can't have sex! I have panic attacks when men try to love me. I can't give myself to the man I love!'

Harry's beloved daughter was falling apart in front of his eyes. A fierce wave of guilt and anguish hit as images from his past crowded in: Ana, blaming him for the death of their unborn child, telling him to stay away from Andre; Katie, asking him to help her through her depression, begging him not to leave; Caitlyn, pleading with him to forgive her. He'd failed them. Every word Eliza said was true.

She'd always been the steady child. Unlike Maria, the dramas of her childhood had seemed to wash right over her, that sunny personality shining on through his marriage breakup, through Ana's death, Janette's death, Caitlyn's death. He thought she'd sailed through it all unscarred, and had always marvelled at that.

How wrong he'd been. Beneath all that confidence, that strength, was a damaged girl.

Same as you.

Unbidden, the memory of his own teenage years rushed in. Losing his brother, his mother and father. A teenage orphan. He'd been lost – until he'd met Katie. And look what he'd done to her.

It was all Harry could do not to cry himself.

'I'm so sorry,' he finally managed. 'Eliza, I'm truly sorry . . . '

She sniffed, then took a breath, making an effort to compose herself.

He held out his arms and, as her eyes met his, he knew she understood.

They held each other tight.

It was some time before either of them spoke again. Eliza's voice was calmer. 'Dr Thomson says if I can let go of the blame, understand you, forgive you, then my subconscious mistrust of men will start to ease. I do understand you a lot more now. When I was little, I thought you were perfect. I thought you knew everything, never did anything wrong. Accepting that you weren't that person, that you were flawed . . . '

'Deeply.'

'Well, yes. Accepting that, it's my first big step. And ...' She pulled back a little and looked at him. 'It wasn't just *your* behaviour, Dad. You're not completely to blame.'

'What do you mean?'

She took another breath. 'Do you remember when Eddie and I went to stay with Uncle Seymour and his wife?'

'After Caitlyn died?'

'A few times before, too. Seymour, he ...' She swallowed.

Suddenly Harry understood, and his blood ran cold. 'My god.'

'No, Dad, it wasn't full-on abuse. But he touched me, all the time, when he thought no one was looking. Patted my bottom, squeezed my knee; he was always staring at my chest, coming into my bedroom. That last time we visited, I was so worried I threw up at the thought of going, but I didn't tell you because Caitlyn had just died. Dr Thomson says his behaviour will have contributed to my ... issue.'

Harry's emotions threatened to overwhelm him again. Fury. Hatred. The need to kill. And guilt, for not protecting her. But, most of all, anguish, for everything Eliza had been through.

'I'm working through it all,' she said. 'The therapy's been great.' He saw her resolve. 'I want Seymour out of Rose. And I want him to pay.'

'I'll sort it. I'll have him removed from the board.'

'No. *I* want to do it. He needs to know it comes from me. I might even do a Twitter thread. Or I'll get Terri to interview me for *The Rack* – it could be part of an update on the #MeToo movement, maybe. What it's achieved, how attitudes have changed. I need to think about it some more.'

Harry gently wiped away her tears. 'If anyone can give him his comeuppance, you can. Do it for yourself and for all those other women out there.'

'Like Caitlyn.'

'Yes, like Caitlyn.'

Eliza gave him a small smile. 'I'm sorry, Dad, for landing all that on you. But I needed to get it out.'

'And I needed to hear it. And I'm so sorry. I can't say that enough.'

'I know you are. And you've changed. I understand what made you behave in that way. You're only human. Once upon a time quite a bad one, but now pretty much the best one I know. Apart from Clare, maybe.'

He smiled. 'Quite right. She's perfect. What did I ever do to deserve her?'

'You don't, according to Maria.'

'Really?'

'But you do, according to me. I hope I find my Clare one day, Dad.'

'Rob?'

'He's amazing; he's waited for me all this time. Maybe he won't have to wait much longer, now I've had this out with you.'

Eliza

'Well, you know what they say – bad things come in threes,' said Eliza to Chess, as they took their plates over to the sofa. She'd invited her cousin over for wine, pasta, and the hot new BBC drama *Kitchen Sink*. It was important to know what was trending.

'Three bad things? What bad things?' said Chess.

'I hardly dare say. Not sure what you know or don't know about the biggest bomb.'

'Stop being mysterious, Eliza. What's going on?'

'Firstly, Kit got into a scrap. A proper fight with bruises and police. Can you believe it?'

'That boy's a complete mystery to me, as is your weird obsession with him.'

'It's not a weird obsession.'

'Try telling that to Rob. Next?'

'Oh. Right.' Eliza took a sip of her wine. 'Mackenzie's in London. She wants to meet up. Maybe this isn't in fact a bad thing, I'm not sure.' Eliza just couldn't make up her mind. Her feelings were ambivalent. 'I *think* I liked her. Did you?'

'I did. She seems interesting.'

'I'm just worried she wants a role at Rose, and I wouldn't know what to do with her.'

'You can cross that bridge if and when you come to it.'

'Dad's having a birthday do – I thought maybe he could invite her.'

'Good plan.' Chess picked up the remote. 'Shall we start?'

'One more thing. Someone else he's going to invite. God, I can't believe I'm saying this.'

'What?'

'His son. My half-brother. I don't suppose that news has reached you on the grapevine?'

'I knew Uncle Harry had another son, Mum told me one time.'

Chess *knew*?

'She swore me to secrecy – said Harry was going to tell you when the time was right. But I didn't know he was in touch with him.'

'They met up in Sydney, on *Janette*. I was there. His name's Stu – he's the image of Dad, a kind of scruffy version. Looks a bit dissolute.'

'Redhead?'

'What do you reckon?'

'So – that must have been quite a shock for you, Eliza.'

She thought back. 'It was. I was floored. But you know what, Chess? After Stu left, I had a real heart to heart with Dad, and it kind of made me understand him better. All the stuff he went through with Katie – losing babies, her depression.'

'Every cloud, I suppose.'

'Yes. So, Chess. The Rose family just got bigger. And I'm wondering how all this is going to play out.'

'Let's hope the new shoots don't turn out to be suckers.'

❊

The next morning, Eliza went to see Terri, to discuss the #MeToo article she'd proposed. In her email, she'd mentioned Seymour's behaviour.

'Why didn't you tell me about this before?' demanded Terri, as Eliza sat down. 'Fuck's sake, Eliza. You could've talked to me.'

Eliza swallowed. 'I want him exposed. But should I just say I was abused, drop a few hints and wait for someone to investigate? Or should I name names?'

'The former, I think. That would work. Other press would run with it, and imagine him stewing while he waited for them to work it out.'

'Let's do it, Terri.'

❊

Maria phoned to let Eliza know she was back in town, and that she'd booked a one-way ticket to Cambodia, where she'd be helping out at an orphanage. She was leaving in August.

'Dad's organizing a birthday party,' said Eliza, as they sat chatting in Maria's austere Westminster flat. The living room was dominated by a large old-fashioned fireplace over which hung a wooden cross. 'You must come.'

'Shall I?'

'Yes! I should let you know, though, there will be two family members there you haven't met before.'

'What? Who?'

'Cousin Mackenzie, Aunt Margot's daughter. I met her at Margot's funeral.'

'And the other?'

Eliza could have kicked herself. 'Dammit. I just dropped myself right into that one. Should've asked Dad to talk to you first. His name's Henry, but he likes to be called Stu.'

Maria met her eye. 'Father's son by one of the women he betrayed Mother with. He told me, in Wales.'

Eliza's relief was enormous. 'You know. Thank goodness.'

'Yes. Eliza – I never said, before. Thank you, for what you did for me back then. Especially for asking Father to come. It . . . well. It changed everything.'

'Gosh. But it was certainly overdue, him facing up to how he treated you. So – will you be OK with meeting Stu?'

Maria pursed her lips. 'It's not his fault our father was a liar and a cheat.'

'Right. Yes. You'll come, then?'

'I will. It'll give me a chance to say my goodbyes.'

'Oh my god,' said Rob in a low voice, as Mac appeared out of the French doors. 'Another Rose clone. Your cousin, I take it?'

'Just you wait,' muttered Eliza. 'There's Stu to come yet.'

Mac was looking lovely in a pair of capri pants that showed off her long slim legs, teamed with a blue shirt. Her hair was piled on her head – it probably pushed her over the six-foot mark.

'Bloody hell,' said Harry, under his breath. 'Who knew?' He stood up. 'Mackenzie, my long-lost niece. Welcome to the southern branch. Undoubtedly more fun than yours.'

Mackenzie laughed heartily. 'Uncle Harry. It's so exciting to meet you at last! You have no idea how many times I nagged Mum and Dad to come visit you. Mum used to say, "Over my dead body." Turned out she was right!'

Harry chuckled. 'Come here, give your uncle a hug.'

As he squeezed his niece, Eliza felt her eyes narrowing.

He introduced Clare, Maria and Rob. 'And you already know Eliza.'

'Yes, lovely to see you again. I've rented a flat in Barnes. I hope we can see a lot of each other.'

'Right, yes. Great.'

The Lisles arrived next, and then the Studleys. Finally, Stu appeared.

Eliza sat up in astonishment. He'd smartened himself up, and was the image of their father, but with lighter hair. His blue eyes stood out against his tanned Aussie skin, and his limbs were loose and long. He had an energy about him that reminded Eliza of Harry.

Chess caught Eliza's eye, her own widening.

'Sorry I'm late,' he said, pulling up a chair. 'Got bloody lost. All these little streets, it's hard to find your way around, eh?'

Harry made the introductions. ' . . . and this is our other long-lost family member, Mackenzie, daughter of my late sister Margot. She's also from an outpost.'

Mackenzie gave Stu a wide smile. 'Well, look at you – an Aussie version of me!' They looked so alike, with their sandy hair, long legs, and smattering of freckles. 'Suddenly I have an abundance of cousins,' she said. 'Och, but life is certainly looking up.'

After lunch, as they swapped seats and chatted over coffee, Eliza looked around at this new version of her family. A new half-brother, a new cousin. Both Roses, through and through, and yet so different, with their accents, their unknown histories. And, most importantly, their unknown intentions.

She acknowledged the discomfort that had been niggling away at her. It was nice for them, getting to know their family. But she wished they'd stayed away. It was all too unsettling, and she hated – yes, *hated* – seeing Harry paying them so much attention.

At least Rob seemed immune to Mac's undeniable charm, she thought gloomily, as Harry joked about how terrifying Aunt Margot had been.

'Hey, wassup?' said Rob in her ear.

'Oh, nothing.'

'Can we take a walk? I have something to share.'

'Sure. I'm feeling like a spare part around here anyway.'

'There's no need to be jealous,' he said, when they were out of earshot. 'You know charmer is Harry's default.'

'Was it that obvious?'

'It's scary, the power of dads.'

'True.'

'Maybe,' said Rob, 'when we're official, his grip will lessen. Like . . . this week.'

'Perhaps. Wait, what did you say?'

'Two words, Lizzie. *Decree absolute.* Or maybe these two: *I'm free.* Or: *I'm yours.*'

'Rob! Oh my god, this is the best news!'

He held out his arms, and when she flew into them he picked her up and twirled her round.

'Shall we tell the others?' he said, putting her down.

'No. Not with those two there. I want to share this only with Dad and Clare for now. Have you told your parents?'

'Not yet, I wanted to tell you first.'

'Oh, Rob!' She gave an excited little squeak. 'This is so, so great.'

'It is.'

'I guess . . . I'll have to think how to play it at work.'

'Well, you're hardly going to make an announcement. Or snog me in the atrium. You've got to be CEO about it.'

She thought for a moment. 'Wimbledon.'

'Wimbledon?'

'You can be my plus one. My very obvious plus one.'

Eliza and Rob stayed behind after the party, and shared the news with Harry and Clare.

'I'm so pleased,' said Clare. 'You make *such* a delightful couple.'

'You did the right thing, waiting,' said Harry. 'The British press is a brutal beast. You may still get some flack but, believe me, you'll learn to live with that.'

'You really think they'll be interested, Dad?'

'Absolutely. You'll need to manage it, Lizzie. Take control.'

'I thought Wimbledon. On Rob's arm.'

Harry smiled. 'I can see the headline now. *Love Match for Eliza Rose.*'

Later that week, Eliza had another session with Dr Thomson. She explained that Rob was now divorced, and related her conversation with Harry.

'I think it's time for you to resume relations with Rob,' said the therapist. 'How do you feel about that?'

Eliza considered her response. 'It's all about letting go of blame? Learning to trust? Forgiveness?'

'As far as your relationship with your father is concerned, I think it is.'

'Then yes. I'm ready to try again.'

Chapter 34

Eliza

'Anyone for tennis?' Eliza said to her reflection in the full-length mirror.

She was wearing a short, off-white linen dress, teamed with red gladiator sandals. *Strawberries and cream.* She'd pinned her hair off her face with strawberry hairclips spotted in Harrods. Subtle eye make-up, red lipstick, and a spritz of a sexy, summery perfume.

Ready for the cameras. *Advantage, Eliza.*

The taxi arrived, and as it headed southwest there were just a few puffy white clouds in the cornflower-blue sky. It was going to be the perfect summer's day, in oh so many ways.

'Good god,' said Harry, looking pointedly at her skirt as she joined him outside the Rose marquee. 'Are you actually competing today?'

'Tsh, get with the times, Dad.'

Their guests began to arrive – there would be a buffet lunch, then an afternoon of tennis, with strawberries and cream for high tea.

Here were Terri and her girlfriend, Layla. Terri's black and white outfit matched her hair.

'Harry,' Terri said, as he kissed her cheek. 'How many years have we been doing this?'

'Since Becker beat Lendl in the final – nineteen eighty-six.'

'And, more importantly, Navratilova beat Mandlíková. And everyone else. Almost every year, for a while there.'

'Fearless trailblazer,' said Harry. 'Like you.'

Terri gave him a half-smile. 'Times certainly have changed, Harry.'

'Maybe you helped make that happen.'

'Sentimental old fool. Ah, while we're on the subject of rainbows ...'

Will and Kit had arrived, and Eliza smiled as she took in their Wimbledon ensembles – designer suits, blue for Will and cream for Kit, and fedora hats. They looked adorable.

'Hello, cuties,' she said. 'Looking forward to the tennis?'

'*To sport would be as tedious as work*,' said Will.

'It's kind of pointless,' said Kit.

'He's brought a book to read,' said Will.

'Sit by me today?' said Kit.

'No way. I'm not sitting with you two looking all dramatically bored. And anyway ...' She spotted Rob striding towards them, rocking a pale-blue suit. 'I have news.'

Rob's grin was wide.

'He's looking pleased with himself,' said Will.

'Hello, gorgeous,' said Rob, kissing Eliza's cheek.

'That's my line,' said Kit.

'Mine now,' said Rob, putting an arm around her shoulder.

Kit raised his eyebrows at Eliza.

'Rob's divorce came through,' she said. 'No more skulking.'

'Ah,' said Will. 'What does one say, Rob? Congratulations?'

'Is the correct answer,' he replied.

'Right,' said Harry. 'Now we've cleared that one up, it's time to go forth and be corporate.' He waved his hand at them. 'Off you go, children.'

❀

After lunch, Harry, Eliza and Rob made their way through the crowds to the Centre Court. Eliza linked her arm through Rob's and smiled for the cameras as press photographers walked backwards ahead of them. It felt *so* good to be able to do this at last.

No doubt they'd describe Rob as 'recently divorced', and imply she was the reason, but there was little she could do about that. Although, if she'd wanted to avoid the marriage-wrecker label . . . perhaps the dress *was* a bit on the short side.

It was the men's quarter finals, and the match was gripping.

Kit was clearly ungripped. Sitting two rows in front of Eliza, he fell asleep with his head on Will's shoulder. No doubt the cameras would zoom in on him too.

Eliza couldn't help smiling. Rose staff were on form today. All they needed was for Harry to be snapped flirting with a celeb for a clean sweep on tomorrow's gossip columns.

The match finished, and as they waited for the doubles to begin, Harry asked, 'How's your tennis, Rob? I seem to remember you weren't too shabby from your times at Richmond?'

'Not bad – better than Dad and Gil.'

'I have a hankering. How about you two come over for a couple of sets after we're done here?'

'Great idea,' said Eliza. 'Rob?'

'Sounds good to me.'

Rob was kitted out, and Eliza changed into her favourite tennis dress – bright blue with an orange trim. And matching knickers.

'As I'm sure you'll remember, Dad takes his tennis seriously,' she said, as they walked down to the court. 'If you beat him you'll have his respect for ever. But, to be honest, that's unlikely.'

'He's more than twice my age, Lizzie. And what about his bad leg?'

'Have you seen him limping lately?'

'Actually, no.'

'It always hurts him after he's played, but during a match he just forgets about it.'

They began knocking up, and Clare came out to watch, sitting up on the umpire's chair.

The sun started its descent, casting long shadows across the court. The gentle *thock* of tennis balls resounded in the quiet of the evening.

They began a mini tournament, best of five games. First up, Rob played Eliza. She gave it her best shot, but Rob was too powerful. She bowed out at three games to love.

Next, Harry and Rob were evenly matched. Rob was quick, and accurately anticipated Harry's moves. But Harry's skill was superior and his backhand was a killer. He aced Rob, time after time. They won two games each, and the fifth went to deuce.

Harry was serving, and another ace flew past Rob before he had time to react.

'Advantage, Harry!' Clare called.

On the next point, Rob returned another powerful serve with equal ferocity. The ball bounced just out of Harry's reach.

'Deuce!' called Clare.

Harry's first serve went in the net, and the second was weaker. Rob took full advantage, blasting his return down the sideline and past Harry.

Lord, would you look at these two go.

'Advantage, Rob!' called Clare.

Oh my god – match point. He could actually win this.

Again Harry's serve was a killer, but Rob somehow managed to reach it. The ball clipped the top of the net and dropped like a stone on the other side. Harry lunged, but was too far away.

'Yes!' cried Rob, punching the air.

Eliza ran onto the court and threw her arms around him. 'I can't believe you won! Dad hasn't been beaten in forever!'

After his initial annoyance at losing to a fluky shot, Harry smiled and held out his hand. 'Well played, Rob. You're officially worthy of my precious Lizzie. Look after her well.'

'I will, Harry. You can count on it.' He put his arm round her. 'Tonight I feel like the luckiest man alive.'

'You are,' said Harry. 'Well, I think Clare and I might leave you to it. And, Rob – if you want to stop over, that's fine with us.' He went to collect up the tennis balls.

'How about we take a walk?' said Rob. 'We could revisit our crime scenes – the lake, the field where we stalked deer?'

Richmond Park was all but deserted, the sun kissing the horizon beyond the trees, its slanted beams turning the long grass of the deer meadows fiery orange.

'I can almost see us,' said Eliza. 'Just there.' She pointed to a spot near a group of trees, where she remembered lying on her stomach watching Rob creeping up on the deer.

'Stalking deer,' he said.

'You were rubbish at it.'

'You always put me off.'

'Did you fancy me even then?'

'Ew, no. I meant with your talking. You never stopped. Is that the tree you fell out of?' He pointed to an enormous oak on the far side of the meadow.

'Yes. How did I even get up into those branches?'

'I lifted you. I think I just wanted to see up your skirt.'

'So you *did* fancy me?'

'Nah. Curiosity.'

They walked over to the oak, and the sun slipped away. The heat of the day radiated from the ground; the air was soft and smelled of warm hay. It was as if their old playground was embracing them, welcoming them back.

Rob leaned against the trunk and she put her arms around him, looking up into the branches, remembering.

'Isn't time strange?' she said. 'Right here, all those years ago. Me and you, running wild, not a care in the world. And now we're here again, all grown up.'

She remembered Kit's words: *Time runs in circles, in loops.*

'Maybe the tree remembers us – there's something about old oaks,' said Rob, pulling her close.

That other ancient oak, bathed in moonlight, flashed into her mind.

A tremor ran through her; her skin was tingling with desire. 'Yes, there is.' She traced Rob's lips with her finger. 'I'm so happy, Rob.'

'Likewise. But I've got to say, if you don't let me take advantage of this apology for a dress very soon, I'm going to cry.'

He kissed her, and the tingling ignited.

'Oh god,' she whispered, as his mouth moved down to her neck.

His hand slipped up her skirt and she gasped as ripples of intense pleasure gripped her, growing stronger, then stronger still, obliterating everything in the world but him, his lips, his fingers.

He paused.

'No, don't stop, please don't stop,' she whispered, her eyes still closed. If he stopped now, she'd die.

'Do we need to talk about this?' he said. 'And ... maybe we should go back to the house?'

She opened her eyes. 'No. Here. I want my first time to be here, on a bed of long grass, beneath an ancient oak. I want it to be ... magical. It's nearly dark, there's no one around.'

'But – your problem?'

'I have strategies – I'm ready to try again. Unless ... I guess ... protection?'

He smiled, and began stroking her again. 'I brought something, just in case.'

'Oh, thank god!' Her knees were threatening to give way. 'But what made you think ... '

'Only the way you've been looking at me all day.'

She acknowledged the truth. The excitement had been building for hours. She was ready to explode with it.

Eliza lay down with her arms above her head, and looked up at the sky. A crescent moon peeped through the branches of the old oak.

Rob stretched out beside her, propping himself up on one elbow. Twilight was fading to night, but she could see his eyes, burning. She closed hers again as he kissed her, picking up where he'd left off.

He was gentle and slow, and she lost herself in one exquisite sensation after another, until there was only one thing left for them to do.

'What should I do?' he said, softly. 'To help you.'

'Keep your eyes on mine. Just keep looking at me, all the time.'

Stroking her hair back from her face, he moved on top of her, between her legs, and she kept her gaze fixed on his. She held her breath, waiting, but there was no anxiety, no panic. All she felt was an intense longing, a need for this to happen.

And then it did. Slowly and cautiously, until she began moving with him, her eyes locked on his.

'Put your legs around me, Lizzie.'

She gasped as the sensation intensified, and a fierce heat flooded her limbs.

All the time his eyes never left hers, as he took her to greater heights, on and on, up and up, until she touched the sky, finally closing her eyes as a burst of ecstasy swept aside everything else.

He collapsed, burying his face in her neck.

Neither said a word for a while as they returned to earth, their breathing slowing. Finally he rolled off her and onto his back, reaching for her hand, and they lay side by side beneath the tree, its branches now silhouetted against the velvety dark blue.

'Well?' he said, turning to look at her.

'That was so nice.'

'*Nice?*'

'I'm just a beginner.'

'Seriously. It was all good?'

'It was incredible. Beautiful. God, Rob, I do love you.'

It was just hitting her . . . she'd done it. She'd overcome her fear. Her virginity was no more. Sent packing, in spectacular fashion. She could finally have a proper relationship with this adorable man. The future stretched ahead, rosy and bright, full of promise. Full of love and fun and – sex! Life was wonderful.

'Same, best girl.'

She sighed happily. 'Will you stay the night? It's time you saw my room – Elizabeth the First slept there, you know.'

'She got around – she slept at our place in Kenilworth too.'

'Coolest monarch ever. No way was she a virgin all her life, though.'

Rob shifted, resting his head on her stomach. 'What makes you say that?'

Eliza played with his hair. 'Why would she have been? She was the queen; she could have any man who took her fancy. She just didn't want to marry any of them – an admirable sentiment, given the attitudes of the times. And the fact that her dad chopped her mum's head off. Not the greatest ad for the conjugal state.'

Rob broke off a blade of grass and started chewing it. The gesture took her straight back.

'But they didn't have contraception,' he said. 'She wouldn't have taken the risk. Imagine, a pregnant unmarried queen.'

'Magic was more powerful in those days.'

'You don't believe in magic.'

'I do. Magic is real.'

❖

They said goodnight to Harry and Clare, then went up to Eliza's room.

Her second time was even better than her first, and by the third there was no need to keep her eyes open.

As the hours passed on this hot and beautiful midsummer night, Eliza and Rob dozed, limbs entangled; woke, kissed, made love, talked, made plans. Out of the old leadlight windows the crescent moon tracked across the sky, then disappeared as dawn crept up on them, calling time.

Chapter 35

Eliza

Eliza slipped out of bed at six-thirty, put on her robe and went downstairs to make coffee. Harry was already up, sitting at the kitchen table, flicking through last night's *Evening Standard*. The radio was on quietly, and beyond the windows the sun was peeping over the trees in Richmond Park.

'Morning, Sweet Pea,' said Harry. 'You're on the front page – want to see?'

There was a close-up shot of her sitting between Rob and Harry on the Centre Court. Rob's arm was along the back of her seat, and she was laughing at something he'd said.

LOVE MATCH FOR HARRY'S ELIZA! said the headline.

'I was close,' said Harry.

'Honestly, can't they find something more interesting to write about?'

'Better get used to it.'

'Help,' said Eliza. 'How do I work this machine? If I don't make him a proper espresso it'll be curtains for me already.'

'Grounds for dismissal.'

'No puns, please, Dad. Too early.'

He came over. 'Come on, Lizzie,' he said, scooping coffee into the filter, pressing buttons. 'It's not complicated. Here you go – one espresso. Give Sleeping Beauty my regards.'

The name was spot on, thought Eliza, as she put the coffee down on the bedside table. She stood staring, drinking him in; his dark curls on her pillow, his long black eyelashes, a shapely leg poking out of the duvet.

His eyelids fluttered open, and his smile knotted her insides.

'I made you a coffee.'

He sat up, brushing his hair back and stretching. 'Oh no.'

'OK, *Dad* made you a coffee.'

'Now you're talking. What time is it?'

'Time for me to come back to bed.'

As she snuggled into him, he picked up his phone.

'Put it down, Roberto. Let's stay offline a while longer.' She trailed a finger down his chest.

He flicked through his messages, and sat up straighter as he read one of them, angling the phone away from Eliza.

'What is it?'

'Work.' He put the phone down and picked up his coffee, sipping it distractedly, staring out of the window.

'Rob?'

'It's fine. But I'm going to have to go in early. There's a situation.'

'What situation?'

'Lizzie – let's make a rule, now we're a full-on couple with sex and all the other things.'

'I'm listening.'

'No work talk in bed.'

'Sounds good to me,' she said. 'So . . . how early are we talking? You wanna drink that coffee up fast?' Her hand crept further south.

'*Early* early, I'm afraid.' He kissed her forehead, then threw back the duvet and slid out of bed.

'Not fair,' she said, pouting, as he disappeared into the bathroom.

But her jokey tone was forced. He was hiding something. What was going on?

Ten minutes later he was showered and dressed. He sat on the edge of the bed, putting on his shoes, then checked his phone again. He kissed her, but it was quick.

'Thanks for yesterday,' he said. 'It was crazy-perfect.'

'I think it was my favourite day ever.'

'Not forgetting the night.'

'I'll never forget the night.'

✻

'Sorry I'm late, Pippa!' Eliza stopped by her PA's desk, a wide smile on her face. 'Something came up.' She laughed at her own joke.

Pippa smiled. 'So I heard. Office grapevine is about to combust. You're official now?'

'Rob's divorce came through, so – yes.'

'That's great. You make a lovely couple. And everyone up here will be happy to be seeing more of Rob.' She winked.

'Isn't he adorable? Sorry, Pippa. Not very CEO of me. Any important messages?'

'Mackenzie James called. Wonders if she can have a meeting, today if possible.'

'Oh.' Eliza had been expecting this. 'Am I free for lunch?'

Pippa looked at her computer. 'Nothing between eleven and two-thirty.'

'Suggest twelve and I'll give her the tour.'

Eliza tried to concentrate on her work, answering emails, reading reports. But her efforts were sabotaged by the images flooding her mind. Lying beneath the great oak, touching the stars. Their limbs entwined in bed, not knowing where her body ended and his began.

She'd put aside her misgivings over the text. Perhaps he'd made a mistake, and hadn't wanted her to know. This boss-as-partner situation was going to need some careful navigating.

ELIZA: How's your day? My productivity is shot to hell. Love you xxxxx

No reply. He was probably in a meeting.

By twelve, things hadn't improved, and she was glad of the distraction when Pippa showed Mac into her office.

'Mac! Great to see you again. I thought we could have a coffee, and then I'll give you the tour.'

'Sounds good.'

Eliza went to indicate the office chair opposite her own, but Mac headed to the sofa. 'Hey, I saw you in the paper. Wimbledon looked fun. Wish I'd been there.'

Oops.

'Oh gosh. I should have invited you – sorry.' She sat down beside her.

'It's no' a problem.' Her Scottish accent was so gentle on the ear. 'Mum certainly wouldn't have come down for an afternoon of tennis. But I'd like to be more involved at Rose than she was. Could we talk about that, do you think?'

Must we?

'Of course. Do you have any thoughts on how it could work?'

'Maybe something like Chess did – she told me she got some cross-departmental experience before deciding to work on the production side of things. My background is politics; my skills are best suited to marketing and PR, probably.'

'I can certainly look into that. Let me speak to our human resources department – embarrassingly called @people, I'm afraid.'

'So . . . the papers are saying you and Rob are together,' Mac said, crossing one leg over the other and sitting back. 'Is that true?'

Bit personal. Back off.

'I've known Rob all my life. He's the son of Dad's friend John Studley. John's on the board so you'll probably meet him.'

'I see. I'm looking forward to getting to know everyone. And I've been having fun hanging out with your half-brother.'

'You've seen Stu?'

'It's so great, hooking up with my family after all these years. Stu and I get on well, we have a lot in common.'

Something about this was making Eliza horribly uncomfortable. It felt like . . . an *alliance*.

There was a tap on the door, and they looked up to see Chess's face poking round it.

'Chess! Come on in – look who's here!'

Then she registered Chess's expression. Something was wrong.

'Eliza, can I have a private word, please?'

'Och, don't mind me.'

'Sorry, Mac. I need to speak to Eliza alone.'

What's going on?

Mac looked like a schoolgirl excluded by the cool kids. 'OK. I'll wait outside.'

'Sorry, Mac,' said Eliza. 'I'll be right with you.'

Mac left the room and Chess shut the door behind her. She sat down next to Eliza.

'Chess, what on earth?' Then she registered – her cousin was white as a sheet. She grabbed Eliza's hand; her own was shaking.

'Eliza. Oh god, I don't know how to tell you. It's Amy. Rob found her this morning, in their house at Kingston. She'd fallen down the stairs. She was . . . oh god. Eliza – Amy's dead.'

Everything seemed to recede, and there was a hissing in her ears. She stared at Chess.

'I can't take it in. I can't . . . ' Chess began to cry.

'Are you sure?' was all Eliza could manage.

'It looks like her neck was broken.'

A chill was creeping through Eliza's veins, turning her hands and feet to ice, and a darkness was entering her soul, extinguishing the light that had filled it since yesterday.

Chess took a tissue from the box on Eliza's desk and blew her nose. 'Poor, poor Amy. I just . . . I hope she wasn't lying there, all alone. Probably would've been quick, right? Broken neck?'

'She fell?'

'I don't have any more information. Rob called Gil as soon as he found her. He's in bits.'

Rob. Oh god, Rob.

What was he doing at Amy's house?
The text. She must have sent him a text.

Eliza stood up quickly, and the room reeled. 'I should be with him.'

'No. Gil's there. Rob's going to stay at ours. He's with the police at the moment.'

'Can I come home with you? Wait for him there?' Now she was feeling faint.

'Why don't we wait; see what Rob wants? Come here, sit down. You've gone horribly pale.'

'He'll need me!' Eliza sat down heavily, breathing quickly. *This can't be real.*

'Gil said … Rob's obviously distraught. I think it's best to wait until all the formalities are out of the way. The police have to check for … that there's nothing suspicious. Standard procedure.'

'*Suspicious?* He was with me! He came home with Dad and me, we played tennis and he stayed the night.'

'I know. He told Gil. I expect they'll establish a time of death and then it'll all be cut and dried – an accident, or … but no one else there.' 'I'll phone him.' Eliza reached for her mobile.

'No! Leave him alone. Wait until he contacts you.'

'But—'

'Look, I'm sorry.' Chess took her hand. 'Gil asked Rob if we should come get you, but … he said no.'

'Why?'

'I don't know. He's a mess, it'll be some time before he can think straight again.'

Only now was it properly hitting Eliza.

Amy's dead.

'He got a text, Chess. This morning. Or maybe last night – his phone was switched off. He didn't say it was from her, but I think it must have been.'

Then Chess's words hit home.

'What do you mean, "an accident, *or* … "?'

'Well, Rob's immediate thought was … she's been depressed

again – really bad. I went to see her; she'd just got the decree absolute. She knew it was coming, but it really set her back. She was devastated.'

'Oh god. Poor Amy.'

Until now, Eliza hadn't spared her a thought. She remembered Katie, with her depression, and Caitlyn ...

Fragile people break, Eliza.

All at once, she felt like she was losing her mind.

'But there was no note,' said Chess. 'They checked. And honestly – if you were going to – well, do that – I don't think that's how you'd do it. So maybe it *was* an accident.'

What did the text say?

There was a tap on the door, and Pippa's face appeared round it. 'I'm so sorry to interrupt; Mackenzie's wondering if there's anything she can do? Or should she just leave? she says.'

'I'll come have a word,' said Chess.

Eliza had started to shake; she felt sick.

Had Amy killed herself?

But surely Chess was right – throwing herself down a flight of stairs wouldn't be the way to do that?

How will we get through this?

Chess came back in. 'Mac's gone. Are you going to be OK? You look terrible.'

'I can't see the way ahead,' she said, beginning to cry as Chess hugged her. 'I don't know what to do.'

'Sit tight, Eliza. That's all we can do. Wait until we have a clearer picture. I'm sure it was an accident. And if it wasn't, then ... you know she's suffered from depression for a long time, on and off. She had it all through her relationship with Rob. Look, why don't you go home? Shall I sort you a taxi?'

'I don't want to be alone. Kit. Find Kit.'

'*Kit?* Why?'

'Just find him, please?'

Chess gave her a quizzical look, but left the room again.

Eliza wiped away her tears, sat back and shut her eyes.

The door opened again, and then Kit was there, holding her tight. Immediately she felt calmer.

'Come on, I'll take you home.'

He got them a cab, and back at the apartment he wrapped her in a blanket and made her Marmite toast and tea.

He sat beside her and she rested her head on his shoulder. Gradually the terrible feelings that had swamped her – the dread, the guilt – receded, and she was able to take a step back.

'Poor Amy,' she said.

'I had . . . ' He shook his head.

'You had what?'

'I don't know. A sense of something.'

She remembered his strange words that time at his house.

'Tell me what you know, Kit.'

'Amy's mind was in a dark place.'

'But you never met her! How could you know that?'

'No idea. I rarely understand my own mind, as you know.'

'My god.'

'Where's Rob?'

'He won't see me.'

'Don't push it.'

'How do we get through this, Kit? Me and Rob?'

'Give him space. He'll have some serious shit to work through.'

'So . . . you don't think it was an accident?'

'I didn't say that. It was going to happen, that's all I know.'

Kit stayed over, and the next morning Eliza rang Pippa to say she'd be in later. There was no word from Rob, and she took Chess's advice to leave him alone, to wait until he contacted her. Kit had made her switch off her phone, but it was time to talk to Harry.

At the sound of his voice, she began to cry. 'Dad, I don't know what to do. Rob . . . he hasn't been in touch. Is this partly my fault?'

'No, Lizzie. I know what you're feeling and, more to the point, what he's feeling. Guilt's a horrible thing.'

'But, Dad. Those things you said to me. About people being fragile, about not smashing their relationships. Treading carefully.'

'You waited – you did everything properly. Rob's marriage was clearly a mistake. And he'll come right, it'll just take time.'

Kit appeared, wiping the sleep from his eyes.

'I'm talking to Dad,' she said.

'Who's that?' said Harry.

'Kit. I asked him to stay.'

Harry was silent. 'Are the press outside?'

Eliza hadn't even considered the possibility. She went over to the window and saw a group of photographers and reporters on the path below.

'Oh god, they are, yes.'

'Have you seen this morning's news?'

'No.'

'Right. The press are all over the story. I'd strongly advise you to avoid the newspapers and TV. It's all idle speculation. And, of course, they're loving it – they build you up to knock you down. I might have some experience of that myself.'

'What are they saying?' She steeled herself.

'All tediously predictable. Sweet, gentle nurse versus fiery media queen temptress.'

'*Temptress?*'

'I warned you about that dress.'

'It was just a look.'

'It's never just a look.'

'Are we back in the twentieth century?'

'As far as the likes of the *Sun* are concerned, we absolutely are.' He paused. 'And I'm afraid . . . there was a copy of the *Standard* on Amy's bed. The press are making much of the fact that you and Rob were on the front page.'

Eliza couldn't help picturing it – Amy staring at the photograph, the confirmation that he'd moved on, right there in front of her eyes.

'Oh no.'

'It's not necessarily significant. And remember, it'll be yesterday's news soon. But you do need to make sure they don't see Kit.'

'What? Why?'

'Eliza, for heaven's sake! You've been in this business long enough. Kit's reputation ... well, my own pales into insignificance. It wouldn't be wise to let the press know he spent the night with you.'

'This is stupid.'

'And, Lizzie. There's obviously a question mark over Rob until they've established a time of death. I'm sure he'll be in the clear soon, but be aware of the finger-pointing.'

'What? You mean ...? But that's ridiculous!'

'He left Richmond early enough to have caught her before work. Their place is only across the park. That's why the police need to be thorough. Look, I'd say come home, but I think you should ride this out. Go to work, carry on as normal. Hold your head high; don't skulk.'

Kit sneaked out a side door, his hair tucked under a baseball hat of Eliza's, and soon after, dressed in a sensible-length skirt and jacket, Eliza headed off to work, stopping for a quick word with the press pack outside before hailing a cab.

Yes, it was dreadful news about Rob's ex-wife. Her thoughts were with Amy's family at this difficult time. No, she hadn't been seeing Rob behind Amy's back; they'd waited for his divorce to come through. No further comment.

Chapter 36

Eliza

The gauntlet to the top floor was lined with staff pretending not to stare. Receptionists, security guards, staff milling in the atrium or waiting for the lifts – familiar faces that always had a smile for Eliza.

Today, none of them met her eye.

Even Pippa. 'Oh . . . Eliza. I thought you probably wouldn't be in.'

'Can you get me a coffee? Then come through and update me.'

She scrolled through her email inbox. Nothing that couldn't wait.

One from Terri.

> Eliza – #MeToo piece on hold. Here if
> you need me X

One from Mac:

> Hi Eliza
>   I'm so sorry about what has happened to Rob.
> This must be a difficult time for you.
>   Further to our meeting I'm attaching my CV

and hope to hear from you once you've had
a chance to liaise with your HR dept (or @
People!). As I mentioned, perhaps a role in
Marketing would be a good fit?
    Warmest regards
    Mac

Mac could bloody wait. How much did she know? Not that it was any of her business. How much did *anyone* know? What were people saying? Why those looks from her staff, who'd always been nothing but loyal and friendly?

Harry's words about avoiding the press coverage were sensible. Yet how could she get things back on track unless she knew what she was dealing with?

She googled *Amy Hart death Rob Studley Eliza Rose*, and clicked on the *Daily Mail*'s website.

It was the lead story. The headline read:

'AMY WAS DEVASTATED BY THEIR SPLIT.' WIFE OF
ELIZA ROSE'S LOVER FOUND DEAD AT HOME

Beneath the headline was the *Evening Standard* photo Harry had shown her, captioned: *A newspaper article featuring this photo was found close to Amy's body.*

Eliza closed her eyes for a moment before reading on.

> Amy Studley, wife of Rose Corp film producer Rob
> Studley, was found dead yesterday at her Kingston
> home. Her body was reportedly discovered by her
> husband at the foot of a staircase.
>
> Studley has recently been seen in public with
> media boss Eliza Rose, daughter of five-times-
> married Harry Rose, former head of Rose Corp.
>
> A source close to Amy, a paediatric nurse, told
> the *Mail* she'd been suffering from depression after

discovering her husband's affair. 'Amy was devastated by Rob's desertion. I was so worried about her, all alone in that big house.'

The reason for Studley's visit yesterday morning remains unclear. He is currently helping police with their enquiries ...

She exited the website as Pippa came in.

'Eliza, all the calls about ... what's happened. We're putting them through to the PR department. There's a statement saying nobody will be commenting until the police have finished their investigation. We thought it best not to include a sympathy quote from you.'

'Right. I need you to tell me the truth, Pippa. What's the office grapevine's take on this?'

'Much as you'd expect. Did Amy fall, or did she throw herself down the stairs because of you and Rob. Some – quite a few – saying maybe they had a row that got physical. Even that she was pushed. And people don't know what the staircase looked like, so they're speculating about whether it was high enough for Amy to have ... well. It's all awful, anyway.'

It was worse than awful. How could anyone imagine Rob would be capable of hurting Amy. Of *killing* her?

'Thanks, that's helpful. Let's attempt to continue as normal until there's further news.'

Next, Eliza called Chess.

'How is he?' she asked, as soon as her cousin answered.

'Hi, Eliza.' Chess dropped her voice. 'The police are all done with him. The time of death's been established – between eight p.m. and midnight. Rob's in the clear. Amy's family are waiting on the post-mortem report so they can organize the funeral. We'll be going up to Kenilworth with Rob when it's all sorted, so long as there's no need for an inquest.'

'But how is he?'

'A little better than he was.'

'He hasn't been in touch.'

'No. I'm afraid he's still beating himself up. It was only yesterday he found her, Eliza.'

'I haven't had a word from him, Chess. Not a word!' Tears threatened. 'Where is he? Still at yours?'

'Yes, with Gil. The press are outside – you mustn't go round.'

'So what am I supposed to *do*?'

'Let me speak to him tonight. I know how hard this must be for you.'

Eliza ended the call and brought up Rob's contact details. Her hands were shaking as she texted: *Please, Rob. Don't shut me out. xx*

By the time Eliza went to bed that night, there was no reply.

The post-mortem confirmed Amy's neck had broken as a result of falling down the stairs. The report stated there was no reason to suppose it was anything other than an accident, in spite of the victim's history of depression.

The press stopped pointing the finger at Rob, instead using the term 'mysterious circumstances', and interest died down.

At last, almost two weeks after Amy's death, Eliza received a response to all the messages she'd sent.

ROB: Sorry. Can I come over tonight?

She almost cried with relief as she texted back.

ELIZA: Of course. Home around 6.30 xxx

Would he want to eat? Would he stay the night? Eliza moved between the kitchen and the living area, tidying up, plumping cushions, in a fever of nervous energy. She poured herself a glass of wine to steady her nerves.

He arrived at seven, looking tired and drawn. He glanced at her quickly, saying nothing as he came in.

'Rob, this is all so awful. I've been out of my mind worrying about you.'

'Sorry. With everything ... I thought it best to stay away.' He walked ahead of her down the hallway.

'It's been hell for me too,' said Eliza. 'The papers painted me as the bad guy.'

He stopped and turned, and his dark eyes flashed. 'Why is it always about you, Eliza?'

She flinched. 'I'm sorry. Please, Rob, don't do this to us.' The tears came, and she reached out a hand. 'Rob?'

He regarded her for a moment, then his expression softened. 'I didn't mean that. I'm sorry.'

They held each other tight, saying nothing for a long time.

'Do you want to talk about it?' she asked, as they sat down on the sofa.

'We should.'

'You got a text from her. That morning at Richmond.'

He sighed. 'It was from the night before.'

She opened her mouth to speak, then shut it again. Did she really want to know what it said? Did she have a right to know?

'It was ambiguous,' he said. 'It said, *I hope you'll ... I hope you'll be ...* ' He couldn't continue; he squeezed his eyes shut.

'Oh god, Rob.'

He opened them, and they were full of tears.

He took a breath. 'It said, *I hope you'll be happy.* I thought ... ' He choked up again. 'I thought, when I got it, she was being snarky – as in, *I hope you'll be as miserable as sin.* Last time I saw her she was pretty angry. But then I wondered – that was why I left early. And now ... I think it was a goodbye, Lizzie.'

He looked away from her, swiping at his tears.

She pulled him close, and he buried his face in her shoulder.

'You can't know that,' she said, rubbing his back, trying to absorb some of his pain.

'The divorce coming through, though ... '

'Rob, surely she wouldn't attempt suicide by throwing herself down a flight of stairs. Chances are you'd end up with a crack on the head and a few broken bones. Painful, but not lethal. Right?'

'It's a steep staircase. Pretty lethal, actually.'

'Well, the police didn't think so, and neither do I.'

He pulled back and looked at her. 'Really?'

Probably not, but she needed to be strong for him.

'The police know their stuff. Don't blame yourself.'

He blew out a breath. 'I don't know how to move on.'

'I'll help you work through it.' She took his face in her hands and kissed him, then wiped away his tears with her thumbs. 'Me and you. We're OK?'

He sniffed, gave her a weak smile. 'Always.'

She fetched a box of tissues and handed them to him. 'Do you want to eat? I got something in.'

'I'm not hungry.'

'Will you stay tonight?'

'Not tonight. I'm sorry, my head's still all over the place.'

'So what would you like to do?'

'Truth? Sleep.'

He stretched out, put his head in her lap and closed his eyes. As she stroked his hair, he fell asleep.

Amy's death was already old news, but Eliza was painfully aware that her golden-girl image had been tarnished. Predictably, the press had had a field day putting their spin on the story, and while her friends and family told her to ignore it, that wasn't so easy. Mud stuck, and it was going to be a long time before she managed to regain her former shine. Meantime, there was no way she could be seen out and about with Rob.

It was Leigh who suggested a way forward.

'We really need a RoseGold presence in the US, Eliza. And Rob's so good at this stuff now – wheeling and dealing. I do the walking, he does the talking. It's better face to face. It'll take a while to recruit the right people, make the right contacts. Rob should be there for all that. And it'll take his mind off things.'

Eliza felt bleak at the prospect of him being away, but recognized the sense in her words.

'You're right. And we need a marketing campaign there for *Most Human*. Rob should manage that.'

She broached the subject a couple of days later.

'Leigh already discussed it with me,' he said. 'It's a no-brainer. I need to go, and it'll stop the gossip about us. By the time I get back – probably two, three months – it'll be ancient history.'

'I'll miss you so much, though. It's going to be hard.'

'What's a couple more months on top of the . . . ' he thought for a moment, 'one hundred and eighty-three I waited.'

She laughed. 'I forgot you're good at maths.'

'I'll be counting down the days. Yes, it'll be hard, but I think it'll see us back on track.'

'Please, god, let that finally happen.'

It was the night before Rob was due to fly out, and he was cooking a farewell dinner at her flat, grimacing at her supermarket-brand ingredients as he lobbed them into his stir-fry.

Eliza smiled as she watched him showing off, but her expression changed as she contemplated the weeks to come.

Rob noticed. 'Cheer up, Snow White. And I'm sorry I haven't been the greatest company recently.'

'Don't apologize.'

'I hope this time away will get me sorted.'

'Me too. You've lost your twinkle, Rob.'

'You're not so sparkly, either.'

He poured them each a glass of wine. 'Let's drink to getting some of that back.'

He stayed the night, and it was the first time since . . . their first time. There was none of the joy or magic, and there was a sense of them together against the world, shutting it all out. But by morning Eliza felt their reconnection, and wondered if they'd turned the corner.

◈

Summer faded into melancholy autumn, and the morning air grew sharper as Eliza walked to work.

She organized a PR position in women's magazines for Mac. The marketing director wasn't happy about it, but Eliza explained that Mac's substantial shareholding meant she had a right to choose her career path at Rose.

She discussed the situation with Cecil.

'It's only likely to be a problem if there are things you want to push through to which she might be opposed,' he said. 'A bit like the situation with your sister. But it's early days; I expect she'll want to find her feet before getting involved in anything strategic. Might pay to keep a close eye, though. Who are our spies in that department?'

'Cecil!' said Eliza, laughing.

'My attempt at a joke. But I'd suggest making sure the editors are aware of her position, just in case.'

Terri asked Eliza if she wanted to move forward with the #MeToo interview, but Eliza felt it was too soon after Amy's death. Terri suggested they postpone until next year, when it would be the five-year anniversary of the movement.

Rob and Leigh were forging ahead in the US, and in his video calls Rob was upbeat, looking relaxed, cracking jokes, regaling her with tales of Hollywood's insanity. He messaged photos of places and people, things he knew would make her laugh. His selfies showed a deepening tan. He, at least, was getting his sparkle back. It looked like the time away was working. For him.

But Eliza was lonely, especially in the evenings. There were plenty of invitations to functions, dinners, premieres, but she didn't want to be out and about in London society by herself. Too many eyes. She started to hang out more with Will and Kit.

Most Human of Saints was in post-production and would be

broadcast simultaneously in the US and UK after Christmas. Rob was orchestrating the marketing campaign, and the buzz was building fast.

The boys were now focusing on their next TV series, *My Dark Soul*, which centred round a Catholic priest battling the Devil on his shoulder. Kit had written the script – a tale of salacious secrets, temptation, corruption and debauchery.

Eliza recognized its brilliance, but found it too disturbing, as the protagonist descended into a hell of his own making. All the vices were there.

'It's incredible, Kit,' she said, as they sat at the bar of The George. 'Please tell me it's not based on your own dark soul.'

'Dark-ish.'

'It's a great story, for sure. But how can you keep the audience on side when the main character basically becomes a degenerate monster?'

'According to whose values?' said Kit. 'Take away the religion and he does nothing wrong.'

'But there's absolutely nothing to redeem the guy.'

'It isn't always about redemption. If it was, who'd be the judge? There is no god. So who are we redeeming ourselves to? Our fellow human beings? What the fuck do they know? Most of them are stupid.' He sipped his beer, his eyes glittering.

'I love him when he's like this,' said Will.

So did Eliza. Kit defending his creative corner was . . . compelling. Dangerous. Deliciously so.

'The people we love? Ourselves?' she said, thinking of Harry battling his guilt over Ana and Caitlyn, wanting redemption in his family's eyes. And of herself and Rob, trying to deal with what had happened to Amy. 'Surely it's about inner peace; coming to terms with our past actions, understanding what drives us, making things right with the people who truly love us.'

'If love even exists,' said Kit. 'Which is questionable.'

'God, Kit. It must be hard to be you,' said Eliza. Then she smiled at him. 'Well, I love you. That exists.' She hopped off her stool, put her arms around his neck, kissed his cheek and nuzzled his hair.

'Ahem,' said Will.

'Love you too, Will,' she said.

'To know ourselves,' said Kit, slipping an arm round her waist, 'we have to look into the abyss.' He kissed her quickly on the lips. 'You, my beautiful Eliza, shine a light into my abyss.'

'Well well,' said a voice behind her. 'Looks like someone takes after her daddy.' The accent was Australian.

Eliza whirled round to see Stu, swaying slightly. His eyes were bloodshot, and cold.

Mac was with him. She looked uncomfortable.

'Oh! Hello, you two!' Eliza said, regaining her composure. She realized – Kit and Will didn't know about Stu. No one outside the family did.

'Who the hell's this?' said Kit, registering Stu's hostility – and perhaps his resemblance to Harry.

She took a breath. 'Stu, this is Kit Marley, from work. And Will Bardington. Guys, this is my half-brother Stu, and I think you've met my cousin Mac.'

'I saw you in the paper, Eliza,' said Stu. 'Shame about your boyfriend's wife. Like I said, seems you take after our dear father – leaving a trail of dead bodies and broken hearts.' He looked at Kit. 'And screwing around behind people's backs.'

Eliza sucked in a breath.

'Stop it, Stu,' said Mac. 'I'm so sorry, Eliza. I'm afraid he's had too much to drink.' She took his arm. 'Come on, Stu, we should go.'

He shrugged her off. 'Nah, that's what she wants. To forget I bloody exist. I'm an uncomfortable reminder of her precious daddy's sordid past. She's ignored me since the day we met. Prefers to hang out with her fag friends.'

Will rolled his eyes. '*Beware, my lord, of jealousy. It is the green-eyed monster which doth mock the meat it feeds on.*'

'Jesus fuckin' Christ.'

Kit was quiet. She sensed him working out the dynamics. He tightened his arm round her waist.

'You should leave,' he said.

'Oh, the pretty one speaks,' said Stu. 'So, do you swing both ways? With your pretty-boy and your pretty-girl?'

Eliza looked at Mac. 'Please, get him out of here.'

'You don't tell her what to do,' slurred Stu. 'Doesn't she own more of Rose than you?'

Kit slid off his stool. 'Time to fuck off, Stu.' He grabbed his arm and marched him towards the door. Stu struggled, but Kit was stronger.

'I'm so sorry, Eliza,' said Mac. 'I'll take him home. Can I come and see you at the office tomorrow?'

'Phone for an appointment,' said Eliza, her voice cold.

Kit shoved Stu out of the door; Stu shouted something unintelligible, then Mac followed him and they were gone.

'Well,' said Will. 'That was . . . unexpected. And rather thrilling. A half-brother, Eliza? Why have you not shared this morsel with us before?'

'Honestly? I don't know. Surely we're past the days of being ashamed of our parents' bastard children.'

Kit returned and put his arm back round Eliza's waist.

'Put her down, Kit,' said Will. 'She's not yours.'

Chapter 37

Eliza

'His flatmate threw him out,' said Mac. 'He trashed the kitchen in a drunken rage after an argument over rent. He had nowhere else to go, so he's staying with me until he sorts himself out.'

Eliza pulled a face. 'You'll need to padlock the drinks cupboard.'

'Och, I didn't realize at first – his problem.'

'Is he an alcoholic?'

'He attempted to give up when he arrived here, but was back on it pretty quick. I've been trying to help him, but . . . ' Mac shook her head and stared out of Eliza's office window. 'You have to want to be helped.'

As Mac shared her worries about Stu, Eliza couldn't bring herself to care. Yes, he was family. But his spiteful homophobia, plus a chip the size of Australia on his shoulder . . .

'That's very good of you, but if it were me, I'd encourage him to move on,' she said. 'You don't need him on your plate, when you've only just come down here yourself. He's not your responsibility.'

Mac looked her in the eye. 'Maybe not, but he's had no joy with his father. His real one. He wants a job at Rose. Thinks he's entitled. He's been hassling Harry.'

'Dad's said nothing to me about that.'

Mac sighed. 'Stu was such good company, at first. We were the outsiders, from the "outposts" as Harry calls it. We really connected.'

'I'd say cut him loose,' said Eliza. 'Maybe he'll go back to Australia if he runs out of money.'

'He's been asking Harry for "loans", too. Guilt-tripping him, basically.'

'I'm not going to get involved in that. Dad can sort out his own mess.'

Eliza didn't want to dwell on this further. 'What about you? How are you getting on, workwise?'

Mac sat up straighter. 'Good. Very good. I'm actually thinking about my next step at Rose.'

Eliza's heart sank. Sheesh, these problem relatives.

'RoseGold is where it's at right now,' said Mac. 'Could we talk about a role for me there, perhaps in a few months, when I've got to know the company a wee bit better?'

I think not.

'Hm. As I'm sure you know, RoseGold has a small core staff. The production teams are on short-term contracts.'

'I would *love* to work with Rob. He's so . . . dynamic.'

In your dreams.

'Leave it with me.' She looked at her watch. 'Sorry, Mac, I've got a two o'clock.'

As Mac left, Eliza frowned at her back. She had nothing against her cousin as a person. She was intelligent, calm, interesting. But she was clearly ambitious, and owned a substantial shareholding in the company – now a little smaller than Eliza's and Harry's combined, thanks to Maria. Nevertheless, how could she not see Mackenzie James as a threat?

She buzzed Pippa, then swivelled her chair to look out of the window, brooding on the situation. Low cloud was teasing the tops of the City skyscrapers, and Tower Bridge was opening up to let a ship pass through. It was all grim, grey. The Thames was churning idly, looking like it couldn't be bothered.

The door opened behind her, and a few seconds later a pair of hands closed over her eyes.

'Pippa! What—'

Then she heard his chuckle.

The hands left her eyes and there stood Rob, in all his beautiful glory, that impish grin on his face, his twinkle writ large.

She gasped in surprise. 'Rob!'

'Hello there, Snow White.'

She flung her arms around him as happiness blew away the gloom like a storm surge on a king tide. He was back – properly back. The old Rob; pre-Amy Rob.

He squeezed her tight, and she gave herself up to the feelings of joy, relief, love.

'Why didn't you tell me you were coming back?'

'I wanted to surprise you.'

'How long—'

'Shh, kiss first.'

'Hey, Rob,' she said, quite some time later.

'Mm?'

'Have you ever done it on a desk?'

He raised his eyebrows. 'Heck, Lizzie. What have you been up to while I was away?'

'Just joking. But maybe we could go home early?'

'Sounds good to me. I'm homeless – Mum and Dad leased Leicester Square. Can I stay with you?'

'Well yes, you most certainly can. Just give me half an hour to move the other guy out.'

He shook his head, smiling. 'Have you been a good girl?'

'I have, unless you count drinking too much with Will and Kit as being bad.'

'God, you three. It was Kit who told me to get my arse back here, double-quick.'

'What? Why?'

'He didn't make a lot of sense; just sent me a cryptic message.'

'Stu was causing trouble, but . . . I don't think that'd be why.'

'So what was his reason?'

'No idea. He'll have one, doesn't mean I know what it is.'

Rob shook his head. 'You've read *My Dark Soul*? What on earth's going on in his brain? And what did he take to make it go there?'

'Don't knock it. Kit's brain's a place like no other.'

'Hm. Hey, are you excited about *Most Human*? The trailer's epic, and we've been feeding teasers to social media. The response has been great.'

'Yes, I'm excited. In many ways.' She grinned. 'Let's go home.'

As a cab took them across the river, Eliza registered her change in mood. She felt like one of Harry's supercars, the ones that went from nought to a hundred in six seconds, or whatever it was.

She sighed in contentment. 'I think we did the right thing, sending you away. I feel like we've got a second chance.'

✻

'Lizzie, you're snoring,' said Rob, later. The room was growing dim as their stolen afternoon crept towards evening. The curtains at the bedroom window billowed gently, like benevolent ghosts.

'No, I'm purring,' she said, sleepily.

Rob kissed her head. 'Don't go back to sleep, I need food. Let's go out.'

An exquisite exhaustion had immobilised her arms and legs. 'Can't we just stay here? I seem to have lost the ability to move my limbs.'

'Just a little while longer, then. I haven't eaten since the plane.'

She made an effort to come out of her stupor. 'So, Roberto, you're properly back?'

'Pretty much. I'll have to go over sometimes, but Leigh's got everything well under control. She should probably be based there full time now.'

'I miss her. And Frankie. She's planning to do the Ocean Race next year – she's already training. RoseGold will probably sponsor her crew.'

Rob snorted.

'Well yes, I know it's all a bit nepotistic, but I think it fits the brand. Exploring, taking risks, going global.'

'Lizzie – are you really OK with me staying here? If not I can find a place, or …' He looked down at her. 'I know last time I asked it wasn't a great success, but now things are … different, how about we look for somewhere together? We could try being actual grown-ups, get a proper house with a garden.'

Eliza was quiet, considering his words. She pictured it: waking up together every day; curling up on the sofa in the evenings. Winter weekends by the fire; summer days lazing in the garden. Somewhere old, with lots of character. Like Will and Kit's Victorian terrace, all cosy book-lined rooms with original features. Except … Rob wasn't really one for books.

'*Gardening?* You?'

'Garden-*er*.'

'Yes,' she said. 'I'd like that very much.'

'What a relief.' He kissed her hair.

'Where?'

'Hampstead? Highgate? It'd be good to be near Chess and Gil. Somewhere modern – big open-plan spaces. Minimalist. Lots of light.'

Oh.

'I'd like to be near the river,' she said.

'Why?'

'I just would.'

'Strange girl. Shall we continue this discussion over dinner?'

'Good plan.'

Where would they go to eat? Somewhere discreet – it would be their first outing as a couple since Wimbledon. Thanks to smartphones, everyone was a potential paparazzo these days.

'People won't make a big deal of it?' she said. 'If we're spotted together?'

'Yesterday's news.'

'And …' Eliza searched his eyes. 'How are you feeling now? About Amy.'

He looked away, and didn't answer immediately. 'Still sad. But time's doing its thing. I'm getting there.'

'That's good. Shall we get up then?'

He rolled on top and kissed her, and everything sprung back to life. 'How about an appetiser?'

'Hm, perhaps a small entrée.'

Chapter 38

Eliza

The Richmond house always looked wonderful at Christmas. The angel Eliza remembered from her childhood sat atop an enormous Christmas tree in the entrance hall, her halo brushing the ceiling. Harry still called her 'Katie'. An oversized wreath hung on the front door, the fireplaces were decked with holly and gold candles, and pretty lights twinkled in the ancient leadlight windows.

Eliza and Rob were enjoying a quiet Christmas Eve with Harry, Clare and Eddie. The only cloud on the horizon was that Stu and Mac were joining them next day, for Christmas dinner.

'How's the house-hunting going, you two?' asked Clare, as they sipped mulled wine by the crackling log fire.

'Eliza's difficult to please,' said Rob. 'She has this strange compulsion to live by the river.'

'What about Chiswick? Or Barnes?' said Clare.

'Not Barnes. Mac lives there,' said Eliza.

'Are you two not getting on?' asked Harry.

'We get on. It's just . . .'

'Is it because she's on the board now? Between you and me, Cecil's keeping an eye.'

'What? Dad – are you spying on her?'

'Knowledge is power, Lizzie.'

Eliza shook her head. 'She told me Stu's been asking you for a job.'

'He's proving something of a headache,' said Harry. 'You'll note that news of his paternity hasn't yet reached the press. I might have had something to do with that. However, the tiresome man is the loosest of cannons, and I have no doubt he'll be taking aim before too long.'

'I wish they weren't coming tomorrow,' said Eliza.

'I felt I should invite them, in the circumstances. I think it's wise to keep Mac close.'

'As in, keep your enemies close?' said Eliza.

'On side, at least. Don't forget she has a political background. She has some . . . interesting contacts. One in particular. But what are we doing, having this discussion on Christmas Eve? Who's for a top-up? I'll go fetch.'

What did he mean, *one in particular*? Part of her was exasperated that Dad carried on as if he were still in charge, with his behind-the-scenes manoeuvring, his spy network. But a bigger part of her was reassured that he was there in the shadows, steering things her way, watching her back.

On Christmas morning, before breakfast, Rob suggested a walk round the grounds, just the two of them. As they slipped out of the back door, that indefinable Christmas magic hung in the frosty midwinter air.

At the bottom of the garden was a high brick wall with a wrought-iron gate leading out to the park.

'I used to climb this,' said Rob, his breath forming little clouds in front of his face. 'Remember?'

'You got me to the top one time. We sat up there like we were the Queen and King of England.'

Rob stopped by the gate. 'Can I give you my Christmas present now?'

'Now? If you want.'

He reached inside his coat pocket and took out a little box tied with a gold bow.

Eliza's heart leaped into her mouth.

'Not going to go down on one knee, these strides were expensive and there is mud.' His eyes were twinkling. 'But ... Lizzie Rose, I wondered if, maybe, you'd like to marry me?' He slid the bow off the box and opened the lid. 'Well?'

She couldn't speak. She didn't trust herself to.

Emotions scrambled for attention. She tried to bring them under control, shuffle the positive ones – joy, delight – to the head of the queue.

But elbowing its way to the front was a sense of walls closing in, doors shutting, keys turning.

'OK, I'll muddy my knee if I have to,' he said, as the silence lengthened. But the line fell flat as he registered her confusion.

'Rob ... it's so beautiful.'

'Shall I put it on for you?' He was less sure of himself now.

'But ... I'm only twenty-four.'

'That's kind of irrelevant. We're looking for a house; you're a CEO. We're grown-ups.'

She loved him so much; she didn't want to hurt him. Eliza didn't know what to say – but she knew it couldn't be 'yes'.

'You know how much I love you. But you also know how I feel about marriage. I told you years ago it wasn't for me.'

'Because of Harry. I know. But look at him now.'

'Only took him five tries to get it right.'

But this wasn't only about Harry. Marriage meant compromise; it meant adapting, putting your partner first. Often.

How could she be that person, with a media empire to run? Rose would always be her priority; work would always come first.

So why are you looking for a house together? asked the voice inside her head.

Because I love him; I want to be with him. But on my terms.

'Rob, we don't need pieces of paper and official things; we know we belong together.'

'So what are you saying? You don't want to marry me?'

She touched his arm. 'I want to be with you, but I don't want to be married. Please, try to understand?'

He shoved the box back in his pocket. 'Every time I think I get you, think I know what you want, you throw me a curve ball.' His voice was exasperated.

'No, Rob. You *do* get me. I'm sorry – that was the loveliest thing you just did, and I'll never forget it. But something deep inside says marriage isn't for me.'

She held his gaze, willing him to understand, until finally he smiled.

'I won't sulk, on one condition.'

'Name it.'

'You let me try again – sometime.'

She loved how he never bore a grudge. Taking his face in her hands, she kissed him. 'I adore you, Rob, and you make me so very happy. Believe me when I say a ring on my finger couldn't make me love you any more than I do right now.'

At midday, Stu and Mac arrived, and as they sipped pre-lunch drinks, Mac buttonholed Rob, asking him about plans for *My Dark Soul*. He seemed only too happy to chat about it; she was asking all the right questions, had done her homework.

Eliza headed to the kitchen.

Stu followed her. 'Eliza, you got a mo?'

She stopped and faced him.

'Look, I'm sorry I lost it in the pub that night.'

She recoiled a little at the alcohol on his breath. It could have been a Christmas Eve hangover, or an early start to Christmas Day.

'I shouldn't have said those things. Can we be friends? You're my half-sister, after all.'

He left her cold, and the words he'd spat at her in the pub rang truer than this apology.

'Maybe. But you need to leave your attitude behind. Bigotry isn't appealing.'

'I need to get a job – can I talk to you about that?'

'Not unless you have experience in media. And if you want to make a go of things here, maybe cut down on the booze?'

'Bugger me, you don't pull your punches, do you?'

'And don't *ever* call my friends fags again. Now if you'll excuse me, there are sprouts waiting.'

She diverted into the TV room, where Eddie was deep into a new video game. 'Carry on,' she said. 'I'll just sit here.'

She waited for her heartbeat to slow. There was something lovely and wholesome about Eddie. She always felt better for spending time with him, even just sitting beside him, saying nothing.

She took out her phone.

ELIZA: Happy Christmas! What you doing?

KIT: Christmas lunch with Will. You know I have a thing for tragedy

ELIZA: Stu's here. Why do I hate him?

KIT: Thoughts that do often lie too deep for tears

ELIZA: Riddle me ree. Rob proposed. Don't tell anyone, not even Will. I said no

KIT: Of course you did

ELIZA: I knew you'd understand

KIT: My turkey's getting cold. It was terrible to start with

ELIZA: Enjoy. Love you xxxxx

During Christmas lunch, Stu ripped into the wine, drinking two or three glasses for everyone else's one, as if in defiance of Eliza's words. His cheeks grew redder and his voice louder. Then he started on the brandy.

Mac was talking to Rob again. He was absorbed in the conversation, and Eliza's eyes narrowed as she watched them. Was this something to do with her 'no' this morning?

Harry remained inscrutable as Stu held forth on various topics – strident opinions, all with lashings of grievance.

As soon as Eliza had swallowed her last mouthful of Christmas pudding, she said, 'I'm going for a walk. I'll help clear up when I get back.'

She expected Rob to follow, but he didn't.

'I'll come,' said Harry.

'Me too,' said Clare.

'Hard to believe Stu's your son,' said Eliza, walking briskly along their well-trodden path. Across the park, children were trying out new bikes, scooters, drones.

'Or Bennie's,' said Harry. 'She's such a sunny person.'

Eliza gave him a look. 'He's staying with Mac,' she said. 'He's probably poisoning her mind with all sorts of crap. She should throw him out, or he might drag her down with him.'

'I'll happily fund him a one-way ticket home,' said Harry. 'Mac's all right. Bright girl. Questionable taste in friends, though. And not just Stu.'

'And you know this how?'

'Cecil did some digging for me.'

'Honestly, Harry,' said Clare. 'You could be accused of paranoia.'

'Once bitten, twice shy, darling,' he said. 'If I'd kept proper tabs on Phil Seville, we'd have been spared a whole lot of trouble.'

'Or if *I* had,' Eliza said. She'd learned a lot about the importance of spy networks since those early days at Rose. 'So who is this other questionable friend?'

'Probably more than a friend, in fact. Hamish Earle. Fingers in all sorts of pies, many of them likely to cause food poisoning. He's involved in Scottish politics in a roundabout way – that's how Mac knows him.'

'It does make me wonder,' said Clare, 'why a lovely, intelligent girl like Mac would choose to associate with people like this man and Stu.'

'Perhaps she's got a thing for bad boys,' said Eliza.

'I can relate,' said Clare, grinning at Harry.

Chapter 39

Eliza

Eliza and Rob's house-hunting seemed to have stalled. February wasn't really the time of year for it.

After the latest viewing, of a beautiful period home in Chiswick, Rob had started to sound antsy. 'It's near the river, it's near your parents. It's everything you said you wanted. What's the problem?'

'It's a little too far out. I like being close to work.'

'So what about the swanky Butler's Wharf penthouse?'

'I thought you wanted a garden.'

'I'll settle for a window box. A house plant. A herb in a pot. Anything, as long as it's ours and not Harry's.'

This was clearly about more than finding a new place to live. But Eliza just didn't have the time to be traipsing all over London assessing whether a property was private enough for a high-profile couple, or the garaging sufficiently secure for Rob's Ferrari, or whatever. Rose was a demanding mistress, and there was always something more urgent needing her attention.

'Rob, you know work has to come first,' she snapped down the phone, after cancelling a viewing due to a threatened pilot strike at Rose Air. 'Cecil and I have to meet with the union.'

'Surely Cecil can handle it by himself?'

'I need to be there. It shows I care. And it'll make our bargaining position stronger.'

'Right. Tomorrow?'

'Unlikely. Rob, can I get back to you? I'm waiting on an important call.'

'Which this obviously isn't.'

'Look, I'm sorry, but you know what you signed up to.'

'Lapdog?'

❀

He appeared in her office an hour later, a bouquet of spring flowers in his hand.

'Sorry,' he said. 'I know you're under pressure. Just tell me to fuck off next time I give in to my insecurities.'

She smiled, taking the flowers. 'Shall we go get some lunch, Roberto?' She looked at her calendar. A one-thirty with a reporter from the *Radio Times*. 'I'll postpone my next meeting. Say I've got the plague or something.'

'Good plan, Snow White.'

As they passed the crèche, Rob stopped and peered through the door. 'Cute,' he said. 'Look at that little guy with the dinosaur.' A toddler with floppy red curls was talking earnestly to a fluffy stegosaurus. 'With that hair, he could be ours.'

Eliza grimaced. 'Children? You've got to be kidding. Oh, nice pun, me.'

'One day, Lizzie? I love kids. They're so on my level. I can't wait to be a dad.'

Eliza hadn't even considered the prospect. *Did* she want children? Certainly not for many, many years. If ever. How could she possibly run Rose Corp *and* bring up a family? If she did have kids, she'd hardly see them. Would that be fair? On them or herself? She was reminded of Maria's desolate childhood.

'Would you be a stay-at-home dad?' she asked.

'No way,' he said. 'But I wouldn't need to be – we have this.' He looked through the door again. 'Aw, look at him.'

'But it shuts at five. And at weekends.'

'Nannies, Lizzie. Babysitters.'

'God, Rob. When would I find time to organize all that? I can hardly find time for a life of my own now.'

'It's what staff are for. You're a Rose, girl.'

Would the maternal instinct strike at some point? Right now, that felt like an impossibility.

◉

Most Human of Saints began screening, and Brits and Americans alike were hooked. As the season continued, viewers binge-watched through the night. BAFTAS and Emmys were surely a shoo-in, and everyone was asking, what next from RoseGold?

Leigh returned from the States to move forward the plans for *My Dark Soul*. She would need Rob to go back with her, to set up the deals.

They put house-hunting on the back-burner.

Chess was promoted to production director, and Rob suggested giving Mac her old role.

Eliza was against it. 'She's only been with us six months. Surely she's not ready for management.'

But she acknowledged her resistance wasn't entirely professional. And the appointment of lower-level management should be down to Rob, as head of department. If she overruled him, it would be personal.

She tried to be objective. Rob knew Eliza's cousin made her uneasy, but that shouldn't influence his decision – or hers – which should be based on what was best for Rose. Mac was efficient, bright, would bring broad experience to the position, and was popular with staff. She'd do a great job.

And reason argued that a production manager role wasn't going to threaten Eliza's position at the top, especially with Chess as Mac's line manager.

She approved it.

'I've made Rizz her assistant,' said Rob, over the Valentine's

Day dinner he'd cooked – sea bass with locally sourced vegetables cooked in interesting ways.

'Lucky Mac,' said Eliza, looking him in the eye and beheading an asparagus spear with her teeth. 'He's adorable.'

Angelo Rizzio, known to all as Rizz, was a cute, dark-eyed Italian who'd been employed on *Most Human* and then kept on in the production department, as no one could bear to see him go. He was everyone's favourite – especially Will and Kit's. He had long flowing hair to rival Will's, and was permanently smiling, rushing around fetching coffee, making sure everyone had what they needed. And, best of all, he would sing while he worked, and he had the voice of an angel.

'Kit certainly thinks so,' said Rob.

'Really?'

'That part in the script where the priest's being tempted by thoughts of a beautiful boy? Sounds like Rizz to me.'

'Kit isn't *tempted* by beautiful boys. Temptation implies an internal battle.'

'He hit on me once,' said Rob. 'I never worked out if he was joking.'

'Probably not. Were you tempted?'

'No. I'm unfashionably straight.' He looked her in the eye. 'Were you? While I was away?'

'For god's sake, how many more times? We're *mates*.'

'You're far more than that.'

'Yes. But you shouldn't feel threatened.'

'I'll never understand you two. You're different with him.' He sat back in his chair. 'Lizzie – don't go too wild while I'm gone. Promise? Save your good times for me?'

A wave of despondency hit as she confronted the lonely months to come. She reached across and took his hand. 'I will, Rob. I'm a responsible CEO now, not a louche student. And you save your wild times for me. No carousing with Hollywood starlets.'

He grinned, and pulled a *what can you do?* face. 'Goes with the territory, I'm afraid. But don't fret.' He lifted her hand and kissed it. 'Starlets are ten a penny. But you, my lovely Lizzie, are a supernova.'

She snorted. 'You mean one that's exploded.'

'Exploded my heart,' said Rob. 'See, I can do words too.'

❦

Time apart had ever been a thing in this relationship, but Eliza's spirits plummeted as Rob left for Heathrow.

It was a Thursday evening. Needing a distraction, she paid Mac a visit. Eliza was aware she could do with more galpals – going out with Will and Kit was always fun but often exhausting – and in spite of her wariness, Mac was family, after all.

It was just gone six as she headed down to the RoseGold floor. Approaching Mac's corner of the office, she saw her cousin wasn't alone. Perched on her desk was a dark-haired man in a black suit. Mac was smiling at him in a way that suggested this wasn't a business meeting.

Mac sat up straighter, the smile leaving her face. 'Eliza!'

The man turned slightly and looked over his shoulder. His eyes were hooded, his expression inscrutable.

'This is Hamish Earle.' Mac looked flustered. 'A friend from Scotland. Hamish – meet Eliza Rose.'

'I know who ye are.' He held out his hand; there were black hairs on the back of it. His grip was strong. He didn't smile and his dark eyes appraised her, partly as a woman but mostly as a fellow person of power. He was good-looking, in the way that a swaying cobra is a thing of beauty.

'Pleased to meet you, Hamish. Are you down on business or pleasure?'

Hamish glanced at Mac. 'A bit o' both.'

'What's your line of business?'

'Finance.'

'Right. Well, I'll leave you to it. I was just popping down for a catch-up, Mac. I'll come see you tomorrow.'

'Sure,' said Mac.

ELIZA: Hamish Earle visited Mac today. They seemed cosy. Exactly who is he?

HARRY: Banker and so much more. Approach with caution.

The following day, Eliza invited Mac for lunch in the cafe. She stopped off at the production floor to fetch her.

Rizz was sitting with Mac at her desk. Their heads were bent together, and they were giggling about something.

'Hello, you two,' said Eliza.

Mac looked up. 'Oh, is it lunchtime?'

'Almost. How are you getting on, Rizz?'

'Oh, *molto contento!*' He flicked back his hair and gave her a big smile. 'I love to work with Mac. She's *bellissima* and very kind.'

'Bless you, Rizz,' said Mac. 'Where would I be without you?'

At lunch, Mac seemed distracted, losing the thread of the conversation as Eliza talked about the plans for *My Dark Soul*.

'What's Stu up to?' Eliza asked, changing the subject.

Mac sighed. 'I wish Harry had given him a job when he first got here. A reason to get up in the mornings. Then maybe things would have turned out differently.' She moved her food around her plate, eating little.

'It wasn't up to Dad. He's retired. And honestly? Stu's not a good fit for the company. It wouldn't have worked.'

'Not a *proper* Rose?' said Mac, raising her eyebrows. 'Well, it's probably too late now. I think he's passed the point of no return.' She dropped her voice. 'I'm really worried. When he's been drinking, he gets so angry. He gets into arguments in the pub; he's been in fights; he's making enemies. I don't want him living at my place any more, but he's got nowhere else to go.'

'Just tell him to leave! Dad would pay to send him back to Australia.'

'I tried, but he flipped. It was quite terrifying; he lost his temper.

Said I was siding with you against him. And if I kick him out he might end up on the streets. Surely we don't want that.'

Eliza remembered Harry mentioning how he'd managed to keep Stu away from the press. Would he sell his story if he were desperate for money?

'I'd better speak to Dad. He's worried Stu might become a loose anti-Rose cannon.'

Mac smiled – a wary half-smile. 'No, leave it to me. It's why I got in touch with Hamish. He's an old friend; he's got my back. Hamish'll sort him out.'

'Sort him out how?'

'Guys like Stu respond better to a show of strength than gentle persuasion. Harry's not going to carry on giving him money forever, son or not. I don't want Stu making an enemy of Harry. He's a complete hothead. He doesn't think before he acts. Like you say, it could be bad for Rose.'

Eliza put down her fork. 'Hamish isn't . . . violent, is he? I mean, this is my half-brother we're talking about.'

'Och, don't worry. Hamish is too clever for anything like that.'

> KIT: Hey, your CEO-ness. Could use your feedback on Dark Soul rewrites. Free tonight?

> ELIZA: Your place?

> KIT: Pub

The script was now a slightly toned-down version of that alarming original Eliza had first read, but was none the weaker for it. There was nothing she'd enjoy more than diving back into it with Will and Kit. And she could use a night out.

She pulled a face at the year-end accounts Cecil had asked her to sign off.

> ELIZA: Yes. Pub. I'll be there by 7 xx

She brooded on the Mac situation as she left. On impulse, she sent a text:

> ELIZA: Going to the George with Will and Kit to discuss Dark Soul, if you want to join us?

> MAC: Love to!

When Mac arrived, Rizz was with her. Eliza couldn't help smiling – he was so cute. His black jeans were tucked into lace-up boots, and he wore a baggy white long-sleeved shirt. His long wavy hair was tied back in a ponytail. He looked like a musketeer.

'Ciao!' he said.

'How bloody gorgeous,' said Will, as Rizz headed to the bar for drinks.

'Thought you'd approve,' said Mac, winking at Will.

'Word has it he's totally crushing on you.'

'Och, he certainly brightens my days, Will.' She sat down next to Kit. 'Which is good, seeing as my nights are mostly shite.'

'How so?' said Will.

'Stu. Don't know how much more I can take.'

'*You must be proud, bold ... resolute ...*'

'*And now and then stab, as occasion serves,*' finished Kit.

'Jesus, who said that?' asked Mac.

'Marlowe,' said Kit, and he winked at Eliza.

'I should text him, let him know I'll be late,' said Mac, taking out her phone.

'You're not his mum,' said Kit.

'No, but I worry like I am. Squish in,' she said, patting the space beside her as Rizz returned.

He blushed and edged up close.

'OK,' said Eliza. 'Shall we make a start?'

An hour or so later they were so absorbed in their discussion that they didn't notice Stu, as he made his way over and stood watching them.

Kit said something outrageously degenerate, and Rizz gasped. '*Mamma mia!* Kit, you make me blush!'

'Result,' said Kit.

'Maybe scrub that line,' said Eliza.

'Wipe it from your memory, bonny lad,' said Mac, putting her hands over his ears.

'Who the *fuck* is this?'

Everyone looked up in surprise. Stu's bloodshot eyes were locked on Rizz, who suddenly looked terrified.

'Stu, hi,' said Eliza, calmly. 'We're having a production meeting. This is Rizz, our PA and—'

'Jesus, *another* fag,' he slurred. 'Is it compulsory at Rose?'

'I'm not gay,' said Rizz. 'I love women!'

'Then you're wasting your time at Rose, mate,' said Stu. Anger radiated off him, poisoning the air. He was glaring at Rizz as if he wanted to kill him.

Kit sighed. 'Stu, how about you just chill? Or are you after an action replay, *mate*?' His drawl morphed into an Aussie accent, surely calculated to tip Stu over the edge.

Oh god, Kit actually wants a fight.

'That's enough!' said Eliza. 'Stu, could you please leave? We're trying to work.'

'That why you didn't invite me, Mac?' said Stu, looming over her. 'Because you're *working*?' His gaze moved to Rizz. 'Yeah, right.'

Kit stood up and squeezed past Mac and Rizz. He was a little taller than Stu, and a lot steadier on his feet. 'Time to piss off, Stu.'

Stu snapped, launching a fist wildly at Kit's head. The blow caught him in the eye.

'Kit!' cried Eliza.

Stu turned and headed for the door; Eliza grabbed Kit's arm to stop him following.

'Eliza, how is that Harry's son?' said Kit, sitting down, touching his eye.

'What?' said Rizz, looking shaken.

'Oops,' said Will.

Eliza frowned at Kit. 'Keep that to yourself, Rizz.'

'I think I go home now, if you no mind?' said Rizz.

'I'll get you an Uber,' said Eliza.

'Is fine,' said Rizz. 'I take tube.'

'No, it's the least I can do. What's your address?'

'*Grazie*. Very kind.' He typed it into her app.

'There you go; three minutes away,' said Eliza. 'Rizz, I'm so sorry about all that. And please – keep what you heard to yourself.'

'I feel bad for Mac. She is beautiful person. She try so hard to help him and he treat her *terribilmente*.' He gazed at Mac for a moment, then picked up his jacket. '*Arrivederci*, my friends.'

'Bloody Stu,' said Eliza, as he left. 'What are you going to do about him, Mac?'

'Like I said, there's a plan.'

Eliza's phone beeped.

Eliza, your Uber is arriving soon.

'Shall we get back to the script?' she said.

'Or we could just get pissed,' said Will.

'Tequilas?' said Kit, his bruise now turning livid.

'I'm not in the mood,' said Eliza. Stu's venomous attack had left a horrible taste in her mouth that not even tequila would shift. If he hadn't been her half-brother, would it have been so foul? Was it because Harry was partly responsible for this bitter, damaged man?

Her phone beeped again, and a notification flashed up:

Where are you waiting? I am on Borough High Street.

'I think I might just go home,' she said. 'I want to FaceTime Rob.' After the evening's unpleasant turn, she longed to see his smile.

'Tequila's good for me,' said Will. 'I'll get them in.'

'Me too,' said Mac. 'I'll give you a hand.'

But Kit was staring at Eliza, and her heart missed a beat as she registered his expression.

Her phone beeped again.

> Do you still want your Uber? Pls respond. Will wait 5 mins.

'Shit!' she said. 'Rizz hasn't met his Uber.'

Kit shot up and rushed for the door, followed by Eliza.

They exited the pub into the alleyway leading to the high street. A group of people had gathered, looking down at the ground.

Kit pushed his way through.

Rizz was lying face-up, unconscious. Blood was oozing from beneath his head, trickling along the gaps between the cobblestones.

Eliza's hand flew to her mouth. 'Has someone called an ambulance?' she said, frantically.

'On its way,' said a man filming on his phone.

Eliza and Kit crouched down beside Rizz. Eliza couldn't properly comprehend what she was seeing. *This can't be happening.*

'Don't touch him, love,' said the man with the phone. 'Mustn't tamper with a crime scene.'

Eliza ignored him. 'Rizz?' she said desperately, touching his face.

There was no response.

The wail of a siren announced the ambulance's arrival, and two paramedics came running along the alleyway.

Kit stood up, pulling Eliza to him.

She closed her eyes for a moment. 'Please, not Rizz,' she said into his chest. 'Fate wouldn't be so cruel.'

Kit gave a bitter laugh. 'You have no idea. Fate loves to fuck with us; haven't you noticed?'

'Don't, Kit,' she whispered. 'Please don't.'

'It was a king hit,' said the man with the phone, nodding at Rizz. 'I saw it. Down with one blow. Then he smashed his head on the kerb.' He lifted his phone to get a better angle.

Kit let go of Eliza and snatched the phone. He threw it on the ground and stamped on it, grinding his heel into the screen.

'Oi! What the f—?'

Eliza picked up the smashed phone and handed it back. 'Maybe show some respect.'

'Hey, you're that Harry Rose's girl.'

She looked at Rizz, still being worked on where he'd fallen. His sweet face was peaceful, as if he were asleep.

A sob escaped her, and Kit pulled her close again.

'I shouldn't have wound Stu up,' he said. 'I should have seen this. It's my fault.'

'He was already wound up. He's like a bomb, triggered by drink. He really hates me. Maybe I'm responsible too. I should've tried harder.'

Two police officers arrived and started asking questions.

The paramedics finally lifted Rizz onto a stretcher.

'Was he with you?' one asked Eliza.

'Yes, his name's Angelo Rizzio.'

The medic shook his head. 'I'm so sorry.'

Chapter 40

Harry

The police were unable to find Stu. He'd vanished, and after a few weeks, during which they alerted the authorities in Australia, the investigation was wound down.

A small item had appeared in the press, with a photo of Stu, asking for information. The media didn't spot the link between Stu and Harry, and as he sat in his home office, Harry offered up a prayer of gratitude to the gods of lazy journalism.

'Thanks, Ramona,' he said to the housekeeper as she set down a coffee on his desk. 'Is it decaf?'

'*Sí*, it is, Harry.'

'Thanks for remembering.' He gave her a smile, and she blushed.

Clare had suggested the switch, although really, what was the point of coffee without caffeine? One small addiction wasn't too much to ask, was it?

But, he acknowledged, it was advisable to do as Clare said. Her 'lifestyle changes' always made sense, even as they whittled away at the 'pleasure' part of his existence. He'd been suffering nasty headaches, and the elimination of caffeine was probably a good idea.

He pondered on his older son as he sipped his stimulant-free beverage. Where did Stu's anger come from?

Harry's lasting memory of Bennie was of her sense of fun. The sassy London girl with her wide grin and mocking blue eyes had been the perfect antidote to his difficult home life with Katie.

Until she got pregnant, and then real life had barged in and she'd left London, wanting to be better than a barmaid in a bedsit, for the sake of her child.

Not long after, she'd met Gilbert Blunt, who'd asked Harry to stay away from little Henry. And, a few years later, off she'd gone to another new life, in Australia.

Somewhere along the way Henry had become Stu and had befriended alcohol. As a consequence he was difficult to like, but Harry did empathise. He knew how that felt, to medicate yourself against pain. In his own case, that ache had started as physical and progressed into something more. He'd managed to break free, thanks in no small part to Clare, but Stu had seemed hell bent on self-destruction.

He sighed. He'd been torn between wanting to help Stu, and washing his hands of him. Should he have tried harder?

Guilt, forever in the shadows, gave him a friendly wave.

Eliza

It was May Day, and once again Eliza was sitting in her office looking out over the Thames, thinking back to May Morning at Oxford. She couldn't shake the melancholy. Rizz's death; Rob's absence; Stu's disappearance.

There was a knock on her door, and Eliza's heart sank as Pippa showed in two police officers. Had they found Stu?

'We're here in connection with Henry Blunt,' said the female officer.

'How can I help?'

'We understand from Mackenzie James that you're his half-sister, and you were witness to events leading up to the death of Angelo Rizzio?'

'That's correct.'

'We're sorry to inform you that Mr Blunt died in a house fire in Churchfields last night, in the lodgings he was staying in.'

'What? Stu's dead?'

A cloud crept across Eliza's soul. Her half-brother's unhappy life, over already. More guilt piling onto Harry's load.

'The fire investigation team's on site. Their preliminary findings indicate arson. Ms Rose, in light of Mr Rizzio's murder, we're asking his acquaintances if they know if Mr Blunt had any enemies – in particular anyone who might have wanted to avenge Mr Rizzio's death. Would you have any thoughts on that?'

Enemies. She pictured Hamish Earle's hooded eyes.

'I didn't know Mr Blunt well. He only came over from Australia last year, and I've seen him less than half a dozen times. But from what I hear, he was often getting into fights. Mackenzie would know a lot more than me.'

'Yes, she's been most helpful.' The police officer looked at her partner. 'Very well, thank you for your time. If anything comes to mind, please get in touch.'

◉

The investigation concluded that the fire had been started deliberately, but the case remained unsolved.

This time, however, the fact that the deceased was the son of Harry Rose was picked up and splashed all over the press.

◉

The mood at RoseGold was subdued. What staff needed was a good cheer up, and Eliza was confident tonight's British Academy TV awards would do the trick. *Most Human of Saints* was nominated in three categories: Best Drama Series, Best Actor and Best 'Must-See' Moment, for Anne Boleyn's beheading.

The ratings for the series had been solid, if slightly lower than hoped. Rob, who'd flown home for the ceremony, was suggesting it was too literary, too highbrow, and that their next production should be more commercially focused. But all the pundits were predicting success tonight, with RoseGold tipped to be the big winner.

Eliza read through her acceptance speech as her hairdresser wrestled with her curls. Will had edited it for her, and now it was worthy of its own BAFTA.

So many people to thank. Final paragraph: *Dad – I don't have the words . . .* Every time she read it, she teared up. Would she make it through tonight without breaking down?

Dressed in figure-hugging scarlet taffeta, Eliza was blinded by flashes as she walked the red carpet outside the Royal Festival Hall, one arm linked through Rob's and the other through Harry's. Both men were dapper in black tie.

Will and Clare followed behind them; Kit had gone AWOL.

Thankfully the reporters on the red carpet had so far been sensible enough not to mention Stu's death.

Eliza spotted Mac up ahead, and realized she was with Hamish.

'Dad, look,' she said, nodding in her cousin's direction.

'Earle,' said Harry. 'That's unfortunate.'

A reporter with BBC on her microphone hurried over. 'Harry, you must be very proud of your daughter tonight.'

'Unspeakably, Jo,' said Harry, giving her a wide smile. 'She has a gift for spotting and nurturing talent and then setting it loose on the world.' He looked over at Will. '*Most Human* is a masterpiece.'

'Eliza,' said Jo, as Eliza made a mental note to memorise media correspondents' names. 'This drama is hot favourite for three BAFTAs. Not bad for your debut series.'

'Will Bardington and Kit Marley are the geniuses behind the script,' she said, waving Will forward. 'And without our producer, Rob Studley, this would never have got off the ground.'

Once inside, Eliza took Will off to one side. 'Where's Kit?'

His smile disappeared. 'He decided all awards ceremonies are bollocks and he'd give it a miss. God, he can be difficult.'

Eliza was stung. 'But, Will, it's our big night. Yours, his and mine. How can he do this to us? All these years, ever since our first term at Oxford – it's all been leading up to this.'

Will shook his head. 'Eliza, darling. Have you learned nothing in all this time? Kit doesn't give a fuck.'

As they filed into the auditorium and settled into their seats, Eliza attempted to shrug off the hurt. She wouldn't let it spoil the night. RoseGold's night, *her* night.

Most Human missed out on best leading actor, but Eliza wasn't surprised. The competition was stellar.

As the nominations for Best Drama were read out, Harry whispered, 'Don't forget to thank your father.'

Aware of the cameras trained on her, Eliza composed her features into a serene smile.

'And the BAFTA goes to . . .'

She hitched her taffeta up a little, aware that the tight dress might prove a challenge.

' . . . *Kitchen Sink*!'

Eliza's mouth dropped open.

'Smile,' hissed Harry. 'Clap.'

She pulled herself together, fixed her smile back in place.

The *Kitchen Sink* team hurried to the stage; many in the audience leaped to their feet.

'Ridiculous choice,' said Harry, even as he clapped and smiled.

'Chav TV,' muttered Rob, grinning widely.

Eliza was shocked to the core, and crying inside. Her team had gone above and beyond, believing in this series as she had, living and breathing it. Pouring in their hearts and souls, working all hours, rewriting, reshooting, re-editing; perfectionists, the lot of them. It was far and away the best of the nominees. She was gutted for them. This was so unfair, so *wrong*!

The ceremony drew to a close, and Eliza brooded darkly on their failure to win any awards – not even Best Must-See Moment – as everyone began leaving the auditorium.

'Un-fucking-believable,' said Rob, watching the winning team passing their award around between them.

'Rob,' said Harry. 'Don't be a sore loser. Head for the bar – use this opportunity to network. You too, Eliza. You need to keep these people on side. Take that look off your face.'

'Got you, Harry,' said Rob.

Soon Harry and Rob were backslapping and congratulating winners. Will perked up when Graham Norton came over for a chat.

But Eliza couldn't shake off her despondency. She headed for the Ladies, needing a breather.

As she switched on her phone, a message flashed up.

KIT: Need a drink?

ELIZA: Where the hell are you?! And yes!

KIT: Come outside – by pier.

The despondency lifted a little.

It was a beautiful clear night; people were still milling on the red carpet, camera crews interviewing celebrities as they exited. Eliza slipped unseen down the steps towards the river.

He was sitting on the wall, dressed in jeans and a leather jacket, smoking a cigarette. He wolf-whistled as she approached.

'That's offensive,' she said, her face breaking into a grin.

'I live to offend,' he replied, hopping down off the wall.

'You do.' She reached up and pulled the cigarette from his mouth. 'Stop this. I won't allow you to die, even though you bailed on us tonight.' She threw it on the ground and stamped it out.

'Pick that up,' said Kit.

'No.'

'Hypocrite.'

'I've stopped caring. The world can go screw itself. We won nothing, Kit. Not one award.'

'I know.'

'You were watching?'

'In the pub. Drink this.' He handed her a wine that had been sitting on the wall. 'You do realize it's all bollocks? Have you seen who was judging? Fuckwits.'

'Not all of them . . .'

'Eliza, read my lips.'

She stared at them, then wished she hadn't.

'It doesn't matter, Eliza. Awards are subjective, and therefore meaningless. *You* know we made something great.'

She felt the tears coming. She couldn't help it. No matter what Kit thought, she'd wanted that award so badly.

'But your script was so brilliant,' she said, as her eyes filled, 'and everyone worked so hard . . .'

'Chrissake, come here.'

He pulled her into his arms and she let the tears fall, burying her head in his shoulder.

He held her tight as she sobbed, stroking her back, saying nothing.

Soon she felt calmer. 'I'm sorry. I suppose people will think I'm a cocky brat, *expecting* to win.'

'Yep,' said Kit. 'Which of course you are. Should've seen your face when *Kitchen Sink* got the award.'

She looked up at him. He was grinning.

'Did I look very shocked?'

'Outraged, perhaps. My god, look at the state of you.'

'Oh no,' she said, wiping under her eyes. 'How bad is it?'

'Car crash,' said Kit. 'Better stay out here in the dark.'

She took a large drink of her wine, then put her head on his shoulder again, taking a deep breath. 'Thanks, Kit. You always make me feel better. I guess I should let Dad and Rob know where I am. And you should text Will. He thinks you don't give a fuck about him and me, as well as the awards.'

'I suppose he's in bits?'

'Pretty upset. But I left him talking to Graham Norton.'

'I'm not sure I can face the drama. Ah, Eliza. Rob's here.'

He let her go and she turned to see him walking towards them, his expression dark.

'Rob,' said Kit. 'I'm trying to convince our girl the awards mean fuck all.'

'To you, maybe,' said Rob. 'But not to her.' He looked as if he'd happily kill Kit. 'I thought you understood her. Come on, Lizzie. I'll take you home.'

The next morning Eliza was horrified to see her shocked face all over the media.

BAFTA BOMB! shouted the *Sun*.

The *Daily Mail* was a little kinder: *ELIZA SHOWS SHE'S MOST HUMAN*.

In the days that followed, her expression became an internet meme, applied to surprise-horror moments. She was mortified.

A message from Kit pinged into her phone. It was the photo, captioned:

KIT: When I tell you the truth.

As ever, she had no idea what he meant.

Rob flew back to the States, and a couple of weeks later Clare phoned to ask if Eliza would come to Richmond for the weekend. 'I'll be honest with you,' she said, 'I'm worried about Harry. He's been pretty stressed over Stu's death. I thought seeing you might help.'

'Stressed? He seemed fine at the awards,' said Eliza.

'Well, of course, he wouldn't have wanted to let on to you.' There was a pause. 'Eliza, seriously. He reminds me of when I first knew him, when I worked for his doctor. He was a ragbag of health problems, on a path to early death. That's why I'm worried.'

A tightness gripped Eliza's chest. The concept of Harry growing old, becoming unhealthy, was an alien one. Apart from his limp, which came and went, he always looked in fine fettle, and much younger than his fifty-eight years.

'When you say stressed, how do you mean?'

'He's preoccupied; he can't seem to sit still for more than five minutes. And he's been losing his temper – he tore the gardener off a strip the other day. It's not like him. Plus . . .' She paused again. 'Headaches, Eliza. So bad he has to go to bed. And he seems short of breath. I'm terribly worried.'

Clare wasn't a worrier.

'I'll come.'

After the phone call, Eliza was restless. She switched on the TV, but couldn't settle to watching anything. She messaged Rob, but it remained unopened. He was probably busy at work.

She googled *My Dark Soul* to see if the buzz was building yet.

The internet rabbithole led her to an image she wished she hadn't seen. *Entertainment Weekly* was speculating on who'd land the coveted lead roles. Already cast as the priest's first temptation was a smouldering almond-eyed blonde with the sort of face you couldn't look away from. And, not looking away, right there in the photograph, was Rob.

Eliza breathed in sharply, and registered how strange that sounded in her empty flat. She was overtaken by an awareness of her solitude.

The actress's name was Letitia Knowles, and the caption said she was celebrating with RoseGold producers at The Ivy after beating off tough competition.

Eliza relaxed when she spotted Leigh behind the pair. Even so, she couldn't help herself. She googled Letitia Knowles and clicked on *Images*.

Big mistake. Her cheekbones were so prominent you could have parked a small car on them. Her feline eyes were wide-set and her lips luscious, her body perfect.

She checked her messages again. Rob's remained unopened.

The following evening she FaceTimed him, but it was the middle of the day in LA so he couldn't chat for long.

'I saw the pic on *Entertainment Weekly*.' Eliza tried to keep her tone nonchalant. 'Does this mean you've confirmed the cast?'

'The pic with Teesha?'

Teesha?

'The blonde.'

'Yep, she's on board. Still screen-testing for the male lead; obviously we've got to take the time to get that right.'

'So can this Letitia actually act? Or is she just a spectacularly beautiful face?'

'She can act all right. Wait and see.'

'And the beautiful part?'

'Not a minger, that's for sure. Look, if you're worried about that pic, don't be. There's always paparazzi at The Ivy. That's why we went there – for the exposure. Remember, this is Hollywood. It's all about making things up.'

'Fair enough. I guess you have to play by the rules.'

'We do. Hey, sorry, Lizzie, I'd love to talk more but I have a lunch. Can we do this again tomorrow?'

'Sure, I'll try and call at a better time.'

'Cool. Love you.' He ended the call.

Eliza sighed as she closed her laptop and sat in the silence of her flat. What she'd give for a Rob hug right now.

As soon as Eliza saw Harry, she knew something was very wrong. There was none of the usual ruddiness in his cheeks, and there were dark rings beneath his eyes.

'Hello, Sweet Pea,' he said, shutting the front door behind her. 'I'm glad you're here. I've been somewhat down in the dumps.'

This was so not Harry. She gave him a hug, squeezing him tight. 'Because of Stu?'

'Mostly. And the young Italian chap. It's hard not to feel at least partly responsible for my son's descent into alcohol-fuelled violence.'

They walked through to the kitchen, and Harry put the kettle on.

Eliza hopped onto a barstool. 'Don't beat yourself up, Dad. And the press will forget about it soon, like they always do. You know that.'

'I spoke to Bennie. It was hard; she's blaming herself. You know what, Lizzie? Life doesn't get any easier. I still seem to lurch from one mess of my own making to another.'

'Dad, this isn't like you. How can I cheer you up?'

'Always better for seeing you,' he said, taking mugs out of a cupboard. 'And Eddie will be home for the holidays soon. We're going up to the Lakes for a week. He and Clare like walking the fells, strangely. And I was thinking, it might be time for Eddie to get some work experience at Rose.'

Oh god. Poor Dad.

'I'm looking forward to seeing him too,' she said. 'You can be proud of him.' But now wasn't a good time to mention her brother's career goal that didn't involve working at Rose.

'And what of Maria?' asked Harry. 'Have you heard from her?'

'She's found her place.' Maria's emails from Cambodia spoke of inner peace, of finding happiness through doing God's will and helping others.

Harry put a cup of tea in front of Eliza and sat down next to her. 'And my other daughter? How's she doing? Are you happy, Lizzie?' His deep-blue eyes were serious.

'Dad, why all these questions?' She gave him a smile. 'Of course I'm happy. Obviously recent events have been a setback, and not winning a BAFTA was a blow. But otherwise everything's fine.'

'Is Rob back soon? I don't like him being away from you. Hollywood's a nuthouse, full of overinflated egos and a million temptations.'

Eliza sipped her tea. 'I hope so. It's hard without him. And it doesn't help seeing photos of him with beautiful women.'

Harry gave a small shake of his head. 'It takes a strong man to resist Hollywood's attractions.'

'What are you saying?' Eliza frowned. 'You don't think Rob's strong enough?'

'I recognize myself at that age.'

'Well, thanks a lot, Dad. That makes me feel a whole lot better.'

Harry's strange mood persisted throughout the weekend.

'I hope this trip to the Lakes lifts his spirits,' Eliza said to Clare, before heading home. 'Dad never does morose. It's scary.'

'It's a shame you can't come with us,' said Clare. 'You could probably do with a holiday yourself.'

'True. Maybe I'll suggest it to Rob. Somewhere warm, doing absolutely nothing for a while.'

'You can always use the Bermuda house if you want.'

What an enticing thought. A week or two in the Caribbean with Rob.

Eliza perked up as she walked to the station. She'd suggest it to him tonight.

'Sorry, Lizzie, but I really can't,' he said. 'I'm on the verge of sealing the deal with the distributor, and there's a million and one other things to sort.'

Eliza groaned. Was this how things would be in their future? Rob away for weeks – months – at a time; Eliza coming home to an empty apartment, an empty bed? One or the other always too busy for a holiday?

After the call, she couldn't help brooding on her conversations with Harry and Rob. She reasoned with herself. What had she expected, taking on the role of CEO? Life was never going to be 'normal'. And would she, in fact, want a 'normal' life? Hell, no. She had the best job, working with the best people; the opportunity to write her name across the sky, as Harry had said.

So why did she feel so low?

Chapter 41

Eliza

Monday morning was far more beautiful than it had a right to be.

Be off with you, sunny summer day. Come back when I'm in the mood.

She slid out of bed and into the kitchen, and switched on the espresso machine.

Her phone pinged.

> KIT: Is your day full of important stuff?

> ELIZA: In the great scheme of things, no. Why?

> KIT: Let's play truant

> ELIZA: What?

> KIT: Phone in sick. Meet me at the Greenwich
> Observatory at 11

> ELIZA: Bunking off like a couple of schoolkids? Are
> you serious?

KIT: Deadly

ELIZA: It was always dangerous to say no to you

KIT: Good girl x

Eliza grinned as she dressed in jeans and T-shirt, slipped on trainers and pulled her hair into a ponytail. This felt deliciously naughty. She phoned Pippa, telling her she'd be working from home because she wasn't feeling great, and that her phone would be switched off.

Bad Kit. But wonderful Kit. Somehow, he'd known her mood.

She caught the ferry to Greenwich and walked up to the observatory. Kit hadn't arrived yet, and she stood leaning on the railings at the top of the hill, looking out across the parkland to the prickly dome of the O2 arena, the stubby chimneys of the power station. Beyond the river, Docklands skyscrapers jostled for position on the Isle of Dogs; further west, the distant towers of the City were a new perspective on the view from her office window.

Freedom.

She breathed deeply.

'Hello, gorgeous.' Two arms slid round her waist.

She smiled and leaned back against him, putting her arms over his.

For a while they said little, enjoying the view, then she turned to face him.

'Why are we here, Kit?'

'You needed time out.'

His hair had grown past his shoulders again, and she pushed it back gently.

'I feel like . . . something's out of kilter,' she said.

'I know. Come on, let's take a walk.'

As they strolled down the hill towards the river, Eliza tilted her face to the sun. 'Oh boy, this was a good idea. We should do this more often, bring Will.'

'Maybe.'

'You two are OK?'

'Of course. I just wanted us to be alone today. I had a dream. At least, I think it was a dream.'

She stopped. 'Kit, you haven't been taking—'

'No. Doesn't work for me any more. I almost went mad writing *Dark Soul*. Not gonna do that again.'

'Thank god. I don't know what I'd do without you.'

They started walking again.

'How's things with Rob?' he said.

'Hm. Dad was sending me weird warning vibes yesterday, talking about Hollywood's wickedness, all the temptations. You've seen the photos of *Dark Soul*'s leading lady?'

'Letitia Knowles? Bit of a babe. But just a girl. Don't stress.'

'I feel so powerless. If I say anything I sound like a jealous nag.'

'So say nothing. Be cool.'

They reached the bottom of the hill and entered the naval college grounds. Eliza enjoyed the elegant symmetry of the old buildings as they walked along ancient stone paths leading down to the Thames, which flashed its welcome in the sunshine.

'Ready for a spot of history?' said Kit. 'This place is loaded with it.'

'Oh yes, I *loves* a bit of history.'

'Look,' he said, stopping at a flagstone on which there was worn writing.

ON THIS SITE STOOD THE TUDOR PALACE OF
GREENWICH BUILT BY KING HENRY VII ...
BIRTHPLACE OF KING HENRY VIII IN 1491 AND
HIS DAUGHTERS QUEEN MARY I IN 1516 AND
QUEEN ELIZABETH I IN 1533.

'This was Tudor central,' he said.

'Henry, Mary and Elizabeth,' said Eliza. 'What a trio. Two monsters and one of the most awesome queens ever.'

'You think?' said Kit. 'Even after we got into Henry's head for *Most Human*?'

'Deeply flawed, then. Corrupted by power.'

'What if he hadn't had absolute power? Would he still have turned into a tyrant? Or would he have stayed that cool guy who loved books and dancing and music and—'

'Women,' finished Eliza. 'Wonder what he'd have been like if he'd been born today?'

'Onwards,' said Kit, 'There's wine in my backpack.'

They wandered along the riverbank then back into the park, until Kit stopped at the fenced-off remains of an ancient tree.

'You can sort the wine,' he said, taking off the backpack, 'I carried it all this way.' He lay down on the grass and closed his eyes.

Eliza poured them a cup each, gazing down at him. He was so beguiling, so gifted, so ... unfathomable.

'Stop staring at me.'

She laughed. 'Here's your wine.'

'Is there food in that backpack too?' she asked, after a while.

'Sorry, no.'

'I don't know how you and Will exist. You still never seem to eat.'

'Go read that sign.'

'I don't want to get up,' she said. 'Don't want to go home, or back to work. Not ever. Wish I could just stay here with you. Shall we run away?'

'Go read the sign.'

She sighed and made her way over, Kit watching.

> This ancient tree, known as Queen Elizabeth's Oak, is thought to have been planted in the twelfth century and has been hollow for many hundreds of years.
>
> It has traditions linking it with Queen Elizabeth I, King Henry VIII and his Queen Anne Boleyn . . .

'Them again,' said Eliza, going back to Kit.

He held out his phone. 'Now read this.'

She spoke out loud:

'Legend has it that Elizabeth picnicked near the tree.
Henry VIII and Anne Boleyn, Elizabeth's mother, were
also supposed to have danced around this tree during
their courting days. This carefree scene didn't last
long – Henry had Anne arrested for high treason and
beheaded three years after their marriage.'

Eliza looked across at the tree again, and experienced something
profoundly odd. It was as if the world stopped turning. As if
time had ground to a halt. All background sound fell silent, and
there was a stillness, a deep awareness, a connection. Some sort
of . . . loop.

Then the Earth began to turn again, and its hum came back.

'You got that too?' said Kit.

'I did. What was it? Ancient oaks?'

'A bit more than that.'

'Our last night at Oxford. The magic.'

Kit lay back down and closed his eyes. '*The universe is full of
magical things*,' he said, '*waiting patiently for our wits to grow
sharper.*'

❀

'I should probably turn my phone back on,' said Eliza, as the taxi
neared Southwark. She unzipped her waist pouch.

'Leave it,' said Kit. 'We'll go into the office. You can catch
up there.'

'Right,' she said, zipping it back up again. 'Or we could just run
away, like I said?'

'Let's walk the last bit.' Kit tapped on the partition. 'Here's good.'

They dawdled along Bankside, the pretty turquoise arches of
Southwark Bridge ahead of them.

As they neared The Rose, Kit took her arm and stopped her.
'Eliza . . . ' He seemed to be searching for words. Not something
he usually had a problem with.

She pre-empted him with a hug. 'Kit, thanks so much for today.

It was just what I needed.' But when she went to let him go, his arms only tightened around her.

'Me too,' he said. 'Look ... if you need me, I'm always here. Day or night.'

'I know.' She pulled back and looked into his eyes. The intensity in them sent a chill through her. 'What is it, Kit? What's going on?'

'Honestly? I'm not sure. But I don't think it's good.'

Chapter 42

Eliza

'Eliza, thank god!' said Pippa, shooting to her feet. 'I've been trying to get hold of you – I was about to come over to your flat.'

Eliza's stomach twisted as she read Pippa's expression: *I don't know how to tell you this.*

She touched Eliza's arm. 'Clare's been phoning. It's Harry. I'm afraid . . . he's had a heart attack. He's alive—' she said quickly, as Eliza's hand flew to her mouth. 'He's in hospital. It was serious, but she says he's stable now.'

Eliza's knees buckled and she sat down heavily on Pippa's desk. 'No. Oh my god. He's stable? You're sure?'

'Yes. He's in Hammersmith. I'll call you a cab. But let's get you a cup of tea first, you've had a horrible shock.'

Eliza squeezed her eyes shut and tried to breathe deeply. *Dad.* An abyss was opening; she was trying not to fall in.

Pippa returned with tea, and Eliza's hand shook as she took it. 'Take your time, Eliza. I'll call a cab when you're ready.'

While I was playing hooky, Dad was having a heart attack. What if he dies? What if I'm too late?

'Now,' said Eliza. 'Get the cab now.' She put down the tea and ran for the lift.

As she waited, anxiously scanning the road, she messaged Kit.

ELIZA: Dads had heart attack. Hes stable On my way to hospital.

KIT: Shit. Want me to come?

ELIZA: Taxi here will be in touch

KIT: Stay strong xx

As soon as she was in the cab, she called Clare. 'It's Eliza.'

'Thank god. Pippa told you? He's stable, Eliza. He's had surgery; he's still unconscious. Are you on your way?'

'In a taxi. I'm so sorry; my phone's been off all day. I'll explain later.'

'Pippa said you were ill. Just get here as soon as you can.'

It was the longest half-hour of Eliza's life, as the taxi crawled through the late-afternoon traffic. At last she was rushing through the hospital corridors following the signs to the ICU. A nurse showed her into a room, where Clare and Eddie were sitting by a bed in which lay Harry, tubes extending from his mouth and nose, more tubes and wires taped to his hands, arms and torso.

He looked so fragile, so dependent. Devoid of his vitality; there was no essence of Harry. He was like a shell. Only the beeping of the machines gave any indication he was still alive.

Eddie stood up and hugged her, and she was comforted by his warmth. Suddenly he was as tall as Eliza. Eddie, her little brother, was nearly sixteen, and all grown up.

'He's going to be fine,' he said. 'They've already done an angioplasty and the surgeon said he's doing great.'

She wiped away a tear. 'Really?'

'He might need another op,' said Clare, 'but he's out of danger.'

Eliza let out a long breath. 'I'm so sorry,' she said. 'I wasn't ill. I took a day off and switched off my phone. What appalling timing.'

'Not at all, darling. I said you needed a break.'

Eliza sat by the bed and looked properly at Harry, trying to ignore the tubes. 'Hi, Dad,' she said softly, holding his hand, taking care not to touch the drip inserted beneath his skin.

'What happened?' she asked, keeping her eyes on Harry.

'He was at home,' said Eddie. 'John Studley was visiting. They were about to go see about joining a golf club.'

Eliza couldn't help smiling, as she remembered Harry asking John if they were old enough for golf yet, back in Sydney.

'They stabilized him in the ambulance, but the cardiologist says his heart's in a bad way. Looks like he'll need a bypass.'

This was worrying news, but Eddie's tone was calm, reassuring. He was going to make a great doctor.

A nurse came in to check the monitors. 'Hello there,' she said. 'I'm sure your father's going to be just fine. He's in the best hands.'

'Will he wake up soon?' asked Eliza.

'Possibly. But he's heavily sedated, so if he does you might not get much sense out of him.'

Harry

Harry became aware of low voices in the room. He wished they'd be quiet, so he could go back to sleep.

Why were there people talking in his bedroom?

Was there a morning coffee on his bedside table?

Ouch.

Something was hurting.

He attempted to open his eyes. Nothing happened.

He gave up, and his mind slipped away again.

When it came back, he managed to open his eyes.

Ana?

Seated beside his bed, the love of his life was gazing at him with those once-seen-never-forgotten dark eyes.

'Ana,' he murmured. 'You came back.'

'Dad!' she said, leaning over him. 'Oh god, he thinks I'm Mum.'

'Shh,' said another female voice. 'Let him come to.'

Clare.

'Harry,' said Clare, touching his hand. 'It's me, Clare. And Eliza's here, and Eddie. You're in hospital, but you're going to be fine.'

Eliza. Eddie.

He blinked a few times, then his mind came into focus.

He managed a smile. 'Hello, Nurse Clare.'

His eyes moved to Eliza. 'Not Ana – Lizzie.'

She burst into tears.

'Hey, none of that. I ... Sorry, rather tired.' He closed his eyes again.

'Come here, sweetheart,' he heard Clare say. 'Everything's going to be all right.'

'Oh, Clare,' his daughter sobbed. 'What would we do without him?'

'We won't be finding that out. We won't let that happen.'

Eliza

Harry's recovery progressed well, and he was moved from the ICU onto the cardiac ward. He was impatient to be home; he hated being bedridden and helpless. Clare, Eddie and Eliza took that as a good sign.

'I remember nursing him after his car crash,' said Clare, as they drove to the hospital. Eliza was staying at Richmond, working from home in the mornings and visiting Harry in the afternoons. 'He was always chirpy, even though he was in a lot of pain. His skills as a patient seem to have gone downhill.'

'Probably because he's not trying to impress the pretty nurse,' said Eliza.

Eddie chuckled.

'You could have a point,' said Clare. 'Gosh, I fell in love with him right there and then. But he was married to your mum, of course, Eliza. I remember her coming in. Yours too, Eddie. Janette would visit during the afternoons to . . . go through his paperwork.'

'You met my mum?' said Eliza.

'Oh yes. And you! She brought you in once. You were fascinated by the contraption his injured leg was in. After that she came by herself. She was certainly a beautiful woman.'

'Did you talk to her?'

'Not properly. I remember finding her quite frosty. Sorry, Eliza, that's rather rude of me.'

'It's fine, I've heard people say that before. I can't relate – all I remember is smiles, cuddles, lots of fun. It was probably because she'd just lost a baby. That was the beginning of the end of their marriage.'

The colour was back in Harry's cheeks. The cardiac surgeon had apparently said he'd be able to have his bypass within the week.

'I need a private word with Eliza,' said Harry. 'Clare, Eddie, why don't you go get a drink in the cafe?'

'The coffee's terrible,' said Eddie.

Eliza smiled. The men in her life and their coffee.

'Live dangerously. I need a word with my girl.'

'What's up, Dad?' Eliza shifted her chair closer.

'Lizzie. This bypass.'

'You'll be fine. You'll be aceing us on the tennis court again in no time.'

'Heart surgery, eh? It got broken too often – I'm surprised it's still repairable.'

Eliza rolled her eyes. 'Really, Dad? From what I've heard, you were the heartbreaker, not the breakee.'

He laughed, then his expression turned serious. 'Look, Sweet Pea. I know we don't like to think these thoughts, but I need you to promise me something, in case . . . Well, in case I don't make it.'

Her heart skipped a beat. 'Of *course* you're going to make it – you're only fifty-eight!'

'But if I don't. You remember our conversation, the ... experience I had before.'

'When you were shot?' He meant the near-death thing.

'This is my third brush with death. I'm not sure I can cheat it again. It's been shadowing me for years.'

'Dad—' Her voice caught, and she glimpsed the abyss again.

'Let me say my piece. I have a loose end that needs tying off. My soul, my spirit – whatever was outside of my body, if it wasn't my brain playing tricks ... I have this feeling, a gut instinct, that it won't rest until I close the circle on your mother's death.'

This was a conversation Eliza didn't want to have. Not now. She wished she could show it the door and tell it to come back in twenty, thirty years.

But as he waited for her response, Harry's expression told her it was finally time.

'Mum's death wasn't your fault, though. You said Andre did it without your knowledge.'

'And there he is, living his life large. I see him, from time to time. Always slaps my back, still thinks he did me a favour. And I let him get away with it, because I was afraid of what would come out. That he'd implicate me. He's a powerful man without scruples. I knew if I ever sought retribution, he'd take me down. Terri wanted to try, but I stopped her.'

Eliza thought back to the time she'd found a file of papers to do with her mother's death. She'd been eighteen, working in Terri's office. Terri had shared her suspicions about Andre, but had explained it was impossible to prove.

'I know she looked into it.'

'Bring her in to see me. I want her to expose Sokolov in *The Rack*, with your help. Then the police will have to reopen the investigation. He needs to pay for Ana's death. Do it for your mum and for me. Promise me, Lizzie.'

He waited, his blue eyes intense.

She'd do anything for him. *Anything.* But she couldn't bring herself to think about the scenario he was describing.

'Dad, we don't need to be having this conversation. You're going to make it. It's a straightforward op, right?'

'There are risks. I need to know Andre will be called to account. Bring Terri tomorrow.'

●

Eliza was FaceTiming Rob in the evenings, keeping him up to date. Tonight he seemed distracted.

'How's Harry now?' he asked, looking away from the screen.

'Looking better every day.'

'Good. That's good. And you – are you doing OK?'

'I'm fine. Dad was being a bit maudlin today. Doing last-wish stuff, just in case. I guess that's understandable – he's had a couple of brushes with death before.'

'Right.'

There was a pause.

'And . . . is everything OK with you, Rob?'

'Fine. We have the final three for the male lead. I can send you links to the screen tests, if you like? Will's been involved, of course, as director.' Will was directing *Dark Soul*, while Kit worked with the RoseGold team on future projects. 'You probably know, he's coming over to meet the three actors.'

'Yes, please do send the links. And run them past Kit too. No one gets the part without his say-so.'

Rob frowned. 'I suppose I could.'

'You *have* been keeping Kit in the loop?'

'Hm, generally the writers don't have a lot of say.'

'Rob – it's Kit's story. You *must* get his agreement.'

He sat back in his chair, swivelling it from side to side. 'There will be some changes to the script. Some of it's too out there.'

'We approved the rewrites a while ago.'

He looked away from the camera, and started scribbling something on a pad of paper. 'Yes, but . . . our distributor. Some of the content, it's too near the mark for US audiences. You have to remember, religion's more of a big thing here.'

'Well, that's kind of the point. Kit's your full-on atheist. He believes religion gives bad people the opportunity to do their thing while hiding behind dogma.'

I shouldn't need to explain this!

He was still swivelling. It was annoying.

He stopped writing and twiddled the pen between his fingers, clicking the end in and out. 'We have to tread a fine line.' His voice was nonchalant as he looked into the camera again. 'We're putting a local writer on it.'

A wave of anger hit, whipped into a tsunami by the anxiety of the past few days. 'What the *fuck*?'

'Look, Eliza. It's how it works. It's a co-production. Once Kit finished those rewrites, it became our intellectual property.'

'Rob! I *won't* have the US team watering down Kit's script!'

'Calm down. You're obviously under a lot of stress. That's understandable.'

His patronising tone wasn't helping.

'Just leave things to us for a while,' he said. 'You can get back into it when Harry's all better.'

This was surely about more than Kit's words.

'When you've completely mangled Kit's script, you mean?'

'It's not Kit's, it's RoseGold's.'

She took some deep breaths, reminding herself that anger solved nothing.

Be professional.

'Look, Rob. The reason *Most Human* did well . . . that was down to Will and Kit. Their vision, their passion, their brilliance. Don't mess with *Dark Soul*. Kit already toned it down. Tell the US guys to back off, OK? I'm going to take a stand on this.'

Rob stopped clicking his pen. 'I'm well aware of where your loyalties lie. I fully appreciate how important Kit is to you. But perhaps your relationship is clouding your judgement? I'm aiming for this series to be huge, not niche. We have to think commercial.

We missed out on the BAFTA because a lot of it went over the audiences' heads. When you're making deals, it's all about bums on seats. You've got to be more objective, Lizzie. And more hands-off.'

His words stung, and her anger gave way to hurt. She was all at once aware of a distance between them that wasn't all physical.

Suddenly she felt exhausted. 'Rob ... please. Let's not argue? I've had the worst week. I wish you were here. I could use a hug. I don't suppose ...'

His expression softened. 'I can't, Lizzie. I'm sorry. Another couple of weeks, I reckon, then I can come back.'

⬧

'So – a heart attack, Harry?' said Terri, sitting down beside his bed. 'Fuck's sake.'

'Never fear, Terri. Still it lingers on, beating ever more faintly, counting down the seconds to oblivion.'

'Oblivion is not a place I've ever pictured you,' said Terri. 'Even beyond death.'

'Can we just stop with the death and oblivion?' said Eliza, sitting on his other side. 'Dad, tell her why you wanted to see her.'

'Right. Yes. It's about Ana.'

'Oh.' Terri took a deep breath and met Harry's eye.

Eliza didn't understand the look that passed between them.

'I think,' he said, 'when I explain what I want you to do, you'll be on side.'

'Tell me this isn't about Sokolov,' said Terri.

'One step ahead, as always.'

'You warned me off before. What's changed?'

'I wasn't expecting to die, that time.'

'Dad!'

'This is what I want you two to do,' he said, sitting up straighter. 'First and foremost, remember that Andre is a man without a moral compass. He's extremely dangerous, with contacts everywhere. Anything and everything you do *must* remain below the radar. Only you two and Charles can know what's going on.'

'Uncle Charles?' said Eliza.

'I saw him yesterday. I explained the situation. He'll give you all the help you need. He wants to put things right, too.'

Eliza was confused. 'What does Uncle Charles have to do with this?'

'He'll fill in the gaps for you. It'll make sense when you talk to him. Terri – I hate loose ends. Ana's my loose end. And I know how much this means to you.'

Eliza looked at Terri. 'You and Mum were pretty close, weren't you?'

'Eliza, love,' she said, after a moment. She looked over at Harry, who gave a small nod. 'I was in love with your mum. She never knew how I felt. I didn't tell anyone, except for Harry, a long time after she died.'

Eliza's mouth dropped open, and a lump formed in her throat as she remembered how Terri had watched over her, from the moment she'd started at Rose.

'That's so sad, Terri.'

'She was a close friend; it was more than enough. I tried for years to link Sokolov to her murder, but as you know I couldn't prove anything. If we can do it now, I'm on board. And, as far as I'm concerned, there's no need for you to die to make that happen, Harry.'

'No. Only if I don't make it. Otherwise he'll take us all down with him. Talk to Charles, gather your evidence. Lock it up, don't put it on any computer. Then write the piece, Terri. Get him put away and tell the world why.' He leaned back on his pillows, suddenly looking tired.

'My god, Dad. Can we just stop this? You've got the best bloody cardiac surgeon in London, right?'

'Eliza, you'll need to be extremely careful,' he said, ignoring her distress. 'Not a word to anyone. Not Rob, no one at the office, certainly not Clare or Eddie.'

'We hear you,' said Terri. 'But like Eliza says, this won't need to happen. You're going to be just fine, and together we'll fade gracefully – make that disgracefully – into old age. Right, Harry?'

'Absolutely, my little pit bull. But I have your word. Swear?'

'I tend to, rather a lot.'

'Swear, Terri.'

'Right you are, Harry. Should you pop your clogs, I do fucking swear that I shall bring down Andre Sokolov, and in so doing avenge the death of the love of our lives, and the mother of our beloved Eliza, and so ensure that your delightful soul – yes, I do love you, Harry – can rest in peace for ever more.'

Eliza burst into tears and left the room.

Chapter 43

Eliza

'Tell me about Charles,' said Terri, as they sat in Eliza's office. 'I met him a few times. He seemed like a carbon copy of Harry – quite amusing, but basically a posh twat.'

Eliza laughed. 'Yes, they're like a pair of naughty children when they're together. Charles is a few years older than Dad. From what I understand, when they were at school, Charles was tasked with making sure Dad was OK when his parents and brother died.' She stopped for a moment. Imagine losing your mum, dad and brother while you were still a teenager.

'God, Terri. We never really think about our parents' lives before they had us, do we? Excuse the pop psychology, but ... maybe Dad's womanising in those early years was overcompensating for losing his parents?'

'Perhaps. It probably explains why he married so young. But back to Charles?'

'Yes. Dad's best friend forever, and obviously married to his sister. He was a banker. He's retired now, just does a bit of consulting. As you know, he was the person who brought Andre on board with the Rose TV investment.'

'Is Charles in London?'

'They live in Suffolk but still have a London flat.'

'Right. Look, Eliza. I know Harry said only if the worst happens, but I want to do this, no matter what. For myself, as well as for him. You OK with that?'

'Yes. Nobody except you, me and Charles needs to know what we're doing until we've worked out a way forward.'

'Good. Can you call Charles and find out where's best for us to meet?' She stood up to leave. 'And, Eliza, love. Try not to worry too much about Harry. It's no surprise that he did the last-wish thing. Anyone would, facing a heart op. Why don't you phone a friend, have a night out.'

'I might just do that.'

ELIZA: You and Will free tonight?

KIT: Want to come over? Can show you screen tests.
We have wine

ELIZA: Food?

KIT: Um . . .

ELIZA: Will bring something. 7ish?

KIT: See you then x

Next, Eliza rang Uncle Charles. As she waited for him to answer, she looked out of her window. Thunderclouds were billowing up over the city. The weather had been hot and sticky, and everyone had been wondering when it would break, in that slightly obsessive British way.

Charles picked up; he'd been expecting her call, he said. 'Harry told you about keeping schtum?'

'Loud and clear. Nothing on the computer, etc., etc.'

'Good. Why don't you and Terri come over to the Bayswater flat tomorrow? About twelve?'

'Perfect. Before I go, can I ask you something?'

'Fire away.'

'Do you still see Andre Sokolov? Like, do you still do any consulting for him?'

'Absolutely not. And let's leave this discussion until tomorrow. After that, the picture should be clearer for you.'

'Right, yes. See you at twelve, then.'

Eliza ended the call and turned back to her desk. And realized she wasn't alone. Her hand flew to her chest. 'Mac!'

'Sorry, I didn't mean to creep up on you. The door was open.'

'That was Uncle Charles; I was updating him on Dad.'

'How's Harry doing?' She sat down opposite Eliza.

'Really well, but he's having a bypass next week.'

'I expect it'll take him a while to get over that,' said Mac. 'Still, he has a nice choice of places to recuperate, has he not? Super-yacht, Caribbean mansion, Richmond mansion . . . ' She laughed, but Eliza detected something sour in her tone.

'How's everything with you?'

'Busy busy. Steady stream of orders from Rob.' She smiled a small smile. 'I love his daily emails. He's so funny. You must miss him.' She held Eliza's gaze.

Eliza didn't return the smile. 'Of course.'

'I came up to tell you something. Hamish and I are getting married.'

What?!

'Oh! That's . . . a surprise.'

'We've known each other a while. I should let you know – we won't be doing the family wedding thing. Hamish hates a fuss.'

'Fair enough.'

'Said he'd prefer to abduct me and lock me up in his Scottish castle.'

Eliza snorted. 'He's got one?'

'Two, actually.'

'Gosh, kidnapped and thrown over the back of a horse. That's quite sexy. Bit of role play on your wedding night?'

Mac smiled. 'Och, you're not all you seem, are you, Eliza? Didn't you once say you'd stay a virgin all your life?'

'I was a teenager at the time.'

'Like I said, you must be missing Rob.' She was watching Eliza carefully. 'I don't suppose his Instagram posts help.'

What's going on here?

'I don't bother with all that. I don't have the time.'

'That's perhaps as well. Still, I guess showbiz is all about image.'

After she left, Eliza brooded on her cousin. Those insidious remarks, that knowing smile. It was all surely designed to unsettle her. Was Mac working towards some sort of power grab? And if so, was it coming from Mac, or from Hamish?

Eliza exited the air-conditioned cool of The Rose into a wall of hot, humid air. She pitied those heading home on the tube tonight, as she made her way to Tesco Metro, where she filled her basket with salads, a quiche, a ciabatta loaf, some hummus and a couple of packets of crisps.

'Good grub, Eliza,' said Will, half an hour later.

They were sprawled on the long narrow lawn of the old terraced house, their feet bare, the cool of the grass a relief on this muggy summer's evening. The sweet notes of a blackbird's song played against the background hum of London traffic, and the musky scent of tobacco plants drifted across from a riotously planted border. To Eliza's and Kit's amusement, Will had developed a fondness for gardening.

'What, Will?' asked Eliza through a mouthful of salad. 'Is that it? Have you no suitable food quote for this excellent fare I have laid before you?'

'I had rather live with cheese and garlic in a windmill.'

Kit and Eliza spluttered with laughter.

'Shut up, I'm tired.' Will tossed his hair. 'Trying to get everything done before I go. It's the best I can do.' He was off to LA in the morning, for the final selection of the male lead on *Dark Soul*.

'*Comedy of Errors*?' guessed Kit, scooping up hummus with a crisp.

Will sighed dramatically. 'Metaphor for my life.'

'Nonsense, Will. Your life's going swimmingly,' said Eliza. '*Dark Soul*'s going to be phenomenal, thanks to my two best boys.'

'I think I *have* made an error, actually,' said Will, opening his laptop. 'But let's get your opinion, dear leader.'

A black actor with liquid eyes appeared on screen. His features were expressive, and before he'd said a single word, the viewer knew this was one tortured soul.

Then the camera pulled back, revealing the person with the priest, the woman tempting him. Letitia Knowles. Her beauty was incandescent, her blonde glow a sharp contrast to the dark figure gazing at her.

Will pressed pause. 'Well?'

'He's perfect,' said Eliza. 'The other two will have to be spectacular to even come close.'

'Agree,' said Kit. 'He's my pick.'

'But?' said Will. 'Kit?'

'Let's see the other two first.'

They were good, but Eliza had made up her mind – the first one.

As they watched the third actor, there was Letitia again, drawing the eye.

Away from the priest.

And therein lay the problem. You couldn't help but look at her.

'She's too much,' said Eliza.

'She detracts from the priest,' said Kit. 'We need a more low-key temptress. Beautiful, alluring, but quietly so.'

'Letitia was Rob's choice,' said Will.

Kit met Eliza's eye.

'Though Leigh was keen, too,' Will continued. 'But Leigh's an economist, let's remember.'

'And Rob's basically a salesman,' said Kit.

'Bitch,' said Will.

Eliza laughed, but realized this situation had the potential to be a real headache. She was going to have to play it carefully.

'So we're agreed, we like actor number one, but it doesn't work with Letitia Knowles.'

'Indeed,' said Will.

'So when you get to LA, can you impart this without implicating me in your decision? So as I don't look like a jealous girlfriend wanting to banish the pretty girl to somewhere far, far away from her boyfriend?'

'I can try. Though he'll know you've seen the screen tests.'

'I have every faith in you,' said Eliza.

'Neatly done,' said Kit, raising his glass to Eliza.

A sudden cool breeze dipped into the garden and grabbed an empty crisp packet, flipping it up and across the lawn. Will retrieved it, looking up at the sky. In the gathering dusk, menacing rainclouds reflected the sickly glow of the city lights, and from the east there came a rumble of thunder.

'*By the pricking of my thumbs, something wicked this way comes,*' said Will. 'I shall get me to bed. Early start tomorrow.'

'Good luck, Will,' said Eliza, holding out a hand to him.

He took it and squeezed it. '*Once more unto the breach.* I sense a creative versus commercial spat about to hit, in the manner of this gathering storm. Don't you just love it when weather foreshadows plot?'

As Will went inside, Kit lit a cigarette and rested back on his elbows. The evening light was tinged an unsettling yellow, and shadows were creeping across the lawn towards them. Thunder rolled again in the distance.

'Is Rob giving you a hard time over the script?' he said.

'We had words, yes. He wants to get a local writer to tone it down, so as not to offend US religious sensibilities. I told him that was kind of the point.'

He was quiet for a moment. 'Will's the director. We'll just have to hope he stays strong. Rob's a good bloke, but—'

'He doesn't get it? Will you talk to him about it, or wait and see?'

He dragged on his cigarette. 'I may have to wade in at some point. Or I could just stab him.'

Eliza laughed. 'Oh god. Maybe I'll have another go; I don't want a civil war.'

A fork of lightning ripped across the sky.

'Leave him to Will. I promise not to kill your boyfriend. Yet.'

'He says I let my relationship with you cloud my judgement.'

'He's an alpha male, remember. People like me confuse him.'

'You confuse everyone, Kit.'

'Come here, let's watch the storm.'

She lay down next to him and they stared up at the sky as night fell, watching the lightning fork and flash, growing more intense, illuminating the cauliflower clouds overhead.

The air sizzled with electricity, and Kit took her hand. A burst of energy zipped along her arm, spreading through her body.

She turned her head and looked at him. 'That was weird.'

He chuckled. 'Shocking.'

He met her gaze, his eyes inches from hers. 'What's coming, you'll be OK.'

There was another bright flash and a clap of thunder, and Eliza flinched.

'What do you mean, what's coming? Don't you dare go all prophet of doom on me again.'

'Maybe this time it's simple human intuition.'

Overweight raindrops began to fall, shockingly cold against her warm skin. They sat up and, for a while, didn't move, as the rain released the most divine earthy scent from the parched soil.

Eliza breathed deeply, closing her eyes. 'Oh, that smell . . .'

'Petrichor,' said Kit. 'Named for the fluid that runs in the veins of the Greek gods.'

'So fleeting, like a moment of truth.' She opened her eyes again.

Another flash lit up his face.

'You look like a Greek god,' she said, smiling and nudging him with her foot.

The rain increased in intensity, and Kit pulled her to her feet.
'Time's up, Artemis.'

'Which one's that?'

'Look her up.'

Chapter 44

Eliza

Cecil poked his head around Eliza's door. 'Have you got a minute?'

'Of course. Coffee?'

'I'm fine, thanks.'

Eliza smiled to herself as he sat down. Cecil had a precise order of doing things. Hitch up his well-tailored trousers, sit down, cross one leg over the other. A few moments looking out of the window while he considered his words, before turning that steady gaze on Eliza. A little chin stroke.

'Before Harry was taken ill, he asked me to keep an eye on things in the US.'

'Oh. By *things*, you mean Rob?' This wasn't a surprise.

'Indeed. Between you and me, Harry can be a little ... overprotective, perhaps.'

Eliza swallowed. She wasn't at all sure she wanted to know what he'd found out. 'Sometimes I wish he wouldn't interfere.'

'Rob's been seen out and about with your latest leading lady,' he said, not meeting her eye. 'But I have no reason to believe he's been ... disloyal.' He met her gaze again. 'Having said that, if you were my daughter, I'd be giving Rob a good talking to.'

Eliza smiled and let out a breath. *No reason to believe ...*

'It's OK, Cecil. I know the score. Hollywood's all about making things up.'

'Perhaps. But what concerns me more, Eliza, is something unexpected that came up.'

'Oh?'

'Mackenzie James has been spying on him too.'

'What?'

'We need to address this. My guess is she's identified Rob as your weak spot, and will be attempting to use that to her advantage. To knock you off balance, perhaps. She's in daily contact with him herself, and I'm not happy with the . . . conspiratorial tone of her emails.'

Eliza felt the ground shifting beneath her feet.

'I have to ask – how have you been reading her emails?'

'One has ways.'

'Sometimes you sound just like Dad.'

'Can I speak frankly, Eliza?'

'Of course.'

'Rob's a tremendous asset to Rose. But I feel he's allowed himself to, shall we say, lose focus . . .'

'You don't really like him, do you?' She'd suspected this for a while. Cecil wasn't easy to read, but there was always a slight pursing of the lips when Rob's name was mentioned.

'That's not important.'

'Yes, it is.'

'Very well. Of course, he's a brilliant executive. But I'm not sure Head of Production was a good fit for him.'

'You think I gave him the job only because he's my partner? Come on, Cecil. You know me better than that.'

'I get the impression he's very ambitious. More so than you'd guess from his demeanour.'

'You think?'

John Studley had said Rob was ambitious, too. In spite of his words to the contrary, was Rob in fact driven by a desire to please his father?

'You can't think he's with me just because of my position?'

'No, no, not at all. But I do wonder . . . sorry, Eliza. But the intel from Hollywood is that he was rather messing that actress about. Using her, perhaps?'

'Using her for what?'

'You'd know better than I. It might be an idea to bring him home. Leigh Walters is very capable, perhaps with . . . Eliza, how would you feel about sending Mackenzie to the US? She's talented, tough, bright; she's got broad management experience . . . but, most importantly, she'd be out of your hair.'

'Oh!' Now, this *was* an idea. Banished from the castle but not from the kingdom. Given her own realm.

'Let me give it some thought, Cecil. And thank you for your . . . insight. As always, it's much appreciated.'

'You're welcome. And please send my regards to Harry when you next see him. Tell him I've got your back.'

'You most certainly have. Did I tell you I love you, Cecil?' She gave him a wink.

He gave an embarrassed cough, and left.

⚜

'Right, ladies,' said Charles to Terri and Eliza, as they sat in the sunny living room of the Bayswater flat. Eliza had parked herself in the window seat, which looked out over a leafy London square.

'First up, while I'm happy to pass on everything Harry wants me to, he did say all this was in the event of . . . well, that thing that isn't going to happen.'

'Yes, Uncle Charles. But if you're OK with this, Terri and I have our own reasons for wanting to move forward.'

'You want to do it now, for Ana. That's understandable. It does seem wrong that . . . no one's ever been held accountable for her death. She was a remarkable woman, taken way before her time.'

'The best,' said Terri. 'Brilliant businesswoman, superb designer, great mum. Her only mistake was falling for bloody Harry.'

'I wouldn't be here if she hadn't,' said Eliza. 'And Dad did love her very much.'

'Until he didn't,' said Terri. 'That was one fucked-up relationship.'

Charles frowned, his eyes flicking to Eliza. 'Steady on, Terri. They had many good years.'

'And then he started screwing his secretary. He just couldn't help himself, could he?'

'Shall we move on to the reason you're here?' said Charles.

'Yeah. Sorry. As you can tell, I still get angry. Spill those beans, Charles.'

'Right. As you know, Andre was the major investor in Rose's football TV channel, back in the late nineties. I'm afraid that to get Andre on board, Harry and I had to dance to his tune. It left something of a bad taste in the mouth. A good proportion of his wealth was from dubious sources, but the world of banking rarely asked questions back then.'

'What's changed?' said Terri.

'Regulations. Things *are* tighter, Terri.'

'Yeah, right.'

'And therein lay the problem,' said Charles. 'After the 2008 crisis, the bank's position with regard to Andre's investments was shaky. Our handling of his finances was investigated. The authorities were looking for evidence of money laundering and any dodgy revenue streams. Andre saw it coming, and made a pre-emptive move. It was only then that Harry and I realized – Ana's death had been all about giving Andre leverage, a hold over us, as much as it was about saving his investment in the football channel.'

'I see,' said Eliza. 'What was the problem with the investment?'

'Ana had a pit bull of a divorce lawyer. They were going to take Harry to the cleaners. Had she succeeded, he wouldn't have had the funds to get the football channel off the ground, even with Andre's investment. In fact, Harry would have been severely over-extended, may even have lost his share of Rose.'

'Are you saying Andre killed my mum because he wanted a football TV channel?'

'It was all about power, Eliza. Everything's about power, in the end. When the banking investigation came, he made it clear that if any incriminating financial dealings came to light, he'd claim Harry had asked him to organize Ana's murder. He couldn't prove it, but the threat was enough to shut down any thoughts of retribution on Harry's part. So I quietly covered up each and every piece of evidence of Sokolov's financial misdeeds, including his links to Russian organized crime. He got away with it all. Everything.'

'Holy fuck,' said Terri. 'No wonder Harry wouldn't let me near Sokolov.'

'Thing is, nothing's changed. He's still got that leverage. I do have incriminating evidence with regards to his finances, and I can quietly gather that together, but I don't have anything to link him to Ana's death. All we have is Harry's word, which ... Well, if the worse came to the worse, you could make public via *The Rack*, prompting a police investigation. However, that's not going to happen, Eliza.'

Eliza swallowed. 'No.'

●

CHESS: Hello! Sorry haven't been in touch, been away. Free for lunch?

ELIZA: Yes! In dire need of heart to heart xx

'Mum kept me up to date while we were away,' said Chess, as they started on their salads. 'She told me about Harry's drug addiction, before he married Clare. I was pretty shocked. She's worried it might have done long-term harm, maybe damaged his heart.'

'The more I find out about Dad's life, the more I admire his ability to bounce back. I'm counting on that happening again. How was your trip?'

Chess and Gil had been on holiday to California, and had stayed a few days with Rob.

'Great! *Loved* San Francisco. Rob gave us a good time in LA.

We saw Leigh, too. Rob asked if I could be based there some of the time, but I talked him round – no need, really. Mac and I are mostly sorting out the UK crews and locations at the moment. Also I don't want to spend time away from Gil. I don't know how you manage, being apart from Rob like this.'

Her cousin's words unleashed a wave of despondency. 'I miss him so much. How is he?'

'Bouncy as ever. Fits right in over there.'

'So I hear. Will's there now.' Eliza paused. 'Rob might be a little less bouncy when he puts his directorial foot down.'

'About what?' said Chess.

'More *who* than what. Actually, I'd like your thoughts.'

'Oh?'

'The thing is, Chess,' Eliza said, considering her words. 'We were all new to this business when we started out. We have an incredible core team, but I think we should have made the roles clearer from the get-go.'

'How do you mean?'

'I set up RoseGold with the goal of producing quality original content. That means the best creative minds get unleashed and the production side of things *supports* that.'

'Ah, I see where you're going with this,' said Chess. 'Rob said something about adapting *Dark Soul* to make it palatable for a wider audience?'

'Yep. And he and Leigh have been deciding on the cast without okaying it with Will and Kit. Not the lead role – they waited on our input for that. But other major roles. Well, role.'

Chess unfolded her napkin and smoothed it in her lap, eyes down. 'Letitia Knowles?'

'Did you meet her?'

'Yes. A couple of times.'

'And?'

Chess met Eliza's gaze. 'I was ... surprised when she came out to dinner with us. Leigh came too, and a couple of others from the office.'

Eliza put down her fork, feeling suddenly nauseous. 'Chess – how do you think Rob would respond to being told she'd lost the part?'

'Really? Why?'

'I watched the male lead screen tests with Will and Kit. She was in them. We all agreed – great actress, but not right for the part.'

'Holy heck. That's not going to go down well with Rob at all.'

'Because?'

'Well, because . . .'

'Don't directors change their minds all the time while casting's ongoing?'

'Maybe, but . . .' Chess looked out of the window.

Was Cecil's intel correct? *No reason to believe he's been disloyal . . .*

'Chess. Rob wouldn't be stupid enough to carry on with someone else in front of you and Gil, would he? Unless he somehow wanted that knowledge to get back to me?'

'No, he didn't. Doesn't. I mean—'

'Please. Just tell me?'

Chess sighed. 'He told Gil. Perhaps he doesn't realize we don't have secrets from each other. He's been seeing Letitia outside of work. I don't know how far it's gone. He told Gil it had nothing to do with you and him, it was just a . . . he actually used the word "distraction", can you believe?'

Eliza breathed in sharply as the hurt hit.

'Dad warned me. He said Rob's just like he was.'

'Rob's mad about you, Eliza. Always has been. That's why I can't understand.'

'Do you think he's having an affair?'

'I won't lie to you; I think he might be. She's incredibly beautiful – it'd take a strong man to resist. Rob's lovely, but we both know he acts first, thinks later. Eliza, what will you do? Confront him? You and him – it's worth saving.'

'Seriously, Chess?' The hurt gave way to anger. 'You'd carry on seeing someone who's going on dates with a beautiful actress just as a distraction? How could I *ever* trust him again?' She looked down in embarrassment, realising her voice had risen.

'He told Gil he proposed to you,' said Chess, 'and you turned him down. Maybe it's something to do with that?'

'You think a ring on my finger would change his behaviour?'

'A commitment; an assurance that he's the one? It might. I think he's never been quite sure of your feelings for him.'

'He's betrayed me, whatever the reason.'

'It's you he loves, Eliza. Maybe it's just the whole Hollywood thing, the way people are there. I know that's no excuse, but . . . you two are so *right* together. God, he's an idiot. I want to slap him.'

Eliza's patience ran out. 'You know what? I can't be bothered with it right now. I've got Dad's op to worry about. I need to focus on the person who *really* matters.'

'Good plan.' Chess put her hand over Eliza's. 'Harry's going to be fine. And things will work out with Rob, I'm sure of it.'

❀

That evening, Eliza and Kit had an email from Will.

> Played through the videos with Rob. Talked him
> through our reasons. Happy (if surprised) to
> report he saw our point of view. Letitia's out,
> calling back others for that role :)

Eliza was surprised, too, but relieved. Letitia was gone. But was still somewhere close to Rob, presumably. Somewhere a lot closer than London. Banished from the castle but not the kingdom. *Seems to be a theme.*

She felt flat as she ate her lonely dinner, half-watching something on Netflix. She'd mulled things over all afternoon. Rob had betrayed her. The thought of him with Letitia, whatever his motivation, made her feel sick. Then furious. She would happily have encouraged Kit to progress his stabbing plan.

But now the anger gave way to a deep sadness. A realisation that she and Rob were just like any other couple battling the temptations that came their way. How many men, thousands of miles away from their girlfriend for months at a time, could have resisted Letitia Knowles?

At least the Rob revelations had provided a diversion from her worries about Harry's operation. It was scheduled for mid-morning tomorrow. She wanted to see him before the op, but was dreading it. Was he going to do the whole 'third brush with death' thing again? Was he going to do 'last words', just in case? How could she face that?

Chapter 45

Eliza

'The porter will be here shortly,' said the nurse, smiling kindly. 'I'll leave you alone until he gets here.'

'I feel a few profound words are expected,' said Harry, 'but I seem to be stuck in cliché-land. How much I love you, how you're all so bloody perfect. How I messed up time and again, but you've tried to understand me.'

Eliza swallowed. *Be brave*, Kit's message had said that morning.

'You do realize, the mortality rate for heart surgery is less than three per cent?' she replied. 'I googled it. This time tomorrow you'll be sitting up laughing at your clichés.' She was surprised the words made it past the lump in her throat.

'Probably not the sitting up part,' said Clare. 'But this time next week you'll be home, Harry. Focus on that. Think about what you'd like me to cook you. Think about walking in the park. You love summer days in the park ...' She choked on the words, and her eyes filled with tears. So did Eliza's.

'Eddie. Keep these two supplied with tea and tissues while I'm in theatre, there's a good chap.'

'Dad, is now a good time to tell you I want to go into medicine?' blurted Eddie.

'Eddie!' said Eliza, jerked out of her misery.

'What did you say?' said Harry, frowning at his son.

'I ... I'm not cut out for business, Dad. I want to—' He was clearly already regretting his words.

'Not now, Eddie,' said Eliza gently.

Harry looked at Eliza, then back at Eddie.

But then he smiled. 'Couldn't be prouder, Son. Rose's future is already in the safest of hands. Male heirs are so last century. Go save lives, live the life you want.'

Eliza and Clare gave up trying to stop their tears as Eddie hugged his father.

'Eliza ... the thing, for Ana,' he said over Eddie's shoulder.

'I promise. But you're going to be—'

'I'll do my best. Give me a hug.'

Her tears soaked his stupid green gown. She felt his warmth, his energy, his strength; breathed them in as he held her tight.

The porter arrived, and she smiled through her tears as Harry was wheeled away.

◈

Eliza pondered on time as they sat in the waiting room. This time tomorrow ... this time next week. Next year. She'd be looking back, remembering how she felt now, in this moment.

Cheerful nurses kept reminding her: *Don't worry, standard procedure, best hands ...*

But she couldn't stop the dread. The feeling there was something waiting in the wings. Something her father had been aware of.

His premonitions; Kit's words: *What's coming. You'll be OK.* His text this morning: *Be brave.* Was she reading too much into it? And what was it with all these premonitions and voices of doom, anyway? She believed in science, didn't she? It was surely just the mind doing its thing, anticipating the worst. Time was linear; these hours would pass. It didn't run in circles, do unexpected things, like Kit had said. It was constant, measurable, reliable. And Fate wasn't a thing; it was a concept invented by humankind needing ways to understand their existence, their purpose. It was mere superstition. So was karma.

An hour passed, then another, and another. Eliza, Clare and Eddie came and went from the cafe, drinking cup after cup of tea and coffee (decaf – they were jittery enough), picking at food they had no appetite for. But the chocolate bars helped.

Another hour, and then another. The three of them carried on, somehow, getting through the minutes.

Harry

He looked down at the empty body below. At the husk of Harry. The surgeon was bent over the gaping hole in his chest, working steadily to mend his broken heart. Like the others in the room, the surgeon was unaware that time had stopped.

The walls and ceiling of the operating theatre had dissolved, and beyond was a void, neither light nor dark. On the edge of Harry's consciousness, present in the room and yet not, shadowy figures muttered, deciding his fate.

Four ghosts – beautiful, diaphanous, feminine bundles of energy – hovered, watching.

Eliza

At last, the surgeon appeared. They tried to read his expression as he closed the waiting room door behind him. Was that a smile? No, not a smile. Was his face relaxed? Would yours be after performing a complicated hours'-long operation?

'Mrs Rose, Eliza, Eddie. There's good news and not such good news.'

Eliza only heard 'good'. He wouldn't say that if Dad was in danger.

'Please, give us the facts,' said Clare, calmly.

'The operation was a success. More complicated than expected, but no hiccups.'

'Thank god.'

'But he hasn't come round. We'd have expected him to by now.'

'How long is it since you finished the operation?' asked Clare.

'Almost two hours. It always takes longer after an op like this one, and he's on a lot of medication, obviously. But even so, this is not what we'd expect.'

'Can we see him?'

'Of course.'

They followed the surgeon to the ICU. Harry looked as he had before – like a shell; full of tubes, surrounded by machines that beeped and flashed numbers. Clare read them, understanding. Eliza had no clue.

They talked to him, touched his hands, his face; stroked his hair. Time passed – an hour, then two. Harry remained motionless, in a deep sleep.

Doctors and nurses came and went, shining torches into his eyes, checking tubes, drips and monitors, speaking reassuring words.

Outside, night fell. The nurses advised going home – they'd call as soon as Harry woke up. But they stayed, dozing in their chairs, talking to each other, and to Harry.

Midnight came and went, then two a.m., four a.m., six a.m., and then the sun was rising.

The surgeon returned.

Eddie stood up. 'Is my father in a coma?'

Clare gasped.

'We believe not. But if he doesn't wake up in the next hour or two we'll do some tests. You should go home, get some rest. We'll be in touch the minute he comes round.'

'We should, Mum,' said Eddie. 'We'll be useless if we don't get some sleep.'

So they returned to Richmond, and Eliza lay on her bed, staring at the ceiling, willing Harry to wake up, willing Clare's phone to ring.

It did, a few hours later, but it was to report the results of the tests. They could find no reason why Harry wasn't waking up. Brain scans were fine; *everything* was fine. It was inexplicable. They were monitoring him closely, making sure he was breathing properly, administering all the fluids he needed. All they could do was wait.

Again and again, Eliza replayed the conversation they'd had by the Thames, about his near-death experience. Was Harry's soul out there, outside his body, watching those mysterious shadows discussing his fate once again? Deciding whether he should live or die?

A week later, Harry was still asleep. But now they were calling it a coma. Every day, Clare, Eddie and Eliza visited, sitting with him, talking to him. Still the doctors could find no explanation for his condition.

Rose's PR department put out a short statement saying Harry was still in hospital with complications following heart surgery, but that the prognosis was good.

Rob FaceTimed every day. He was kind, supportive, wishing he could be there. Neither he nor Eliza mentioned Letitia. Eliza ached to feel his arms around her, in spite of her hurt and confusion.

She went back to St Katharine Docks and picked up her office routine, visiting Harry after work.

Eliza brooded on his last wish as she walked across London Bridge. Ahead, The Shard glinted in the morning sun. Its presence felt sinister today – it reminded her of the Tower of Sauron in *The Lord of the Rings*, and she had a passing fancy it was pointing skywards, guarding the entrance to Heaven, refusing Harry permission to enter. *You shall not pass.*

Instead of going to her own office, she headed to Terri's.

'Hello, love. No change?'

'No. You know what? I thought modern medicine had all the answers. But the doctors have no clue what's going on.'

'Gotta admit, I've been googling comas. There seem to be an awful lot of unknowns.'

'Terri. I know this sounds a bit out there, but I have this feeling that if we could tell Harry we'd nabbed Andre, it might help him out.'

'You've been reading far too many film scripts.'

'I knew you'd say that. But I need to do something to try and help him. Can we at least see what Charles has got? Surely he'll let us move forward now Dad's . . . in limbo. Kind of.'

'Fair enough, if it'll help you. Eliza – where the fuck's Rob? Why is he not here?'

The question threw her. 'What could he do?'

'He could get his pretty arse back here and support you, that's what.'

'I have Clare and Eddie. And you, and Kit.'

Kit. She hadn't seen him since the night of the thunderstorm.

'Hm,' said Terri. 'OK, I'll talk to Charles and let you know.'

Back in her office, Eliza got to work on her emails. There was one from Mac.

Hi Eliza

   I was so sorry to hear about Harry. I hope by the time you read this he's awake and making everyone laugh as per.

   I wondered if you might be free for an hour sometime this week. Hamish and I have a proposal we'd like to run past you. Very early days but would be good to get you on board from the get-go. Let me know when you're free.

   Kind regards

   Mac

What was Mac up to now? A proposal? A remake of *Braveheart*?

```
Hi Mac
   Back at my desk. No change re Dad. Come up
midday if you're free.
   E
```

Mac appeared at twelve. After discussing Harry's progress, Eliza said, 'So what's all this about a proposal? Oh, speaking of proposals, when's the big day?'

'In three weeks.'

'Three weeks! Has he a horse kidnap-ready?'

Mac laughed. 'A brand-new Lamborghini. It'll have to do. Remember I mentioned his Scottish castles?'

'Just the two.'

'One of them is close to Loch Lomond, within easy reach of Glasgow Airport. It's in need of renovation, but it's got fantastic potential as a hotel and casino.'

'What? A casino? At Loch Lomond?'

'All Scotland's casinos are in the cities. Big-bucks visitors – Americans in particular – love the whole Scottish-castle experience. Hamish had this brainwave that we could combine the two. It's a brilliant idea; it'll make us a fortune.'

'Us? You mean him and you?'

'Why not Rose? Casinos – it's easy money. Hamish has all the right contacts. Local council, government, banks.'

Mafia?

'It's a no-brainer,' Mac continued. 'But it needs investment. That's where I thought Rose could come in.'

Are you mad?

'I'm sorry, Mac. It's out of the question. A casino would be way off brand. Gambling? I mean – really?'

Mac looked her in the eye. 'A business shouldn't be run according to personal prejudices, Eliza. This is a sensible proposal. The return on investment would be solid. Let me email you the figures

Hamish has drawn up. And Rose wouldn't be bearing all the risk. There are other interested investors.'

'Who? A bunch of Trump clones? *Just* the type of people we want to be dealing with.'

'Not Americans. Europeans.'

Eliza sat back in her chair. 'Mac, come on. This is all about Hamish, not you. He's using you. Tell him to go find his own investors.'

Mac pursed her lips. 'Like I say, he does already have interested parties. But he needs more to launch a high-end product that will really appeal to the big-bucks tourists. That's why local government's on board. It helps, of course, that Hamish knows all the right people.'

'So I hear. Dad told me about his *interesting* contacts. Who are these co-investors?'

'There's a Swedish consortium, and some Russian involvement.'

'Russian?' Eliza's spine prickled.

'I believe he's known to you. I heard you mention his name on the phone the other day. Sokolov, the football team owner.'

Eliza went cold. Her cousin was suggesting she did business with her mother's killer. She hardly trusted herself to speak.

'This stops now. Dad had dealings with him, years ago. He's a crook. I'm going to forget you mentioned his name, and I don't want to hear it again.'

Mac went to respond, but Eliza interrupted. 'Look, Mac. I know you a little better now. Can I suggest again that this is all coming from Hamish? You seemed very happy in your new role at RoseGold. Why this sudden interest in ... for god's sake, a casino?'

Mac sat up straighter. 'Eliza, your high-handedness as CEO can be quite insulting. I own a large proportion of this company and therefore expect to be taken seriously. Yes, of course it was Hamish's idea, but it's a sound investment. I'm sure Rose's finance people will agree.'

'Cecil? Agree to Rose entering the gambling scene? I think not. Mac, just stop this now. We won't be going there. And one last thing, before you leave. Avoid Sokolov like the plague. He's dangerous. I realize this is something that doesn't actually put you off men, but in this case you need to listen to me. And, anyway, I can assure you that his days as a corrupt, despicable . . .'

God, what am I saying?

'Just go, Mac. It's not a good time for me to be discussing future projects. In fact, it's not a good time for me, full stop.'

'I hear you. I'll put it on the back-burner, out of respect. When you're in a more positive frame of mind, we'll revisit.'

Chapter 46

Eliza

By four o'clock, Eliza had cleared her admin, briefed Cecil on her conversation with Mac, and was on her way to hospital.

>   ELIZA: Shit day. Help

>   KIT: Shall I come over?

>   ELIZA: Would you? Will be home by 8

She talked to Harry, grumbling about how stupid Mac was letting herself be manipulated by stupid Hamish, and how stupid Rob was still in stupid LA and had probably cheated on her with a stupid blonde.

Harry didn't respond, but Eliza felt a little better. 'And we're moving on Andre. He's in league with Hamish, would you believe? Yes, you probably would. We'll get him, Dad. Not sure how, but Charles is sorting the paper trail.'

Having given him her daily update, she took his hand. 'Dad. I love you. Please wake up? Come back to us? We're hurting so much without you. You're our anchor, we're all at sea.' She stared at his beloved, empty face, kissed his forehead, cried a little, and left.

❀

'Look – food,' said Kit, walking through to Eliza's kitchen. He upended a carton of curry and one of rice onto two plates, and flicked the tops off two beers. 'Tuck in,' he said, putting the plates down on the table.

She felt the tension of the day easing as Kit rambled on about this and that, before getting round to *Dark Soul*.

'Our man in LA seems to have sorted things.'

'Really?'

'Yep. Rob's backtracked on the whole toning-things-down business. Will convinced him if they went down that route, it would end up just another bland, forgettable piece of nothing, like most of the crap out there. Told Rob if he left well alone, we'd have another blockbuster.'

'Finally, some good news. We love Will.'

'We do.'

'And Letitia's gone.'

'Yup.'

Eliza's smile faded. 'Rob's been seeing her, Kit.' She could hardly believe her own words. 'Chess told me. She and Gil visited him. He admitted it.'

He met her gaze; his expression was hard to read. 'Tosser.'

'I've been trying not to think about it, with Dad being in hospital. What should I do?'

'Can I stab him now?'

Her small laugh caught in her throat. 'How could he, Kit?'

He shrugged. 'Depends if you think fidelity's important. Maybe it isn't.'

'It is to me. Dad once said Rob's like he used to be.'

'What did I tell you, about girls and their dads?'

Eliza sighed. 'I can't deal with it right now. I'll wait until things are back on an even keel. Let me tell you about Mac's ridiculous proposal instead.'

She related the conversation. 'And as for Sokolov,' she concluded, 'the man's a complete crook. Dad foolishly got involved with him, years ago. He nearly went bankru—'

Kit had dropped his fork with a clatter.

Eliza looked at him – it was as if he'd seen a ghost.

'Kit?'

'Sokolov? As in . . . premiership football Andre Sokolov?'

'That's him. He's—'

'*Fuck*.'

'What? You hate football. What do you know about him?'

'It's . . . Eliza, I can't . . . holy *shit*.'

The intensity in his eyes was frightening. It was as if he'd just realized something, like he'd had one of his premonitions.

'What's going on?'

'I need to work something out. These connections are never random.'

'What connections? Kit, don't go cryptic on me again. Tell me what's worrying you.'

'I can't. Look, don't do anything rash.'

'You mean with Mac? I sent her packing. I mean – gambling? She's totally being manipulated by Hamish.'

'Hamish . . . this is the guy who may have killed Stu?'

'My money would be on that, yes. I was rather hoping the police would work that one out, but it all seems to have gone quiet.'

'And Hamish has dealings with Sokolov?'

'It would appear so. Why does that not hugely surprise me? Dad warned me about Hamish months ago.'

'Eliza, do nothing. Don't interfere with Mac and Hamish. Definitely not Sokolov. Promise me?'

Eliza thought for a moment. 'Kit, I can't explain why, but I *can't* ignore Sokolov. There's unfinished business. I think it might help Dad if I can resolve the situation. Terri's helping, and Uncle Charles. But we're sworn to secrecy. I shouldn't be telling you this, but you know I'd trust you with my life.'

'Fuck. Eliza – you've set something in motion here. It needs to stop. Promise me you'll stop.'

'I can't.'

'Then at least wait.'

'Until what?'

'You'll know.'

'Stop being mysterious! What do you know?'

'I have to go.'

'You've just got here!'

He made for the door.

She ran after him. 'Kit, for god's sake! You're terrifying me.'

He was. Anxiety was radiating off him.

He opened the door, then turned back and hugged her. 'Wait.'

'I will. But why?'

'Just be careful.'

A few days later Charles called, telling her he'd put together a file of documents that would implicate Andre in all manner of financial crimes – fraud, money laundering, tax evasion.

'You name it, he's done it,' he said. 'The dossier's locked in the safe in the London flat. But I can't see how this will help. It has nothing to do with Ana. And Harry will come right – no reason he shouldn't, they said. Correct?'

'That's right,' said Eliza. 'Maybe just knowing we have enough to get Andre will help? I'll tell him today.'

'Whatever I can do, just say the word.'

That same morning, an email from Mac to Rose board members dropped like a bomb into Eliza's inbox. Mac was convening a meeting in an attempt to move forward the proposed casino investment. Her tone was friendly:

> I'm sorry to land this on everyone at short
> notice, especially while Harry isn't able to
> participate, but I'm afraid this opportunity
> won't wait and it's too good for Rose to miss!

Attached was a précis of the proposal with links to supporting documents and spreadsheets. Mac had been thorough.

Eliza went through to Cecil's office. 'Can she do this, over my head?'

'She's a majority shareholder so, yes, the board should give the proposal due consideration. And she's moving quickly to take advantage of Harry's absence. Be objective in your response, Eliza. Take the time to construct a rational argument as to why Rose should turn this down. Financially it's solid, so you'll need to make a good case. Talk to Chess; I'll sound out Eddie's trustees.'

'Dad?' Eliza said at the hospital later. 'We've got everything we need to get Sokolov put away for financial crimes. Even if we can't link him to Mum's death, we can still get him sent down. Isn't that great news?'

Of course, there was no response. If this had been a movie, Harry's fingers would have twitched. But nothing twitched; his eyelids didn't flicker. Nothing.

But hadn't all this been about avenging Ana's death? Would convicting Andre only for financial crimes be enough for Dad? No, it wouldn't.

Cecil's digging ascertained that Rich and Seymour were in favour of the casino project, while John Studley, it seemed, was on the fence.

Be objective, Cecil had said. Difficult, considering the opposition's line-up. Eliza remembered Harry's words in Sydney: *too many family members can lead to infighting.* Mac, with her chippy attitude. Heinous Uncle Seymour, who was on borrowed time, and his equally arrogant brother, Rich. Easy to picture those two gambling the night away. John – Rob's father, Chess's father-in-law, and one of Harry's oldest friends. He'd be on side, wouldn't he?

She'd spoken to Chess and was confident of her backing, no matter what the Major decided.

It was going to be a close-run thing, and she was all too aware of what it represented: a bid for the Rose throne.

※

As Eliza contemplated her reflection in her full-length mirror, she was reminded of the last time she'd planned her look this carefully. That hot July day, when she'd come out as Rob's partner, at Wimbledon. The too-short dress, the scarlet shoes, the bright red lips, the cascading curls.

Look at me, all grown up . . . ready to rule, ready for bed.

She'd sat between Harry and Rob, aware of the camera lenses pointed at her. The new Rose queen, men at her feet, on the brink of having it all.

Today, there would be no short skirt. No colourful shoes; no curls. To hold on to everything she'd worked so hard for, to stop it all from slipping through her fingers, she needed to remind herself how far she'd come – to *feel* it. To show herself, and the board, that she was no longer that ingénue, still in her father's thrall.

She was on her own. Harry was in limbo; Rob had let her down. There would be no more relying on men.

She fastened the buttons of her black jacket, smoothed down her skirt – knee-length – and slipped on the sensible black shoes. Her straightened hair was scraped into a bun; every errant wisp had been tamed with a vicious blast of hairspray.

Her make-up was the full Snow White. This was no time for blusher. Pale and proud.

She smiled at her mirror image. Goodness, but this look was working. She almost frightened herself.

One last thing, before she left. The lipstick would still be red. The suit – her armour – was CEO; the lips were Eliza Rose, to the max.

As she applied the lipstick, it felt symbolic. She was transformed, ready to defend her kingdom. But she was still true to herself.

Eliza stood at the boardroom window, watching the Thames mooching along below. She'd arrived early, wanting the time to mentally prepare.

As ever, watching the river centred her, calming her nerves. Since time immemorial it had been doing its thing, oblivious to the dramas and battles through which it passed, every day.

She swallowed as she glanced over at the chair Harry always sat in, at his portrait on the wall. There was a Dad-shaped hole in the room, and in her heart.

No, Eliza. You can do this. You don't need a man to help you this time. Not even Harry.

The others filed in. She registered the fleeting surprise on Mac's face as she took in Eliza's battle dress. Mac wore a green blouse and matching skirt, and ... oh dear. She'd tied a small tartan scarf around her neck. Was that meant to be 'fun'? It looked ridiculous.

She gave Eliza a tight smile, then briskly connected her laptop to the screen. As she did, Seymour's eyes appraised her trim body.

Isn't she a bit old for you?

The preliminaries were kept short, and Mac began her presentation.

The projected profits of the casino venture were compelling. Surreptitiously watching the board members' reactions, Eliza saw Chess being hooked in. Seymour, Rich and John were taking notes, nodding. There were pound signs in their eyes.

Things were swinging Mac's way.

Eliza's palms were sweating.

Mac's final slide was an artist's impression of the castle-casino at sunset, lit up against the backdrop of Loch Lomond.

'So there we have it,' she said. 'While I appreciate you may initially be cautious about supporting Rose's involvement in a casino, remember it's also about investing in Scotland's local economy, protecting Britain's heritage. Most visitors won't be serious gamblers; they'll be wealthy tourists having a wee flutter for fun. And, of course, the figures I've shared demonstrate beyond doubt that this project will give us a healthy ROI – one that's far more robust than, say, the investment in RoseGold.'

OK, now I actually hate you.

'Thank you, Mackenzie,' said Eliza. 'Most informative. I'm sure we all have questions. I'll kick things off with one of my own.'

'By all means.' Mac held Eliza's eyes, inviting the challenge.

'How confident are you that the source of co-investor Andre Sokolov's funds is above board?'

'He's achieved remarkable success in Britain, particularly in the world of football. If his wealth were suspect, that would surely have come to light already, after all his years here. And his high profile can only be of benefit to Rose.'

'I beg to differ. While I can't reveal my source, I have evidence that Andre Sokolov is not a person Rose should be partnering with. He's a criminal. My father realized this soon after Sokolov became involved in Rose TV. He offloaded the investment.'

'That was years ago,' interrupted Seymour. 'The days of treating every Russian with suspicion are long past, Eliza. I, for one, consider this to be a sound proposal. I think we should back it.'

'*Do* you?' She fixed her gaze on Seymour, and in that moment, all the stress of recent weeks was concentrated into a beam of loathing aimed squarely at this man she'd avoided looking at for so many years. She thought about what he'd got away with. How it had affected her precious relationship with Rob.

She felt a surge of strength. The #MeToo piece was planned for October, but Eliza felt it in her gut. It was time.

'So you believe, Seymour, that just because something illegal, something . . . monstrous, happened years ago; if the person got away with it at the time, such an action should be overlooked for the sake of – what? The greater good? Profit? Although *good* isn't a word I'd associate with Sokolov. Or you, in fact, Seymour.'

He shifted in his seat. She saw the penny dropping. His eyes flicked around the others at the table. 'It's a sound proposal,' he repeated. 'Perhaps we should hear from the others.'

'No,' said Eliza. 'I'm not done. Going off topic for a moment – sorry, everyone, we'll come back to *gambling* in due course – I'm proposing that Seymour be removed as a trustee.'

'What's this about, Eliza?' said John, frowning. 'Please explain.'

Eliza took a breath, closing her eyes for a moment.

You can do this.

'Seymour abused me. He touched me inappropriately, on many occasions, when I was a child in his care. I would suggest that invalidates the "trust" part of "trustee". Thoughts, Seymour?'

Seymour had turned pale. 'Don't be ridiculous. It was just horseplay. And it was years ago. I'd suggest your memory is playing tricks.'

'We'll see what the police think, shall we?'

'It would be your word against mine. No evidence.'

'Seymour,' said Eliza. 'Have you not noticed? The world has changed. Our words are being given weight, now. Words like *Me* and *Too*. Words we can put out via the internet, even before we take them to the police. A tweet should do it.'

John looked deeply shocked. 'We all know Eliza wouldn't make a thing like that up.'

'You *bastard*,' said Chess.

Cecil stood up. 'Please leave, Seymour.'

Seymour looked round the table again. Met only with stony silence, he did as Cecil suggested.

'A paedophile, a Russian crook and gambling,' said Chess. 'Leaves a bad taste in the mouth. Sorry, Mac. I won't be supporting you, and Helena has already said no.'

'Likewise,' said John. 'Seymour's gone. Harry's absent—'

Rich interrupted. 'Eliza, I don't know what to say. This has come as a terrible shock. Of course you have my full support.'

'And I,' continued John, 'as a military man, would never throw my lot in with a Russian. Let's vote this out now, shall we?'

'There's no need for a vote,' said Mac. She sighed, and sat down.

Eliza could see her weighing up her options. If she gave up now,

Hamish would be angry, but she might still be able to salvage her relationship with Eliza.

'I've clearly misjudged the board's core values. I was focused on the bottom line. I'll tell Hamish you turned down our proposal. I hope you'll view this in the spirit in which it was intended – as a good deal for the company.'

Rather more than that.

'Perhaps we can talk later, Eliza?'

'My door is always open. As you discovered when you eavesdropped on my conversation with Charles. Perhaps knock next time. If you wish to continue working for Rose, you'll need to appreciate that I expect absolute loyalty. I work only with people I can trust, whose values mirror my own. You'll need to prove yourself. I look forward to the time when you do.'

Chapter 47

Eliza

It had been a long, hard, traumatic day. Eliza suspected she was heading for emotional collapse when she found herself buying a box of Belgian chocolates on the way home.

She ripped into them as soon as she was back.

Dad's in a coma. Nobody knows why, or if he'll ever wake up.

Rob probably cheated on me.

Stu's dead. Rizz is dead. Amy's dead.

Kit's acting like there's another disaster on the horizon.

Mac could still be a threat. Her strings are being pulled by the man who likely killed my half-brother.

Her mirror image from this morning spoke up.

You won. You roasted Mac and Seymour.

All by yourself.

Eliza ate another chocolate.

But what's the point of any of it?

I'm alone.

A headache took hold, gripping her skull like a vice.

She flung the chocolates across the room, went into the bedroom and crawled under her duvet.

❀

She jerked awake later, petrified. There was someone in her bedroom.

As she lay frozen, images flew into her mind – her mother's assassin, with a loaded syringe. Hamish, with a can of petrol.

It was dark, but she could see his shadow.

'Lizzie?'

Lizzie?

'I'm going to put the light on. Close your eyes.'

'Rob?'

Oh god, Rob!

He flicked on the bedside light and sat down next to her.

He looked different. He'd evolved again. There were the obvious things – the tan, the longer hair, styled differently.

But there was something else. Something indefinable.

As he took in her appearance, his smile faded. 'What's going on? Have you been crying? Is it Harry?'

'I was having a moment.'

'There are chocolates all over the living room floor.'

'Chocolate wasn't helping.'

Eliza's head was still pounding.

'No change in Harry?'

'None. And Mac's being a pain. And ... other stuff. But I'd rather not talk about it now. I've had one hell of a day.'

He lay down and pulled her into his arms. It felt so good, but she was too drained, too emotionally spent – and too wary – to respond. She closed her eyes and tucked her head into his chest.

'OK,' he said, when she remained still. 'Go back to sleep. I'll stay here until you drop off, then I'll have a shower. It's only the middle of the afternoon in LA. I'll be here when you wake up. We'll ... talk then.'

❀

But come morning, he was dead to the world. It was the early hours in LA. Best let him sleep.

She slipped out of bed, showered and dressed.

'Oh dear,' she muttered, as she took in the chocolates sprayed across the living room floor. Yesterday had been an emotional roller coaster, and she had an inkling today would be more of the same.

After coffee and cereal she went back to the bedroom and gazed at Rob's sleeping form, trying to work out her feelings. Adorable Rob – her lifelong friend, her ally, her love. Rob, who'd wanted to marry her, who assumed her 'no' had been because of her father's extra-marital adventures. And yet it seemed he'd gone the whole Harry, and hadn't taken the trouble to hide the fact – from Chess, Gil, Leigh and Will. He must know that she knew.

How could he do that to me?

She quietly shut the bedroom door behind her, and left for work.

❋

'Rob's back,' she said to Pippa as she hung up her jacket.

'Yay!' said Pippa. 'About bloody time. Oh, this came for you.' She held out a courier letter marked *Private and Confidential*.

Eliza fired off a quick email to Terri:

```
Need to update you on the #MeToo piece. And
might need lawyers to check our position
re Seymour.
```

She pressed send, then opened the letter. Unfolding the sheet of A4, she gasped, her heart skipping a beat.

DROP YOUR INVESTIGATION IF YOU VALUE YOUR BROTHER'S LIFE

Along with the anonymous letter there was a photo of Eddie coming out of his uncle Rich's Isleworth house, where he was sleeping over for a few nights with his cousins.

Eliza examined the letter and photograph, but there was no clue as to the sender. It had to have come from Andre. But how could he possibly know what Charles was doing? Did he have a contact at the bank?

Hamish.

It had to be. Mac must have tipped him off after hearing her mention Sokolov's name on the phone to Charles.

'I'll be with Terri,' she told Pippa, heading for the lifts.

'We have to drop it,' said Terri, when Eliza showed her the letter. 'Harry wouldn't want Eddie's life put in danger over this.'

'No. But what if we take the evidence Charles has collected to the police? Then at least Andre might be arrested?'

'Eliza, love. It wouldn't be a priority, investigating bank fraud from years ago. And, in the meantime, Andre's team of Bond villains would be on the loose, ready to do his bidding. Not worth the risk.'

Terri was right. Hopelessness rushed in. What could they do? Absolutely nothing, it seemed. Dad was in limbo and Mum's killer was still out there, doing whatever he bloody pleased.

With a heavy heart, she went back to her office.

KIT: Can you come round tonight?

ELIZA: Not really. Rob's back

KIT: Please? Just for an hour? Important

ELIZA: Are u in office?

KIT: No, at home

ELIZA: Will come now. Can't concentrate on work anyway

KIT: Good x

Eliza pondered the situation in the taxi. She'd hit a brick wall; she couldn't see a way forward. Terri was right – the situation *was* too dangerous, thanks to Mac. She balled her fists for a moment. *Bloody Mac.*

Kit answered the door. 'Thanks for coming.'

'Nowhere I'd rather be,' she said, hugging him. 'Shit coming at me from all sides at the moment.'

'But Rob's back?'

'Like I said, nowhere I'd rather be.'

'Coffee?'

He glanced at her as he fired up the machine. 'Afraid I'm about to add to your shit.'

'Oh god. Is this why you wanted to see me?' She thought back to his weird behaviour at her flat.

He leaned against the worktop as the coffee dripped through. 'Where to start?'

'Kit – what on earth is this about?'

'It's all linked. Everything. I need to explain, but . . . fuck it, I don't know how.'

'You, lost for words? That's a first.'

But she registered his expression. For the first time since she'd known him, Kit was looking vulnerable.

He passed her the mug of coffee. 'Come and sit down.'

He picked something up off the table, then sat beside her on the kitchen couch, which looked out across the garden. The herbaceous borders were going to seed; summer was already a memory.

'In storytelling terms, we're at the denouement.'

'What? For once in your life, Kit, just give it to me straight.'

Wordlessly, he handed her a photo. In it was a beautiful blonde woman holding the hand of a boy of five or six years old. Looking closer, she recognized Kit.

'This is my mother,' he said. 'My father killed her. And—'

'*What?* Your father killed your mother?' She stared at him in horror.

'And . . . Eliza. He murdered your mother too.'

Chapter 48

Eliza

She couldn't take in his words. They whirled around her brain, refusing to stay still and be understood.

He took her hand. 'The bastard didn't kill my mother himself. He organized it, back in Russia, when she wanted to divorce him. I used to hear them arguing. He'd say, *If you leave me, I'll kill you.* She died of blood poisoning, same as Ana.'

Eliza shook her head, squeezing her eyes shut for a few seconds. This couldn't be possible.

'Are you telling me . . . Andre Sokolov's your father?'

'Yes. Mum was English; they met when she worked for the British Embassy in Moscow. They moved between Russia and London. When she died I was sent to school in England.'

'But . . . how do you know he killed my mother?'

He was quiet for a moment, looking down at her hand in his. His hair fell forward, hiding his expression. 'When I met you at Oxford, I remembered – Harry came to our house in Chelsea when I was a kid. I liked him; he made me laugh. I nearly told you I'd met him, that night in Browns. But then you said Ana died of toxic shock, and . . . it was the same as Mum.'

His words were finally sinking in. 'My god, Kit . . .'

'Something came back to me – a comment my father made when we were watching Football TV one time. He said that if it hadn't been for him, Harry would have been ruined by his "angry wife" and Dad wouldn't have had his stupid Football TV. I put two and two together.'

Finally he looked at her, waiting for a response.

This was all beyond incredible – and yet, things were falling into place.

'But you never said anything. Why?'

'You were so close to Harry, you wouldn't have wanted to keep it from him. My father's a dangerous man. I couldn't take the risk.'

'Your dad killed my mum. Jesus, Kit.'

He held her gaze, then smiled. 'Cool plot twist, though?'

'My god. No wonder you didn't want to ... with me ...'

'That's some baggage.'

She put her head on his shoulder, closing her eyes for a moment. 'Oh, Kit. You finally make sense to me.'

'Do I?' he said, putting his arm around her, resting his head on hers. 'Perhaps you could enlighten me.'

'The love that was taken from you – your mum.'

'She was an angel.'

'And your stance on sport.'

'Well spotted.'

'What are we going to do? Andre's made a death threat against my brother.'

He pulled away and looked at her. 'What?'

'This morning. I had an anonymous letter, telling me to stop digging into his financial history if I valued Eddie's life. There was a photo of Eddie, taken in the last day or so.'

He frowned. 'My father has people. A lot of people.'

'I should explain. Dad asked me and Terri and Uncle Charles – Dad's best friend – to help with his last-wish thing. He said if he dies ...' She took a breath. 'He wants us to expose Andre as Mum's killer, to avenge her death. Reckons he won't rest in peace if it's not resolved. Dad's not religious, but—'

'He wants redemption.'

'Yes. We have enough dirt on Andre to get him put away, but nothing to prove he killed Mum. And now it's too dangerous to continue.'

'I guessed as much, that night at your flat. Eliza, you're going nowhere near him.' He took her hand, stroking the back of it with his thumb. 'There's a plan. That's why I wanted to see you. Will's on board – he's coming back today.'

'A plan?'

'Everyone has an Achilles heel. I'm my father's. He's always trying to reconcile, even though he must realize I know what he did to Mum.'

Their conversation by the Tower came back to her. *I'm a fuck-up . . . nobody could sort out my shit – believe me.*

She touched his face. 'I wish you'd told me before. I could have . . . ' She was unsure of how to finish.

'Maybe.' He looked at her for a long moment.

'You're going to meet him?' she said.

'Tomorrow, at his house. I'll try to get him to confess. Not sure how, and I know it's a long shot. But I have to do it. I'll record the conversation on my phone.'

'I see. How long is it since you've seen him?'

'Not since I was at school.' He let go of her hand and stood up. 'Hungry?'

'What? How can you think about food!'

'I don't. But you're looking peaky. I know pale is your default, but that is a whiter shade of pale.'

She smiled. *Kit.* What had she done in life to deserve a friend like this?

'OK. Maybe a slice of your signature toast?'

'So, Rob's back?' he said, rummaging in a cupboard.

'Rob. Yes.' She was still processing Kit's bombshell, but she attempted to respond. 'I left him asleep this morning. We need to have a conversation. About *Teesha*.'

'What will you say, assuming he's been playing away?'

'If I can't trust him, there's no point. I can't spend my life wondering what he's up to when we're apart. And if it's all about me being his boss, then that's another reason to shift things back to a professional relationship. If he can't accept that Rose will always come first . . .'

He brought over the toast.

'I won't compromise. I won't spend my life apologising for being home late, or missing a night out, or not wanting children. And I will never, *ever* get married.'

As she said the words, she realized this was the first time she'd thought about her future properly, pragmatically.

'You don't want children?'

'I don't think so.'

'One problem at a time. What about Rob?'

She sighed. 'Trouble is, I still love him. I can't imagine not being with him.'

'Act like a Marley. Be with him, but don't commit. Ever.'

'He's obsessed with me committing.'

'He wants a degree of power over you. Don't give it to him.'

'You think he'd settle for less?'

'You turned down his marriage proposal. Tell him why – the real reason. Nothing to do with Daddy issues, and everything to do with letting someone mess with your priorities. And you know what, Eliza? It's no fun sticking to one. Chrissakes, girl – how many boyfriends have you actually had?'

'One.'

'Fucking hell.'

Eliza spluttered with laughter. 'Oh my god, Kit. It's *pathetic*.'

'Tragic. There's a world out there full of beautiful men. And you're its queen.'

'True. And I'm my father's daughter. It took him long enough to find Mrs Right, but what a time he had getting there.'

'Legend.'

'Why would I even need a boyfriend? Why can't I just be me, and date guys for fun? Maybe even make like a Marley, as you say.'

'Now you're talking. So . . . what will you tell him?'

She thought for a moment. 'Before we got together properly, we called it *friends and a bit more*. Maybe that again.'

'Be prepared, though. He'll probably kick off.'

'He might. I—'

The front door slammed, and Will appeared.

'Greetings! Two such pretty heads, deep in conversation. What gives?'

'Will!' said Eliza. 'Heart to heart about my dysfunctional love life.'

'Drama? Excellent!' said Will, sitting down on Eliza's other side. He kissed her cheek. 'Mwah! I've missed my people.'

'You did great in LA,' she said.

'Dreadful place. So corrupting.' His eyes met hers, and she knew he meant Rob. 'It sucks you in; it's easy to slide into their ways.'

'And did you?' said Kit.

'Not I. For me, fidelity is ever a thing.'

'Sweet boy,' said Kit. 'Let's have a beer.'

He stood up, but, before heading to the fridge, he planted a lingering kiss on Will's lips. 'Missed you too.'

❊

Night was falling. Eliza had ignored her phone these past hours. There was so much to face: Kit's meeting with Andre tomorrow, the conversation she needed to have with Rob. Harry, still lingering in limbo. So she'd been living in the moment, making the most of this time with her two best pals.

Reluctantly she took out her phone and read her messages.

ROB: I'm home. Where are you?

The time sent was 6.10 p.m.

The next one was an hour later:

ROB: What's going on? Call me?

She replied:

> ELIZA: Won't be long now

'You need to go?' said Kit.

'I ought to. What's the plan for tomorrow? What should I do?'

'Sit tight,' said Kit. 'Carry on as normal. We'll keep you posted.'

She ordered a taxi.

'Hey, thanks for today. And, Kit – what you're doing for me. I don't have the words . . . ' As she looked at them both, she experienced a rush of emotion. 'You two mean so much to me. Did I tell you that?'

'Back at you, my sweet,' said Will.

Kit waited with her on the street.

'Are you nervous about tomorrow?' she asked.

'Only that I'll lose control when I confront him.'

'Deep breaths,' she said. 'You can do this.'

'Good luck with Rob.'

'Thank you. And Kit . . . '

She slipped her arms round his neck and kissed him quickly, but not that quickly.

Delicious.

'You love me,' he said. 'I know.'

Rob was watching TV when she let herself in. Her heart was in her mouth. All the way home she'd been wondering what to say, what words to use. Should she start with an accusation – *I know you've been cheating on me with that actress.*

Now that she was considering their future, all she could think about was the good times. Rob's twinkly eyes as he mocked her attempts at making coffee; lying on the sofa with a chocolate between his teeth. Walking home arm in arm across

London Bridge, his curls blowing in the wind. Always laughing, always fun.

'Where have you been?' He kept his eyes on the TV.

'I'm sorry, I should've texted you.' She took off her jacket and draped it over a chair back. 'There's all sorts of stuff going on. It's to do with Dad, but I can't tell you. Sorry – it's Uncle Charles and Terri and me . . . '

This isn't going well.

She sat down beside him. 'And Kit. I've been at Kit's.'

He turned to face her. His eyes were cold. 'Kit's. Finally, the truth. Why don't you tell me what you've *really* been up to?'

Two could play at that game. 'You first, then. Tell me all about Letitia.'

His eyes slid away for a moment, then he met her gaze again. His expression was guarded, but there was guilt. 'Chess told you? It didn't go far, Lizzie. I ended it before anything much happened. I'm sorry, especially about how I didn't try to hide it.'

'It's like you wanted me to know.'

'I've tried to work out why, but I'm not good at introspection like you are. I thought . . . maybe it was because I wasn't sure how you felt about me. And maybe I was kicking against you being my boss? I don't know. But it won't happen again.' Now he looked contrite, and his eyes pleaded for a second chance.

'Your turn.' His expression hardened again. 'You and Kit. Has it been going on for ever? Or did you just get . . . extra close while I was away?'

Eliza was still processing his words about Letitia when she realized what he'd asked. 'What? *Kit?* No! I told you before. How many times – there's nothing physical.'

'Come *on*, Lizzie! How stupid do you think I am? You're always touching each other. You read each other's minds. You disappear off together; he's the person you turn to when you've had a bad day, when things go wrong. Him, not me. I've fessed up, now why don't you do the same?'

She needed him to understand about Kit, before she . . . what was she going to do? Had he really not slept with Letitia? Was he telling the truth?

'Kit gets me like nobody else,' she said. 'Not even you. I can't explain it. Anyway, you know Kit – he plays by different rules. Love and . . . well, sex. They don't go together for him.'

'He loves you?'

'We love each other, but not in *that* way.'

'So he's never come on to you?'

'After that first time at Oxford? Only for fun, not seriously.'

'For *fun*, Lizzie? *Really?* The guy's a complete slut.'

'He just behaves differently.'

'*Differently?* And his mind's twisted. You've only got to read his writing. Oh, wait – no. It's *brilliant*.' He glared at her. 'Don't touch, you told me. Hands off Kit's genius. And sending Will over to LA to bring me back in line. *They're* the talent; *they* get final say. I'm just the salesman.'

'Stop it, Rob. *Please* . . . '

This was horrible. This wasn't Rob.

She owed him the truth.

'I was at Kit's because of Dad. I can't tell you more than that – it's a dangerous situation to do with why Mum died.'

'What?'

'I'm so sorry, I can't explain.'

'So. Like I said. You have a major life crisis, and you turn to him. Not me.'

'No! It's not like that . . . '

'It *is* like that. It always has been, all through our relationship. You won't commit to me, you never have. Maybe we should just call it a day.' He grabbed his jacket and headed for the door.

'No, Rob!'

What could she say? How could she make him understand?

He stopped.

'Come on, Rob.' She went over to him, holding his gaze. 'You know it was real, me and you. That brief time we had, when things finally worked out. After Amy, before Letitia. I thought we were for ever, that's the truth.' Tears filled her eyes.

'So did I.' His voice caught.

'But then I found out you were cheating on me. You may not have slept with her – I don't know – but Chess and Will told me how you two were.'

He shook his head. 'This isn't about her.'

'You're right. It's not.' She blinked, dismissing the tears. 'All this wanting me to commit is just you wanting me to put you first. That's not going to happen. Rose will always be my priority. If you can't handle that, then it's best we go back to how we were. Friends and a bit more.'

'That's not enough.' He paused. 'Lizzie – don't you ever wonder, what's the point? You've got more than enough money, you have power and status. But the way you're going, you'll have no one to share it with, no one to pass it on to. What's driving you?'

And there it was. The reason why this could never work. He just didn't understand her.

'None of those things you said. I want to create great things, leave a legacy. It may be a cliché, but I want to change the world. And I want to give back. For Rose, for Dad, as well as for myself.'

She sighed. 'Look. I know you can't handle coming second. And as for Letitia – you know what? Dad said you're just like him when he was your age. Incapable of resisting temptation. That's not what I want – always wondering, always worrying; picturing you with someone else.'

He was quiet. The fight had left him. 'So ... we're over?'

'Rob, I ... don't ... ' Finally, she ran out of words.

'Goodbye, Lizzie.' He shut the door quietly behind him.

Chapter 49

Eliza

Eliza couldn't focus on work. She checked her phone again. No messages.

The time Kit was due to meet his father came and went. She took herself down to the cafe, nibbled at a sandwich, tasting nothing, and stared out of the window at the Thames chugging along, oblivious.

'Here you are!'

Eliza looked up to see Mac pulling out the chair opposite. With the exception of Andre himself, Mac was probably the last person she wanted to see.

'Not now, Mac,' she said, and resumed looking out of the window.

'It's important. Can we go somewhere private?'

When Eliza didn't respond, Mac sighed. 'Look.' Glancing around her, she slipped down one shoulder of her blouse, briefly exposing her upper arm. Wordlessly, she waited for Eliza's reaction. There was a row of livid bruises, as if someone had gripped her strongly and shaken her.

'Hamish?' said Eliza. It didn't come as a surprise.

'I won't be marrying him. I've always known he had a violent streak, but never thought he'd direct it at me.'

Why would you not?

'Good.' It *was* good but, right now, Eliza couldn't bring herself to care. All she could think about was what Kit was going through. And the scene last night, with Rob.

Rob. She felt her heart bleeding.

'Eliza,' said Mac, 'I know things between us are difficult—'

'Look, could you just leave me alone? I'm waiting for news on something important.'

'Harry?'

'Unfortunately not.'

'Hamish went ballistic when I told him the board's decision. I'm scared. I want to break it off with him. I'm asking you for help. You're the nearest thing to a friend I have down here.'

Eliza thought for a moment. Perhaps her cousin could still be useful.

'I see. Mac, could you not break up with him just yet? There's been a death threat against Eddie.'

'*What?*'

'I think Hamish might have something to do with it. I'm afraid I can't tell you what's going on – it's nothing to do with Rose. But if you could let me know what Hamish is up to, that might help.'

'You mean . . . spy on him?'

'Yes. Keep an eye on his whereabouts. Be on my side now, Mac. Enough with the bad boys.'

'That's what I want. Please – can we start over? You, me and Chess. We could be a fabulous team.'

'Perhaps. In fact, I have a role in mind for you. But like I said, you need to prove your loyalty. If and when you do, then we'll talk about that further.'

Back in her office, Eliza finally received a text from Will:

WILL: Kit got what he wanted. Andre suspicious, took phone but we have backup. On my way to you.

ELIZA: Brilliant! Hope it wasn't too awful for Kit xx

They'd done it! *Kit got what he wanted.*

A confession. Had Andre Sokolov really admitted to murder?

Will arrived, and sat down on her office sofa. 'Oh my lord, Eliza. Kit was *incredible*. So cool under pressure. You'd never have guessed he was laying a trap.'

Will described how he'd listened in via a hidden microphone. 'Kit held out the olive branch, hinted at a reconciliation, then spun a yarn. He almost had me believing him; it was a *sublime* piece of acting.'

'What yarn?'

'About falling in love with a girl at university – one Eliza Rose, daughter of Harry and Ana Rose. He told Andre he wanted to resolve things so he could move forward with you.'

Eliza swallowed. 'What happened next?'

'Kit said he couldn't properly be with you while Ana's death was hanging in the air between you. He told Andre he suspected he'd organized her murder. Andre didn't deny it, Eliza. He just scoffed.'

Will put on a Russian accent. 'He said, *That woman wanted to ruin Harry, my English brother. It was easy to remove her. I did him big favour. He soon found a new wife.*'

Eliza's hand went to her mouth.

Will put his arm round her. 'I know. It's horrible. So you see, Andre couldn't resist boasting about Ana, but immediately he realized his mistake – he'd confessed to a murder in front of Kit, who's hated him most of his life.'

'What did Andre do?'

'I should imagine Kit's expression gave him away. He demanded to see Kit's phone, and when Kit refused he had his bodyguard snatch it. He pocketed the SIM, then smashed the phone. But the hidden mic was still transmitting to me in the next street. I've got the conversation here on a USB.' He patted his pocket dramatically. 'We'll make a copy, give one to Terri and the other to the police.'

'Right. I think it's time we talked to Terri.'

Eliza rang down to make sure she was there, and they headed to the lift.

'Terri,' said Eliza, shutting the door behind them. 'Will's … um, he's helping us with …' *Where do I start?*

'Shall I take it from here?' said Will.

'Please the fuck do,' said Terri. 'You're rather better with words than Eliza.'

'I can't deny it. Right. Kit told Eliza something rather mind-blowing yesterday – something he'd kept hidden from her until now.'

He paused for effect.

'Get on with it, Will,' said Eliza.

'Kit is Andre Sokolov's son, and he's going to help you nab Sokolov for Ana's murder.'

For once, Terri was speechless.

'It's true,' said Eliza.

'What the *fuck*?'

'And this morning Andre confessed,' Eliza continued, 'to Kit. He and Will recorded the conversation. Terri – we've got him.'

Terri sat back down heavily. 'For real? Kit's Sokolov's son? You couldn't make this up.'

'I know.'

'And … he confessed to killing Ana?'

'He did,' said Will. He handed the USB to Terri.

'After all these years …' she said quietly.

'Finally, justice for Mum.' Eliza gave her a hug.

'Wait a minute. I thought I saw …' Terri swivelled her chair and brought up her email window. 'There's something here from Kit. It's flagged urgent. It's to me and you, Eliza.'

Will frowned. 'What does it say?'

She read out, '*No phone. Tell Will not to come home yet. Think I'm being followed.*'

Eliza felt a stab of fear. 'Email him back, Terri. Quickly.'

'*Shit.*' Will stood up, white-faced.

Terri typed in:

Understood. Please reply immediately.

'We need to go,' said Will.

'I'll get you a taxi,' said Terri. 'What's the address?'

Will told her.

'Keep refreshing,' said Terri, as she made the call.

'Maybe you should stay here,' Will said to Eliza.

'No way.'

When there was no email response, Eliza and Will ran out the door.

They said little as the taxi sped towards Dalston. Eliza gripped Will's hand, dreadful thoughts tumbling in her head.

She scanned the street as they ran to the front door, but saw only a woman with a buggy.

Will's hand shook as he fumbled with his keys and let them in.

Kit was lying on the living room floor in a pool of blood. A knife was embedded in his neck. His eyes were closed.

Eliza gave a strangled cry as her hands flew to her mouth.

Oh god – no. Not Kit.

Will stood stock still, staring at him.

Eliza crouched down and put her fingers to Kit's wrist. She wouldn't allow herself to look at the knife.

'There's a faint pulse.' She gently touched his face. 'Kit? It's Eliza.'

Don't let him die. Please don't let him die.

Will finally spoke. 'Call an ambulance. And the police.' He knelt down and stroked Kit's hair. 'We're here, Kit. It's going to be OK.'

Eliza took out her phone.

How do I call an ambulance?

What's the number?

Please, Kit. Don't leave me. Please, please don't leave me.

His eyes flickered open; he stared at the ceiling.

'Help's on the way, Kit,' she said.

But as his eyes met hers, and then Will's, she saw their light fading.

'No, Kit! Please – don't leave us!'

He managed a faint smile, then the fire went out.

'No, Kit! *No-no-no.*' She grabbed his hand, kissing it, bathing it in hot tears.

For a while they sat either side of him, watching over him, crying quietly. Then Eliza lowered her wet cheek to his chest, resting on him, closing her eyes.

His heart was silent. Her own broke into a million pieces as her tears mingled with the blood soaking his T-shirt.

'He's dead because of me. Beautiful Kit. He's dead because of *me.*' Darkness filled her soul. 'How can I live with that? How can I live without him? I can't bear it.'

'He wanted to help you, Eliza. He'd have done anything for you.'

She sobbed, holding Kit's empty body. With a shaking hand she grasped a handful of his hair and buried her face in it, trying to burn his smell into her memory.

'Come here. Let him go,' said Will gently. 'We want his killer caught; you need to stop touching him.'

'No!'

This can't be happening. How can a life so precious suddenly end?

Then, all at once, their conversation beneath that ancient oak came back to her.

How do you know these things?

I just do. Like I know I'll die young.

She let him go, even as her world caved in.

◉

The police arrived, and after some initial questions asked them to leave the room. Eliza began to cry again, not wanting to abandon Kit to these people who didn't know him, didn't love him.

Will gently propelled her towards the door, and for the first time she registered the disarray. A small table lay on its side, and the Lalique glass cat she'd given the boys as a housewarming present lay in smithereens on the floor.

'Perhaps we could all have a cup of tea,' said a policewoman.

Two officers questioned them. Eliza answered while Will stared into space, saying nothing.

The officers' eyes widened when Eliza mentioned the name of Kit's Russian billionaire father. 'Andre tried to stop Kit sending evidence of a crime to a reporter,' she said. 'But he failed. The evidence is already with Terri Robbins-More at Rose HQ.'

The officer scribbled in a notebook. 'And what crime would that be, Ms Rose?'

'The murder of my mother, Ana Rose, in 2002.'

The other officer spoke. 'So you're alleging Mr Marley's father—'

' ... killed my mother, yes. And Kit's mother. And Kit. His own son.'

Will finally paid attention. 'But ... Andre wanted a reconciliation. He wouldn't have had Kit killed.'

'It looks like there was a brawl, Mr Bardington.'

Eliza squeezed her eyes shut, trying to block the image of Kit fighting a knife-wielding attacker.

'We'll send someone over to Rose HQ right away,' said one of the officers.

'And you should contact my uncle – Charles Lisle.' Eliza scrolled through her contacts. 'He has a dossier of incriminating evidence regarding Sokolov's financial history. Money laundering, fraud, all those things. Here's his number.'

'Right. I think we're done here,' said the officer. 'We'll need you to vacate this property until the crime scene investigation is completed, and we'll need to know where you both are. Is there somewhere Mr Bardington can stay?'

'With me,' said Eliza. She stood and hugged Will where he sat. He rested his head against her and she held him tight.

'I don't know how we'll get through this, Will.'

Chapter 50

Eliza

An officer drove them home. Once inside, Eliza poured them each a glass of brandy, then curled up beside Will on the sofa, her head on his shoulder.

She was exhausted, all cried out, her mind numb. 'It's like a terrible dream,' she said.

'He was everything to me,' said Will. 'But he belonged to no one.'

'He told me he knew he'd die young. Will, how could you live with that knowledge? And knowing that your father killed your mother.'

'Exactly like he did. Not giving a fuck.'

'Oh, he gave a fuck,' said Eliza. 'For you, Will. For me.'

In the early hours of the morning, unable to sleep, her pillow soaked with tears, Eliza lay trying to unsee Kit with a knife in his neck, the pool of blood, the light leaving his eyes. Instead she pictured him singing with his guitar on May Morning; inviting her to embrace Bacchus; lying hand in hand as lightning flashed around them. Dancing in the moonlight on their last night at

Oxford; playing truant at Greenwich, stopping time at Queen Elizabeth's Oak:

You got that too?

I did. What was it? Ancient oaks?

A bit more than that.

What had he meant? What had he known?

The next morning, Eliza's phone buzzed with notifications as word of Kit's murder quickly spread. She checked online to see what information the police had released. News websites reported the death of RoseGold's creative genius Kit Marley, co-writer of *Most Human of Saints* and close friend of Eliza Rose. In a sensational twist, Russian billionaire Andre Sokolov was being questioned in connection with the murder, and the more switched-on journalists had spotted the link between Sokolov and the conspiracy theories about the death of Eliza's mother, Ana.

Eliza ignored all the calls and messages, apart from Mac's. She'd been with the police, she said, giving evidence against Hamish, who'd been arrested on fraud charges courtesy of Uncle Charles's dossier. And it seemed he'd had a hand in Kit's murder.

'Thank you, Mac, I appreciate your help.'

Then Rob's image flashed up. She answered.

'Lizzie, I'm so sorry. I don't know what to say. Is Will with you?'

'Yes. Where are you?'

'At work, but I'm staying at Gil's. What happened? The papers are saying Andre Sokolov killed Kit. None of this makes any sense to me.'

'I can tell you now, it's not a secret any more.'

'What isn't?'

'I never told you this, Rob, but Mum didn't die of natural causes. She was murdered. I've known who did it since I was eighteen, when I started working for Terri. She told me. Andre Sokolov had Mum killed when she threatened to ruin Dad during their divorce. He did it without Dad's knowledge.'

As Eliza said the words, she knew she believed them. One hundred per cent.

'Holy fuck. Why did you never tell me?'

'It was unproveable, and Dad hated talking about it, so I kind of buried it. Rob ... Andre Sokolov is Kit's father. And he killed Kit's mum too. Kit was helping me with Dad's last-wish thing, which was to make Andre pay. But yesterday ... well, you know what happened. He was killed by one of Andre's hitmen.'

Rob was silent. 'My god. I can't take this in. How are you doing?'

'Terribly. You know what Kit meant to me. And then there's Will ...'

'I'm so sorry, Lizzie. And for those things I said about you and him. I was a jealous prick. He made me feel so ... I don't know. Boring?'

'*Boring?*' Eliza managed a small laugh. 'Rob, you could *never* be boring. I want us to be close again. Can we? Please?'

'Always and for ever, Lizzie. Look, call me if you need anything. Anything at all. You know I'm here for you.'

'I do. Goodbye, Rob. And ... I love you.'

'Likewise.'

She realized she was smiling, for the first time in how long?

'Are you hungry, Will?' she said. 'I'll make us some toast.'

But as she headed for the kitchen, she remembered Kit making her Marmite toast and it all came crashing down again. She burst into tears, and made for Will instead.

She was almost asleep when Will gently nudged her. 'Clare's calling,' he said, picking up her phone.

She answered.

'Eliza, it's Harry. He's waking up.'

It took a moment for the words to sink in.

'I'm at the hospital. He's come round twice, just for a minute or so. He's confused, but the doctor says it looks like there's no brain damage. He's going to be OK.'

'I'll be there as soon as I can.'

'What's happened?' asked Will.

'It's Dad. He's coming round.'

'Because of Kit.'

'Yes. This is Kit's doing.' There were tears in her eyes. 'I'll call you from the hospital.'

❀

Clare and Eddie were sitting at Harry's bedside. He was still asleep, but Eliza could tell – he was back. He wasn't a shell any more. Some of the tubes had been removed; he was breathing by himself.

'I'm so sorry about Kit,' said Clare, hugging her. 'He was remarkable. So gifted.'

Immediately, her tears were back. 'He was.' She swiped them away. 'I can't imagine life without him.'

She took Harry's hand. 'How long did Dad wake up for? Did he say anything?'

'He woke twice, the first time when the nurse was checking on him. The doctors decided he was coming out of the coma.'

'Thank god.'

'And then when we arrived ... I saw it, Eliza. He opened his eyes again.'

'Did he recognize you?'

'No.' She paused. 'He said, "Ana".'

Eliza could hardly speak. 'Kit. That's because of Kit.'

'No, Harry can't possibly know about Andre's arrest yet,' said Clare. 'Nobody's told him.'

'He knows,' said Eliza.

Then she felt it. Harry squeezed her hand.

Eliza gasped.

His eyelids flickered open, and his blue eyes fixed on her. 'Lizzie.'

'I'll fetch the doctor,' said Eddie.

Harry's eyes were confused, moving between Eliza and Clare.

'Harry,' Clare said gently, leaning over him. 'The operation went well. You're going to be fine. You'll feel strange for a while, it's the medication, and ... you took a little longer to come round than anyone expected.'

'Dad,' said Eliza, her voice unsteady. 'I don't know if you can understand. Andre's been arrested. He confessed to Mum's murder. It's over, Dad.'

He squeezed her hand again. 'Andre's ... confessed?'

'He has. Yes.'

Harry smiled. 'Bit tired. Talk later.'

The three of them stayed until the evening, and Harry woke again, this time for half an hour or so. He was still disorientated, but began to make sense of what they were telling him, about how long he'd been asleep, and about how Will and Kit had recorded Andre's confession.

Eliza didn't mention Kit's death.

'Kit,' he said. 'Sokolov's son. Hard to believe. I think I might even have met him when he was a boy, at Andre's mansion.'

'You did. He liked you ...' She burst into tears again.

'Sh, it's OK, Lizzie. I'm back now. What I told you before – remember? It happened again. They let me live.'

And they took Kit. Why?

●

The police and MI5 acted swiftly, before the Russians had time to regroup. Andre and Hamish were remanded in custody and Kit's murderer was arrested after Hamish turned informer. According to Mac, he'd done a deal, spilling the beans about Andre in return for leniency in his sentencing.

Kit's funeral was held a few days later, and Will's eulogy was the most beautiful piece of prose Eliza had ever heard. He finished, of course, with a quote:

> *Grief fills the room up of my absent child.*
> *Lies in his bed, walks up and down with me.*
> *Puts on his pretty looks, repeats his words.*
> *Remembers me of all his gracious parts.*
> *Stuffs out his vacant garments with his form.*
> *Then, have I reason to be fond of grief?*

Rob sought out Eliza, afterwards. 'Probably a stupid question, but how're you doing?'

'Dead inside.'

'Would you like some company?'

'That'd be nice. Leigh's taking Will home now the cordon's been lifted.'

Back at the apartment, as he made them a sandwich, Rob asked, 'Were they a couple? I was never sure.'

'As close to a couple as Kit got with anyone, I think,' said Eliza, pouring two cups of tea. 'As you know, he didn't do fidelity. But he loved Will in his own way.'

'Poor Will. He looks like a ghost.'

They took their tea and sandwiches over to the couch.

'Rob. *Dark Soul*. Promise me you'll produce it as is. Kit's words, nobody else's.'

'It'll offend a lot of people.'

'Which is—'

' . . . exactly as Kit intended. Yes, I promise.'

'Thanks. That means a lot.'

He held her gaze, then suddenly leaned across and kissed her.

For a moment she shut her eyes, feeling that sense of relief, of coming home.

But then she pulled back. 'Rob! We only buried Kit this morning.'

He reached for a curl, wound it round his finger. 'Your Kit was never one for acceptable behaviour, wouldn't you say?'

Eliza smiled. It was a sad smile, but it grew wider.

Act like a Marley. Be with him, but don't commit. Ever.

'You have a point, Roberto. Honouring his memory with tea and sandwiches? What *was* I thinking?'

Chapter 51

Eliza

Two months later

She'd intended to find a bench overlooking the river, but the biting wind barrelling down the Thames had her ducking into Caffé Uno.

She bought a hot chocolate and sat at their usual table, tucked away in the corner, picturing him in the seat opposite, feeling his absence. She slit open the envelope and started to read.

> *Dear Lizzie*
>
> *Bit rad, writing an actual letter! It feels more personal though. Plus sometimes I'd swear people are reading my emails.*
>
> *How are you doing? I mean, how are you REALLY doing, Snow White? Yes, I love your chirpy emails but it's me, Rob. You can tell me when you're sad, or pissed off, or exhausted.*
>
> *~~So I just thought I'd tell you.~~ God, this is hard. I wish I had your way with words. I'm writing like this, all serious, because I wanted to say that I understand why you sent me away.*

I know you want me to keep Mac in line, forge ahead with RG here in the US because this is where it's at, but I'm here mostly because you needed space after losing Kit, to think on things and work out what you want – from life, from me.

Lizzie, I want to be part of your future, you know that. As in, the main part. As in, can we get back together? I'll never love anyone like I love you. I get that you don't want to marry, that you're not convinced about having kids. But I know it's worth saving – us. Please, Lizzie. Whatever it takes, I'll do it. Don't give up on us?

I probably don't need to say more, you get the picture. Sorry I'm not a Bardington (how's he doing, by the way?). But you already know my heart, even if I'm crap at putting my feelings into words.

Can we meet up, maybe? Somewhere far away from work? Talk it through? You could come over, we could go to Hawaii or take a road trip? That holiday we never had. What do you reckon?

Sending all my love and enormous hugs from my desolate, lonely flat, and love to Harry, Clare and Eddie.

And, Lizzie, you'll see pics of me, like you did before, with others. It's all part of the game. I see pics of you too and I hope to god it's just you having a bit of fun before you maybe settle down again – with me?

Your ridiculously devoted and ever hopeful

Rob xxxxx

ONE WEEK LATER

Dear Rob

Picture me in Caffè Uno (coffee hasn't improved), reading your letter and having a little cry.

I miss you so much, and I loved every word you said and Bard couldn't have said it better. (He's getting there BTW, but slowly.)

Sorry it's taken me a while to respond, aside from my usual 'chirpy' emails. I've been trying to find the words too. So so hard, but here goes . . .

Yes, I sent you to the US because I needed space, not just because of Kit but also because of what happened to you and me.

When we had that horrible row, I had a kind of epiphany. It wasn't so much about you cheating on me (although after Dad's example, that was always going to be a big deal), it was more that I realized we want different things out of life.

You want a family, Rob. A wife. I don't want to be a wife and mum, I'm sure of that now. I just can't see myself as one of those superwomen who has it all – the beautiful kids and the successful career and the devoted husband and somehow juggling it all and making it work. Many do, but that's not for me.

The time we spent looking for a house, planning our future, showed me how much I would have to change to make that work. I felt guilty every time I put work first, which I have to do in this job. So I had to make a choice. Rose, or you.

You deserve better than what I can offer, Rob. You deserve someone who's always there for you, who can commit to you one hundred per cent, who can give you a family, who has the same goals as you.

Do you understand?

None of this changes the way I feel about you, not one little bit. I love you with all my heart and I always, always will. Me and you – it was a moment in time and nothing like it will ever happen again, to me. Thank you for giving me that time, for making me so happy. I'm beyond sad that we couldn't make it work. (Oh god, I'm crying again.)

She put down her pen and wiped her eyes, picturing Kit's face as he told her, 'There's a world out there full of beautiful men. And you're its queen.'

Picking up her pen, she carried on.

You'll see me with other men. But know that I will never love anyone the way I love you. Never. And when I see you with those other girls, my heart will break a little bit, but I will be strong and I will hope you find someone who makes you happy, who gives you what you want.

But hey – before you do, can we take that road trip? I am SO due some time off. You could get us a big fuck-off American car (actually, no – carbon emissions. Unless they do an electric version). One with a soft top. We can drive through the desert with the wind in our hair (a new level of hair chaos?) and sleep under the stars and eat burgers in diners and do all the American things.

How about it, Roberto? Friends and a lot lot more, for ever?
With all my love
Lizzie

Harry

'Oh my gosh, who's this one?' asked Clare, spotting Eliza with a tall, fair-haired man on her arm.

'He's French,' said Eddie. 'She met him at the gym.'

'French?' said Harry. 'That's disappointing.'

'He's rather lovely,' said Clare.

'Mum!' said Eddie.

'I can't keep up,' said Harry. 'What happened to that other one? Dev, was it? The chap from Essex.'

'Oh, he's still around. I like him, too,' said Clare.

'Hello, family!' said Eliza, as the Frenchman pulled out her chair. 'Hi, Terri, Layla. This is François. How is everyone?'

'Good!' said Clare. 'You look beautiful, darling.'

She did. There was a glow about Eliza, these days.

Tonight was the launch of her new charity, the Ana Rose

Foundation. Initial funding had come via Eliza's rather massive settlement from Seymour Morrissey. Her 'suggestion' that he make a donation in exchange for not naming names in the recent *Rack* interview had been a pragmatic one, but her use of the term 'family member', and some clues in the surrounding context, meant that most in their circle had worked it out. Seymour was persona non grata in London now.

Harry had suggested tightening the charity's focus, which to him seemed a little amorphous. It was mostly to do with empowering women. Scholarships to see bright, underprivileged girls through university; business mentorships; seed funding for female entrepreneurs, and the like. But also the Kit Marley Residency, which paid for a promising writer to spend six months at the Roses' Provençal villa – the wedding present he'd bought for Ana, all those years ago.

Harry looked across at his daughter. He'd been worried by her reaction to Marley's death, six months ago. She'd been bereft; heartbroken at losing her soulmate. But she finally seemed to be bouncing back.

Harry, too, had been deeply affected, blaming himself for a while. It had been him, after all, who'd set them off on the mission to entrap Andre.

'No, Dad,' Eliza had said. 'He died because of me, not you. And the only way I can handle it is by reminding myself how Kit believed we should go with the flow, shouldn't fight against Fate. I didn't always understand his words, but now I see he had a sense of things to come. He saw a pattern – of events, relationships. He'd say, *Don't look for reasons. Let it play out.*'

Rob had been a great support, but then Eliza had sent him back to the States. She'd joined him for a holiday, but on her return had told Harry, 'It's over, Rob and me.'

Her explanation as to why had almost broken Harry's heart (again).

'I can't make it work with him,' she'd said on their Sunday afternoon walk in the park. 'He wants all of me. And children. I can't run Rose *and* make that commitment.'

'Surely it's possible, in this day and age.'

'Is it, Dad? Didn't being head of Rose scupper your marriages? You drifted apart from Katie, always busy with work, never home, and Mum was there in the office and you couldn't resist. Then Mum's ambition was too much for you; you couldn't work together so you turned to Janette, who was sweet and easy and didn't challenge you. But if she hadn't died, would she have been enough? Or would you have tired of her, too? And then Caitlyn. According to you, it was your wealth and power she loved, not you. So perhaps your position wrecked that marriage too.'

He saw his life playing out through her eyes.

'But, finally, you're doing it right with Clare. Maybe that's because you've taken that step back. Rose isn't everything to you any more. Your family is just as important now.'

Along with Rob, she'd sent Mac to the States, making her Vice President of RoseGold's US operation.

'What's that all about?' he'd asked.

'I've given her a kingdom of her own, Dad. It was the only way. And Rob will keep an eye on her, make sure she toes the Rose line. Cecil's right behind me on this. He's always been suspicious of Mac.'

'Here's Maria,' said Eddie, bringing Harry back into the moment.

'Number one daughter!' he said, rising out of his chair to give her a hug.

'Hello, Father.'

She looked so different. This was her first visit home since she'd left for Cambodia. Eliza had been to see her recently, to discuss yet another arm of the foundation, this one providing support for girls who'd fallen victim to sex traffickers in the region.

'Maria, you look stunning!' said Eliza.

Something of an exaggeration. But much improved, for sure. Her hair was in a sophisticated up-do, and she was wearing a rather lovely red dress. Red! And heels. High ones.

After Eliza's speech, which was received with thunderous applause, she swapped seats with Eddie.

'How did I do, Dad?'

'I liked the part about me.'

'Oh my god.'

He took her hand. 'Ana would be so proud.'

'It's all down to you,' she said. 'Thanks so much for not dying.'

'You're welcome.'

'Dad . . . any time you want to come back, properly, to Rose. I know how much you miss it all.'

'I might feel somewhat superfluous, in light of your competence.'

'Are you sure? You're nowhere near retirement age, and I'd love to have you properly back on board, not just doing your remote thing. You're always working anyway; you may as well come in. It seems a shame you don't, especially considering all the effort you put into the Rose building.'

'Perhaps.'

'Come on, Dad. We make a great team. Just a day or two a week?'

'Is that an order?'

'Well, yes. It is.'

'Very well, then. You're the boss.'

Epilogue

Eliza

'So you finally gave up smoking?' said Frankie to Leigh, as they laid out blankets beneath a willow tree.

'One untimely death was more than enough,' Leigh replied. 'However, I'm wide open to the possibility of excessive alcohol consumption tonight.'

'Excess is mandatory,' said Will. 'We're here to honour Kit, after all.' He sat down, flicked his curls back and began opening a bottle of champagne.

Insects dipped into the water, creating ripples, as a church bell chimed the hour from some distant dreaming spire. The air was warm, and the setting sun bathed everything in golden light.

'I still can't believe he's gone,' said Frankie. She'd just completed the Ocean Race, after nine gruelling months, her Rose-sponsored team coming in second.

'Neither can I,' said Eliza. 'I miss him so much. But his work will live for ever; he'll never be forgotten.'

Will had poured his heart and soul into bringing Kit's visionary script to life, his empathy for Kit's work producing a compelling masterpiece that had resonated with viewers worldwide. Reviews spoke of a writer of unique brilliance, a Shakespeare for the twenty-first century, cut down in his prime.

The first time Eliza had watched *My Dark Soul*, in the dark of The Rose's little cinema, her insides had been ripped to shreds. All Kit's pain, confusion and, ultimately, his beauty, as he tried through his writing to make sense of human existence, was displayed right there, large on the screen. She'd cried all the way through.

She remembered their first-year discussions, here on this river-bank, about changing the world. Kit had made his mark. Not only had *Dark Soul* set the arts world on fire, it had opened up a whole debate on the nature of right and wrong, good and evil, and the place of religion in contemporary society. The term 'spiritual athe-ism' was being used to describe his way of thinking, though Eliza loathed such attempts to label Kit and his work. He'd been unique.

'He was both dark and light,' Frankie said. 'Kind of ... unknowable.'

'He saw things, knew things,' said Eliza. 'He understood time and Fate.'

'I thought he was just weird, or on drugs,' said Leigh.

Will laughed. 'He was those things too.'

Will was carrying on Kit's work, developing the ideas they'd had together, keeping the flame burning.

'Come on, Eliza. Drink up,' said Leigh, pouring more champagne.

The sun slipped away, and the river was a wide, dark path in the dusk.

They were quiet for a while, remembering Kit.

Twilight deepened; night wrapped itself around them. The moon rose, huge and golden.

'It's time,' said Eliza. 'Will?'

They moved down to the river, Will carrying the simple white urn containing Kit's ashes. They passed it along, each tipping out a handful, scattering them onto the moonlit water.

'Goodbye, sweet Kit,' said Eliza, as she crouched down and let the ashes slip through her fingers. Tears ran down her cheeks as she remembered the two of them together here, on that magical last night.

Later, as the moon climbed higher and the water meadows turned silver, Eliza held out her hand to Will. 'Come with me.'

She led him back from the river, to where the ancient oak waited.

'He brought me here. On our last night.'

'I remember you running off.'

'He told me things. Truths.'

They sat in the shadows, leaning against the gnarled tree trunk, looking back towards the Thames. Their friends' voices carried across in the stillness of the moonlit night.

The air suddenly snapped with magic.

Eliza felt his presence. He was here.

For ever, now. It's all the same.

'Time,' she said. 'It's the strangest thing.'

Acknowledgements

First and foremost, thanks to my editor Emma Beswetherick at Little, Brown UK for the conversations we've had about this story, especially the lunch we spent chewing over Harry and Kit. The writing life doesn't get much better. Thanks too for the care and thought you put into helping me get Eliza right.

My thanks also to Eleanor Russell for forging ahead with editing through these crazy times of Covid.

Huge thanks and hugs to my agents Vicki Marsdon and Nadine Rubin Nathan at High Spot Literary, whose support goes above and beyond. I mean, how many agents design a cocktail based on your main character? (Visit oliviahayfield.com to learn how to concoct a Harry Rose. Smooth and spicy, with a hit of ginger.)

Big thanks to Giles Portman and Chris Buckley for answering my questions on life at Oxford, for sharing your memories and letting me steal some of those, and for your helpful and occasionally acerbic comments on the text. Mwah!

I'd also like to thank Jennifer Ward-Lealand, actress, supporter of the arts and well-deserved New Zealander of the Year, for generously giving advice on the machinations of film production; and actor and director Michael Hurst, mostly for reciting a Shakespeare sonnet to me on his doorstep. Shivers down the spine. I hope you enjoy Will Bardington.

Director and writer Kirstin Marcon also read through the film production parts for me – thanks so much for your enthusiasm and support.

Thanks to my beta readers: my daughter Helena (Team Kit), for blisteringly honest feedback; Jane Bloomfield, Suzanne Main and Julie Scott – your ongoing support and fun messages keep me going and mean the world.

And finally, enormous thanks to my husband Michael, who brings me wine and nuts in my writing hut and cheers me on, even when I forget who's real and who's made up; and my children James and Helena (again), for only rolling their eyes occasionally.

Readers Guide –
Questions for discussion

1. Did Eliza do the right thing in deciding marriage wasn't for her? Or should she have tried harder to make it work?

2. Do you think the tension between Maria and Eliza accurately reflects the relationship Mary Tudor would have had with her sister Elizabeth?

3. Neither of the Tudor sisters had a happy ending when it came to romance. Has the author been true to their stories with regards to Philip of Spain and Robert Dudley?

4. If Kit hadn't had a sense he was on borrowed time, would he have hooked up with Eliza? Would she have reciprocated? Was Kit in fact the real reason why she couldn't bring herself to commit to Rob?

5. To what extent do you think Elizabeth I's refusal to marry was down to her father's example, in particular his beheading of her mother? Or was it simply about giving up power?

6. In real life, Elizabeth I and Mary Queen of Scots never met. If they had, do you think they could have resolved their differences, woman to woman?

7. How well do you think Olivia Hayfield reflects the tension between the queens of England and Scotland in her depiction of Eliza and Mac's relationship?

8. Lady Jane Grey (Chess) and Mary Queen of Scots were beheaded; Mary Tudor died an unhappy woman, and Elizabeth I was a successful queen but had to give up thoughts of marriage and a family to make that work. Do you feel Olivia Hayfield's resolution of their lives in modern times is realistic?

9. Shakespeare's and Marlowe's plays were often social commentaries on key people (especially those in power). How effective do you think a modern-day Shakespeare or Marlowe would be in holding people in power to account – who is doing this sort of thing now?

The history behind the characters . . .
A Q&A with Olivia Hayfield

Eliza's historical equivalent, Elizabeth I, is famously known as 'the Virgin Queen'. Do you think Robert Dudley really was her lover? And do you think she would have married him if he'd been free?

These are still hotly debated questions in historian circles. I'm going to go for a disappointing 'Honestly, I don't know' on both.

I think there's a strong possibility Elizabeth would have considered marrying Robert if he'd been free, early on in her reign when she perhaps allowed her heart more of a say, before she became the tough cookie of later on. She was certainly indiscreet about her feelings for Robert, openly flirting with him. They'd known each other since childhood, too, and that would have meant a lot to someone in her position.

But she'd have had a hard time convincing those around her – especially William Cecil – that marriage to Robert was a good idea. Marriages weren't made for love, they were political alliances, and the Queen of England was not to be squandered on a fellow Englishman. She was a prize for a foreign prince, emperor or king. And when Robert *did* become available, there was no way she could have married him – it would have been a wildly unpopular move, given the suspicions surrounding his wife's death, and Elizabeth cared a great deal about her image. I also think that by then, she'd realised that marriage to *any* man would mean giving up a great deal of power. As an imperial diplomat at the time said, 'If she marry My lord Robert, she may one morning lay herself down as Queen of England and rise the next morning as plain Mistress Elizabeth.'

I wonder if she was influenced by her father's track record with marriage. He did behead her mother, after all. She may have decided early on that marrying for love wasn't wise – or maybe marriage was just a big 'Nope!' from the word go.

As for whether or not she remained a virgin, I like to think not, though I'm basing that mostly on sentiment. Many argue that she wouldn't have had the opportunity – she was always surrounded by her ladies, even in her bedchamber at night. And then there was the risk of pregnancy. But! She was the queen, she could have dismissed those attendants for a while, right? Put a trusted lady on the door for an hour. As for pregnancy, maybe there were ways; maybe she only took the risk once or twice, who knows? I hope she did. She was smitten with Robert, and I believe he genuinely loved her too (though he was undoubtedly ambitious, and looking at the portraits, I'd say a bit full of himself).

It has been suggested that the episode with her step-father Thomas Seymour (see later question) contributed to an aversion to sex and hence the resolve to remain a virgin. I explored this idea when writing of Eliza's problem – it seems plausible to me that this would have affected her, but to what extent we don't know.

Unlike Henry VIII, Harry Rose got a happy ending. Did you have to think hard about that?

Not too hard. By the time I started writing *Sister to Sister* I'd already decided he was genuine in his search for redemption, and sorry for the damage he'd done, and I wanted him to have the chance to put things right with Eliza and Maria (and Ana), for their sakes as well as his. But Harry has to work hard for his happy ending, and he does suffer, blaming himself for Stu's unhappy life, and Maria's, and Eliza's inability to have a proper relationship with Robert. He's also haunted by the deaths of Ana and Caitlyn, and is determined to atone for those.

By the end of *Sister to Sister* he's resolved all that confusion we saw at the start of *Wife After Wife*, where he couldn't understand modern women and didn't get why they weren't enjoying his 'compliments'. Now he's a proper feminist (mostly). He deserves his happy ending. Well done, Harry.

Why did you decide to write Kit as a promiscuous pansexual? And why did he have to die?

Kit was a peripheral figure when I was first plotting *Sister to Sister*. Christopher Marlowe was just that other guy who was around at the same time as Shakespeare. But when I started researching him properly ... *oh*. And once I'd started writing, Kit quickly took centre stage.

Very little is known about Marlowe's life, but what we do know is intriguing. Words used to describe him include 'rakehell', which I love. He was a brilliant playwright and poet, of course, but he loved a good brawl, and was a noted atheist at a time when it really wasn't a good idea to say so. Best of all, it's highly likely he was a spy for Elizabeth's government. When at Cambridge he used to disappear for long periods, and the university hesitated to give him his degree because of his dubious trips to Catholic France. But Elizabeth's Privy Council intervened, describing his absences as being on: ' ... *matters touching the benefit of this country* ...'. Kit got his degree.

I think he was probably gay (he did say *All those who love not Tobacco and Boies were fools*); there's disagreement over this, but I see him as an experimenter – he seems to have lived his life large – so maybe gender wouldn't have meant a lot to him. Hence my Kit's sexuality.

Christopher Marlowe died at the age of 29, stabbed to death in mysterious circumstances. All sorts of conspiracy theories exist, including an assassination organised by a jealous wife, or by Sir Walter Raleigh, or William Cecil, even by Queen Elizabeth herself. Then there's the theory it was a fake death, and he in fact lived on and wrote under the pseudonym William Shakespeare. I decided Kit should die young, it seemed fitting, and because he has the ability to sense the future and knows it's going to happen, it makes his behaviour and his reluctance to let anybody close easier to explain. It was so hard, killing him off. I may have wept a little when I wrote that part.

What influenced Maria's story and character arc?

Mary Tudor (Bloody Mary) is known mostly for burning Protestant heretics at the stake. So she isn't the sort of person you warm to (sorry, terrible pun). But are people shocked by this mainly because she was a woman? A horrible way to die, obviously, but the numbers weren't excessive by the standards of the time. She was also heavily influenced by her husband, Philip II of Spain – the Spanish Inquisition isn't remembered for its religious tolerance.

I've always felt sorry for the young Mary. She went from beloved apple of Henry's eye to being declared illegitimate, and was sent away to live apart from her mother, to whom she was very close. Henry wouldn't even allow her to see Catherine when she was dying. The story of her relationship with Philip of Spain is a sad one – she seems to have genuinely loved him, and had more than one phantom pregnancy.

All in all not a happy life, and as part of Harry's journey to redemption I thought I'd give her a second chance too. Mary is my antagonist initially (the Bloody Mary character was too juicy not to have fun with), but thanks to Eliza confronting Harry about his treatment of her sister, Maria has ... maybe not a happy ending, but a contented one, at peace with herself.

Was Mary Queen of Scots really attracted to bad boys?

I recently read a history blog called 'The Worst Monarchs of All Time', and Mary Queen of Scots was on the list, described as 'useless'. A bit harsh, maybe, but she does seem to have had questionable taste in men. Her story is one of those 'truth is stranger than fiction' ones.

Mary had three husbands. Her first was Francis II of France, who died at the age of 16. Her second, her half-cousin Lord Darnley, was a shocker. She was won over by his tall, fair good looks; he could sing and dance and was well educated, all the things a girl likes, but once married it soon went horribly wrong. He was a drinker with a violent streak; he wanted to co-rule but Mary refused. This didn't go down well. Darnley was also part of the team that stabbed to death Mary's secretary, David Rizzio, with whom she was rumoured to be having an affair. Not long after, Darnley met his own sticky end when the house he was staying in was blown up.

The person thought to be responsible for Darnley's murder was the Earl of Bothwell, who had designs on marrying Mary himself – although he already had a wife, in Denmark. Actually, make that two wives. The other was in Scotland. There were rumours about Mary and Bothwell, and they did have a close relationship. Bothwell was brought to trial but acquitted. He and Mary left Edinburgh together soon after Darnley's death, and suspicion was rife that she'd colluded with him over the murder. Wife #2 divorced Bothwell citing adultery with her servant, and Mary and Bothwell married seven days after the divorce was granted. One version of the story has Bothwell kidnapping Mary and raping her so that she'd have to marry him. The other is that she was willingly 'kidnapped', and the rape was made up to protect her reputation.

Whatever the truth, their antics were too much for the people of Scotland. There was a showdown between Mary's supporters and those who opposed her, during which Bothwell fled, and Mary never saw him again. He set sail across the North Sea, his enemies in hot pursuit, but was blown off course and ended up in Norway, then ruled by the King of Denmark. Thanks to his first wife's intervention, the king wasn't sympathetic. Bothwell was kept in appalling conditions and spent the last ten years of his life chained to a pillar. Not surprisingly, he went mad.

Why did you depict Philip of Spain, renowned as a proudly Catholic ruler, as a fundamentalist Evangelical Christian?

Philip of Spain was enthusiastic in his persecution of heretics, so I needed a modern-day parallel for that. Catholics are more enlightened these days, but not so much those extreme fundamentalist Christians, the ones who view women as men's 'helpmeets' and still firmly believe a woman's place is in the home. Let's say, I'm not especially tolerant of such views. I gave myself the opportunity to share my intolerance, via Eliza, who's a trailblazer for modern women. I wanted to write a full-on juicy clash between Eliza and a powerful misogynist, and Philip was my man. Also Seymour . . . I so enjoyed Eliza giving those two their comeuppances!

What do you think really happened to Amy Dudley?

There are several theories. Amy Dudley (née Robsart) is thought to have had breast cancer, which may have weakened her to the stage where even a small fall down the stairs would have broken her neck. The fact that Amy sent everyone in her household out to the local fair so she was alone in the house, is odd. If she was in constant pain and knew she was dying, knew her husband was never coming back, maybe she was tired of life and decided to end it.

Or was she murdered, and if so, by whom? Suspicion at the time fell on Robert Dudley, and this ended any chance of him marrying Elizabeth. In her book *The Virgin's Lover*, Philippa Gregory is convincing in her idea that Elizabeth realised Robert was becoming too powerful through his relationship with her, and sanctioned Cecil's move to make it impossible for her to eventually marry him (it was known that Amy was increasingly sick) by organising Amy's murder and implicating Robert in her death. It's out there, but it's plausible. Others have blamed Cecil, but without Elizabeth's knowledge, again to scupper any chances Dudley had of becoming king consort. Cecil wasn't a fan of Dudley.

What was the real story with Elizabeth 1 and Thomas Seymour (Seymour Morrissey)?

This is a strange episode in teenage Elizabeth's life. After Henry VIII's death, Catherine Parr married Jane Seymour's brother Thomas. He was a glamorous, charismatic man and it seems Catherine was strongly attracted to him before she caught Henry's eye. Elizabeth went to live with her step-mother and her new husband, and there are well-documented reports of him coming into her bedroom for a bit of a romp (tickling, even the slapping of buttocks) – she was fourteen. This was abuse! And Catherine even joined in sometimes. What was she thinking? But Elizabeth seems to have been attracted to Thomas, and Catherine discovered the two in an embrace. At which point Catherine came to her senses and sent Elizabeth away. Like I say, Elizabeth was fourteen. Thomas was in his thirties.

Was it very different writing from the point of view of a millennial woman, compared to writing from the perspective of Harry and his wives in *Wife After Wife*?

Yes, it was. Henry and his wives were my age and era so it was easy remembering the attitudes and events of the times, the pop culture references, the way things were changing especially in relation to equality, sexuality and gender. With Eliza I was getting into the head of someone of my daughter's generation (18–19 at the time of writing) and it was great to be able to get her feedback as I wrote. For instance, I had Kit as bisexual, but she explained he'd probably be pansexual. It's been an interesting exercise, and it made me feel pretty positive about how far we've come over the past couple of decades. Millennials won't have a bar of half the stuff I had to put up with!

Who's your favourite character in this book – or their historical equivalent?

It's very hard letting go of characters you create. When you reach the end of the book there's a mourning period. I'm now deep into my next book, but I miss Harry, Eliza, Rob, Will, Kit and Co. as if they were real friends (though … I may have borrowed from some real friends when creating these characters. Not telling.). If I had to choose just one I'd go for Kit. I mean, honestly, who can resist a beautiful, messed-up creative genius?